BROKEN PLACES

BROKEN PLACES

R. ANTHONY MARTIN

BROKEN PLACES

iUniverse books may be ordered through booksellers or by contacting:

iUniverse
1663 Liberty Drive
Bloomington, IN 47403
www.iuniverse.com
1-800-Authors (1-800-288-4677)

ISBN: 978-0-5955-2961-2 (sc)
ISBN: 978-0-5956-3014-1 (e)

Print information available on the last page.

iUniverse rev. date: 05/13/2016

CHAPTER 1

Robert stopped at the entrance to the bus terminal and took one last look at Cambridge Falls, Ohio. It was the first week of September, and the colors of summer still dominated the landscape. The giant oak trees that lined Main Avenue still flaunted their green foliage. The farmers' market across the street from the bus depot still had white corn and yellow squash to sell. And the sun that brightened the eastern horizon still cast a soft orange glow against the early-morning sky. But the threat of autumn hinted in the air. Robert could smell the ripening apple orchards and flourishing ragweed that grew in red and green patches along the outskirts of town. He knew it wouldn't be long before the bitter winds of autumn stripped the small Midwest town of its brilliant color.

Robert hated autumn as much as he hated Cambridge Falls. But after eighteen years, he was finally leaving. Leaving the place he despised, the place that haunted him with his past and denied him his future.

"C'mon, son. I have a schedule to keep."

Robert stepped inside the terminal door and handed the bus driver his baggage. After watching his bags neatly stored in the cargo hold, he climbed aboard the eastbound Greyhound bus. He maneuvered down the narrow aisle and took a window seat near the rear. A few minutes later, the bus rolled out of the terminal and turned onto Main Avenue. He placed his hand against the glass and watched the familiar sights of his childhood fade into the distance.

He was moving on, headed for Pittsburgh City University and the start of his new life.

Since Pittsburgh City University was only a three-hour ride from Cambridge Falls, he had convinced his father to let him take the bus.

"Why don't you and Mom come down next weekend and bring the rest of my stuff," he had said.

As the bus crossed the border from Ohio into Pennsylvania, Robert watched the endless succession of red farmhouses that dotted the otherwise green landscape stream past his window. With each passing mile, he became more excited about his future. He closed his eyes and visualized himself attending a large university in a big city where nobody knew his name. He prayed the new surroundings would allow him to escape his painful past—a past filled with cruel whispers and unfounded rumors.

His life hadn't always been shrouded in secrets. He remembered a time he once ran free in the sun. But everything changed after his parents sent him away to that private boarding school. They said it was a trial experiment. They said it would better prepare him for college. They said if he didn't like it, he could transfer back to Cambridge Falls High.

"It's final, Robert. You're going. Stop arguing!"

Our Lady of Fatima was the name of the boarding school he'd been forced to attend for his sophomore year of high school. The school was tucked away in the foothills of the Allegheny Mountains, about fifty miles southeast of Cambridge Falls. His first impression of the school reminded him more of a prison than a boarding school, with its collection of dark brick buildings and black wrought iron fences. Even the head administrator looked more like a warden than a priest, with his flattop haircut and bulging biceps.

Looking back now, Robert realized he should have seen the warning signs. But how could he have known the school would turn him into a murderer.

"Welcome, Robert. I'm Father Bullock, the head administrator of Our Lady of Fatima."

"Nice to meet you, Father."

"You're just in time for supper, Robert. Let's get your bags up to your room, and then I'll take you over to the refectory so you can meet the rest of the students and get something to eat. I'm sure you must be starving."

Robert clinched his eyes. He didn't want to remember the worst chapter of his life. But the memories kept flowing.

"Gentlemen, this is Robert Robinson. Today is his first day, and I want you guys to show him the ropes. These boys will be your tablemates for the reminder of the semester, Robert. The boy at the end of the table is Stephon. He's a class leader."

"Nice to meet you, Rob. I think you'll like it here."

"Thanks, Stephon."

Robert tensed at the thought of Stephon. Two and a half years had not erased the pain. It was ironic; his parents had sent him away to a private boarding school for structure and discipline, but it was the structure and discipline that caused his life to spiral out of control.

"You know the rules, Robert. Touching another boy is against the rules of this school and against the word of the Bible.

"I know, Father."

"Was Stephon at your bunk last night? Answer me!

"Don't shake your head. What were the two of you doing?"

"He was showing me something?"

"What was he showing you?"

"Pictures."

"Pictures of what?"

"People."

"What people?"

"Naked people."

"What were the naked people doing?"

"Having … ssssex."

"Did Stephon touch you, Robert?"

"No."

"I've gotten reports, Robert. I know you and Stephon have been having sex. Is it true?"

"No."

"You're lying to me, Robert."

"No, I'm not."

"If you lie to me, you're going to burn in hell. Do you want to burn in hell? Do you want eternal damnation?"

"No!"

"Then tell me the truth!"

"I'm telling you the truth!"

"Then put your hand on the Bible, and swear before God that you're telling the truth. Swear before God that nothing happened!"

"I can't!"

"Yes, you can."

"Please don't make me!"

"Eternal damnation, Robert."

"No."

"Swear before God!"

"He made me do it. Stephon made me touch him!"

Robert sat up in his seat. He wanted to block out the final memory of Stephon. But the image of Stephon's blood-soaked body being rushed past him on a stretcher was forever etched into his memory.

"Stephon, I'm sorry. Please forgive me. Forgive me."

Robert folded his hands and prayed. He prayed his boarding school days would be replaced with positive new experiences. Living through one scandal in his life and returning to Cambridge Falls to face the rumor and innuendo that followed was more than any fifteen-year-old should endure.

He remembered his very first day at Cambridge Falls High. His brother, Randy, was a good athlete and the center on the varsity basketball team. His sister, Rhonda, was pretty and the head cheerleader for the Cambridge High Nightriders. Robert, on the other hand, was the punching bag for jokes. He had little athletic ability, a scrawny five-nine, 130-pound frame, and an infamous reputation that preceded his arrival.

The only thing he had going for him was his intelligence. Unfortunately, the popular boys at his school were the athletes, the rappers, or the class clowns. The intelligent brothers like himself were relegated to the roles of nerds, faggots, or sellouts.

Consequently, none of the cool kids wanted to be seen with him. Even his brother and sister kept a safe distance away while in the public eye. His mother tried to convince him he was handsome and had self-worth. Unfortunately, her words didn't carry as much weight as the insults hurled against him by his peers.

"Hey, Robert, I hear you're a damn faggot."
"Hey, Robert, can I take you to the prom, pretty boy?"
"Hey, Robert, are you looking for a new boyfriend?"

Robert watched his reflection stare back at him through the Greyhound window. Somehow he had survived high school in one piece. So long as he didn't count his self-esteem as a part of the whole.

The acceptance letter from the university had sparked a sense of hope, and for the following five months, he worked out religiously on his brother's weight bench. His mother's knowing smile and affirmative nod acknowledged her approval of his regime, although she never uttered a word about it. By the end of the summer, his body had grown from 130 pounds of skin and bones to 160 pounds of developing muscle. His jacket size went from a thirty-six slim to a forty regular while his waist remained a trim thirty. A thicker neck broadened his slender face, and his sharp facial features of a narrow nose, thin lips, and large eyes seemed less obtrusive against his almond-brown complexion. Based on the double takes he began receiving from some of the girls, he knew step one of his plan was working.

His preparations to win back his self-esteem consisted of a three-prong attack. Step one was to develop an awesome body and make all the girls want him. Step two was to get a quality education and land a high-powered job so he could return to Cambridge Falls rich and important. Step three was to deal with the emotional turmoil waging war inside his head.

The green-and-silver metallic sign posted on the side of the highway read twenty miles to downtown Pittsburgh. As the bus emerged from the dimly lit Fort Pitt Tunnel, Robert's eyes met with the most spectacular sight he had ever seen. A bright, gleaming skyline of sparkling glass skyscrapers that continuously narrowed down to form a triangle. At the very point of the triangle, two small rivers merged to form a third powerful river. He remembered from his ninth-grade geography class that it was the Monongahela and the Allegheny Rivers meeting to form the Ohio River. He also remembered the point where the three rivers merged was called the Golden Triangle. To the left of the Golden Triangle sat the stadiums where his beloved Pittsburgh Steelers and Pirates played. To the right of the Golden Triangle sat towering Mount Washington, where pretentious mountaintop restaurants hugged the jagged curvature overlooking the city. At the very center of the Golden Triangle sat a water fountain that sprayed cascading streams of rainbow-colored water that twinkled with the reflections of the sunlight.

Robert reclined against his headrest and closed his eyes. He envisioned the three merging rivers as the threads of his life—his troubled high school life coming together with his approaching college life to ultimately form his future life. A life he hoped to be full of beauty, wonder, and power, like the Ohio River flowing just outside his window.

CHAPTER 2

The sunlight seeping through the partially closed blinds awoke Shawn from a peaceful sleep. He blinked at the clock on the black lacquer nightstand next to the bed. The illuminated numbers beamed 9:50 a.m. His girlfriend, Latisha, was already awake and sitting on the side of the bed.

"Good mornin', baby." He poked Latisha with his big toe.

"Shawn, you better get up." Latisha pushed his foot away. "It's almost ten o'clock. Coach Green said he'd be here at eleven to drive you to campus."

Shawn pulled the sheet up around his neck. "Ten more minutes. Let me sleep ten more minutes."

Before Latisha had a chance to answer, there was a knock at the door.

"Shawn. Are you up yet? Rise and shine, son. Rise and shine. Your coach called. Said he would be here in about an hour. You better get moving so you have time to eat breakfast before he gets here. And tell Latisha I think it's time she goes home. I know you snuck her in here again last night."

"Come on, Moms," Shawn answered groggily. "Latisha's mother knows she's with me, the next NBA superstar."

"Humph," Martha grunted before stomping down the stairs.

Latisha rose from the bed and recovered her beige bra draped over the nightstand.

"Your mother's right. You better get moving. You don't wanna be late for your first day of practice, do you?"

"They'll wait for me. Now come back over here and show me love." Shawn threw back the sheet, exposing his morning eagerness.

"Shawn, you already know how I feel about you. Besides, didn't I show you enough last night?"

"I never get enough of you, baby."

"Is that the same thang you told Monica last weekend?"

Shawn sat upright in the bed. "You know you're my girl, Tish. Why you gotta keep throwing Monica's name in my face all the time?"

Latisha rolled her eyes. "Don't even go there! We both know what happened last weekend between you and that slut Monica Chambers."

"Yeah, nothin'."

"Today's an important day for you, Shawn. Let's not start it with a fight."

"Look at me." Shawn flexed his muscles, showcasing his tattooed arms and chest. "You know you want some more of this."

Latisha didn't respond.

"You know you're my girl. Why you all worried about Monica?"

"Is Monica as good as me?" Latisha cupped her breasts.

"You know you're the best. Now get back in bed and prove it."

Latisha pushed him away and headed toward the door. "I'm gonna take a shower. I'll give you some more when you deserve it."

Shawn jumped from the bed and slammed the door behind her. He slid his black polo shorts around his waist and walked over to the mirror above his dresser. He wondered if he was losing his touch.

"No way." He smirked at his reflection. "You're too fine."

Shawn loved his looks. His six-four frame was well proportioned to his weight of 195 pounds. His height was complemented with wide shoulders that tapered down to a narrow waist and washboard stomach. His light hazelnut complexion, wavy brown hair, and piercing gray eyes added to a package that always turned heads when he walked into a room.

"Yeah, you da man."

After removing a fresh pair of black boxers from his dresser, he headed for the master bathroom just off his mother's bedroom. He grimaced at the pastel flowered wallpaper and ornate gold fixtures that adorned the room. "Pop's never would have approved." He turned the gold handle to release the spray of water and stepped inside the sliding glass door. He worked up a thick lather against his tightly muscled body and thought about his life. "Look out, NBA. Here comes Shawn Collins."

After returning to the bedroom, he inspected his body to make sure Latisha hadn't left any marks. He picked up his soft bristle brush and swept back the thick crown of wavy hair on top of his neatly faded haircut. He made a mental note to call his barber to schedule his next appointment before his hair started looking out of place. He patted his hair neatly into place and then combed out his mustache and goatee before meticulously trimming them with his clippers. Next, he applied a moisturizer to his face and used the excess liquid to smooth out his thick eyebrows so all the hairs flowed in the same direction. He nodded his approval and then headed for the cedar-lined walk-in closet on the far side of the bedroom.

In recognition of the special day, he selected his most impressive blue sweat suit with white stripes embroidered down the left arm sleeve of the pullover hooded jacket. He stepped in front of the full-length mirror behind the closet door. "Lookin' good, bro."

Realizing he wouldn't be able to come home during the week, he grabbed his suitcase from the top shelf of the closet and packed enough clothes to last the duration of the week. He placed the packed suitcase next to the bedroom door and headed toward the bathroom. Latisha was singing in the shower.

"Meet me in the kitchen after you finish."

Latisha stopped her rendition of "I Will Survive" and answered with a melodic, two-pitched "Okay."

Shawn grabbed his suitcase along with his basketball and headed down to the first floor of the split-level ranch house he shared with his mother and brother in the Stanton Heights section of Pittsburgh. He could smell the bacon frying before he hit the bottom step. The ache in his stomach reminded him how hungry he was. His little brother, Damar, was eating breakfast in the living room and watching cartoons.

"Hey, whatcha watchin', little man?"

"Cartoons."

Shawn threw the basketball to Damar. "Think fast."

Damar caught the ball and immediately passed it back.

"Great pass, little man."

Shawn headed into the kitchen twirling the basketball on his index finger.

"Don't you two ever get tired of playing with that ball?"

Shawn kissed his mother on the cheek. "Good morning to you too, Moms."

"And what did I tell you about sneaking that tramp in here?"

"Come on, Moms. Latisha might hear you. And why do you have to dog her out all the time? You know she doesn't like going home."

"I don't care if she can hear me. And why does she have to come here?" Martha shook her head. "Never mind. Don't answer that."

Shawn removed a carton of milk from the refrigerator. "Good, I won't."

"Shawn, you can do a lot better than Latisha."

"I know, so stop preachin' and fix me something to eat. I'm starvin'."

Martha turned to the stove to finished frying the bacon. After draining the bacon on a paper towel, she loaded up Shawn's plate with bacon, eggs, toast, and grits.

****

Latisha gave her appearance one final appraisal before heading downstairs. Since her hair was cut short, it was much easier to style. A couple quick swipes with a wet brush followed by a sprits of holding gel maintained the slicked-back look she wanted. For the finishing touches, she put on her large doorknocker earrings that framed her cocoa-colored face and punctuated her full lips with dark red lipstick. Although she never considered herself beautiful, her cute face, overdeveloped breasts, and bubble butt could attract almost any man. In fact, she was dating the finest brother from Peabody High School. After smoothing out the remaining wrinkles from her tight black spandex dress, she headed down to the kitchen.

****

"Do you want some breakfast, Latisha?" Shawn asked as Latisha entered the kitchen.

"No thanks, Shawn. I have to get going. Will you call me later and give me your number at the dorm?"

Shawn wiped his lips before kissing Latisha. "Sure, baby. See ya later."

"Good-bye, Mrs. Collins."

"Good-bye, Latisha," Martha quipped without turning around.

Latisha bounced out of the screen door and down the side steps.

"Shawn, I sure hope you're using protection with that girl. The last thing you need is for her to get pregnant. I'd hate to see you waste your future on trash like that."

"How many times do I have to tell you, Moms? Latisha is just the flavor of the moment. There are too many fine women out there for me to be tied down."

"I don't think Latisha feels she's the flavor of the moment. That girl has a lot more on her mind than just pleasing your taste buds." Martha sat across the table from Shawn. "Listen, son. I've known Latisha's family for a long time. They're nothing but hoodlums. They've never belonged to any church, her father's in jail, and her mother's too busy running the streets to run her own household. That girl's looking for a way out, and she sees you as her meal ticket."

"Moms, please stop preachin'. I know what I'm doin'. Besides, once practice starts, I won't have time to even think about Latisha."

Martha shook her head. "I hope you're right."

Shawn ignored his mother's comment and mixed a slice of butter into his grits. He was relieved when the doorbell rang.

"Mom, Coach Green's at the front door!"

"Okay, tell him to come in, Damar!"

Shawn gulped down his milk and rushed to put his plate and glass in the sink.

Coach Green entered the kitchen with an outstretched hand. "How are you, Mrs. Collins?"

"Oh, I'm fine, Coach Green. Can I get you a cup of coffee or something to eat?"

"A cup of coffee would be nice. I like it black." Coach Green took a seat at the table.

Martha poured the coach's coffee into a shiny black mug.

Shawn noticed it was the mug his deceased father won for his mother at the policemen's ball over eight years ago.

Coach Green smiled, exposing his obvious overbite. "Well, Shawn, I hope you're ready to meet the squad today. We have a fine team, and I believe the Tigers have a good shot at winning the Big Central Conference crown this year."

"Coach, I've never been more ready in all my life. It's been my dream to play for the Tigers." Shawn stood and imitated his patented fifteen-foot jump shot. "Now that the time has arrived, paint me the Big Central most valuable player!"

"Not so fast, Shawn. I think you have a decent shot at making first string, but you're going to have to beat out Brian Short for that starting guard position."

"Coach, I can outshoot, outdribble, and outrebound Brian Short with one hand tied behind my back and both eyes closed!"

"That's the spirit I like to hear. Now let's see if you can match that enthusiasm with your action on the court."

"Coach Green," Martha interrupted, "I'm not worried about Shawn making the squad, or even beating out Brian Short, but I am concerned about his studies. He's barely been able to maintain a C average in high school, and college is going to be a lot tougher."

Coach Green nodded his agreement.

"Coach, I want Shawn to get a good education while he's playing basketball. It's something that's very important to me."

Coach Green smiled. "I hear you, Mrs. Collins."

"Shawn's father, Albert, died when Shawn was a young boy. His dream was for his two sons to go to college. Albert never had that opportunity. Shawn does, and I want to make sure he takes full advantage of it. Do you understand me, Coach?"

Coach Green reached across the table and patted Martha's hand. "Don't worry Mrs. Collins. We already took care of Shawn's registration. We'll arrange for him to have a tutor if he needs one. Besides, we were able to get him to score above a 700 on the SATs, now weren't we?"

Martha drew back from the coach's grasp. "That reminds me. What major did you say Shawn was registered under?"

Coach Green cleared his throat. "Right now it's undetermined. But don't worry. The school doesn't require Shawn to declare a major until his sophomore year. I'm sure we can come up with something appropriate for Shawn by then."

"Yeah, like how I'm gonna manage all my millions from my sneaker and cereal commercials. Right, Coach?"

Coach Green peered at Martha from the rim of his coffee mug. Beads of perspiration had formed across his pale, white forehead. "Don't get too far ahead of yourself, Shawn."

"More coffee?" Martha asked.

"No, thank you. I think it's time Shawn and I get going." Coach Green stood to leave, accidently knocking the mug off the table in his haste.

Shawn grimaced as the shattered pieces danced across the linoleum. "I'm so sorry, Mrs. Collins."

Martha began picking up the pieces.

"Let me help you."

"No, that won't be necessary, Coach Green. I can manage."

"Well, at least let me give you some money to replace it."

Shawn knew no amount of money could replace the sentimental value of the mug.

Martha looked up at Coach Green from the floor. "No, just promise me you'll take good care of my son."

"That's a promise, Mrs. Collins."

Martha placed the fragile pieces of ceramic in the palm of her hand.

Shawn watched in silence as she tried to arrange the pieces back together.

"Shawn, we better get going. We still have to pick up a couple of your teammates before we head over to the Omni Center."

"A'ight, Coach."

"Shawn, can I come and watch you practice?" Damar asked.

"Not today, little man, but I'll make sure Moms brings you to our first home game."

"All right!" Damar yelled.

Coach Green patted Damar on the head. "What grade are you in, Damar?"

"The fourth."

"Let's see, that means in about eight more years, I'll be here picking you up for practice, right?"

Damar slapped the coach a high five. "Right, Coach."

"Good-bye, Mrs. Collins!"

Martha managed a fake smile as she walked into the living room to show Coach Green to the front door. "Good-bye, Coach."

"Moms, don't forget to bring the rest of my stuff over to the dorm. I'll call you after practice with my dorm number."

"All right. Don't forget your suitcase." Martha pointed to the suitcase sitting next to the door.

"Oh, yeah."

"Now be sure and do what Coach Green tells you to do. You hear me, boy?"

Shawn turned and mouthed, "All right, Moms."

Martha mouthed, "I love you."

Shawn situated himself in the front seat of the van. He turned to give his mother a final wave, but she had already disappeared back into the house. He smiled, knowing she was already in the kitchen, trying to glue the shattered pieces of that mug back together.

CHAPTER 3

A barrage of mixed emotions clawed at Jamal's mind. In less than two hours, he would board Amtrak to embark on the first leg of his future—a future that included four years at Pittsburgh City University, followed by two years at Wharton for his MBA. Jamal had mapped out his entire life and, with the grace of God, hoped to fulfill his mission. He knew it wouldn't be easy. It would take a lot of hard work and cold cash to obtain his dream. But if there was one thing Jamal knew he had, it was ambition. Ambition fueled by the meager surroundings of living in the hood.

Scraping up an additional $8,000 for his first year's tuition was difficult. But Jamal was determined not to end up in jail or on the street like so many of his friends. Growing up in one of the poorest neighborhoods of Newark, New Jersey, his life hadn't been easy. Crack dealers, drive-by shootings, and street gangs were just a few of the obstacles he endured on a daily basis. But what he hated most was watching his father return home from his second janitorial job with barely enough strength to climb the stairs to their third-floor apartment. Jamal wanted a better life, not just for himself but also for his family.

Jamal knew his parents did the best they could to support their family of six children. But paying rent on their three-bedroom apartment took almost all the monthly income they could muster. Although the family never lacked food or clean clothes, for which Jamal was grateful, they couldn't afford the things all the other kids seemed to have. His parents, instead of providing material possessions, tried to instill values in their children to make them realize family and mutual respect were much greater gifts than worldly possessions. But Jamal still longed for the things he could not have.

With strong faith and strict guidance, his parents were successful in keeping his two sisters and three brothers off the streets and out of any serious trouble. However, Jamal could see cracks developing in the moral shield his parents so proudly provided. His oldest sister, Aaliyah, was secretly dating a known drug dealer, and his younger brother Malik was hanging out with one of Newark's most notorious street gangs, the West Side Kings. Jamal prayed his absence would not be the factor that allowed his family to fall victim to the violence lurking outside their front door, waiting to attack like a contagious disease.

During his eighteen years of living in the hood, Jamal witnessed the disease of violence grab hold of his community and infect everything it touched. Although his community was structured with a solid foundation of strong brothers and sisters, it was left vulnerable to violence. Not because the community bred violence but rather because it didn't have the weapons to fight it off. The violence was produced externally and fed into the community intravenously through the needles of poverty, hopelessness, and despair.

Jamal had watched the disease of violence eat away at his community, and he was determined to return to Newark after completing his education to make a real difference. He knew he had to return because so many of the other successful brothers and sisters had turned their backs on the community. They moved away to the suburbs and severed the rope of opportunity. But not Jamal; he knew he was the chosen one. He knew he would return to transform his community into the promised land.

Jamal finished packing his bags. He surveyed his sparsely furnished bedroom he shared with his two younger brothers to decide what else he needed to take with him. The Knicks and Nets posters all belong to Jerel, the athlete of the family. The rap posters all belonged to Malik, the aspiring artist of the family. His oldest brother, Ali, had joined the navy and removed his things two years ago. The only items left in the bedroom that truly belonged to Jamal were the books, of which he had many.

As the middle child, number three to be exact, Jamal always felt ordinary and overlooked. He didn't have the distinction of being the oldest; that belonged to Ali, his mother's favorite. He didn't have the distinction of being the youngest either; that belonged to "Cleo," short for Cleopatra, his father's favorite. Other than his dreads, which he had just begun to grow, even his looks were ordinary. His dark oval eyes didn't make him stand out in a crowd. His complexion, a mixture of his father's rich dark chocolate and his mother's smooth, creamy caramel resulted in an ordinary shade of mahogany. His height equaled the statistical male average of five ten, and his weight was a predictable 170 pounds. Jamal yearned for something to set him apart. He found that something through his schooling.

Learning came easy for Jamal. While his brothers and sisters struggled with their homework, he glided through his with ease, winning almost every contest and award his school had to offer. Consequently, he spent most of his spare time reading. His collection of books grew so large his father built a bookcase into the bedroom wall to contain the ever-growing collection. When he graduated valedictorian from Newark's West Side High School, no one in his family was surprised. Nor were they surprised when he won a partial scholarship worth $20,000 a year to attend Pittsburgh City University. His only problem was raising the remaining $8,000 to pay the total tuition bill of $28,000. That's when his ambition kicked into high gear and he devised a plan to raise the remaining funds. Although he never felt particularly close to his aunts and uncles, he took great pains to write each of them letters informing them of his upcoming address he was to deliver at graduation. He extended an invitation for them to attend both the ceremony and the after-graduation party he convinced his parents to throw.

During his "It Takes a Village" commencement speech, he praised the importance of family and personally thanked his extended family members for their positive influence in shaping his life. His plan worked liked a charm. He raised more than $3,000 from family and friends. Combined with the $2,000 he saved from his job at the hospital, and the $5,000 from miscellaneous grants and loans, he raised enough money to get through his freshman year, with a little left over to apply to year two. The work-study job the school promised would more than cover any additional living expenses and even provide enough money for at least one trip home during the school year. However, raising the funds for years two, three, and four would again be a task not easy to fulfill. Therefore, he made a mental note that his first mission upon arriving in Pittsburgh would be finding an additional job to supplement his work-study job.

The knock on the door snapped Jamal back into reality.

"Jamal, are you ready to go?"

Jamal's father, Lloyd, had offered to help carry his bags down to the street.

Lloyd sat on the lower bunk bed opposite his son. "Jamal, you know if we could afford a car, I would drive you to Pittsburgh instead of you having to take that damn train."

Jamal had grown accustomed to his father's solemn tone. "Dad, you know I don't mind taking the train."

Lloyd looked into his son's eyes, reached under his jacket and removed a gift box and a small white envelope. "Some of the guys down at the janitorial service kicked in to get you this going-away gift." Lloyd handed Jamal the box and envelope. The envelope had the words "Jamal, College Man" printed boldly on the front. Jamal opened the envelope, and read the card:

> Some people talk of success,
> some people dream of success
> and some people achieve success.
>
> Congratulations on your great achievement.
> The guys from Sanitation Cleaning.

Folded inside the card were four crisp twenty-dollar bills. Jamal closed the card and put the eighty dollars in his shirt pocket. Next, he unwrapped the gift box. Inside the neatly wrapped box was a gold leaf book.

As Jamal flipped through the blank pages, Lloyd said, "It's a journal. I know how much you like to write. I thought you could keep a log of your freshman year. I know it's not much, son, but it's the thought that counts, right?"

Jamal gave his father a hug. "Thanks, Dad. It's perfect. Tell all the guys down at the service I said thanks."

"I will. Now come on. Your mother's waiting to say good-bye."

Lloyd wrapped his arm around Jamal's shoulder and guided his son down the long, narrow hallway that led to the kitchen.

As they entered the kitchen, Jamal's mother, Louise, was busy loading foil-covered goodies into a plastic bag.

"Jamal, I fried you some chicken and made you a couple of sandwiches. You know how expensive that food is on the train." Tears sat in the corners of his mother's eyes.

"I'm really going to miss your cooking," he said, "and you of course."

"Jamal, take care of yourself. Remember you promised to write me once a week."

"I will, Mom. I promise."

"Good-bye, baby." Louise smiled through her tears.

Jamal put down his two suitcases and gave his mother a hug. As he wrapped his arms around her, he slid the four crisp twenty-dollar bills into her apron pocket. He took the plastic bag from her hands, tucked it under his arm and kissed her on the cheek. He was relieved his brothers and sisters had already left for school because saying good-bye to his parents was hard enough.

Lloyd looked at his watch. "Jamal, we better get going. I called you a cab; it should be here any minute."

Jamal smiled at his mother and then looked around the apartment. Eighteen years of memories floated through his mind. He picked up his bags and followed his father out the door. As he descended the stairs, the biblical story of Lot flashed through his mind. Lot had advised his wife not to turn around to look at the twin cities of Sodom and Gomorrah, to avoid turning into a pillar of salt. Jamal knew if he turned around and witnessed his mother waving at the top of the landing, he would turn into an emotional wreck. So he kept his eyes focused directly ahead of him.

Jamal and Lloyd stood on the front stoop in silence, too emotional for idle chitchat.

Jamal thought about the many times he walked, ran, and bicycled up and down South Orange Avenue. How he played baseball with his friends in the empty lot between the liquor store and the check-cashing establishment. How he witnessed the murder of his best friend, shot to death over a stupid leather jacket while waiting to catch the #31 bus. He remembered kissing his first girlfriend Teresa Myers behind the abandoned tire store. His life was about to change, but he knew he wouldn't forget his roots.

"Well, son, I guess this is it," Lloyd stated as the familiar logo of the city cab rounded the corner.

"Dad, promise you'll call if you or Mom need anything."

"I'm the father here, remember. We'll be just fine." Lloyd wrapped his big, strong arms around his son's shoulders and gave him a forceful hug. "Be good."

"I will, Dad. Good-bye."

"Good-bye, Jamal. I love you." Lloyd opened the cab door.

Jamal hustled his three bags into the backseat and told the driver to take him to Newark Penn Station. As the cab pulled away from the curb, Jamal watched his father standing on the stoop, coughing and trying to light a cigarette.

After the cab turned the corner, Jamal did not see his father clutch his chest and fall against the stair railing.

CHAPTER 4

Robert stepped off the bus into downtown Pittsburgh. He raised his collar and buttoned his jacket against the cool September winds that blew off the rivers. The sun was shining brightly, making the rivers shimmer with dances of excitement—the same excitement that tingled through his body.

He exited the Greyhound bus terminal and stood smiling on the sidewalk. He looked at the merging rivers and inhaled the wet, fishy odor the water cast into the wind. The interlocking array of bridges connecting the city to the surrounding mountains reminded him of giant escape hatches. He prayed the iron and steel structures represented a positive sign for his future. A sign he would never again suffer the awful feeling of being trapped.

Suddenly, the sound of Stephon's cries echoed in his ears.

"It's all your fault, Robert. You did this!"

Robert wished he could change the course of action he took that dreadful evening two and half years ago. He knew what was happening in the back of the classroom. He saw the headlights flash against the window. He heard the torturous sounds of Stephon's sobs and the rustle of his books and papers as he was ushered away. He knew what was going on, but he wouldn't turn around. He couldn't turn around. He couldn't bear to see the look on Stephon's face.

Robert put on his sunglasses to hide his eyes. He picked up his bags and walked one block to Liberty Avenue to look for an uptown cab to Oakland. Oakland was the section of town where most of the colleges, universities, and hospitals were located. It was the intellectual heart of the city, packed with coffee shops, bookstores, video arcades, and libraries. He longed for such an environment where he could escape among the anonymous souls rushing back and forth to class.

After hailing a cab, he climbed into the backseat and told the driver to take him to Pittsburgh City University. As the cab crossed the Sixth Avenue Bridge, he remembered his desperate attempt to escape Our Lady of Fatima. Unfortunately, the only road that led out of the school required the permission of his parents.

"Mom, its Robert. Can you come get me?"

"What do you mean, can I come get you? Robert, are you crying? What's wrong? Are you all right?"

"No, I'm not all right. I need to leave this place tonight or I'm going to lose my mind. Mom, please come get me!"

"Robert, calm down and tell me what's going on. I can't help you unless you tell me what's wrong."

"I hate it here. You promised if I didn't like it, I could transfer back to Cambridge High."

"Robert, just a month ago, you said you loved it there. What's happened to make you change your mind?"

"I can't live like this anymore. Please come get me!"

"Robert, wait a minute. We paid a lot of money for you to go to that school. We can't come up there and yank you out because you had a bad day. We need to sit down and discuss this with your father."

"Mom, no! Listen to me. We can't tell Dad!"

"Robert, you're scaring me. What the hell is going on?"

"I promise to tell you everything, but you have to promise you won't tell Dad."

"Robert, I'm driving up to that school first thing tomorrow morning, and you're going to tell me everything. You understand me, boy? Everything!"

"I promise, Mom. Just come and get me. Please come get me."

"Robert, your father and I love you very much. We won't let anything happen to you. Now, pull yourself together and wait for me to get there in the morning."

"What's that's address you want me to drop you off at, son?" the cab driver bellowed from the front seat.

"Ahh, just a minute." Robert removed the packet of housing information from his jacket. "The address is Wehrle Hall, 104 Locust Street, sir."

The driver turned onto Broad Avenue, the main drag that ran the entire length of the campus.

"Are you a freshman?"

"Yes, sir," Robert answered, taking in the sights of the students milling in and out of the fast-food establishments that lined the avenue.

"I thought so. You're much too polite to be an upperclassman. The dormitory is up ahead."

The driver pulled the cab behind a long line of cars with other students unloading their luggage. He helped Robert remove his bags from the backseat.

"Good luck to you, son."

Robert smiled and handed the driver a generous tip. "Thank you, sir. I think I'm going to need it."

"Relax. You'll be just fine." The driver pulled away from the curb with a beep of his horn.

Robert watched the brake lights disappear into the flow of traffic. "I certainly hope so." He glanced up at the dormitory. It was a large glass and concrete circular building that extended over forty stories high. Although he had seen the building before, it looked entirely different now, with the multitude of arriving freshmen swirling around it. He took a deep breath, picked up his bags, and gathered enough strength to fight the crowd.

Once inside the lobby, he was swept into the swirling beehive of students rushing back and forth between their cars and the revolving front doors. He knew the university was large but never imaged the chaos that would greet him upon his arrival. Everyone was talking at the same time, and the noise inside the building was deafening. He noticed a long line of students holding luggage, wrapped twice around the circular lobby of the dormitory.

"Is this the line to get room keys?" he shouted to the girl in front of him.

"Unfortunately, yes!" she shouted back.

Robert settled into his spot and pulled out his housing information. The letter from the housing director identified his two roommates as Shawn Collins and Jamal Lewis. He wondered what his roommates would be like.

As the line inched forward, he remembered how quickly he made friends at Our Lady of Fatima, thanks to the popularity of Stephon. Stephon's infectious laugh and charismatic personality made everyone want to be around him. Stephon also had the gift of persuasion, which he skillfully used to organize the other eight black sophomores into a club named the Defiant Ones. The Defiant Ones did everything together; they went swimming together, played basketball together, studied together, and even went into town together. During one of the trips, Stephon convinced the club members to buy matching T-shirts. They were white with the words "The Defiant Ones" printed in bold black letters across the back.

Robert remembered seeing the outline of Stephon's chiseled chest through the thin white material and wishing he could make his T-shirt fit like Stephon's.

"Next!" the registrar roared from behind the makeshift table. "Wake up, son. We don't have all day!"

Robert fumbled through the manila envelope and removed his housing packet.

"Mr. Robinson, welcome back to the world of the living." The registrar laughed. "Let's see here. You've been assigned to room 2020. Here are your keys and your safety instructions. Take the elevators up to the twentieth floor. If you have any questions, see the resident advisor assigned to your floor. Next!"

Robert hated elevators. They gave him the sense of being trapped inside a moving prison. He was relieved when the light illuminated the number twenty. He maneuvered down the circular hallway until he reached the door that read 2020. He unlocked the door and hauled his bags into the middle of the room.

The suite was a good size, plenty large for three people, he thought. It had a small galley kitchen with a stove, refrigerator, sink, and storage cabinets. The kitchen faced a dining area that had a large rectangular table with four chairs. The table and chairs took up most of the room.

To the right of the dining area was a small living room that contained a sofa and a loveseat. He walked into the living room and sat on the sofa. The thick tweed cloth felt hard and scratchy. It was obvious the furniture was built for durability and not style. The living room also contained a large picture window that looked out over the campus. He walked over to the window.

Although he was only on the twentieth floor, the people below looked like ants scurrying back and forth. Robert smiled at the thought of becoming one of those anonymous ants.

He picked up his bags and headed down the small hallway that divided the three bedrooms.

Being the first to arrive, he assumed the right to choose the best bedroom. He analyzed each room before making his final decision. All three bedrooms were furnished with the same furniture—a chest of drawers, a small metal-framed bed, and a wooden desk and chair. He selected the bedroom largest in size and closest to the bathroom. He tossed his bags onto the bed and started to unpack.

CHAPTER 5

S hawn peered through the van window at the Pittsburgh City University Omni Center. The first leg of his journey was about to begin, and he could hardly contain his excitement.

"Go ahead in, men, and get dressed," Coach Green stated as he stopped at the front entrance. "I'll meet you inside in about ten minutes."

Shawn grabbed his gear and headed for the locker room. His heart palpitated. This was the moment he had longed for, the first step toward achieving his dream of superstardom.

Before changing into his workout gear, he looked around the locker room for his good buddy, Jelin Church. Jelin was a childhood friend who graduated a year ahead of him from Peabody High School. Although Jelin was currently the star forward for the Tigers, Shawn wasn't opposed to taking over his position. Not seeing Jelin around, Shawn changed into his workout gear and jogged onto the court.

Before he noticed the three thousand individual seats and the gigantic size of the gymnasium, he noticed her. Before he admired the championship banners hanging down from the rafters and the computerized digital scoreboard, he admired her. She was the most beautiful girl he had ever seen. She was a cheerleader, and she was practicing cheers with the rest of her squad in the rear section of the gymnasium. The most important practice of his career was about to begin, but the only thing he could think about was her.

Coach Green's whistle snapped Shawn back into reality.

"Okay, men, gather around! We have a lot of work to do to prepare for this season, and we don't have a hell of a lot of time to do it. However, before we get started, there are a few rules I want to get straight right off the bat."

Coach Green paused and then pointed toward the door.

"First, if you're not here to give 100 percent of yourself, there's the door. You can leave right now, because I don't have the time or the patience to deal with you. Second, I'm not your mother or your father; I'm your coach." Coach Green pointed to the word *coach* printed on his sleeveless sweater vest. "If you have any personal issues, check them at the door." Coach Green looked toward the entrance of the gymnasium and then over at Shawn. "The only thing I want you thinking about once you enter this gymnasium is winning the Big Central Championship."

Shawn wondered if the coach had noticed his distraction with the cheerleader.

"Third, as of right now, all the positions on the first-string roster are open. We have five new freshmen with a lot of talent joining the squad, and they'll be competing for your spots. As you all know, two of last year's starting seniors are now in the pros. That means one guard position and one forward position are going to be highly competitive spots. I'll make the decision on who gets those spots, along with the other three positions, based on the talent and hard work you show me over the next five weeks."

Shawn looked around at his teammates and spotted Jelin standing with a group of sophomores. Shawn loved competition. Plus, he knew he was the best guard out of the freshman crew.

"Our first game this season is against West Virginia, and it's only six weeks away. So, men, let's buckle down and get to work."

After finishing his speech, Coach Green read down the list of names on the attendance roster.

When his name was read, Shawn shouted "Here!" hoping his dream cheerleader would take notice. She didn't, but Jelin did.

"Now, for a warm up, I want you guys to give me thirty laps around the perimeter of the gym. Some of you look a little out of shape to me. Once you've completed that, we'll do some shooting drills. Okay, men, let's go."

With a blow from the coach's whistle, the race around the gym floor commenced.

When Shawn rounded the corner near the rear of the gym, he got a closer look at his dream girl. She was even more beautiful close up. He knew he had to meet her but didn't want to come on too strong or too fast. He had an image to uphold.

He looked around for Jelin. He knew Jelin would intervene on his behalf. He picked up his pace to catch up with Jelin.

"Yo, Jelin!"

"Collins, I thought I heard someone callin' me."

Shawn put his arm around Jelin's shoulder. "Jelin, what's up, brotha?"

"Collins, what are you doing up front with the real men? I thought you'd be bringing up the rear like you did at Peabody."

"When will you learn, Jelin? The cream always rises to the top. And we both know who the cream is around here, don't we?"

"Yeah, and it ain't you." Jelin laughed as they completed the lap.

"Jelin, see that fine honey over there?"

"I see a lot of fine honeys over there."

"No, I mean the really, really fine one."

"And which one would that be?"

Shawn pointed. "The one with her hair pinned up in a ponytail."

"Man, stop pointing." Jelin slapped Shawn's hand down. "I know the one you're talking about. Her name is Tammera, Tammera Patterson. She's a home girl, graduated from Alterdice last year. I know her. She used to date my cousin, Trae."

"Are they still dating?"

"No they broke up after Trae went to Georgetown last year. Why? You interested, Collins?"

"Hell yeah. Look at her. She's fine."

When Shawn and Jelin passed by Tammera for the third time, Shawn noticed her smile at him.

"Did you see that, Jelin?"

"Did I see what?"

"Man, she smiled at me. You didn't see that?"

"I think these laps are getting to you, Collins. You're starting to see things."

"Watch when we pass her this time. I think she has the hots for me." Shawn pounded his chest, doing his best Tarzan impression.

When they made their next pass around the cheerleaders, Tammera smiled and waved at Jelin.

"You idiot. She's smiling at *me*, Collins. I told you, I know her."

"You're my friend—right, Jelin? And friends are supposed to look out for one another, right?"

"What do you want, Collins?"

"Hook a brotha up. Introduce me to my future wife."

"Man, you talkin' crazy. Your future wife? I thought you were dating Latisha Wright?"

"Latisha who?"

Jelin and Shawn both laughed as they completed lap twelve.

Shawn couldn't believe his good luck; Jelin actually knew his dream girl. On the next pass, he ran as close to Tammera as he possibly could without touching her. The girl was absolutely stunning. She had a maple brown complexion with big bright eyes. Her eyebrows were thick, just like his. She stood about five seven, which was about the height he preferred his women. She was thin but not too thin. She had tight, perky breasts, not as big as Latisha's but a nice size, and her ass looked nice and round. She was very athletic and in the best of shape. Her skin was soft and smooth; she didn't even have a blemish, at least not one he could see. Although her hair was pinned up in a ponytail, he could tell it was long and thick. He hated when Latisha cut her hair off. He loved being able to run his fingers through his girl's hair when they made mad love.

Shawn fantasized what it would feel like to make love to Tammera. He imagined wrapping his arms around her, pulling her body against him, and exploding his passion inside her.

Jelin grabbed Shawn's shoulder. "Slow down, yo! This is supposed to be a slow jog, not a sprint. You better save some of your energy for later. This is gonna be a long practice."

Shawn had never been so turned on by a girl he hadn't met. He wondered what was happening to him.

After the final lap, Coach Green blew his whistle.

"Okay, men, form a single line and take turns shooting from the foul line. Last year's foul shooting cost us a couple key games. I want to make sure it doesn't happen again. Line up. I wanna see who my best free-throw shooters are."

The cheerleaders stopped their routine to watch the foul-shooting exhibition. Shawn knew foul shooting was one of his strengths and a great way to make Tammera notice. As he rotated his turn around the foul line, he successfully sunk all his free throws. His fluid stroke and smooth follow through caught the coach's eye.

Coach Green made some notations in his notebook. "Not too shabby, Collins!"

Shawn looked around to see if Tammera had noticed. Yes! She was looking straight at him. But when their eyes met, she looked at the floor.

"Okay, men, we're going to play a couple scrimmage games. The freshmen are going to play the sophomores, and then the juniors will play the seniors. I want the freshmen to be skins, so remove your jerseys, men."

Shawn smiled. Tammera would definitely notice him now. He removed his jersey and glanced over at the cheerleaders. He caught Tammera eyeing his body and gave her a quick wink and a big smile.

Tammera smiled back.

Having Tammera watch from the sidelines made Shawn play like a man possessed. His fifteen-foot jump shot was right on the money. He didn't miss one shot throughout the entire game. After every bucket, he glanced over to see if Tammera was still watching.

Shawn's freshmen squad beat the sophomore squad forty to thirty-two. Shawn had twenty of his team's forty points. Coach Green blew his whistle and ordered the juniors and seniors to take the court in preparation for their match.

Shawn took a seat on the sidelines, opposite Tammera. Occasionally, their eyes met, and he flashed his brilliant white smile.

"Yo, Jelin, I think Tammera likes me. Look at the way she keeps smiling at me."

"Collins, give it a rest, I give in. I'll introduce you, all right? Just shut up about Tammera. You're starting to work my nerves, bro."

Shawn looked over at Jelin and faked his best sincerity. "Did I ever tell you I love you, man?"

"Yeah, well, you're going to owe me big time, Collins. And I mean big time."

Shawn patted Jelin on the back. "Okay, man. Just take care of business for me."

While the juniors and seniors played their scrimmage, the cheerleaders started packing up to leave. Jelin ran over to where Tammera was and started talking to her.

A few minutes later, Tammera picked up her bag, looked across the court, and waved good-bye to Shawn. Jelin came back and sat down beside Shawn.

"C'mon, man, the suspense is killing me. What did she say?"

"She said she knows you're a player, and if you looking for another harem girl, she's not the one."

"Get out! Is that what she said?"

"Man, would I lie to you?"

"Yeah, Jelin, you would. Now tell me the truth. I saw the way she smiled at me when she hightailed it out of here."

"That's what she said. But she did agree to meet us tonight at seven o'clock at the Big O. But, my brother, let me give you a word of advice. You better be on your best behavior, because that girl doesn't take any shit."

Before Shawn had a chance to answer, Coach Green blew his whistle, indicating it was time for the next drill.

Shawn hustled back onto the floor. "I just hope I have some energy left after this practice."

CHAPTER 6

The eight-hour train ride from Newark to Pittsburgh allowed Jamal to relax. But his thoughts kept returning to his father. Something about the way he said good-bye seemed odd.

Jamal reached into his backpack and removed the gold leaf journal his father had given him. As he wrote down his observations, the problem became apparent. Jamal stopped writing and looked out the window. His father was ill.

Although his father was only fifty-two, all the hard work he put in over the past thirty years to keep the family afloat had finally taken its toll. His father had always been a quick, strong man, but lately he seemed a little slower. He took the three flights of stairs to their apartment at a slower pace. He didn't eat much, and he never laughed anymore.

Jamal wasn't sure why his father's health was deteriorating, but he needed to confirm his suspicion.

Dear Mom,

Greetings from aboard Amtrak. Yes, I decided to write the first letter from the train. I intend to keep my promise and write you once a week. Mom, I have something very important to ask you, and I hope you can be honest and tell me the truth. There comes a time in life when a boy crosses that threshold into manhood. I've crossed that threshold, and I'm strong enough to handle the truth, no matter how painful it may be. Since the day my friend Tony was murdered, you've tried to protect me from pain. But pain is a natural part of life, and to be a man, I must handle the good as well as the bad. I must be strong and accept whatever life throws my way.

I'm telling you all of this because I need to know the truth. I need to know if there's something wrong with Dad. I've noticed his health isn't as good as it used to be. And this morning, there were tears in his eyes. Mom, I've never seen Dad cry before. I know something must be wrong. I'm not a little boy anymore. I can handle the truth. So please, in response to this letter, tell me if my instincts are correct. Is Dad sick?

Since we're being honest with one another, there are a few things I've been keeping from you and Dad that I think you need to know.

First, Aaliyah has secretly been dating Bobby Rodgers. Yes, Bobby Rodgers, the drug dealer who hangs out over at Paige's Grill. He picks Aaliyah up at the corner so he doesn't have to come to the house. I think Aaliyah is impressed with the expensive gifts he buys her and the fancy car he drives. I 've warned her to stay away from Bobby, but I don't think she listened. Mom, I know Aaliyah is smart and can handle herself, but I don't trust Bobby. So please keep a close eye on that situation.

The other problem is with Malik. The West Side Kings have been pressuring him to join their gang. So far, I don't think Malik has joined, but I'm afraid now that I'm gone he may decide to cross over. If you notice him dressing in red and black, call me immediately.

Well, I think that's enough bad news for one letter. I love you.

Your son,
Jamal

Jamal folded the letter into an envelope and decided to mail it once he arrived in Pittsburgh.

After hearing the conductor announce the next stop would be Pittsburgh, Pennsylvania, Jamal gathered his bags and waited at the doors. He glanced at his watch. It was a quarter to four. He needed to hurry to the financial aid office so he could pick up his registration packet and select a work-study job before all the good jobs were taken.

He rushed through the station, wondering where he could catch a bus to campus. He stopped at the information booth in the rotunda of the station. The nameplate on the desk identified the clerk as Mrs. Buttons. He ran up to the counter with a shortness of breath.

"How can I get to Pittsburgh City University?"

"Slow down, sweetie," Mrs. Buttons answered with a smile. "I can always tell you people from out of town. You're always running around here like your house is on fire. I bet you're from New York City, aren't you?"

"New Jersey," Jamal answered.

"I knew it." Mrs. Buttons slapped her hand against the counter. "Why are you people from New York and New Jersey always in such a rush? You know, honey, life is short. You need to slow down and enjoy life while you can. If you don't, you just might rush your life away."

Jamal returned Mrs. Button's smile. "I'm sorry, can you please tell me how I can catch a bus to Pittsburgh City University?"

"Now that's better, sweetheart. You look so handsome when you smile. Now you go right out those doors and cross the street to the hotel. They have a shuttle that runs to the campus every half hour. The next shuttle should be in about fifteen minutes. Now take care of yourself and come back and see Mrs. Buttons again. Okay, sugar?"

"Thank you, Mrs. Buttons." Jamal waved good-bye and followed her directions to the hotel. He mailed the letter he had written his mother in the mailbox in front of the hotel.

He looked around at downtown Pittsburgh and was amazed at the vast difference between Newark and Pittsburgh. He thought the city would be dirty from the pollution generated from the steel mills. But there were no steel mills in sight. Downtown looked like something from a picturesque postcard. All the glass skyscrapers looked shiny and new, the air was fresh and clear, and the city was impressively clean. Unlike Newark, the streets were swept clean of debris, and no graffiti was visible. However, one thing did bother him—the lack of black and brown faces. He could count the number of minorities on one hand. He knew that would take some getting used to.

The campus bus stopped in front of the hotel just as Mrs. Buttons had advised. Jamal paid his fifty cents and climbed aboard. The ride to campus was interesting and short. In Newark, everything was relatively flat. But here, everything was built on steep, narrow streets. He realized he was on campus when he saw the towering Cathedral of Education, a gigantic gothic structure he remembered from the information packet the school sent him. The bus pulled up in front of the Student Activity Center. Jamal followed the arrows to the financial aid office. He could not believe the size of the hill he had to climb in order to reach the office. He was relieved to see only a few students ahead of him in line.

The day was moving fast; it was already four thirty. He couldn't wait to get to his dorm room, take a shower, and change out of his sweaty clothes. He was thankful the financial aid officer worked fast. In less than twenty minutes, he was called into the office. He was instructed on his scholarship obligations and then handed a list of available work-study jobs. They all paid the same wage, $7.50 an hour. He selected the job of hall monitor in his dormitory. The job would be convenient and allow him to get some studying done while he worked.

After completing his responsibility at the finical aid office, he picked up his keys from the housing director's office and headed for his dorm room.

By the time he reached the door of his assigned suite, it was already six o'clock. He put down his bags to unlock the door. Raised voices were coming from inside his suite. He pushed open the unlocked door to find his roommates had already arrived and were arguing over who should have the biggest bedroom.

"What's going on in here? I could hear you guys all the way down the hall."

"I take it you must be roommate number three?" one of them said. Jamal nodded.

The boy stuck out at his hand. "I'm Shawn Collins."

"Nice to meet you, Shawn," Jamal answered, not sure of the situation he had walked into.

The other boy also shook Jamal's hand. "I'm Robert Robinson. And you must be Jamal Lewis, right?"

"Right," Jamal answered.

"Well, bro, let me fill you in on what's goin' on here." Shawn looked back toward the bedrooms. "Robert grabbed the biggest bedroom before the rest of us got here."

"Since I was the first to arrive, I chose that bedroom over there. I didn't know I'd be setting off World War III over a bedroom that's about two feet larger than the other two rooms," Robert said.

"You thought wrong," Shawn answered. "Listen, you guys, I'm gonna be the next superstar guard for the Pittsburgh City Tigers. I'm gonna need that extra space for all of my gear and shit."

"Just because he's an athlete doesn't give him special privileges, does it?"

"All right, check this out," Jamal said. "In order to be fair to everyone, this is what we're gonna do. I'm going to write the numbers one, two, and three on three pieces of paper. Whoever pulls out the paper with the one written on it gets first pick of the bedrooms. Can you both agree to that?"

Robert and Shawn nodded.

Jamal wrote the numbers on three slips of paper and let Shawn and Robert pick from his hand. Robert opened his paper and found a two, Shawn opened his paper and found a three, and Jamal opened his paper and showed that it was the one.

"Well, my man, it looks like you're the grand prize winner," Shawn said sarcastically.

Jamal rolled his paper into a tight ball. "Yeah, it looks that way, doesn't it? But look, Shawn, since I really don't have that much stuff, I'll let you have the bigger room. Any objections, Robert?"

"I guess I'm outnumbered," Robert answered.

"Well, fellas, I think we're gonna get along all right. Oh shit, I almost forgot." Shawn looked at his watch. "I have a date at seven. I gotta get moving so I'm not late meeting my future wife." Shawn picked up his bag and raced into the bathroom.

Jamal looked at Robert inquisitively. "His future wife?"

Robert shrugged and then went to retrieve his stuff from Shawn's new room.

Jamal looked around at the rest of the suite. Compared to the one bedroom he shared at home with his two brothers, the suite seemed enormous. He found it hard to believe his roommates were arguing over one of the bedrooms since all three rooms provided the luxury of privacy, something he never had.

"If you need to call your parents, we already have a phone installed," Robert said, walking back into the living room. "It's over there against the kitchen wall."

Jamal took in the view from the living room window. "This place is great. I had no idea it was going to be this large."

"Yeah, me neither," Robert agreed. "These are the suites assigned to athletes and scholarship recipients."

Jamal turned from the window. "So which one are you?"

"I won an academic scholarship for public administration. I wanna be a city manager after I graduate. How about you, Jamal? Are you a jock or a brain?"

"I won an academic scholarship for business administration."

"Cool. Hey, maybe we share some of the same classes. Let me see your schedule."

Jamal handed Robert his schedule.

"We have the same Urban Management class with Dr. Altenburger," Robert stated. "That's great; if we miss any classes, we can copy notes."

"Yeah, right," Jamal laughed. "Robert, I'm starving. Do you want to go over to the cafeteria and grab some dinner before it closes?"

Before Robert had a chance to answer, Shawn came out of the bathroom with a towel wrapped around his waist and a toothbrush stuck in his mouth.

Jamal noticed Robert admiring Shawn's powerful physique.

"Do you guys have any plans?" Shawn asked.

"We're going to grab something at the cafeteria," Jamal answered.

"Why don't you guys come over to the Big O and meet some of my friends. I met this fine cheerleader today, and she's going to be there with some of her roommates. From what I hear, her roommates are fine too. Come on, if you're interested."

"What's the Big O?" Robert asked.

"It's the local watering hole down the street from the dorm. The food's a little greasy, but it's not bad. I'm friends with the bartender. He'll serve us drinks even though were not twenty-one." Shawn shoved his toothbrush back into his mouth and returned to the bathroom.

"What do you say, Robert? Sounds like it might be fun."

"I don't know, Jamal. I still need to unpack."

"Me, too. But this may be a good way to get to know our roommate." Jamal placed his hand on Robert's shoulder. "First impressions aren't always the right ones. Give Shawn a chance. Besides, maybe you'll like his friends."

"I doubt that but all right," Robert answered reluctantly.

"Great. Give me a minute to change out of these sweaty clothes. Let Shawn know we're going with him."

Robert walked down the hallway and stuck his head inside the partially opened bathroom door. "Okay, Shawn, we're gonna meet you at the Big O."

Shawn had removed his towel and was naked when Robert looked in. He quickly wrapped the towel back around his waist. "A'ight, but you guys need to hurry and get dressed because I told my friends I would meet them at seven."

Robert knocked on Jamal's open door. "Shawn said hurry up. We need to be there by seven."

"Is Shawn ever going to come out of the bathroom, so somebody else can use it?" Jamal asked.

Robert looked down the hallway at the closed bathroom door. "You know, Jamal, I think we better get used to Shawn hogging the bathroom. Maybe you can jump in the shower while he's at the sink. I think that's the way we're going to have to operate around here. If we don't, we may never make it to class in the mornings."

Jamal jumped off the bed. "Yeah, I think you're probably right."

CHAPTER 7

By the time Robert and Jamal arrived at the Big O, Shawn was already there with his friends. They were seated at a large table in the rear of the crowded bar. The Big O wasn't much to write home about. It was very narrow, with tables lined against the side and rear walls. It was packed with students, and the jukebox was playing some ridiculous country western music. Robert wondered what made the place so popular and why it was called the Big O. It looked more like the "Small L."

Shawn motioned his roommates over to the table. "There you guys are! Let me introduce everybody," he shouted above the music. "This is my homeboy Jelin Church, another member of the soon-to-be Big Central champions. The lovely lady across from me is Tammera Patterson, and beside her are her roommates, Anika and Jazmine.

"Everyone, these are my roommates, Jamal and Robert."

"Shawn, you didn't tell me your roommates were going to be so cute," Tammera said.

"We have a pitcher of beer here. You guys thirsty?" Jelin asked.

Jamal and Robert sat at the table. "Sure, I'll have a glass," Jamal answered.

"How about you, Robert?"

"Yeah, thanks."

"Have you all eaten yet?" Jamal asked.

"No, Shawn wouldn't let us order until you guys got here. Can we please order now, yo?" Jelin picked up the plastic-coated menu from behind the salt and pepper holder. "I don't know about you all, but I'm starving."

"Yeah, me too," Jamal replied.

"All right, all right, you can order now. But remember—tonight everything's on me," Shawn boasted.

"My, my, my, aren't we the big spender. If one didn't know any better, Mr. Collins, one might think you were trying to impress me," Tammera said.

"And if I am, Ms. Patterson?"

"Then you just scored two points." Tammera laughed.

"And what do I need to do to win the game?"

"Wouldn't you like to know?"

"How long have you two known each other?" Jamal interrupted.

Shawn looked at his watch. "Oh, about five hours. But I hope it's just the beginning of a beautiful relationship."

"You're such a player, Shawn Collins. But you're gonna have to do a little better than that. I'm not gonna fall for those tired lines." Tammera laughed.

Anika smiled across the table at Robert and chimed in with a soft southern accent.

"Where are you two from?"

"I'm from Cambridge Falls, Ohio, and Jamal's from Newark, New Jersey," Robert answered.

"Oh, what a small world. I'm from Montclair, New Jersey," Jazmine said, finally getting a chance to jump into the conversation. "What high school did you graduate from, Jamal?"

"West Side High School."

"You're kidding. Do you know Gail Summers?"

"Yeah, she was in my calculus class last year."

"She's my cousin," Jazmine replied.

"Get outta here! Next time you see her, tell her Jamal Lewis said hello."

"I certainly will." Jazmine smiled.

"Where are you from, Anika?" Robert asked.

"I'm from Richmond, Virginia."

"Richmond. I've been there," Robert said. "It's a beautiful city."

"The view ain't too bad from here either," Anika replied.

"I don't know about you all, but I'm ready to order," Jelin said.

"Why don't we get a couple buckets of buffalo wings and some curly fries?" Shawn suggested.

"Sounds good to me. And another pitcher of beer," Jelin added.

"How about the rest of you. Does that sound a'ight?" Shawn asked.

"You're the one paying," Tammera said. "Go ahead and order. We girls are going to go to the restroom."

"Yo waiter! We're ready to order over here," Jelin shouted.

Tammera and her roommates gathered their purses and stood from the table.

"Why do women always travel in packs when you go to the restroom?" Shawn asked, checking out the bodies of Tammera's roommates. "What is it you really do in there?"

"Talk about you men. You should know that by now, Shawn. C'mon, girls, we have a lot to discuss."

As the girls walked past the table, Anika ran her hand against the back of Robert's neck.

Robert returned a weak smile.

When the girls were safely out of hearing distance, Shawn let out a long, slow whistle.

"Damn that Tammera is fine. I can't wait to hit that."

Jelin poured himself another beer. "Knowing you, it won't take long. And what are you gonna do after you get it? Move on to her roommates?"

"Man, I think Tammera might be the one to make me settle down."

"What!" Jelin choked on his beer. "Did I hear those words come from the mouth of Shawn Collins? Mr. Romeo himself. Did you say settle down?"

"Yes, I did," Shawn answered as the waiter approached the table.

"Well, I don't know about the rest of you guys, but I think Anika likes my boy Robert here." Jamal patted Robert on the back. "I saw the way she looked at you and stroked your neck. You go, boy."

"Yeah, I got that impression too," Jelin added.

Shawn glared down the table at Robert. "So when you gonna make your move, man?"

Robert picked up the pitcher of beer and refilled his glass. "I think she's nice, but I need to get to know her a little bit better. I mean, I don't wanna rush into something without knowing what else is available."

"I heard that." Jelin tapped his glass against Robert's. "You never know what you might find."

"Yeah, Shawn," Jamal agreed. "Not everyone moves as fast as you do."

"And what about you, Jamal? I think Jazmine wants a piece of you."

"To be honest with you, Shawn, my main focus right now is school. I think Jazmine is cool, but between my school work and my work-study job, I don't think I'm gonna have a lot of time for an active social life."

"Active social life? Don't tell me I'm gonna be the only one gettin' any action around here." Shawn stood to address his congregation. "You guys need to adopt my motto. If you see something you like, go for it, because life is too damn short to spend your time waiting. And, men, Tammera is definitely something I don't want to wait for."

"That's fine for you, Shawn," Jamal answered. "But I'm far from wealthy, and if I lose my scholarship, I'll have to drop out of school. School has to be my number-one priority."

"I'm just trying to make you have some fun. Lighten up, yo."

"Did you miss us, gentlemen?" Tammera asked as her crew returned to the table.

Shawn placed his hand across his heart. "I miss you every second you're away."

"Give me a break." Tammera laughed.

"Here's your order." The waiter placed the food on the table. "Can I get you anything else?"

"No, I think we're fine," Shawn answered.

Jelin grabbed for the bucket of wings.

"Slow down, homey! Ladies first," Shawn insisted.

"Aren't we the gentleman," Jazmine exclaimed. "I'm happy to see there are still a few good men around with manners. Tammera, I think you better hold on to this one. He seems too good to be true."

Jelin reached for the basket of curly fries. "Take it from me, Jazmine, anytime you're around Shawn, expect the unexpected."

"That's right. I like to keep a little mystery."

"Well, I intend to give you a lot of that." Tammera laughed, dipping a wing in the blue cheese dressing.

"These wings are delicious," Anika said, licking the sauce from her fingers. "Do you like it hot or mild, Robert?"

"Do I like what hot or mild?"

Anika batted her lashes. "Why the sauce of course. Whatever else do you think I could have been referring to?"

Everyone laughed as Robert seemed caught off guard by Anika's less than subtle flirting.

As the evening dragged on, Anika's advances and sexual innuendos toward Robert become more aggressive. He tried to play along, but the more he played along, the more suggestive she became. On top of that, her actions were drawing unwanted attention from Shawn. He could tell Shawn's was watching him, analyzing him, waiting for him to do or say something wrong.

"Do you need any help getting that sauce from between your fingers?" Robert asked, watching Anika use a napkin to get at the sauce.

"Maybe later," Anika giggled.

As the dinner conversation went on, Robert felt pressure being applied against his foot. He looked under the table. Anika had removed her shoe and was tapping her foot against his sneakers. *Damn, doesn't this girl ever give up?*

As Anika's toe crept up his pant leg, he pushed away from the table.

Shawn dropped a curly fry to see what was going on under the table.

"Excuse me." Robert almost knocked over the table in his haste to leave. "I have to go to the men's room."

"It's right over there." Shawn grabbed hold of the table.

"Robert's a little shy," Jamal piped in.

"Oh is that it?" Shawn answered sarcastically.

"I think he's cute," Anika replied.

"That's obvious," Tammera responded. "You've been chasing the poor boy all night long."

"Do you have a problem with that, Tammera?" Anika asked.

"I think what she means," Jazmine intervened, "is maybe you need to tone it down a little bit. I mean, if you had batted those lashes any faster, you would have created a funnel cloud up in here."

Everyone laughed as Jazmine imitated Anika's eye-batting routine.

Robert escaped to the small, single-urinal men's room. He locked the door behind him and took a deep breath. *You idiot. You're acting like such a pussy. You're going to ruin everything. You haven't been here a full day, and you're already raising suspicion. Pull yourself together and get a grip.*

He looked at himself in the mirror. Perspiration had seeped through the underarm of his cotton shirt. He snatched a paper towel from the dispenser, wet it with cold water, and wiped his face. He needed to settle his nerves and collect his thoughts. He couldn't return to the table in an agitated state and cause another scene. He unbuttoned and removed his shirt so he could wipe away the perspiration that had dripped from his armpit. Before he could wet another paper towel, there was a knock at the door.

"Robert, it's Jelin. Let me in, yo. I gotta take a piss bad, man."

"Ahh, just a minute, Jelin." Robert took a second to collect himself and then unlocked the door.

Jelin rushed into the bathroom like a hurricane. He brushed passed Robert and walked up to the urinal. "Thanks, yo."

Robert put his shirt on.

"Ooh, what a relief," Jelin exclaimed.

The forceful sound of Jelin's urgent demand splashed into the reservoir at the bottom of the urinal. It took all Robert's strength not to look over at Jelin, but he kept his eyes focused in the mirror.

Jelin looked at Robert. "Are you all right, yo? You look wack. Too much to drink, huh?"

Robert buttoned his shirt. "Yeah, I'm not a heavy drinker, and I'm still a little tired from all the rushing around I had to do today."

"I heard that, my brother." Jelin shook off the remaining drops and then zipped up his pants.

Robert stepped away from the sink to allow Jelin to wash his hands.

Jelin reached around Robert to grab a paper towel. His free hand cupped Robert's shoulder. "Sorry, yo, but it's a little tight in here."

Robert looked in the mirror and saw Jelin smile. "Here, I'm finished." He squirmed out of Jelin's grasp and threw his paper towel in the wastepaper basket.

"See ya back at the table." Robert reached for the door.

"Right," Jelin said.

Once outside the door, Robert caught his breath. *I'm not going to let it happen.* Robert closed his eyes and forced his thoughts of Jelin into the depths of his subconscious. He made up his mind; he was going to return to the table and try to enjoy the rest of the evening. He wasn't going to let his inner desires take control, and he most certainly wasn't going to let Shawn rattle his nerves. He raised his head and walked back toward the table with pride in his step.

"What took you so long?" Shawn smirked. "We were starting to get worried about you."

"I was talking to Jelin" Robert answered, aware of Shawn's head games.

The conversation at the table had changed to the new routines the cheerleaders were working on for the first home game.

Jamal looked at his watch. "Well, everyone, this evening has been fun, but I really need to get back to the dorm."

"So soon?" Jazmine asked.

"I haven't unpacked yet, and I have an early class in the morning."

"Yeah, me too," Robert agreed, relieved to have an excuse to leave.

"It was very nice meeting you all," Jamal said, looking around the table.

"It was nice meeting you too," Tammera answered, wiping the sauce from her lips so she could kiss them both on the cheek.

Anika winked across the table at Robert. "I hope to see a lot more of you, Robert."

"How about if I plan something for next weekend?" Shawn said, looking for everyone's agreement. "We'll all get back together again."

"Cool," Jamal said. "That is, as long as I don't have to work next weekend."

"Where's everybody going?" Jelin asked, returning to the table.

"My roommates are wimping out on us. They have to go back to the dorm."

Jelin slapped Robert's back. "But it's still early, bro. Come on, have one more beer."

"We really have to get going, Jelin. But I think we're going to get together again next weekend," Robert said.

"Oh, we are? Cool."

Robert and Jamal waved their final good-byes and then maneuvered their way out of the crowded bar.

Anika ran over and slid her telephone number into Robert's shirt pocket. "Call me."

Robert nodded then quickly followed Jamal out the door.

As they stepped into the cool September air, Robert breathed a sigh of relief.

"Are you all right, man?" Jamal asked. "You looked a little tense in there."

"Yeah, I'm all right. I just needed some air."

CHAPTER 8

The Braid Boutique was busier than usual for a weekday. Every time the phone rang, Latisha looked over at the receptionist, hoping it was Shawn. But when the receptionist lowered her head into the appointment book, Latisha knew it was just another customer calling.

Five long weeks had passed, and Shawn hadn't called once. Latisha wondered why he hadn't returned any of her messages. Why he was tearing her heart out? *Stop*, she told herself. The time for crying and feeling sorry for herself was over. It was time for action, and she had a plan.

Latisha wiped her eyes with the back of her hand and then reached for another section of hair to add to Miss Gloria's new do. *Why do women with a nanosecond of hair have to get braids down to their damn ass?* Latisha thought as she skillfully weaved the long blond braid into Miss Gloria's nappy, black roots. It would take at least another hour to finish Miss Gloria's hair. Thankfully, she was her last customer for the day.

"Latisha girl, I can tell your mind's on somethin' other than braiding my hair." Miss Gloria put down her *Jet* magazine and looked up at Latisha. "You've hardly said two words, and that's not like you, precious. Is everything all right? How's Ruby and your mother doin'?"

"Oh, they fine. Just got a lot on my mind right now is all."

Latisha wished her last customer was anyone other than Miss Gloria. She was a nice lady but nosy as hell.

"I saw your brother, Mookie Man, over at the Rendezvous Club last Friday night. Is he still seeing Mildred's daughter? What's that's child's name?" Miss Gloria snapped her fingers. "Oh yeah, Pumpkin. Is he still seeing Pumpkin? 'Cause I didn't see the two of them together."

"Yeah, they still together."

"Oh, I was just wondering. Not that I'm trying to be nosy. Where they livin' now?"

"They at my mother's house."

"You all livin' there together? Must be awful crowded."

"You still dating Tethonie, Miss Gloria?" Latisha asked, trying to change the direction of the conversation.

"Yeah, child, that man treats me good. And like I always say, when you find a good man, hang on tight 'cause they hard to come by these days. You know what I mean, Latisha?"

"Yeah, I hear you, Miss Gloria."

"Are you still dating that Collins boy?"

Latisha had been wondering how long it would take Miss Gloria to get around to Shawn.

"Yeah, we're still dating, but since he went off to college, we don't get to see much of each other anymore."

"I thought he went to the university down in Oakland?"

"Yeah, he did."

"Child, that school's right down the street. Don't tell me you're lettin' a couple miles come between you."

"No, it's not the distance. It's just … Shawn's been real busy with basketball and all."

"Basketball! Let me give you a word of advice. As fine as that boy is, those college girls gonna be all over him like black on a skillet. You better get down there and stake your claim before it's too late. You see, I know what I'm talkin' about. I won't let Tethonie alone for one minute without knowing exactly where he is and when he's coming home. Believe me, sugar, it don't take long for another woman to step in and steal yo' man. Honey, I don't give' em the chance."

Miss Gloria picked up the handheld mirror and checked out her new color. "You think Tethonie gonna like me as a blond? I was getting tired of that autumn sunset color."

"I'm sure he will, Miss Gloria. I think you look like Shirley Murdock."

"Oh, Tethonie just loves her."

As Miss Gloria broke out into a rendition of "As We Lay," Latisha thought about Miss Gloria's words. She hated to admit it, but Miss Gloria was right. Shawn probably did have another woman on the side. That's why he hadn't called.

Latisha narrowed her eyes and shook her head. *He's not gonna dump me like a bag of old garbage and walk away.*

"Did you say somethin', Latisha?"

"No, I was just thinking."

Latisha finished the first side of Miss Gloria's head and looked down at her watch. It was almost six o'clock. She had to hurry if she was going to make it down to Oakland before Shawn went out for the evening.

"Latisha, you makin' the braids too tight. Loosen them up a little before you stop my blood flow."

"Sorry, Miss Gloria."

As Latisha continued working Miss Gloria's braids, she remembered her unsuccessful attempt to get Shawn's number from his mother.

"Hello, Mrs. Collins, this is Latisha. I was wondering, did Shawn give you his number at the dorm yet? You see, I need to get in touch with him, but he hasn't called me yet."

"Latisha, if Shawn wanted you to have his number, he would have given it to you, don't you think?"

She's such a bitch, Latisha thought. But the situation was about to change. If Shawn wanted to drop her, he was going to have to tell her to her face. *Weeping may endure for a night, but joy comes in the morning.* Latisha smiled, realizing the full potential of her plan. If everything worked out the way she intended, Shawn would have no choice but to remain a part of her life. Hell, it could even lead to marriage if she played her cards right.

By seven thirty, Latisha had finished Miss Gloria's hair. She said her good-byes to the girls at the Braid Boutique, collected her pay for the day, and headed home. Thanks to Miss Gloria, she had earned over $150. She hated to carry so much cash on her, but since the banks were all closed, she couldn't deposit the money into her checking account until Monday.

Since starting her job at the Braid Boutique, she had saved over $2,000. She was determined to save enough money so she could move out of the hellhole her mother called a house and get her own apartment.

If her plan was successful, she definitely was going to need her own place.

Her calculations indicated she would need another $2,000 to set herself up right. She needed enough money to pay the security deposit and the first month's rent. Plus, she needed money to buy furniture. She had already selected the apartment complex. It was on East Liberty Blvd., halfway between her job and her mother's house. The location was perfect since it allowed her to walk to either location within ten minutes. She couldn't wait until she could sit on her balcony, barbecue, and drink beers with her friends. If her arithmetic proved correct, she would have enough money saved up by spring.

Before heading home, Latisha stopped in the drugstore on the corner of Penn and Highland Avenue to pick up the items she needed for her plan. She walked to the rear of the store and stared at the overwhelming selection of condoms. Although she had purchased condoms before, she never noticed the large selection available. Usually any type would do but not tonight. Tonight she needed the perfect condom. She carefully studied each brand, contemplating which one best suited her purpose.

"I don't know why you're standin' there looking at those. I heard Shawn dumped your tired ass."

It was Monica Chambers, one of the tramps Shawn slept with.

"Well, at least I had him, which is more than I can say for you, bitch. All you did was open up your legs like some low-down, triflin', skeezer ho!"

"Who you callin' a bitch?"

Latisha turned to confront Monica face-to-face. "Do you see anybody else standing here? Why don't you just go on and do what you came in here to do because if you start somethin' with me, you're gonna get your flat ass kicked."

"You're right, Latisha. You ain't worth my time. By the way, I think you better lay off them Doritos 'cause I almost mistook your fat ass for a Macy's Parade float."

"Yeah, well you can kiss my fat ass from the crack to the back," Latisha replied.

"My lips couldn't stretch that far," Monica answered.

Latisha put her palm to Monica's face and pretended she was no longer there.

Monica snapped her gum and walked away.

Latisha's blood was boiling. What the hell did Shawn ever see in that hoochie?

After waiting for Monica to exit the store, Latisha selected the extra-thin lubricated condoms with the reservoir tip. As she stood at the checkout counter, she thought about her plan and started to get nervous. What if it didn't work? What if he didn't let her into his dorm room? What if he had another girl with him? "Stop," Latisha told herself. She wasn't going to think about failing. Besides, her personal psychic had advised her, "Your day will be filled with romance from an unexpected source." The psychic had to be referring to Shawn. Latisha grabbed the white plastic bag from the cashier and stuck it under her arm.

Once outside, she hailed a jitney to take her to Garfield. She hated the thought of going home. Her mother's apartment was always in a state of chaos. Although she only had two brothers and one sister, the apartment was always filled with people. Her older brother, Mookie Man, his girlfriend, Pumpkin, and their two kids had recently moved back in. Her older sister, Ruby, and her three kids still lived there. And her younger brother, Hennie, who was always entertaining his drug-dealing friends, also lived there. Since the project apartment was a large three-bedroom-with-basement model, her mother was able to accommodate the extra bodies by turning the basement into an apartment for Mookie Man and his family. Her brother Hennie slept on the pullout couch in the living room, which left a separate bedroom for her parents, one for Ruby and her three kids, and one for herself. Latisha cherished her little bit of privacy, but since the noise inside the house was always so loud, she rarely enjoyed it.

She got into the backseat of the jitney and told Jimmy to take her to Proctor Street.

She braced for the chaos she knew would greet her inside the apartment. As usual, the house was a crowded mess. Her brother Hennie and two of his friends were in the living room watching the New York Yankees play the Baltimore Orioles. Hennie's friend "Peanut," who had been trying to get into her pants since he was fourteen, was sitting facing the door. She knew she wouldn't make it through the room without him opening his big mouth.

"Mmm, mmm, mmm, look who's here." Peanut licked his lips. "Baby, you sure are lookin' good today."

"Don't you ever go home, Peanut?" Latisha asked sarcastically.

"I wanted to see you, baby."

Latisha stepped over the toys the kids left scattered across the living room floor. "Hennie, why don't you clean up this mess?"

"Why should I? You know Ruby's brats just gonna mess it up again."

Latisha picked up the toys and loaded them in the bin placed in the corner of the living room. "Where's Mama?"

"She in the kitchen with Ruby. And bring us back three beers since you're goin' in there."

"Why don't you make your little, skinny ass useful for a change and get them yourself."

"Mmm, you sure are sexy when you're mad, girl." Peanut smirked.

"You're all a bunch of dumb-ass, pathetic losers!" Latisha declared, before leaving the room to a chorus of laughter.

"What's so funny in there?" Ruby asked as Latisha entered the kitchen.

"Nothin'. It's just Hennie and his dumb-ass friends actin' stupid as usual. Did anyone call while I was at work?"

"If you're asking if Shawn called, the answer is no," Latisha's mother, Pearl, answered. "If that boy ain't called you by now, he ain't gonna call. Baby girl, you know how men are; once they get what they want, they move on. Just like cattle, once they eat all the grass, they move on to greener pastures."

"I don't understand you, Latisha," Ruby chimed in. "You got almost every man in town chasing after yo' ass, and you stuck on Shawn. I know he fine and all, but he ain't the only fine brother in town." Ruby waved her finger in the air. "Girl, you need to get a grip and stop walkin' around here like you on your way to some damn funeral."

"Ruby, I wouldn't expect you to understand." Latisha placed her hands against her hips. "You don't know the difference between love and sex. You open your legs to any Raheem, Tarek, or Abdul that comes around and call it love. That's why you got three damn kids and no man. I don't want to end up like you." Latisha looked down at the table where Ruby and Pearl were seated. "Havin' babies, goin' on welfare, and livin' with my mother. Don't you understand? With Shawn, I have a chance for a future. A chance to be with a man who's gonna be somebody. A chance to get away from all this"—Latisha looked around the kitchen— "mess."

"Who you think you are? Princess Di?" Pearl stood up.

"No, Mama. But ..."

"But nothin'." Pearl walked up to Latisha. "You listen here! I won't have you talkin' like that in my house. I might not have much, but at least I can call it mine. I don't know where you got the notion life's a flower bed of ease. That all you got to do is find the right man. Then you can twirl like a lily from side to side without a care in the world while your man takes care of you." Pearl pointed her finger in Latisha's face. "Well, let me tell you something right now. It don't work that way!"

"How you know, Mama?" Latisha stood her ground. "How you know? You never took the time to find the right man. You and Ruby both settled for the first thing that came along. I'm not gonna be like that. Ending up livin' here with nothin' to show for my life except a monthly check from the state and some triflin' man's baby to feed."

"Giiirl, I don't know what's gotten into you today, but if you keep talkin' to me like that, God help me," Pearl grabbed the plastic bag from Latisha's hand and threw it against the table. "I'll pack your bags and put 'em out on the street. If you think you can do a better job than me, I'll give you the chance to prove it."

Latisha realized she crossed the line. Her anticipated encounter with Shawn and her run-in with Monica had her on edge.

"I didn't mean to talk to you like that, Mama. I'm sorry." Latisha picked up the plastic bag from the table. "I really had a bad day. Ruby, I didn't mean to talk to you like that either. Y'all know I don't mean it."

"What happened today to get you so fired up?" Ruby asked.

"I ran into Monica Chambers in the drugstore, and she really got under my skin. I'm sorry. I didn't mean to take out my frustrations on the two of you." Latisha reached over and gave her mother and Ruby a hug.

"Anyway," Latisha smiled, gripping the plastic bag in her hand, "I've got plans for this evening."

"You mean you ain't gonna sit around here and wait for Shawn to call tonight?" Pearl asked.

"Nope, not tonight." Latisha reached into the refrigerator and removed three beers. "I'm going out tonight and don't expect me back until tomorrow."

"Well, all right, girl!" Ruby exclaimed.

After passing through the living room to hand the beers to Hennie and his friends, Latisha headed upstairs to prepare the items she needed for the evening.

First she removed the condoms from the plastic bag and laid them side by side on the bed. Next she retrieved one of Hennie's razor blades from the bathroom medicine cabinet. She picked up the first condom and slowly slit the outer blue foil wrapping. She carefully removed the condom through the slit. She placed the condom on the bed with the eye of the nipple pointing up at her. She took the razor blade and sliced a small hole in the tip. She examined the hole under the light, making sure the hole was large enough to allow Shawn's sperm to get through but small enough so he wouldn't see it. Her hands were shaking and she wondered if she had the courage to follow through with her plan. "I'll show him he can't treat me like a whore and then just walk away. No, my love, it's time you pay the price for your actions."

She followed the same procedure with the remaining two condoms, making sure the razor penetrated the latex just enough to suit her needs. Upon completing her handiwork, she took a quick shower and changed into her black leather mini skirt and blue mock turtleneck sweater. She placed the box of condoms inside her purse and headed out the door to catch the bus to Oakland.

CHAPTER 9

Robert's mind drifted away from the boring management definitions he was studying and focused on the status of his life. So far, everything was going reasonably well. He'd received good grades on his first three exams and was headed into midterms with a solid 3.0 average. In addition, he had adapted to dormitory life and managed to avoid any major confrontations with Shawn.

Robert's thoughts were interrupted when Shawn and Jelin entered the apartment. The two of them were hooting and hollering and making so much noise he went into the living room to find out what all the excitement was about.

When he entered the kitchen, Shawn was talking on the phone.

"Moms, I did it! Coach Green named the starting lineup for next week's game against West Virginia, and guess who the starting point guard is?"

"That's right, yours truly. You're coming to the game—right, Moms?"

"Okay, good. I'll leave tickets for you and Damar at the front gate. Come early so I get a chance to see you before the game starts."

"I gotta go now, Moms. Jelin's here. I'll see ya next week … Love you too. Bye."

Shawn hung up the phone and danced his way back into the living room.

"Congratulations, Shawn." Robert reached out his hand. "I always knew you'd make first string."

"Yeah, so did I," Shawn answered without shaking Robert's hand.

Robert was disappointed by Shawn's obvious snub but decided not to let it get to him. "Can I get you guys a couple of beers to celebrate, or do you have practice later?"

"No, bro, we're finished for the day," Jelin answered. "A beer sounds good right about now. What do you have?"

Robert opened the refrigerator and inventoried their beer selection. "Let's see, we have Iron City, Heineken, or Corona."

"I'll take an Iron City, bro."

"How about you, Shawn?"

"Yeah, I'll take one of those too."

Robert retrieved three beers and passed them around.

Jelin twisted off his cap and raised his bottle in the air. "I wanna make a toast. To my home boooy, Mr. Shawn In-Your-Face Collins, may your freshman year be as spectacular as my freshman year."

"Wait, hold up, hold up, hold up. I want to change that toast a little bit." Shawn pushed Jelin aside. "May my freshman year be even more spectacular than the freshman year of Jelin Church."

"No way, man!" Jelin put down his beer and threw fake punches at Shawn's face.

"Okay, how about if I make the toast." Robert raised his beer and climbed on top of the coffee table. "To Shawn Collins and Jelin Church, may the PCU Tigers win the Big Central Tournament, then go on to win the NCAA Tournament, with the two superstars of Collins and Church named co-MVPs."

"Wait a minute." Shawn threw a sofa pillow at Jelin. "Why do I have to share my MVP title with that punk? I do everything better and faster than Jelin, even when it comes to drinking beer." Shawn turned his bottle upside down and guzzled. "When you gonna stop nursin' that beer, Church?"

Jelin turned his bottle upside down and guzzled.

Robert observed the similarities between Shawn and Jelin. Jelin was just as handsome as Shawn but in a sexier, more masculine way. Whereas Shawn had a pretty-boy look, Jelin had a more rugged, natural look. He was almost as tall as Shawn, maybe an inch shorter. His Hershey chocolate complexion was smooth and flawless. His handsome face was accented with bold, expressive eyes, a strong nose, and full, kissable lips. His muscular build was as near to perfection as Shawn's but about twenty pounds heavier. He sported a shaved head, a goatee, and always dressed in clothes that highlighted his powerful physique. On this day, he wore a tight blue spandex shirt that displayed his wide shoulders and flat stomach. The shirt was matched with a pair of white nylon running pants that hugged his muscular ass and large thighs. Robert knew he was hopelessly attracted to Jelin.

Jelin finished his beer and winked at Robert. "Now who you callin' a nurse, Collins?"

Robert smiled.

"Who wants another beer?" Shawn asked.

"I'll take another one. This is a night to celebrate," Jelin proclaimed. "How about you, Robert?"

"No, not me. I need to finish studying."

"Oh come on, yo!" Jelin complained. "Celebrate with us."

"I need to finish studying for my test. I'll celebrate with you guys after you destroy those West Virginia Wildcats."

Jelin slapped Robert on the back. "Okay, man. I'm gonna hold you to that."

The touch of Jelin's hand sent a wave of electricity shooting through Robert's body. When the goose bumps developed, he had to escape. "I'll see you guys later." He threw his half-full beer bottle in the trash and rushed to the privacy of his bedroom.

"Wimp-ass punk," Shawn muttered under his breath.

Once inside his room, Robert shut the door and closed his eyes. He needed to get his fantasy of Jelin out of his head. With his back pressed against the bedroom door, he could hear Shawn and Jelin discussing him in the living room.

"I think your roommate's a cool brother. Why do you give him such a hard time, Shawn?"

"Like I told you before, Jelin. He's a fag. That's why."

"You don't know that for sure."

"Man, didn't you see the way he was lookin' at you? If that wasn't lust in his eyes, then I don't know what is. And that's not all. He's soft—you know, like a sissy. Don't you notice the way he carries himself with his damn nose up in the air? And the way he talks, all prim and proper like? I'm tellin' you, he's a faggot."

"Maybe that's the way the brother was raised. You did say he was from farm country somewhere out in Ohio, didn't you? Since he wasn't raised in the city like you and me, maybe he's just different, yo. I mean, he doesn't look like a faggot."

"That's because you don't live with him. You haven't seen the shit I've seen."

"What shit?"

"I'm talkin' about the way he looks at me all the time with his eyes hawkin' my crotch. I'm talkin' about the way he conveniently comes into the bathroom whenever I'm taking a shower. I'm talkin' about the fact he hasn't dated any women since he got here. Tammera's roommate Anika gave him her number, and he hasn't even called her. As fly as that girl is, he's not interested. Hell, he doesn't even talk about pussy. That's why I think he's a fag, and that's why I'm staying away from his faggot ass. I can't have him ruining my reputation around campus."

"Even if he is gay, give 'em a break, Shawn."

"Yeah, as long as he keeps his faggot hands off of me."

Hearing Shawn use the word faggot broke Robert's spirit. It was happening all over again. Just like before. He slid down to the floor and buried his head in his hands. It didn't matter how careful he was; his secret always found a way to escape and ruin his life, just like it did at Our Lady of Fatima.

After it was all over, Robert ran to the bathroom to cleanse himself. He stood under the shower and tried to make the water cleanse him of his sin. He rubbed the washcloth against his body, over and over again until his skin turned raw from the friction. He had to get the evidence off. He had to make himself pure again. But no matter how hard he scrubbed, he couldn't remove that indelible stain of guilt permanently etched under his skin.

After the shower, he ran to the chapel. He prayed for the Lord's forgiveness. He prayed nobody would find out what he had done. He prayed for his soul, and he prayed he wouldn't burn in the eternal flames of hell. He walked back to the dorm room filled with guilt and shame.

When he walked past Stephon's bed, he was just lying there, acting as if nothing had happened. Robert went up to Stephon and asked that he never do that again. Stephon just looked up at him and smiled.

Robert lay petrified someone would find out what he had done. He hated himself for letting it happen. But even more, he hated himself for liking it. He could have stopped it, but he didn't. He could have pushed him away, but he hadn't.

Robert cried himself to sleep, listening to the wind whispering, "Ssshame, ssshame, ssshame," against his window.

The next morning, he was awakened as usual by the bell. He wondered if anyone had seen what happened. Unfortunately, it didn't take long for his worst fears to be realized. Stephon and he were called out of history class to report to the head administrator's office.

The head administrator, Father Bullock, was a big man. He stood over six four. He looked more like an ex-jock than a priest with his crew cut and muscular arms. Robert thought Father Bullock was a racist because he always treated the black students differently, more harshly than the white students. Robert knew he and Stephon were in for a confrontation that even the devil himself would fear.

"Have a seat, gentlemen," Father Bullock stated as they nervously entered his mahogany office. Everything in Father Bullock's office seemed to be made of wood. Even the walls and the floor were covered with wood, giving the room a dark, menacing appearance.

The office contained a big mahogany table with large, high-back chairs that looked like they were constructed for giants. The entire office reeked of freshly polished wood. The smell of it made Robert nauseous as his stomach churned with fear. Father Bullock sat behind a big, imposing mahogany desk that matched the table where Stephon and Robert were seated. Robert felt small and fearful, crouched in the giant chair.

Father Bullock stood from his desk and walked behind them. Robert's heart pounded, and he couldn't stop his hands from shaking. He glanced over at Stephon. He appeared cool and calm with a look of defiance in his eyes.

"I've received reports about the two of you, and I want to know if it's true." Father Bullock's deep voice reverberated between the walls and Robert's head. "Is it true, gentleman? Answer me! Is it true?"

"Is what true?" Stephon asked.

"Is it true about the two of you hanging out at each other's bunks at night, after lights out?"

"We're not the only ones who do that, Father, and you know it. Why are we being singled out?"

Father Bullock bent down between them and whispered, "All right then. Let me put it another way. Are you two faggots?"

The audacity of him to ask us that, Robert thought as he sat quietly at the table, his knees knocking together and his fingers gripping the wooden arm posts of the chair.

"Answer me! Are you faggots?"

There it was again, that awful word. *Faggots.* The word kept echoing inside his head, mixing with the smell of the wood, making him dizzy.

Faggots!

Faggots!

Faggots!

Stephon bolted up from the table, knocking over his chair. "No! We just like to talk to each other at night, that's all. Is that our crime, Father!"

"Don't you dare raise your voice to me, Mr. Matthews!" Father Bullock picked up Stephon's chair. "Now sit your butt down and don't you say another word until I ask you to. You got that?"

The room was filled with a disturbing silence. Father Bullock walked around to look out the window.

Robert looked at the floor and prayed the interrogation would end.

"That better be all it is, Mr. Matthews." Father Bullock turned around to face them. "If I ever find out there's been more going on than what you're telling me, I'll have you kicked out of this school so fast you won't know what hit you. Am I making myself clear, gentlemen? How about you, Mr. Robinson? You've been awfully quiet. Have I made myself clear? Answer me, boy!"

"Yes, sir, Father, I understand."

"Okay then, I don't want to hear anything else about this situation. You understand me? If I do, you'll have to face the consequences. We don't like faggots around here."

There it was again, that word *faggots*. Oh how Robert hated the sound of it, especially the way it rolled off Father Bullock's tongue, sounding ugly and cruel.

Robert picked himself off the floor and dried his eyes. *Not this time*, he told himself. *Not this time.* He wasn't going to let Shawn or that word destroy his life again. He shoved his management book into his book bag. He would study in the library rather than the suite. He went into the bathroom and erased the tearstains from his face. He refused to give Shawn the satisfaction of knowing he hurt him.

As he prepared to walk through the living room, he wondered what cruel taunt or humiliating laugh he would have to endure. Fortunately, Shawn was preoccupied with a call from the front desk.

"I'm going to the library to do some research," Robert mumbled to Jelin.

Jelin smiled and grabbed Robert's hand. "Be strong, my brother."

Robert closed the door and headed down the hallway. Before stepping into the elevator, he thought about Jelin's comment and the gentleness of his touch.

CHAPTER 10

"**D**amn it!" Shawn slammed the intercom phone. "What the hell is she doing here?"

"Who?" Jelin asked.

"Latisha! She's downstairs, and she's on her way up here. Man, I don't want to see her right now."

"What did you expect?" Jelin joined Shawn in the kitchen. "You haven't spoken to the girl in over five weeks. Of course she's gonna try to find out what's going on. Latisha might be many things, but she's not stupid."

"I know, Jelin, but every time I picked up the phone, I wasn't sure what to say. 'Hello, Latisha, this is Shawn. Sorry but you've been kicked to the curb. See ya.'"

"That would have been better than leaving the girl hangin'. Now that she's on her way up here, you're gonna have to think of something to tell her."

"I know, and to make matters worse, I'm expecting Tammera any minute."

"Well, I'd say you have a situation on your hands." Jelin patted Shawn on the shoulder.

"I'm gonna get rid of Latisha and get rid of her fast, that's all."

"That's easier said than done. Don't forget. I know Latisha; she's not the kind of girl you can easily dismiss."

"I'm just going to tell her the truth. I've met someone else—period."

"And what are you gonna say after she slaps the shit out of your ass?"

"See, Jelin," Shawn explained with a smirk, "I have this way of controlling my women. Even after I tell Latisha I'm dating someone else, she's still gonna want to be with me. And you know something else? After all is said and done, we'll still be gettin' busy. Latisha doesn't wanna lose all this."

"You think so, huh, Shawn?"

"I know so. Where's she gonna find another brother as fine and talented as me?" Shawn pointed to himself. "She'll deal with me having another woman on the side, as long as I'm still giving her a little bit of play. You see, Jelin, I got it like that. And when you got it like that, you can keep your women in check."

"I wish I could stick around to see how this all turns out, but I think it's best if I bounce before Latisha gets here."

"You don't wanna pick up a few pointers from the pro?"

"I'll pass." There was a knock at the door. "That must be contestant number one. Let her down easy, okay, Shawn?"

"Yeah, right, whatever you say, Jelin. Now get out of here, punk."

Jelin opened the door with a smile and greeted Latisha on his way out. "Hey, my fine Nubian sister. Sorry I can't stay. Shawn's inside waiting for you. See ya later. Peace."

"Hello and good-bye, Jelin."

Latisha stepped inside the apartment.

"Hey, baby, would you like a beer?" Shawn asked.

"Yeah, I'll take one."

"It's good to see you, Latisha."

Latisha maintained her silence.

"Do you want a glass?" Shawn asked.

"No, that's all right." Latisha reached for the bottle. "Are we alone?"

"Yeah, we're alone." Shawn placed the bottle in Latisha's hand, momentarily grasping her arm and softly kissing her cheek. "My roommate Robert went to the library, and that was my other roommate, Jamal, working behind the front desk when you came in."

"Oh, okay," Latisha said.

"I know what you're thinking, Latisha, but before you say anything, let me explain."

"Explain what, Shawn? Why you treat me like shit? Why you can't return any of my phone calls?"

"I was going to call you, Latisha. But I've been busy. Between basketball practice and classes, I've been working my ass off. My first game is next Tuesday. After that, I should—"

"It's been over five weeks, Shawn." Latisha slammed her bottle on the table. "You mean to tell me you couldn't find two damn minutes to pick up the phone!"

"Like I said, I've been busy. I didn't know college was going to be this rough."

Latisha folded her arms across her chest.

"Am I forgiven?"

"What do you want from me, Shawn? Where do we go from here?"

"To tell you the truth, Latisha, I think you need to give me a little space. At least until after basketball season is over."

Latisha picked up her bottle and took a gulp. "And exactly what does a little space mean? Are you sayin' we're still together or are you sayin' we're through? What the hell am I supposed to do? Sit at home and wait for the goddamn phone to ring? Hoping you'd find a minute or two for me! No, my love, Latisha doesn't play that. Either you want me or you don't. It's that simple."

"See, Latisha, I knew you were gonna come over here with a damn attitude! That's why I haven't called your ass, because I knew you'd have an attitude! I thought you loved me. If you really loved me, you'd understand how busy I am and be more understanding to my situation."

"More understanding?" Latisha took a deep breath. "I do still love you, Shawn. I wish to hell I didn't, but I do. I didn't come over here to pick a fight. Really I didn't. I just needed to find out where I stood. If I'm still a part of your life. Is that so hard for you to understand?"

"Latisha, you're still a part of my life." Shawn stepped toward her. "But I need some breathing room ... just until I can free up some time to spend with you."

"We have some time right now, don't we?" Latisha removed the beer bottle from Shawn's hand and pushed him against the counter.

"Latisha, what ... what are you doing?"

Latisha removed her sweater, exposing her bare breasts to Shawn's eager eyes. "I'm takin' advantage of this time we have together."

"Latisha, girrrrl! Don't you know one of my roommates could walk in here any minute?"

"Then why don't we go back to your room." Latisha rubbed an erect nipple against Shawn's lips. "We have some business to attend to. You know what I mean?"

Shawn opened his mouth to object, but the sight of Latisha's breasts was too much to refuse. Instead of voicing his objection, he stuck out his tongue and licked her right nipple.

"That's right, baby, come to mommy."

Shawn licked his tongue around the perimeter of Latisha's nipple.

Latisha grabbed Shawn's hand and placed it under her skirt. "You want some of this? Then let's go back to your bedroom. I've got something I've been saving just for you. I'm sure you're gonna like it."

Shawn looked at his watch. He could do Latisha and have her out of the apartment before Tammera arrived.

Latisha guided Shawn toward the bedroom.

Shawn followed her lead. He could feel the moisture that had seeped through the thin, nylon fabric of her underwear. He pushed her into his bedroom and closed the door. He removed his shirt and then pressed his chest against her smooth, ample breasts.

Latisha ran her hands up and down Shawn's back. "I've missed you, baby."

"I've missed you too." Shawn pushed Latisha onto the bed and crawled on top of her.

Shawn's urgent hardness pressed against her thigh. She slowly unzipped her leather skirt and slid it down her legs.

Shawn stood and unzipped his pants.

"Do you want me to take these off?" Latisha tucked her thumbs inside the elastic band of her panties.

Shawn nodded his head.

"You remember what I like, don't you?" Latisha asked.

Shawn smiled.

"Then come on," Latisha said.

Shawn straddled Latisha on the bed. He ran his tongue behind her ear, across her shoulders, then down her stomach.

Latisha pressed her hands into Shawn's back.

Without missing a beat, Shawn maneuvered out of his pants and underwear. He covered Latisha with an intense, sweaty heat.

Latisha reached underneath Shawn and grabbed his throbbing manhood.

Shawn moaned.

"You like the way that feels?" Latisha asked. "I got something even better."

"I want you. I want you now," Shawn said, sliding down Latisha's body.

"Wait a minute, Shawn. Let me get a condom."

Shawn lay back and waited for Latisha to grab a condom from her purse.

Latisha carefully slid the condom from the foil wrapping and gently placed it on Shawn.

Shawn positioned himself on top of her. Just as he slid into her, there was a knock at the door. "Damn it!" He knew it was Tammera at the door. He quickly pulled out of Latisha and sat up on the bed.

"Don't answer it," Latisha whispered in his ear.

Shawn jumped from the bed and reached for his jeans. He hadn't locked the front door and knew Tammera could walk in on them. He grabbed Latisha's clothes off the floor and threw them at her.

"Here, go in the bathroom and get dressed!"

"Get dressed? Shawn, why you buggin'? Come back over here and finish what you started. Who gives a damn if anyone walks in."?

"I didn't lock the front door, damn it! Now go in the bathroom and get dressed while I go see who it is." Shawn scrambled back into his jeans. "Didn't I tell you to go! Now go!" He slapped Latisha on the behind.

Latisha grabbed her clothes and stomped into the bathroom.

Shawn raced through the living room in his bare feet and opened the front door before Tammera had a chance to realize it was unlocked.

"There you are. What took you so long?" Tammera asked.

"I didn't hear the door."

"Jamal told me I could come right up. What's wrong with you? You look like shit."

"I'm sorry, baby, I was asleep."

"Did you forget we had a date tonight?"

"No, Tammera, I have this really bad headache. Would you go to the store and get me some aspirin while I get dressed?"

"Are you all right, baby? You're not coming down with a cold, are you? You can't get sick now. You have that big game on Tuesday."

"I'll be all right, Tammera. I just really need those aspirin. Do you mind?"

"Of course I don't. I'll be right back. But before I go, I need a kiss."

Shawn gave Tammera a peck on the cheek then quickly closed the door.

He took a deep breath then rushed back toward the bathroom. He noticed the door was ajar and wondered if Latisha had heard any of the conversation with Tammera. "You can come out now, Latisha." Shawn banged on the door. "Hurry up. You have to go. That was my assistant coach. We have a team meeting, and I have to report to the Omni Center right now. Sorry, baby, but it's important that I make this meeting."

Latisha didn't respond.

"Latisha, did you hear what I said? You have to go now."

Latisha opened the door. "I heard you twice the first time, Shawn."

"I'm sorry, baby, but these things happen." He pulled Latisha out of the bathroom. "Come on, let me walk you down to the lobby. I'll make this up to you, baby. I promise."

"Will you call me later, Shawn? Maybe we can pick up where we left off."

"Yeah, baby, I'll call you later. Do you have everything?"

"I think so."

"Okay then, let's go." Shawn motioned Latisha out of the apartment and down the circular hallway.

Latisha stared at Shawn in the elevator but remained silent.

Shawn directed Latisha through the revolving front doors and waved good-bye as she walked down the hill. After she was safely out of distance, he returned to the dormitory and directed his anger toward Jamal, who was working behind the front desk.

"Why the hell did you send Tammera up to the apartment, knowing damn well Latisha was still there!" He pounded his fist against the desk and pointed his finger into Jamal's stunned face. "Man, I almost get busted with Latisha. Don't ever play me like that again!"

"Wait a minute, Shawn! Tammera said you were expecting her, and Latisha told me she was an old friend from high school. How was I supposed to know you planned on doing them both the same night?"

"C'mon, Jamal. You can't be that stupid."

"From now on, Shawn, you need to inform me of your plans because I can't read your shallow little mind."

"Use your common sense, Jamal. Don't ever send two females up to my room on the same night."

"Shawn, I don't play my women against each other. I treat my women with honesty and respect. And I think it's about time you do the same. And another thing," Jamal pointed his finger into Shawn's stunned face, "you're not a little boy anymore. You're a grown man, and you need to understand your actions have consequences. So don't you come around here pointing fingers at me and banging on my desk. If you get busted, it's your own damn fault, not mine. I've got my own problems to worry about. So if you want to blame someone, go call your mother. She's the one who raised you."

Shawn looked at Jamal curiously and then stepped away from the desk. "Damn, yo. You need to relax. You're too damn intense." Shawn walked away from the desk, knowing he wasn't going to win an argument against Jamal.

When Tammera returned with the aspirin, he rushed out and kissed her before she reached the revolving front doors.

"What's all this about?" Tammera asked as Shawn swept her off her feet.

"Nothing. I just missed you, baby." Shawn grabbed Tammera's hand and led her back into the building.

CHAPTER 11

J amal removed his time card from the metal rack and punched out. Since Shawn had left with Tammera, and Robert was still at the library, he would have the entire suite to himself. He grabbed his book bag and slung it over his shoulder. The quick motion caused the flap of the bag to fly open. The letter he received earlier that morning fell at his feet. He knew the letter contained bad news. He picked it up and returned it to his bag.

After reaching the suite, he stretched out across his bed. The image of his father appeared in his mind. He thought about the question he asked his mother in the letter. *"Mom, I'm not a little boy anymore. I can handle the truth. Tell me if my instincts are correct. Is Dad sick?"*

The last line kept repeating through his mind.

Jamal switched on the desk lamp and picked up the silver-handled letter opener his mother gave him as a graduation gift. He remembered the last time he saw her standing at the top of the third floor landing with tears in her eyes.

"She knew," Jamal whispered.

> My dearest son,
>
> It was good hearing from you so soon after your departure. It hasn't been the same around here since you left. We all miss your bright smile and warm laughter. Although you tried to hide it, it was obvious you were nervous about moving to a strange city where you didn't know anybody. But I'm sure you've made many new friends by now. I'm also sure you're doing well in your classes, so I'm not going to bore you with that question. You've always been a bright child. I often sit and wonder what I've done right to deserve such a son.

Jamal, you've filled my life with great joy since the day you were born. I often remember back to that wonderful day and the first time I looked upon your beautiful face. Oh, my son, I knew from that very moment you would be a special child. Your face was filled with a strange calmness; a look I really can't describe. You didn't cry; you just looked up at me as if to say, "You can relax now. I'm here. Everything's going to be all right." Since that day, you've possessed the gift of calmness. That uncanny ability to steer this family through turbulent times.

Well, my son, this is another one of those turbulent times. Your instincts about your father were correct. Three months ago, the doctors found a small spot on your father's lung. They performed a biopsy and found the spot was cancerous. My dearest son, your father has lung cancer. We decided together not to burden you with the news. You were getting ready to leave for college, and you were so excited. Your father and I couldn't find it in our hearts to burden your joy with our pain.

My son, it's time you spread your wings and soar. Your father and I know you're capable of great things. So please believe me when I tell you this. It is through you that your father feels fulfilled. He experiences the ecstasy of success through your achievements. When he speaks of you, his eyes sparkle with pride. So, my son, it is very important that you remain at school and not come home to take on the burdens of the family. With the help of God, we will survive this turbulent time.

Your father's surgery is scheduled for next week. The doctors will remove one of his lungs and hopefully stop the cancer from spreading. Since they believe the cancer was caught early, they are very optimistic of his prognosis.

So, my precious, precious son, there's really no need to worry. I know after reading this letter, you'll want to come home and be with your father during his surgery, but it's not necessary. There is nothing you can do at this time except pray. So, son, please don't spend your money on a ticket home. You're going to need every penny for next year's tuition.

Your father and I planned to help you with your expenses, but it doesn't look possible now. The insurance company is only picking up 80 percent of the hospital tab. But with a little help from your aunt Fannie and uncle Joe, we think we can cover the rest.

I am so sorry this letter couldn't contain better news, but I decided it was time you heard the truth. Your brother Ali will be home on leave to help out while your father's in the hospital. I'll call you with the results of the surgery when I have any news.

Please take care of yourself and pray for us.

Your loving mother,
Louise

Jamal shoved the letter in his desk drawer. As the tears streamed down his face, he thought about the last words his father spoke to him.

"Good-bye, Jamal. I love you."

He knew his father loved him, but that was the first time he ever heard him say those three words. His father was from the old school and believed it was a sign of weakness for a man to show his emotions. Jamal shook his head. The one time his father displayed emotion was a testament to his strength, not his weakness.

Jamal's mind was blanketed with worry and concern. His family couldn't afford to pay a huge hospital bill. He had to find a way to help out, but how? His own financial situation was bleak. Although he covered for some of the other students and worked more than the twenty hours a week his work-study job offered, his weekly check still averaged less than $200. According to his calculations, he would fall short of the $8,000 he needed by fall.

Jamal switched off the desk lamp and returned to his bed. He had to think of a way to earn some additional money. He heard someone else entered the apartment and hoped it wasn't Shawn. He definitely wasn't in the mood for any more of Shawn's childish games. He was relieved when Robert walked past his door.

****

Robert glanced into Jamal's room and noticed him lying across his bed in the dark. He knew something was wrong. Usually Jamal would be watching television or reading on a Friday night.

Fear struck Robert's heart. He wondered if Shawn had told Jamal the same fag story he told Jelin earlier. *Damn Shawn!* Robert threw his book bag against the bedroom wall. Shawn hadn't wasted any time spreading his unsubstantiated rumors.

Robert flashed back to the day he transferred from Our Lady of Fatima to Cambridge Falls High. His best friend at the time was named Chuckie. Chuckie had heard rumors about the situation with Stephon and confronted him with questions.

"So, Rob, why did you leave Our Lady of Fatima?"

"I didn't like it there, Chuckie."

"Why not? Was it too far from home? Did you get homesick?"

"No, I just didn't like it there."

"What was wrong with the place?"

"I didn't get along with the other students."

"Why not?"

"I didn't fit in!"

"Why not, Rob?

"Have you heard something, Chuckie? Is that why you're acting so weird?"

"Yeah, I've heard something. I heard you're a punk, a sissy, a homo. I heard you were caught doing it in bed with another guy!"

"That's not true, Chuckie! It didn't happen that way. That's just a rumor someone put out about me."

"Then what really happened?"

"Chuckie, I thought we were best friends. I thought if anyone would believe me and stick by me, it would be you."

"Rob, I can't be your friend anymore. People are already starting to look at me funny. They say since you're a faggot, I must be one too. I can't be your friend anymore, Rob. I'm sorry, but I can't. So please don't come around my house anymore. And when you see me at school, do me a favor and act like you don't know me."

Robert slammed his fist against the metal bed frame. "No! I'm not gonna let it happen again. I can't." He made up his mind he was going to march into Jamal's room and find out exactly what Shawn said. Then he would convince Jamal nothing had changed. That he was still the same person he was yesterday. Robert took a deep breath. He walked down the hallway to Jamal's open door.

"Jamal, can I come in? I need to talk to you."

"Yeah, come in, Robert. I need to talk to you too." Jamal's eyes were puffy and red.

"Is everything all right?" Robert asked softly, afraid of the answer.

"No, Robert, it's not all right." Jamal sat up on his bed.

Robert braced himself for the worst. He knew what was coming next. It was always the same old story. *Sorry but I can't be your friend anymore. What would people think?*

"I received a letter from home today."

"A letter?"

"A letter from my mother."

"Your mother?"

"She was writing to tell me my father's going into the hospital next week."

"The hospital? What's wrong with him?"

Jamal took a deep breath. "Robert, my father has lung cancer." Tears filled the corners of his eyes.

"Oh my God, Jamal. I'm so sorry. Is there anything I can do?"

"Not unless you can figure out a way for me to earn some extra money. My dad's insurance company is only picking up a portion of the hospital bill. I don't know how my family's going to survive. We don't have that kind of money."

Robert felt guilty for coming into Jamal's room, thinking the situation concerned him. Jamal was going through hell, and he needed to find a way to help his friend. He sat down next to Jamal on the bed. After a tearful moment of silence, an idea popped into his head.

"You know, Jamal, I think I do have a way for you to earn some extra money. And the best thing about it is you can do it while you're working your work-study job."

"What are you talking about, Robert?"

"I saw a poster over in the Activity Center requesting the services of tutors. That would be perfect for you. You're so smart; you could tutor almost any subject. And you could have the students meet you down at the front desk while you're doing your work-study job. Basically, you could work two jobs at the same time!"

Jamal jumped from the bed and paced back and forth across the room. "You know, Robert," Jamal hugged his friend, "that's a brilliant idea. That just might work. Except, how much does it pay?"

"I think the poster said ten dollars an hour. Wait here. I'll run over to the Activity Center and get a copy of the poster."

Robert dashed out of the bedroom and out the front door before Jamal could respond.

****

Jamal sat at his desk and calculated the amount of hours he needed to work in order to bring in some serious cash. He didn't hear Shawn enter the apartment.

"What the hell is this?" Shawn yelled from the bathroom.

Jamal walked down the hallway and into the bathroom. "What's going on, Shawn?"

Shawn held up a condom. "Look at this shit!"

"What is it?"

"Its a damn condom."

"I can see that."

"Look at the tip. It has a fuckin' hole in it. She cut a god damn hole in it."

"Who cut a hole in it?"

"You remember when Latisha was up here earlier?"

"Yeah, I remember."

"She must have dropped these when she was in the bathroom." Shawn pulled the second condom through the slit of its foil wrapping and examined the tip. "That little bitch! She was trying to get herself pregnant. No wonder she was so eager to drop her panties."

"How do you know they belong to Latisha?"

"Because she's the only one who could have left them. They must have fallen out of her purse when she came in here. Tammera didn't come into the bathroom. And I'm sure you or Robert wouldn't have a need for tampered condoms. Damn her! She's not gonna get away with this shit."

"Was Latisha successful, Shawn? Did you have sex with her?"

"No. Thanks to you, Jamal, we were interrupted before it got that far. Listen, man, I want to apologize for the way I acted earlier. I had no right going off the way I did. You were right. I was acting like a little boy. I'm sorry, man. I really owe you one, yo."

"Well, since you owe me one, how about when Robert comes back, you take us both out for a beer. I really need one tonight."

"That's a deal." Shawn shook Jamal's hand. "But first I have to save the evidence for when I confront Latisha."

"What are you gonna do?"

Shawn folded the two condoms and their altered packaging back into the condom box. "I don't know yet, Jamal. But I've been looking for a reason to kick Latisha to the curb. Now I have all the reason I need."

CHAPTER 12

Shawn rushed into Coach Green's office. "Coach, we have problem. My mother is on her way over here. She got my mid-semester grade report, and she's not happy."

"I received the report too, Shawn." Coach Green walked around to sit on the edge of the desk facing Shawn. "Let me make this as clear as I possibly can. Your ass is in deep shit! And if you don't bring your grades up to a C average by the end of the semester, you'll be ineligible to play for the Tigers. Do you understand what I'm telling you?"

Shawn swallowed hard and felt his heart beat out of rhythm. "Coach, you promised if I came to play for the Tigers, I wouldn't have to worry about my grades. You said you'd take care of things."

"Why do you think I kept asking you about your grades, Shawn? Why do you think I needed to know how you were doing in your classes? I didn't expect to find out at the last minute you were failing half your classes. Now both of our asses are in a sling."

"Coach, I thought you would handle it the way you handled my SATs. You said I wouldn't have to worry about my grades or going to classes."

"You're right, Shawn." Coach Green walked over to the window. "But it's too late to worry about that now. We need to concentrate on the situation at hand." He turned to face Shawn. "I'll take care of it, but you're going to have to help me."

"Help you how? I don't know what's going on in those classes."

Coach Green handed Shawn a printout. "Here is a list of available tutors. I need you to select a person from this list to help you with your classwork."

"What do you mean, help me with my classwork? Are you sayin' I have to start going to class? No way, Coach. That wasn't the deal!"

"Shawn, you'll have to at least attend your classes. In the meantime, I'll talk with your professors. Hopefully I can persuade them to give you passing grades."

"I don't like this, Coach." Shawn snatched the printout. "I bet if I was going to West Virginia Tech, I wouldn't be havin' these problems. And by the way, they're still interested in me."

"Is that a threat, Shawn?"

"No, Coach, it's a warning."

"Just look at the list, Shawn."

Shawn looked over the printout and spotted Jamal's name. "Hey, my roommate's name is on this list."

"I thought I recognized one of those names." Coach Green walked around to look at the list again. "You introduced him to me on Freshmen Orientation Day, didn't you?"

"That's right."

"Are the two of you good friends?"

"Yeah, he's cool. But he's been under a lot of stress lately."

"What kind of stress?"

"His father has lung cancer and had to get one of his lungs removed. I think the hospital bills are more than Jamal's family can handle right now. Jamal's been working a lot of hours trying to make some extra money, but I don't think it's making much of a difference. He's been stressed out over the situation for the past couple weeks."

"Jamal's father has lung cancer?"

"Right, Coach. Jamal told me his father's insurance company is only picking up a part of the hospital tab."

"Is that right?" Coach Green shook his head.

"Jamal really wants to fly home to Newark to visit his pops in the hospital. But because of his financial situation, he can't afford it."

"You don't say." Coach Green picked up a pad from his desk and jotted down some notes. "You say Jamal's from Newark?"

"Yeah, that's right."

"Do you know what hospital his father's in?"

"I think Jamal said … Mount Hope Hospital."

"Shawn, can you arrange for your roommate to meet me here at my office this evening?"

"Why, Coach? What are you going to do?"

"I'm gonna make your roommate a little offer he can't refuse."

"What kind of offer?"

"Let's just say I think your academic problems are going to be a thing of the past."

Shawn smiled. "You mean like my SAT problem?"

"Now you're getting the picture."

"You know, Coach, I knew we could work this little problem out. But let me tell you something about my roommate. Jamal's very smart, but he's very high strung. I don't think it's gonna be easy convincing him to cheat for me."

"Who said anything about cheating?" Coach Green grinned. "I'm merely suggesting a little business opportunity. If Jamal rubs our back, we'll rub his. Just promise me you'll have him here by seven o'clock. I'll take care of the rest. Do you think you can handle that?"

"Yeah, Coach. I can handle that."

"All right, Shawn. I need you to get back to the practice gym before your mother gets here. We need to keep you focused on our game against the DC Capitols. The Tigers are in first place in the Big Central Conference, and I intend to keep it that way. Let me handle your mother. I'll let her know we're getting you a tutor and convince her you can bring your grades up by the end of the semester."

"A'ight, Coach."

"Shawn, don't forget to have your roommate here this evening."

"I won't."

****

After watching Shawn leave, Coach Green reached across his desk and thumbed through the Rolodex for the number of Deluxe Auto Sales. He picked up the phone and dialed the number for the dealership.

"Hello, Tony? Melvin Green here."

"Melvin, how you doing?"

"I'm fine. I was calling to see if you finalized that paperwork we discussed last week."

"C'mon, Melvin. You know I wouldn't let you down. I did just what you asked. I got him a candy-apple red BMW convertible with leather seats, CD player, and a cell phone."

"That's perfect, Tony. Did you lease it under the name of Shawn Collins?"

"Absolutely. It's leased under his name for four years. But remember, Melvin, if the kid leaves the Tigers, I take the car back on the spot."

"That's the whole idea, Tony. I refuse to let another school snatch away one of my premier players like they did Calvin Holloway. I still haven't recovered from that slap in the face. Now, like we agreed, I'll take care of the insurance payments and the cell phone payments, and you'll handle the lease payments, right?"

"Right, Melvin, and the paperwork will make it appear as if Collins is making the payments. There's no way this deal can be traced back to you or me. But I do need you to bring Collins down to the lot so he can sign off on the paperwork."

"No problem. I was planning on bringing him down on Friday after practice."

"Just make sure you bring him after seven o'clock. I'll be the only one here."

"Are you coming to the game Thursday night, Tony?"

"Are you kidding? I wouldn't miss it. It's going to be a great game, the Tigers against the DC Capitols. I can't wait to see how Collins matches up against Henderson."

"I've been getting Collins ready for that matchup all week. Henderson's weak on the left side, so I've instructed Collins to go up strong against his left side on every drive. We're going to have Henderson so frustrated he'll foul out by the end of the third quarter. We're going to beat the shit out of the Capitols—take my word for it."

"I hope so, Melvin. I have five hundred big ones riding on the Tigers."

"My job is riding on it, Tony. If I don't produce a championship team this year, I can kiss my coaching job good-bye."

"I hear you, Melvin."

"Why don't you stop by the locker room after the game, Tony. We'll go out and have a drink over my victory and your winnings."

"Sounds like a plan to me, big guy. See you Thursday night."

"Okay. Take it easy, Tony. Bye."

Coach Green hung up the phone and rubbed his hands together in glee. But his moment was interrupted by the intercom.

"Coach?"

"Yes, what is it, Marjorie?"

"There's a Mrs. Collins here to see you. She doesn't have an appointment, but she's insisting on seeing you."

"It's okay, Marjorie. Send her in."

Martha barged into the office and threw down a copy of the letter from the athletic director. "You can spare me the pleasantries, Coach Green. I'm here to discuss this letter. What's going on with my son?"

"I know you're upset, Mrs. Collins ..."

"Upset. You better believe I'm upset. You promised you were going to take good care of Shawn, and then I get this. I told you how important it was for Shawn to get a good education while he was going to this school."

"I know you're concerned, Mrs. Collins, but—"

"But nothin'. I trusted you." Martha pointed to the letter. "I trusted you would do right by Shawn. But I can see you're no better than the rest of those grinnin' fools that came knockin' on my door, promising my son the moon if he played for their team. Well, let me tell you something right now." Martha leaned across the desk and glared into Coach Green's narrow-set, gray eyes. "If my son's grades don't improve, I'll take him off the team myself."

Coach Green bolted from behind his chair. "Wait just a minute, Mrs. Collins. Don't forget we're on the same side here. Believe me, I have Shawn's best interest at heart. Please have a seat so we can discuss this calmly. There's no need for you to be this upset. Shawn's no good to me if he's academically ineligible. Have a seat so we can work this problem out together."

Martha pulled back from Coach Green's desk and took a seat opposite him.

"Now, isn't that better?"

Martha ignored the coach's question.

"I received a copy of Shawn's mid-semester grade report too. And let me tell you, I was just as upset as you were when I read it. Whenever I asked Shawn how his classes were going, he replied fine. Whenever I asked him if he needed any help, he answered no. You see, Mrs. Collins, I wasn't aware of the situation myself until recently. But let me assure you, I'm already working on the problem. And as I told you before, I want all my boys to leave this university with a degree. That's one of my highest priorities."

"You could have fooled me. The way things look right now, I'd be surprised if Shawn makes it through his first semester."

"He'll make it through, Mrs. Collins," Coach Green stated with authority. "I'll see to that."

Martha looked into Coach Green's eyes. "Shawn's a fine young man, but he has his faults. He likes to have fun. That's why you have to keep close tabs on him. You have to stay on his behind to make sure he does what he's supposed to do. I thought I explained all of this to you."

"You did, Mrs. Collins, and I apologize. I thought I was keeping close tabs on Shawn. Evidently I haven't been doing my job. But that's all about to change."

"Change how?"

"I've decided to assign Shawn a personal tutor. The person I assign will help Shawn with his classwork, arrange his study schedule, and ensure Shawn attends all of his classes. But most importantly, he'll report to me on Shawn's progress. From now on, I'll know firsthand how Shawn's doing."

"That sounds encouraging. I just hope it's not too little too late."

"In addition, Mrs. Collins, I'll speak with Shawn's professors. Hopefully I can persuade them to give Shawn a break and not fail him this semester. I'll convince them that with a little help from his tutor, he'll bring his grades up." Coach Green rose from his chair. "Don't worry, Mrs. Collins, Shawn will make it through the semester. I promise you that." Coach Green placed his arm around Martha's shoulders.

"I'm going to hold you to that promise. Oh, and one more thing before I go." Martha turned to face Coach Green. "I want to get copies of the same reports you get. I think it's best if we both keep close tabs on my son."

Coach Green escorted Martha to the door. "I'll personally see to that. Between the two of us, we'll make sure Shawn leaves this school with a diploma in his hands."

"That's what I'm counting on, Coach Green. That's exactly what I am counting on."

"I'll call you in about a week to let you know when you can expect to receive your first progress report."

"Coach, I can't tell you how relieved I am." Martha paused in front of the outer office door. "I'm sorry if I came in here like a wet cat in a hen house."

"I understand, Mrs. Collins. Shawn's education is very important to you."

"I'm glad you realize that."

"Of course I do. It's important to me too." Coach Green patted Martha's hand. "Now don't you worry. We'll have everything under control very quickly."

"Good-bye, Coach."

After watching Martha leave, Coach Green turned to his secretary. "Get me the number for Mount Hope Hospital in Newark, New Jersey."

CHAPTER 13

Robert added another ten pounds to the military press machine. He positioned himself on the narrow seat and then raised the weight above his head. He found himself using the weight room at the Omni Center more and more as his internal and external pressures mounted. The weight room provided him a means of escape, at least for a little while, from his external pressure and internal confusion.

He added another five pounds to the press machine and observed his form in the wide mirror in front of him. The sight of his strained face reminded him of the early weight-training days with Stephon.

"Rob, you have to keep good form or your workout will be useless. Now, remember what I told you. Raise your arms slowly above your head. Exhale as you push the weight up; inhale as you lower the weight down."

"Stephon, it's no use, I'll never be able to get my body to look like yours."

"Yeah you will, Rob. Just do what I tell you. As a matter of fact, I think I can see your pecs starting to poke through your T-shirt already."

"All right, all right, Stephon. Stop pinching me. I'll do another set."

"That's my boy. Now count to three and lift. One, two, three, lift."

"How's my form?"

"It's great, Rob. But you're not straining enough. I think it's time we increase your weight."

"Increase my weight! Give me a break."

Robert recalled Stephon's infectious laugh and vibrant smile. *Why did I have to destroy everything?* In order to shake himself from the painful memories, he added another ten pounds to the press machine and flexed his muscles. He was proud of how far he'd come since those early weight-training days with Stephon.

He wondered if he would ever develop another friendship as intense as the one he shared with Stephon. In the short time they were friends, they shared everything, even their most intimate, private secrets. But it was that secret, Robert thought as he was transported back to that hot August night. It was that secret that caused their world to spiral out of control.

It had rained all day, and the sweltering night air hung low with late August humidity. Robert lay across his bed, dressed in a pair of powder blue boxer shorts, trying to catch a hint of the slight breeze that sifted through the screened windows. His focus, as usual, was on Stephon. He wondered what it would feel like to crawl into bed next to him. His fantasy caused his sleeping manhood to awaken.

Stephon, aware of Robert's actions, sat up on his bunk and motioned him over.

"Rob."

He didn't answer.

"Rob, come over here. I have something to show you."

He knew it was a mistake, but he crept out of his bed and tiptoed across the room.

"What?"

Stephon reached under his mattress and pulled out a glossy magazine.

"What kind of magazine is that?"

"What kind do you think?"

Stephon had shown him nude girlie magazines before, but this one was different. This magazine depicted two men on the cover.

"Stephon, are you crazy? Put that away before someone sees it."

"It's dark in here. No one can see it except us."

Robert had never seen two men having sex before, and the picture on the cover intrigued him.

Stephon opened the magazine and slowly turned each page, making sure Robert got a good look at every erotic scene.

"Do you like what you see?"

Robert nodded his head.

"Then let's try it."

Robert was speechless. His brain wanted to say no, but his mouth wanted to say yes. He spat out something unintelligible.

Stephon placed his hand on Robert's leg.

He didn't pull away.

Stephon inched his hand up Robert's thigh. "Admit it, Rob, you wanna do it. You wanna do it just as much as I do, don't you?"

Robert wanted to scream but didn't. He wanted to make Stephon stop but couldn't. His penis snaked down the inside of his thigh. He was powerless against his desires.

"You're just like me, aren't you, Rob?"

Robert nodded his agreement but didn't understand his answer.

Stephon wrapped his fingers around Robert's penis and stroked the smooth surface.

"You got a big one to be such a little guy."

Robert was paralyzed with fear. But it felt good to be touched by Stephon. He silently hoped Stephon wouldn't stop.

"You like that, Rob. Does that feel good?"

Robert couldn't speak. The heat from Stephon's hand combined with the August humidity made him weak.

"Relax and enjoy it, Rob."

Robert felt something was happening, something strange, something building up inside of him. He pushed Stephon's hand away.

"What's the matter, Rob? Don't be scared."

Robert wanted to run, to escape all the strange feelings that were shooting through his body. But Stephon grabbed Robert's hand and guided it inside his shorts.

"Touch it, Rob. Make me feel good."

Robert gripped Stephon in the palm of his hand.

"C'mon, Rob. Make me feel good."

He wanted to follow Stephon's directions. He wanted to make him feel good, but his head was spinning with fear.

Stephon begged Robert to continue, but he couldn't. He let go and ran back to his bunk.

As he lay trembling, he could smell the scent of Stephon still on his hand. He raised his fingers to his face and inhaled Stephon's lingering aroma. When Robert looked up, Stephon was watching him. Smiling at him. Robert was ashamed of his actions, he put his head under the covers and hid.

Robert grabbed his workout towel and walked out of the weight room toward the water fountain in the hallway. He needed a drink of water to cool his thoughts. The sound of the basketball team practicing in the large gymnasium caught his attention. He approached the double doors and peered through the windows. Jelin was racing toward the door to retrieve a basketball. Robert tried to duck out of the window, but Jelin spotted him and came into the hallway.

"Yo, Robert, I thought that was you? What are you doing out here? Thinking about joining the team?"

"I was working out down the hall. I came to get a drink of water."

"You look pumped, bro."

"Thanks. Today's my shoulder day. It's my weakest body part, so I try to do at least one workout a week that concentrates entirely on my delts."

"Well, it's working. You're looking good." Jelin smirked.

"I'm almost finished." Robert removed the towel from around his neck and wiped the sweat from his forehead. He wasn't sure if he was perspiring from his workout or being so close to Jelin. "I need to finish so I have time to hit the showers. I have a lot of studying to do tonight."

"I'll check you out later, bro." Jelin smiled. "I better get back inside before Coach Green comes looking for me. And by the way, Robert, the water fountain is that way." Jelin pointed, before returning to the practice gym.

Robert blushed. He couldn't hide his attraction to Jelin. He wished he could control his feelings. But his sexuality wasn't a choice. It was somehow predetermined; a path he was destined to walk.

By the time he hit the showers, it was six thirty. The basketball team had finished their practice and was also in the locker room. Robert cursed his luck as he navigated his way down the narrow aisle of lockers. The last thing he needed was a locker room full of naked, finely conditioned athletes. Grateful no one occupied his row, he sat on the wooden bench to remove his sweaty clothes. His muscles were tight and he struggled to remove his wet jersey over his head. He wrapped a towel around his waist, grabbed his soap case and trudged to the shower area.

The shower area was composed of three large shower rooms. Each room contained a total of ten showerheads. He hated the lack of privacy the open shower rooms provided and wished the school would invest in individual shower stalls. Fortunately, most of the basketball players were either finished or in the first shower room. He made his way to the third shower room, which was empty.

He positioned himself under the showerhead closest to the back wall and turned on the water. But his privacy was interrupted when someone else entered the room. Robert blinked twice to make sure his eyes weren't deceiving him. He couldn't believe Jelin had come all the way down to the third shower room. He quickly turned to the wall and tried to shield his face. He didn't want Jelin to know he had seen him.

Jelin turned his back to Robert and stepped under the water.

Robert peeked a look and was mesmerized by Jelin's magnificent body. It was even better than he had imagined. Jelin's dark skin rippled with muscles, and his large feet and hands were matched in proportion to the size of his manhood.

Robert couldn't control his erection. *Damn it. Not now. Not in front of Jelin.* He reached up and frantically changed the temperature dial from warm to cold.

"You can't speak, Robert?"

Robert moved closer to the wall. The cold pellets of water bounced of his body.

"Jelin … I didn't realize that was you. Howww wwwas practice?"

"I'm glad it's over, yo." Jelin smeared a glob of white liquid soap over his well-defined torso.

"Where's Shawn?" Robert asked, trying to act casual.

"He went back to the dorm. Said something about a meeting with Jamal and Coach Green at seven o'clock."

"With Jamal? What kind of meeting?"

"I'm not sure, but I think it has something to do with a tutoring opportunity for Jamal."

"Oh, a tutoring opportunity, that's great. Jamal needs the money."

"Robert, is everything all right?"

"Yeah, why?" Robert was relieved the cold water had diminished his erection.

"'Cause you're talking to the wall. That must have been a hard workout."

"Yeah, it was," Robert answered, turning around to face Jelin.

"Nothing like a hot, steamy shower after a long workout. Right, Robert?"

"Yeah, right," Robert answered, admiring the contrast of the white soapy water against Jelin's rich, dark skin.

"There's nothin' better to relax the muscles." Jelin smiled, stretching his hands above his head.

Robert struggled not to stare, but his eyes were riveted to the human reality of his fantasy.

Jelin leaned back, allowing the warm water to cascade over his shaved head.

Robert's manhood stiffened again. *Damn it.* He turned to face the wall.

"You're not shy about taking public showers are you, Robert?"

"No." Robert turned his head to look at Jelin.

"You could have fooled me," Jelin smirked, squirting more white liquid soap onto his body.

Robert knew Jelin was teasing him. He didn't want to give Jelin additional ammunition to take back to Shawn. But unfortunately, he was in the shower with Shawn's best friend, and he had an uncontrollable, full-fledged boner.

Robert turned to face the wall again.

Finally, Jelin rinsed away the lather and turned off the water.

"Hey, man, you ready for your towel?"

"Yeah, would you mind throwing it to me?" Robert was afraid to turn around.

"Here, man, catch."

Robert stepped away from the wall to catch the towel before it hit the wet floor. He caught the towel in midair and snatched it around his waist. But he knew he was busted. He couldn't look Jelin in the eyes. He dashed past him without saying a word.

"Hold up, yo."

Robert froze, afraid to turn around.

"You forgot something."

"What?"

"Your soap case."

"Oh yeah, thanks." Robert grabbed the case and continued toward his locker.

"Hold up, bro. I need to ask you somethin'."

Robert was ashamed he hadn't controlled his urges. He looked down at his feet, knowing what was coming next.

"I was wondering." Jelin grabbed Robert's shoulder, turning him around. "I'm having a hard time in my accounting class. I was wondering if you could give me a hand."

"What?" Robert looked up, surprised at Jelin's question. "Give you a hand? A hand with what?"

"With my debits and credits. I thought maybe you could … you know, help a brother out."

"Help you out? Is this some kind of a joke, Jelin?"

"No, bro. It's definitely no joke. Shawn tells me you're getting an A in accounting. I thought maybe you wouldn't mind showing me a few things. You know what I mean. Showing me how to stay … balanced."

"Balanced?"

"Yeah, help me fill in some of those little boxes."

Robert tried to keep his imagination from running away. "Well, I guess so, Jelin … if you really need the help."

"Now we're getting somewhere." Jelin followed Robert to his locker. "My professor, Dr. Coatly, is a real pain in the ass."

"Yeah, I heard about him. He doesn't like to give up any As." Robert bent over to unlock his locker.

"Would you?" Jelin smiled. "You know, if you were a professor."

Robert didn't know what kind of a game Jelin was playing but decided to play along. "Sure, I wouldn't have a problem with it. As long as the student earned it." Robert opened his locker.

"And what would a student have to do to earn some As from you?" Jelin asked.

Robert sat on the bench and looked up at Jelin with a nervous smile. "He would have to come to every class and show me his best."

Jelin placed his left leg on the bench and dried off his groin area. "I would certainly show you everything I had."

Robert was beginning to enjoy the game and the bird's-eye view. He knew Jelin was teasing him. But that look in Jelin's eyes. *Could it be possible?*

Jelin switched legs, lifting his right foot onto the bench. "So, Robert, when can we get together to go over … my material? My accounting test is next Thursday."

"Hmmm, next Thursday, that doesn't give us much time." Robert stood with his back to Jelin. "What if we're not on the same chapter? I mean … what if you're confused? I don't want to make it worse."

Jelin moved closer to Robert. "Don't worry, Robert. I think we're on the same chapter. I think you know just what I need."

Something thick and hard pressed against Robert's back. He couldn't believe what was happening. If it was a trick, Jelin was putting on one hell of a performance.

"Why don't you meet me at the library on Saturday afternoon, Robert? We'll get one of those private study rooms. If there's any confusion, we can talk it out. You know, brother to brother."

Robert's imagination shifted into overdrive. He turned around to look Jelin in the eye. "Are you sure this is really what you want?"

Jelin winked. "I'm sure. How about we meet at three o'clock."

"All right, three o'clock."

Jelin wrapped his towel around his waist and walked away.

Robert watched Jelin disappear down the row of lockers. He folded his hands together to stop them from shaking. *Did that actually just happen?* He wondered if he was about to make another mistake. He still wasn't convinced of Jelin's motives. It could all be a plot to expose him. A vicious trap. But that look in Jelin's eyes looked real. The hardness Jelin pressed against his back wasn't imagined.

Robert wished he had someone to confide in. Someone who understood his feelings. Someone to tell him what to do. His repressed desires were unleashed, and there was no holding back. He finished getting dressed and walked out of the locker room. It was only Wednesday; he had to wait three full days to find out the real motive behind Jelin's actions.

CHAPTER 14

Jamal was uneasy about his meeting with Shawn and Coach Green. He reached up and twisted one of his loose locks. He made a mental note to find a barbershop to retwist his locks as soon as he got out of the meeting. He looked over at Shawn and tried to pry more information out of him.

"Come on, Shawn, tell me why I'm here."

"Chill. The coach will be here any minute. He'll explain everything."

"You're being very mysterious, and I don't like the strange vibes I'm picking up from you, Shawn."

"Strange vibes? Is that what you said? Strange vibes?" Shawn leaned forward in his chair. "If you want to talk about strange, let's discuss that roommate of ours. Now that's what I call strange."

"Shawn, why are you so hard on Robert? He's gone out of his way to make friends with you. But all you ever do is dog him out."

"His kind of friends I don't need." Shawn waved his hand in the air. "Hell, I don't even want anyone to know he's my roommate. Jamal, you have to know by now Robert's a fuckin' faggot."

Jamal exhaled a heavy sigh. "I know Robert's dealing with some personal problems. He hasn't opened up to me yet, but I'm sure he will."

"I don't understand you, Jamal. Are you a faggot too? Is that why you're always sticking up for Robert?"

"No, Shawn." Jamal answered with a tone of irritation. "I'm not gay, but that doesn't mean I have to shun any black man that is." Jamal looked Shawn directly in the eye. "Robert's my friend, and I'll be damned if I let his sexual preference come between our friendship."

"Well, that's fine for you," Shawn answered. "But I don't wanna have anything to do with that punk-ass wimp. So if you wanna be his friend, go ahead, knock yourself out. But don't look for me to accept his perverted ass. I don't have any faggot friends, and I don't want any."

Jamal shook his head. He hated Shawn's attitude and searched for a way to get through to him.

"Shawn, have you ever heard the story of William Lynch?"

"William Lynch? Who's he? Another faggot?"

"No, William Lynch was a slave owner who back in 1712 came up with a foolproof method of controlling his slaves."

"Slaves! Seventeen twelve!" Shawn rose from his chair and walked over to the window. "Come on, Jamal. You're not going to get deep on me again, are you?"

Jamal joined Shawn at the window. "Just hear me out, okay?"

"Do I have a choice?" Shawn looked out the window.

"As I was saying, William Lynch was a slave owner who back in 1712 used the common human traits of fear, distrust, and envy to heighten the differences between his slaves. He systematically pitted the dark-skinned slave against the light-skinned slave, the course-hair slave against the straight-hair slave, the house slave against the field slave. Whatever differences he could come up with, he used to keep his slaves fearful, distrustful, and envious of each other. That's how he maintained his system of control, by keeping his slaves divided."

"I'm not trying to control anybody." Shawn stepped back. "I'm just trying to stay the fuck away."

Jamal raised his hand to silence him. "William Lynch was so proud of his system, he shared it with other plantation owners. It wasn't long before his foolproof method of controlling slaves spread throughout the entire South."

"So what does all this slave shit have to do with me?" Shawn pointed to himself.

"It's been over two hundred years, Shawn, and that noose William Lynch tied around our neck is still choking our race. We still let our differences divide us."

"What are you saying, Jamal?" Shawn returned to his seat. "That I have to start hanging out with our faggot roommate because our ancestors were slaves?"

"I'm telling you it's time you stop being controlled by William Lynch. I'm telling you to accept Robert for who he is, our brother."

"Man, that's bullshit." Shawn couldn't remain seated. "Robert's not like us."

"Robert is like us. He may have a sexual preference that's different from you and me. But he's still our brother. And I refuse to disassociate myself from him because he's not exactly like me." Jamal grabbed Shawn's arm. "Don't you see, Shawn, if we allow ourselves to be divided from Robert because of our differences, then we're still victims of William Lynch. That's exactly what William Lynch wanted."

Shawn was speechless. But before he had a chance to respond to the William Lynch diatribe, the door to the office opened, and Coach Green whirled inside.

"Gentlemen, sorry I'm late. The traffic on Bigalow Boulevard was tied up all the way down to the Civic Arena. I forgot there was a Penguin game tonight. Jamal, I'm glad to see you could make it. I'm Melvin Green, Shawn's coach."

"I know. We met earlier this year."

Coach Green removed his jacket and hung it on a hook behind the office door. "Shawn tells me you're a big Tiger fan."

"Yes, sir. It's kinda hard not to be when your roommate's one of the best players on the team." Jamal returned to his chair.

"That's one thing you got right," Shawn answered.

"Not one of the best." Coach Green took a seat behind his desk. "Shawn is the best player on the team."

"Hey, Coach, how come you've never told me that?"

"Because I didn't want it going to your head, Collins. It's already swelled with all that chatter you've received from the press."

"Coach Green," Jamal interrupted. "Why am I here?"

"I'm glad you asked that question. See that wall over there, Jamal?" Coach Green rose from behind his desk and walked across the room to stand in front of a blank wall. "Tell me, what do you notice about it?"

Jamal looked at the wall and shrugged. "Nothing. It's blank."

"That's right, Jamal. It's blank. And do you know why it's blank?"

"Can't say I do."

"Then let me tell you. It's blank because the Tigers haven't won a single championship since I've been head coach here. That's been over four years, Jamal. When I took this job and this office, I told myself this was going to be my wall of achievement." Coach Green ran his hand across the smooth surface of the wall. "But as you can see, I haven't had any achievements. The Tigers haven't won one blessed title since I've been in charge. And I'm tired of it. Do you hear me, Jamal?" Coach Green placed his hand on the side of Jamal's chair. "This year, things are going to be different. Thanks to Shawn and some of my other fine ball handlers. This year we have a chance. A chance to bring a championship back to the city of Pittsburgh, a chance to finally hang something on that wall we can all be proud of."

"That's an excellent speech, Coach Green, but what the hell does all of this have to do with me? I don't play basketball."

"It has everything to do with you, boy."

"Boy." Jamal repeated the word. "Excuse me, Coach, but my name is Jamal. Jamal Lewis.

Coach Green apologized. "Jamal, I'm sorry if I offended you. Believe me, I wasn't trying to be malicious."

"Apology accepted," Jamal replied, confident he had set a new tone for the direction of the rest of the meeting.

"Now, where were we?" Coach Green cleared his throat. "Jamal, I understand you're a very bright … man. It's your intelligence that has everything to do with the success of the team."

"My intelligence? Now you're really losing me, Coach. How could my intelligence possibly be the key to your team's success?"

"Because we need your academic abilities, Jamal. We need you to be Shawn's personal tutor. Shawn and I discussed it. We came to the conclusion that you would be the ideal candidate, being the two of you are such good friends." Coach Green placed his hand on Jamal's shoulder in a patronizing display of friendship and brotherhood.

Jamal looked over at Shawn with disbelief. "Shawn, why didn't you ask me this yourself? You didn't have to drag me all the way over here for this dog and pony show. Of course I'll be your tutor. My schedule is a little tight right now, but if I get one of the other tutors to take on a couple of my—"

"You don't understand, Jamal," Coach Green interrupted. "We want you to tutor Shawn exclusively."

"What do you mean exclusively? Wait a minute, Coach. I need all the money I can get from my tutoring. I can't afford to limit my tutoring to just one student."

"Jamal," Coach Green said, "you don't understand what I'm asking."

"I do understand, and I'm telling you I can't do it." Jamal turned to face Shawn. "Tell him, Shawn. You know what I've been going through." Jamal stood from his chair. "I'm sorry, but I can't do this. So if this meeting is finished, I'm outta here."

"Jamal," Shawn said, "I think you need to listen to what the coach has to say."

Jamal looked at Shawn and then at Coach Green. "All right, would someone tell me what's really going on here?"

"Jamal, I know what you've been going through. I know all about your father's operation and the tight financial situation your family's in right now."

"What!" Jamal lost his balance. He sat down to avoid falling.

"That's why we called you here, Jamal. To make a very lucrative offer for your services."

Jamal's pulse quickened. "Coach Green, I'm not sure I understand what you mean."

Coach Green opened his briefcase and removed a plane ticket and some papers. "Jamal I've done a little research. I know your father was admitted to Mount Hope Hospital where he had one lung removed. I also know his hospital bill is expected to rise above $50,000 before it's all over. Since his insurance is only picking up 80 percent of the total tab, your family is looking at a bill of roughly $10,000. I know your family can't afford that. That's why I'm offering you a deal. If you help me out, I'll help you out."

"A deal!" Jamal stood from his seat. "Let me see if I understand you correctly. You want me to make a deal, using my father's health as a bargaining chip. Is that the kind of deal we're talking about here? Well, let me tell you something." Jamal pointed his finger into Coach Green's reddened face. "I don't make deals with the devil. So you can take your deal and shove it up your ass!"

Shawn grabbed Jamal's arm. "Damn it. Don't be stupid, Jamal. This is an opportunity to help out your Pops. Think about it, man. You know how bad you need the money. Why knock yourself out tryin' to earn it the hard way? Make it easy on yourself for a change, bro."

"Easy on myself!" Jamal snatched his arm from Shawn's grasp. "That's the difference between you and me, Shawn. You're always looking for the easy way out. You never want to make sacrifices or accept responsibility. You think life is easy. That all you have to do is snap your fingers and people will come running. Well, let me tell you something." Jamal looked directly into Shawn's eyes. "Nothing comes without a price. And one day you're going to wake the hell up and realize the price you've paid."

"Oh, Jamal, shut up and climb down from your holier-than-thou high horse. You owe it to your Pops to at least listen to what the coach has to say."

"Jamal, listen to me," Coach Green interjected. "There are no strings attached to this deal. If you don't want to accept my offer, just say no. I can find a hundred other people ready to take your place. But Shawn was thinking of you. He thought it would be a good way to help you out of a tough situation. To help us all out of a tough situation. And all I'm asking you to do is listen."

"All right." Jamal sat back down. "What exactly are you asking me to do?"

Coach Green reared back against his chair with a grin. "It's simple. We need Shawn to get passing grades this semester. Time's running out, and I don't think he can make it through three of his courses without a little assistance."

"A little assistance?"

"Jamal, you must swear to me that what I'm about to say never leaves this room." Coach Green got up and made sure no one was in the outer office. "As I said before, you're free to turn my offer down. No questions asked. But you must swear to keep this between the three of us in this room. Can I get your agreement to that?"

Jamal reluctantly nodded his head. He knew what the coach was about to ask him. He just needed to hear it spew from the coach's slimy mouth.

Coach Green sat back down behind his desk. "That's my boy—I mean, man. The deal is this. I'll be willing to pay your father's entire hospital bill, no matter what the final figure comes to. But in return, you must do all of Shawn's class assignments and agree to take three of his final exams."

The silence of the moment clogged Jamal's ears. He couldn't believe the situation that confronted him. His parents taught him to be a man, to always do the right thing, to never let anyone take advantage of him. But under these circumstances, what was the right thing? His family desperately needed the money, but he couldn't live with himself if he accepted a deal with the devil. It went against everything he had been taught. For eighteen years, his family instilled values in him to treasure respect over worldly possessions, to resist temptation and greed. But he never dreamed he would have to choose between self-respect and the worldly possession of his father's health.

Coach Green sliced through the deadly silence. "I can see you're having trouble making a decision, Jamal. That's why I want to give you this plane ticket and some time to think it over. Fly home over the weekend and mull it over. See how your family's doing. Give me your decision next week after you get back. And by the way, even if you don't accept the offer, the ticket's yours. No strings attached."

Jamal accepted the ticket. What harm would it do to get a free visit home? He really wanted to visit his dad, and this might be his only opportunity.

Coach Green reached to shake Jamal's hand, but Jamal refused. "I'm not agreeing to your offer. I'm only agreeing to think it over." Jamal checked the dates on the ticket.

"That's all I'm asking," Coach Green responded. "And, Shawn, I want you to get some sleep tonight. We have that big game against the DC Capitols tomorrow, and I want you to be fresh."

"Yeah, Coach, I hear you," Shawn replied.

"Okay, gentlemen, that will be all." Coach Green walked over and opened the door. "Jamal, I hope to hear from you next week with your decision."

Jamal pushed past the coach without saying a word.

Shawn ran up and tried to put his arms around him, but Jamal shrugged him off and hurried down the darkened corridor.

As Jamal stepped into the cold November air, he buttoned his coat and raised his hood against the brisk wind that swirled around him. He looked up at the trees that lined the perimeter of the Omni Center. He watched the swirling wind strip the trees of their remaining leaves. As he watched the leaves float aimlessly through the air, he thought about his struggle for direction.

"Why me, God?"

CHAPTER 15

Latisha slumped onto the sofa in the back room of the Braid Boutique. Another long workday had passed, and Shawn hadn't called. She wondered if she would ever get Shawn out of her system. Every night she went to sleep with him on her mind, and every morning awoke to find him still there. *Good morning, heartache. Sit down.* Just one more time, she promised herself. Just one more time, and if he didn't respond, then she would move on. She picked up the phone, but before she could push the numbers, her best friend, Nickea, bulldozed into the room and snatched the cell phone from her hand.

"Latisha, girrrrl, I know you're not getting ready to do what I think you're gonna do. Don't you dare call that boy again. Why do you think I set up this blind date for you tonight?" Nickea slid the phone into her pocket. "I did it so you could get your mind off Shawn Collins. And here you are callin' his ass again."

"I know, Nickea, but this is the last time. I promise. If Shawn doesn't call back this time, it's over."

Nickea put her hands on her hips and shook her head. "Uhm'hm, I've heard those famous last words before. Girl, I'm gonna have you checked. You definitely need help."

"Nickea, just go back in the shop. I'll be there in a minute, and you can finish doin' my hair."

"You're a damn fool wasting your time on Shawn." Nickea threw the phone back to Latisha. "Girl, if I had a body like you got, there wouldn't be enough hours in the day for all the men I'd be havin'." Nickea snatched opened the curtain and returned to the front of the boutique.

After watching Nickea's wide ass flounce through the curtain, Latisha searched through her phone for Shawn's dorm number. She took a deep breath and recalled what her master psychic advised. "What you've claimed in your heart will soon be yours." Her stomach tightened as she waited for someone to answer.

"Hello."

"Shawn?"

"No, this is Jamal. Who's calling?"

"Oh, Jamal, I thought you were Shawn. This is Latisha. Remember me? I met you at the front desk a couple of weeks ago."

"Oh yeah, Latisha, I remember you. How you doing?"

"I'm fine. I was trying to get a hold of Shawn. Is he there?"

"No, Latisha, he's not. I just left a meeting with Shawn, and he didn't come back to the dorm."

"Do you know where he went?"

"I'm not sure, maybe over to Jelin's dorm."

"Or maybe Tammera's?" Latisha asked.

"You know about Tammera?"

"Yeah, I know." Latisha sighed.

"I'm sorry, Latisha. But I'll be sure to give Shawn the message you called."

"Thanks, Jamal. I'll be here at the Braid Boutique for about another hour. If he gets in before nine o'clock, tell him to call me here. He already has the number."

"Latisha, do you have anyone there who can tighten my locks?"

"I can do it myself. When do you need it done?"

"I'm flying home on Saturday morning. I was hoping to get it done before I left."

Latisha opened her appointment book. "Let's see ... how about tomorrow evening? I have an opening at six."

"No, that's no good. I'm going to see Shawn play the DC Capitols tomorrow."

"Okay, how about Friday evening after six thirty?"

"That's perfect. How much do you charge?"

"If you get me a ticket for the game tomorrow night, I'll do it for free."

"Are you serious?"

"Yeah, Jamal. Can you get me a ticket?"

"Hell, yeah, Latisha. Why don't you meet me at the front desk at seven thirty? I'll have your ticket, and we can walk over to the game together."

"It's a date, Jamal." Latisha smiled. "See you tomorrow. Bye."

Latisha clapped her hands. She couldn't believe her good fortune. Hell, she even had the strength to go through with the ridiculous blind date Nickea had arranged. But first, she needed to make some changes to her appearance. Based on the length of Tammera's hair, Shawn liked long hair. She needed Nickea to redo her hair. The crimp style wouldn't do. Since there was no time in her schedule to get it done Thursday, she had to get it taken care of tonight.

She rushed back into the front room. "Nickea! Nickea! Hurry, wash all of this damn gel out of my hair."

"What!" Nickea looked up from her magazine with disbelief. "I just spent two hours giving you a wrap. Now you want something different. No way, sister girl."

"I thought we were best friends."

"We are, but even best friends have to draw the line somewhere." Nickea cut her eyes up at Latisha. "What's going on?"

"Girl, I'm going to see the Tiger's play the DC Capitols tomorrow."

"You mean to tell me that good-for-nothing Shawn Collins wants you at the game?"

"Not exactly. His roommate Jamal's getting me the ticket. Shawn wasn't home."

"Oh, I see." Nickea folded her plump arms against her leopard, sleeveless tank. "And you don't think your wrap is good enough for Shawn."

"I think it was a mistake for me to cut all my hair off. Based on Shawn's new girl, I think he likes long hair. So when Shawn sees me tomorrow night, I'm gonna have a head of hair. Just like that bitch Tammera."

"Latisha, you know our dates are going to be here in an hour. I don't have time to give you a weave!"

"I don't want a weave. Just wash all this damn gel out of my hair and pin me on some curls.

"Girl, I don't know what I'm gonna do with you." Nickea motioned Latisha over to the sink and wrapped a towel around her neck. "I arrange for you to meet a fine brother tonight, and all you can think about is Shawn's yellow ass."

"It's not only his ass I'm thinking about." Latisha giggled.

"What makes you think he's gonna see you at the game anyway?"

"Oh believe me, Nickea, he'll notice me."

"And isn't Tammera a cheerleader? Are you prepared to see the two of them together?"

"That's what I'm counting on. I'm gonna make Shawn realize what he's giving up. I have a lot more to offer than that little heifer."

Nickea worked the shampoo through the stiff finger waves pasted against Latisha's scalp.

"What exactly are you gonna do, Latisha? Strip naked and streak across the court?"

"No, I have something a little subtler in mind. You see, Shawn's roommate is picking me up before the game. After the game, I'll tell him my ride is meeting me at the dorm. That's where you come in."

Nickea stopped massaging Latisha's scalp. "Me! Oh no, you're not draggin' me into this silly mess."

"All you have to do is call me at Shawn's around ten thirty and tell me you're gonna be a little late picking me up. Then get your brother Peanut to drive down and pick me up around midnight. That way, I can ensure myself enough time in Shawn's dorm room. If everything goes according to plan, Shawn and I are gonna pick up right where we left off. In bed."

Nickea rinsed warm water through Latisha's hair. "I have to hand it to you, girl. You don't give up easily, do you?"

"I know I'm acting like a fool, Nickea, but I can't get Shawn out of my system. I really do love him."

"That's why I'm fixin' you up with Darius. You need someone to get your mind off of that asshole, Shawn."

"Yeah, yeah, yeah." Latisha sighed.

"I'm serious. There's only one sure-proof way to forget about a man."

"And what's that?" Latisha asked.

"Replace his ass." Nickea laughed, adding more conditioner to Latisha's overstressed hair.

"He's not easy to forget. Shawn's a man who's goin' places. He has a lot to offer. In less than four years, he's gonna be a pro, playing in the big leagues. And I plan on being there, right by his side. Mrs. Latisha Collins."

"Sounds to me you're more in love with Shawn's potential income than you are with the man."

"Nickea, I don't want to live in the projects the rest of my life. I've watched my mother and my sister struggle. They've struggled all their damn lives because they picked men with no ambition, no drive. And look where they ended up? Right where they started. I don't want to end up like that. I wanna be somebody. When I walk down the street, I want people to know who I am. I want my children to have a father they can be proud of. I have dreams, Nickea, and Shawn's a big part of my dreams."

"Damn it, Latisha." Nickea lifted Latisha's head from the sink and toweled her hair. "When are you gonna get it through this thick head of yours? Shawn don't love you. If he did, he wouldn't treat you like dirt. Listen, honey, there are plenty of good men out there with ambition. You just have to be willing to let one in. Now we both know how many brothers you got sniffin' after your ass. You won't give any of them the time of day."

"That's because they don't have anything to offer, Nickea." Latisha took the towel from Nickea and dried her hair. "I can do bad all by myself. I don't need an anchor pulling me down."

"Well, Darius isn't an anchor. He works with Lester over at UPS. He has his own apartment and a car. And did I mention he was fine with a capital F?"

"That remains to be seen."

Nickea removed the cover-up from Latisha's shoulders. "You're going to thank me for this. Just remember—you have to name your first child after me." Nickea laughed and then placed Latisha under the dryer for the second time that evening.

After twenty minutes, Nickea lifted the hood on the dryer and checked Latisha's hair. "Okay, where are those curls you picked out for me?"

Latisha handed Nickea a handful of spiral curls. During her twenty minutes under the dryer, she had painted the tips of the curls with blond highlights.

Nickea brushed Latisha's hair up into a small tight knot and pinned the cluster of curls into a smart-looking bun that cascaded down her neck.

Latisha picked up the handheld mirror and checked out her new do. "It's not exactly what I had in mind. But it works." Latisha swiveled her head and watched the curls bounce.

"Okay, would you go get dressed now?" Nickea peeked through the blinds to see if she could see Lester's car. "Our dates are gonna be here any minute. And I hope you brought something sexy to wear. With a body like you got, I'll never understand why you don't display it more often."

"I'm wearing my black spandex dress, Nickea. Is that all right with you?" Latisha shouted from the back room.

"Yeah, girl. You know that's one of the only dresses you got that I like." Nickea looked in the mirror. After straightening out her leather miniskirt, she put on the matching jacket.

Latisha looked at her watch. It was almost nine o'clock, and she couldn't wait to get the evening over with. She needed to concentrate on her plans for Thursday night. As she freshened up her makeup in the small employee's restroom, Nickea unlocked the front door for Lester and her mystery date.

"Hey, baby, you look good. Give me a kiss, you sweet, juicy thang."

"Lester, calm down unless you want to embarrass me in front of your friend here." Nickea laughed.

"Nickea, you remember Darius, don't you?" Lester asked. "And where's that fine Latisha at? I've told Darius all about her."

"Good to see you again, Darius. Latisha's in the back getting ready. She wanted to make sure she looked good for you."

"If she looks half as good as Lester claims, I'm in for a real treat." Darius grinned, displaying a wide set of dimples.

"I think she's in for a real treat, too. You're lookin' good, Darius," Nickea said.

"Hey, hey, hey, now don't you go looking at any other man except me, baby," Lester warned.

"You know I would never do that." Nickea kissed Lester on the cheek. "Let me go see what's keeping Latisha."

Nickea entered the back room. Latisha still had her face stuck in the mirror. "Girl, will you come on. Our dates are waiting, and wait till you see Darius. Like I said, he's fine."

"All right, I'm ready." Latisha threw her lip gloss into her purse and followed Nickea into the shop.

"See, what did I tell you, Darius? She's fine, isn't she?"

"You weren't lying, Lester. Where have you been hiding her?"

"What's he been saying about me?" Latisha asked, walking up to touch Lester on the shoulder.

"Just how beautiful you are," Lester replied.

"And I must say," Darius shook his head, "for once, he wasn't exaggerating. It's nice to finally meet you, Latisha."

"It's nice to meet you too," Latisha replied, pleasantly surprised at her date. Darius had all the attributes she desired. He was tall and long-legged, with a nice smile and a clean-cut look. His tight black shirt and blue jeans displayed a body that saw the gym at least three times a week, and those dimples were enough to make any woman swoon. But he wasn't Shawn.

"Okay, now that the introductions are over, let's go." Lester opened the door and motioned everyone out.

Nickea locked the door to the shop. "Where are we going anyway?"

"I thought we would go over to the Chitchat Room in Shadyside."

"Oh, you know I love that place," Nickea replied.

Darius opened the front car door for Latisha and the back door for Nickea and Lester.

Latisha was impressed with Darius's show of manners. But men were always nice to her, until they got what they wanted.

During the ten-minute drive to the Chitchat Room, Latisha kept noticing Darius looking at her.

"Is this your car, Darius?" she asked, trying to break the awkward silence.

"Yeah, it is."

"It's a Ford Taurus," Nickea chimed in from the backseat. "And it's not leased. He owns it."

"Well, thank you, Nickea." Latisha cut her eyes back at Nickea. "But I think I know a Ford Taurus when I see one."

Darius stopped the car in front of the restaurant and advised everyone to go inside while he searched for a parking spot.

As the trio climbed out of the car, Nickea grabbed Latisha's arm and pulled her aside.

"So what do you think? Didn't I tell you he was fine?"

"Yeah he's cute, Nickea, but don't go planning any weddings just yet."

"You better give this brother a chance, Latisha."

"Is this a private conversation or can anyone join in?" Lester asked, directing the women toward the restaurant door.

"I was just trying to find out what Latisha thought of Darius."

"I know one thing," Lester stated. "Darius can't keep his eyes off of you, girl."

"I think your friend is very nice," Latisha said.

The hostess at the door said, "A table for three?"

"Four," Lester answered.

"This way." The hostess led them into the dining area and seated them at a table with a view of the street. "Here are your menus. Your waiter will be right with you."

Darius located the table and sat next to Latisha. "I was lucky. There was a parking spot right across the street." Darius looked around the restaurant. "This is a nice place. I can see why it's so popular."

"Nickea and I come here often after work. They have a jazz band every Thursday night and no cover charge," Latisha said.

Darius smiled. "I'll have to start coming here more often."

"I bet he'll come every Thursday night," Lester laughed.

"Since you're such an expert, what do you recommend, Latisha?" Darius asked.

"I like the steak salad."

"Well, whatever you like, I'm sure I'm gonna like too." Darius flashed his dimples.

Nickea looked at the two of them. "Isn't that sweet. You two make a nice couple, if I do say so myself."

"Watch out, Darius," Lester warned. "Miss Cupid's on the war path again."

"That's all right with me. Go ahead, Nickea, make me a victim of love."

The waiter walked up to the table. "Can I get you drinks?"

"I'll have a champagne spritzer," Nickea answered. "Maybe the sound of the bubbles will drown out the negative vibes coming from my left."

"Make that two," Latisha added.

"What beer do you have on tap?" Darius asked, looking up from his menu.

"Iron City and Iron City Light."

"I'll have an IC Light," Darius answered.

"I'll have a regular Iron City," Lester said.

Darius arched his brow. "I thought you were working on flattening that stomach?"

"All right, make mine an IC Light too." Lester sighed. "Man, I'm sorry I ever let you talk me into working out with you."

"I'm not." Nickea reached over and rubbed Lester's potbelly. "By next summer, my man's gonna be buff."

"Yeah right," Lester replied. "I thought you said you liked your men with a little weight on them."

"I do," Nickea replied. "But when their breasts are as big as mine, that's where I draw the line." She laughed.

Latisha cut her eyes at Nickea for her lack of sensitivity. "I'm thinking about joining a gym too."

"Why don't you come to the gym with me sometime?" Darius asked. "I would love to work you out."

"I bet you would." Lester laughed

The waiter brought their drinks. "Are you all ready to order?"

"Yeah, I think we're all going to have the steak salad." Darius looked around the table for everyone's agreement.

"Four steak salads coming up." The waiter closed his notepad and rushed back into the kitchen.

Latisha smiled at Darius. This was her first date since Shawn dumped her, and she was actually enjoying herself. She relaxed against the back of her chair and looked out the window. It was a gorgeous moonlit night, and the stars were shining like polished silver hubcaps. She remembered as a little girl picking out the largest star and making a wish. She always wished for the same thing.

"Are you all right?" Darius asked, noticing Latisha's stargazing. "You looked a million miles away."

"I was." Latisha answered.

Darius looked up at the stars. "I know what I would wish for."

"Don't tell me," Latisha said. "Or your wish won't come true."

Darius winked and flashed his dimples. "I'm gonna make it come true."

Latisha smiled and then returned her focus outside the window. Unfortunately, instead of seeing stars, she noticed a familiar face getting out of a parked car. *No, it can't be.* She squinted her eyes to get a better look. Damn it. Just when her mood was improving. There was no mistaking that damn ponytail. It was Tammera. Latisha leaned across the table and directed Nickea to look out the window.

"Who is that?" Nickea whispered in Latisha's ear.

"That's Tammera," Latisha answered.

"Shawn's Tammera? Oh shit." Nickea watched as Tammera and her two friends were led into the restaurant. "You're not gonna cause a scene, are you, Latisha? Please, not in front of Darius. He really likes you. I'm warning you, Latisha. Don't spoil it."

"I have a score to settle with that little bitch," Latisha whispered back into Nickea's ear.

"What's all the whispering about?" Darius asked. "Am I being kicked to the curb already?"

"No, of course not." Nickea laughed. "It's just a little girl talk. Right, Latisha?" Nickea kicked Latisha under the table.

"Yeah, right. Girl talk." Latisha watched as Tammera and her friends were seated at a nearby table.

"Damn it," Nickea muttered. "Latisha, would you come with me to the restroom? Excuse us, gentlemen." Nickea grabbed Latisha's arm. "We'll be right back."

Nickea strong-armed Latisha past Tammera's table and pushed her into the restroom. "Now you listen to me, girl." Nickea used her weight to pin Latisha against the wall. Your relationship with Shawn is over. Do you hear me? It's over. And it's high time you moved on with your life. Getting into a catfight with Tammera is not gonna prove anything. In fact, it will probably just drive him further away. You'll never be able to get him back once he finds out. Besides, maybe you can get something going with Darius. C'mon, honey, give him a chance. I can tell he likes you."

Latisha's eyes filled with tears. She wasn't ready to let Shawn go. Not yet. But Nickea was right. Getting into a fight with Tammera in a public place wasn't such a good idea. No, it wasn't the right place or the right time to get her revenge. Tears rolled down Latisha's face. "All right. I won't let Tammera get to me this evening."

Nickea took a tissue out of her purse and wiped Latisha's face. "Good. Now freshen up that pretty face and come back out and join us at the table. All right?"

Latisha nodded. "Just give me a couple minutes to pull myself together."

"He ain't worth it, Latisha." Nickea shook her head. "Shawn ain't worth your tears."

Latisha nodded.

Nickea turned and walked out of the restroom.

Latisha stepped up to the sink to wash the tearstains from her face. *Why do girls like Tammera get everything?* Over the past three weeks, she had done some snooping around about Tammera. She found out Tammera was the daughter of one of the most prominent black judges in town. They lived in a large house in Squirrel Hill, and Tammera was the only child. Probably a spoiled brat. Latisha took out her compact and reapplied her makeup. Not only did Tammera have money and looks, but she also had Shawn, at least for the moment. Latisha frowned at her reflection.

Before leaving the restroom, Latisha decided to take advantage of the facilities. She walked back to one of the stalls and closed the door. Just as she sat down, the door to the restroom opened and two voices could be heard.

"I'm not sure who she is, Anika. Shawn won't tell me her name. All I know is she won't leave him alone. She calls him night and day. Even though he never calls her back. I also hear she's from Garfield."

"You're kidding me, Tammera. Shawn was dating someone from the projects?"

"That's right, the projects. And like I told Shawn, those people not only physically live there, but they mentally live there too. She'll never amount to anything but a baby-making machine living off the state."

"It's a good thing he got rid of her. Have you seen her yet, Tammera?"

"No, but I can just imagine what she must looks like." Tammera laughed. "A hoochie mama."

Latisha had heard enough. She rifled through her purse, looking for her blade. *I'll show her a hoochie mama. I'll show her a hoochie mama with a blade in her hand.* She located the switchblade lying at the bottom of her purse and gripped the smooth pearl handle. She peered through the small opening between the stall wall and the door. *I'll cut that bitch's ponytail off.* She released the blade from its holder, pulled back the latch on the door, and crept out of the stall.

"Latisha!" Nickea called entering the restroom.

Tammera and Anika quickly made their exit as Nickea's presence suddenly made the restroom feel crowded.

Nickea spotted Latisha crouched in the doorway of the stall, the switchblade still clutched in her hand. She rushed over and pulled her friend up from the floor. "Lord have mercy; it looks like I done come in here just in time to stop you from doin' something stupid. Are you crazy?"

"She called me a hoochie mama," Latisha cried.

"That's no reason for this." Nickea pried the switchblade from Latisha's hand. "What the hell were you thinking? Do you want to end up in jail? Huh, is that what Shawn's gonna drive you to?"

Latisha sobbed against Nickea's shoulder.

"It's all right, baby. Go ahead and cry. Let it all out." Nickea slipped the switchblade into her purse. "Oh, child, what do I gotta do to make your pain go away? You can't go on like this. You gotta pull yourself together."

"I don't have nothin'," Latisha sobbed. "She has everything, and I don't have nothin'."

"That's not true." Nickea lifted Latisha's face. "You just need to open your eyes and realize you got your self-respect, honey. And can't no one ever take that away from you, unless you let them. Now you listen to me." Nickea said. "You can't let this destroy you. You gotta be strong.

Where's that old feisty girl I used to know? Where's that girl with the good head on her shoulders, the girl who would never let anyone walk over her? That girl who refused to be ignored, where is she?" Nickea tried to shake some sense into Latisha.

"She's gone." Latisha looked up at Nickea. "She's gone."

"She's not gone!" Nickea exclaimed. "She's right here. And God help me if it takes a month of Sundays, I'm gonna get her back. You understand me! I want my friend back, not this imposter. Now, let me tell you what we're gonna do." Nickea wet a paper towel and wiped Latisha's face. "We're gonna walk back out to that table, and you're gonna hold your head up high. You hear me? You're gonna hold your head up high and be proud of the wonderful person you are. That person with a loving heart and a kind soul. That person you were before you met Shawn Collins."

Latisha took a deep breath and hugged her friend tight.

"Nickea, what did I ever do to deserve a friend as good as you?"

"You've always been there for me, honey. And I'm gonna be there for you." Nickea placed her arm around her friend. "Remember what you used to always tell me? Weeping may endure for a night, but joy comes in the morning."

Latisha nodded.

"All right, c'mon."

Latisha gathered herself and walked back to the table arm-in-arm with Nickea. As she walked past Tammera's table, their eyes met. Latisha's eyes burned a hole in Tammera's flesh. Her grip tightened against Nickea's hand.

"Gentlemen, I'm very sorry, but Latisha's not feeling well. Darius, would you mind driving her home?"

Darius stood and grasped Latisha's hand. "No, of course not."

Lester said, "Darius, I know where Latisha lives. Let me use your car to drive her home. I'll come right back."

"I'm coming too." Nickea grabbed her purse.

"Ah, all right." Darius handed his keys to Lester. "I'll have them hold our food until you come back."

"You're a sweetheart, Darius." Nickea took hold of Latisha's hand and guided her toward the door.

"I'm sorry." Latisha turned around to look at Darius. "I'm so sorry."

CHAPTER 16

Shawn was nervous as he opened his locker. The game against the DC Capitols was a must-win for the Tigers. All week long, Coach Green had gone over practice films, pointing out Derrick Henderson's weak points. It didn't matter that Henderson was an All-American senior on the DC Capitol squad or that Henderson was considered one of the best point guards in the nation. Coach Green still expected a standout performance.

"I'm not going to let it rattle me," Shawn whispered to himself as thoughts of his father entered his mind.

"I'm gonna be a superstar, Daddy."

"And I'm going to be there to watch you play, son."

Shawn sat on the bench and removed his leather-bound, weekly schedule book from his gym bag. He flipped to the rear of the book and removed the photo he kept tucked away under the back flap. The photo was a picture of his father dressed in his policeman's uniform and cap.

He held the photo up to the light. "Tonight's the night, Pops. I'm gonna make you proud of me."

Shawn couldn't think about his father without remembering the accident. It was a cold, angry memory he tried many times to forget. But the sights and sounds of the accident were forever etched in his mind. He remembered the family being together that fateful August day. He remembered the sky turning gray and the sound of the raindrops against the windshield. He remembered the truck appearing out of nowhere and careening across the highway. He remembered the impact of the collision and the sound of the shattering glass.

When his teammates began entering the locker room, Shawn returned the photo to his schedule book and continued to get dressed for the game.

****

Robert squeezed more toothpaste onto his brush. He was excited about seeing Jelin again, even though it would be from the stands at the game. He hadn't talked with Jelin since their conversation in the locker room and was anxious about their looming study date. He still wasn't convinced of Jelin's motives and found it hard to believe someone as handsome and popular as Jelin could actually be interested in him.

Robert looked at his reflection in the mirror. His low self-esteem had reared its ugly head again. But it was hard to have a positive self-image when society labeled him deviant. When the Bible said he was sinning against the Lord, Robert wondered why God made him gay.

He stepped back and analyzed his appearance. He didn't look gay. He didn't act feminine or prance around making a spectacle of himself. He just desired the feel of a masculine touch, the hardness of a male physique. He prayed the feelings would go away, but it seemed the harder he prayed, the more intense they became.

After the tragic incident with Stephon, he thought he could suppress those feelings forever. But Jelin caused them to reemerge.

Robert retuned his toothbrush to the stand. He prayed the meeting with Jelin on Saturday wouldn't be another big mistake in his life.

****

Jamal picked up the phone to call his mother. He wanted to let her know he was coming home for the weekend. "No." He hung the phone back against the wall. His mother would ask too many questions. Questions he wasn't prepared to answer, at least not truthfully.

Although her letters indicated his father was recuperating from the surgery, Jamal could tell something was wrong. He had to make the trip home to find out the truth. But unfortunately, that meant accepting Coach Green's offer.

"One step at a time," Jamal told himself. First, he would make the trip home to visit his father. Once he was convinced his father was out of danger, he would return to Pittsburgh and turn down Coach Green's offer. But tonight he was going to relax and try to enjoy the game, if that was possible.

****

Latisha marched through the revolving doors of the dormitory and signed in at the front desk. "Could you buzz Jamal in room 2020?" she asked the student behind the front desk. "Tell him Latisha is downstairs."

She took a seat in the lounge and rehearsed her plan. So far, everything was proceeding according to schedule. Nickea had agreed to have Peanut pick her up at the dormitory at midnight. That gave her roughly two hours after the game to get Shawn back to the dorm and into bed. Her only problem was making sure Tammera didn't show up and ruin her plans again.

Latisha smiled over the simplicity of her plan. She lowered her purse onto the table and searched through the contents for the specially prepared condoms. "Where are they?" She turned the purse upside down and emptied out the contents. "They have to be here." She rifled through the contents over and over, but each search turned up empty. "Damn it!" She took a deep breath to calm her nerves. She could still pull her plan off, but she had to find a convenience store and buy another package of condoms right after the game.

"Latisha?"

"Over here, Jamal." Latisha scooped the contents back into her purse.

"Good to see you again, Latisha."

"You too, Jamal."

"Latisha, this is Robert."

"Nice to meet you, Robert."

"Nice to meet you too, Latisha. I've heard a lot about you."

"Uh-oh, I don't know if that's good or bad," Latisha answered.

"It's all good." Robert smiled.

"Are you ready to go?" Jamal asked.

"Ready as I'll ever be."

"Okay, then let's bounce." Jamal put his arm around Latisha and guided her toward the revolving doors.

"I feel like a queen being escorted by two handsome men."

The trio exited the dormitory and headed up the hill toward the Omni Center.

****

"There he is, Momma. I see Shawn." Damar ran up to his brother. "Shawn! Shawn!"

"Hey, little man." Shawn raised his brother onto his shoulders and kissed his mother on the cheek.

"Shawn, put him down before he falls." Martha grabbed Damar down.

"Glad you could make it, Moms."

"You know I wouldn't miss a chance to see you play."

"Hello, Mrs. Collins," Jelin chimed in.

"Jelin, good to see you again." Martha kissed Jelin on the cheek.

Shawn put his arm around Tammera and presented her to his mother. "Moms, I want you to meet Tammera."

"So you're the girl that has my son so smitten."

"Moms, come on. Give me a break. Smitten?"

Tammera gave Martha a hug. "It's nice to finally meet you, Mrs. Collins."

"You're as lovely as Shawn said you were." Martha stepped back to get a good look at Tammera.

"Moms, stop bustin' me."

"I'm Damar, and I'm happy to meet you too." Damar touched Tammera's pompoms. "Are you a cheerleader?"

"Yes I am, Damar. And I'm going to cheer your brother on to victory tonight."

"Shawn tells me your last name is Patterson. You're not by any chance Judge Patterson's daughter?" Martha asked.

"You know my father?"

"I know your father very well. Believe it or not, your father and Shawn's father were close friends."

"Shawn, how come you never told me that?" Tammera asked.

"Because the two of you were too young to remember," Martha answered. "It was a long time ago. Your father was an up-and-coming lawyer, and Shawn's father was a rookie police officer. They worked together on a community outreach program. They were honored by the NAACP. After that, they became good friends." Martha smiled.

"Your father used to bring you over to our house when you were just a little girl."

"Wait a minute. You mean she's that little bucktooth brat that used to come over and hide behind her father's pant legs?"

"She's the one." Martha laughed. "We sure did have a lot of good times back then. Tammera, tell your father I said hello. And why don't you bring your family over for the holidays?"

"I'm sure Father would love that." Tammera smiled.

"Martha Collins, is that you?"

Martha turned to see Coach Green walk up behind her.

"How are you, Coach?"

"I'm fine." Coach Green flashed a nervous smile. "I came to get Shawn and Jelin. It's time for our pregame meeting."

Martha pulled Coach Green aside. "Coach, can I talk to you in private for a moment?"

"Yes, Mrs. Collins, what is it?"

"I wanted to remind you about those progress reports you promised."

"I haven't forgotten. As a matter of fact, I've already selected the person who's going to be Shawn's personal tutor."

"You have?"

"Yes, it's Shawn's roommate, Jamal Lewis. Do you know him?"

"No, I haven't met him yet, but Shawn speaks very highly of him."

"He's a great student, Mrs. Collins, and I think he's just what Shawn needs."

Martha nodded her approval.

"In fact, there he is over there. Just a minute. I'll go get him."

As Coach Green stepped away, Shawn approached his mother. "What were you two talking about?"

"The coach was just telling me about your new tutor." Martha placed her hands against her hips. "We still need to discuss your grades, Shawn."

"Yeah, Moms, I know. But I still have time to bring them up before the end of the semester. Don't worry. Where did Coach Green go?"

"He went over to get your roommate."

"My roommate?" Shawn looked up to see Coach Green, Jamal, Robert, and Latisha all headed toward them.

Realizing Tammera and Latisha were about to meet, he stepped back and grabbed Jelin's arm. "Man, I need you to get Tammera out of here fast. Look who's on her way over."

Before Jelin had a chance to react, Coach Green regained Martha's attention. "Mrs. Collins, this is the young man I was telling you about."

Martha shook Jamal's hand. "I've heard a lot about you, Jamal. I can't tell you how pleased I am you're going to be my son's tutor."

Jamal cut his eyes at Coach Green. "Nice to meet you," Jamal answered. "This is our other roommate, Robert, and I suppose you already know Latisha."

"Yes, I do," Martha replied. "Pleasure to meet you, Robert. Hello, Latisha."

Shawn scratched his head. "Latisha, I didn't know you were coming to the game."

"I thought I would surprise you."

"You did." Shawn glanced over at Tammera.

Tammera stepped up and introduced herself to Latisha. "Hello, Latisha. I'm Tammera. I'm sure Shawn has spoken to you about me."

"No, he hasn't," Latisha fired back.

"Shawn, Jelin, let's get going, men." Coach Green motioned with his hand. "We have an important game to win tonight."

Relieved the coach had rescued him from an uncomfortable situation, Shawn gave his mother a final kiss on the cheek. "Wish me luck, Moms."

"Good luck, son."

"Yeah, good luck, Shawn," Damar said. "Beat those stupid Capitols."

"Have a good game, Jelin," Robert added.

Jelin nodded to Robert and then followed the coach into the locker room.

"Don't I get a kiss, too?" Tammera asked Shawn.

"Sorry, baby." Shawn walked past Latisha and kissed Tammera on the lips.

Latisha looked down at the floor.

Shawn walked past Latisha without saying good-bye.

Tammera flashed a devious smile. "Mrs. Collins, let me help you and Damar to your seats." She put her arm around Martha and flung her ponytail into Latisha's face.

"Well, how nice." Martha grabbed hold of Tammera's hand as she and Damar were escorted away.

Latisha ran over and caught up with Shawn before he entered the locker room. "Shawn, meet me at your dorm room after the game. I have something I want to give you." She ran her hand across her breast and smiled.

Shawn looked at Latisha and shook his head. "No fuckin' way." He quickly disappeared behind the locker room door.

"Latisha, Latisha," Jamal shouted through the crowd. "C'mon, let's go find our seats."

Jamal and Robert walked up to Latisha. "Are you okay?" Jamal asked.

Latisha eyes were full of tears. "Yeah, I'm fine. But I don't think I can sit through this game. If you guys don't mind, I'm gonna catch the bus back to Garfield."

"Are you sure, Latisha?" Jamal asked.

"Yeah, I'm sure. I need to be alone for a while."

"How about if we walk you down to Broad Avenue?" Robert asked.

"No, that's all right. You guys go ahead and watch the game. I'll be all right by myself. I'm a big girl."

"Okay, but I'll see you tomorrow at the Braid Boutique for my appointment, right?" Jamal asked.

Latisha nodded. "Come down after six thirty. Bye, guys." Latisha turned and walked away.

The band started to play. "C'mon, Robert. Let's go watch the pregame festivities. I'm sure Latisha will be all right."

****

Latisha exited the Omni Center and walked down the hill toward Broad Avenue.

When she saw the Negley Avenue bus loading up at the corner, she dashed the last twenty-five feet to catch it before it pulled away. She reached into her purse for a dollar to pay the fare but then changed her mind. She motioned for the driver to leave without her. She re-crossed Broad Avenue and marched back up the hill toward the Omni Center.

After showing the guard her ticket stub, she proceeded toward the gymnasium. She reached the double doors and peered through the windows. The game had started, and the Tigers were winning 12 to 8. A time-out had been called, and the cheerleaders were on the court going through their routine.

She saw Tammera doing a cartwheel across the floor. Without thinking, she stormed through the double doors and charged onto the court. Just as Tammera finished her last flip, Latisha ran up and punched Tammera in the face. The audience roared as they watched Tammera bounce off the floor.

CHAPTER 17

"Collins Outshines Henderson in Tiger Win." Shawn's eyes danced across the headlines of the *Post Gazette*. His outstanding performance against the DC Capitols made him the toast of the town. The article named him the hottest freshman in the country and predicted the Pittsburgh City University Tigers to win the Big Central Conference title. The article also mentioned the spectacle Latisha had caused. Shawn frowned. It had taken almost half the night to convince Tammera not to press charges.

Shawn looked at the messages scrolled across Coach Green's memo pad. ESPN had called for a spotlight interview, and *Sports Illustrated* wanted him for the cover of their next issue. Everything was happening so fast, Shawn thought, closing his eyes and imagining his future.

"Collins! I've got great news for you." Coach Green entered the office. "I scheduled that interview with ESPN for next weekend, and *Sports Illustrated* is going to take some pictures of you tomorrow for the cover of their College Basketball issue. You're a star, Collins. Just like I promised." Coach Green patted Shawn on the back. "Didn't I tell you, if you stuck with me, I'd make you a star?"

"I have to hand it to you, Coach. That strategy to get Henderson frustrated worked liked a charm last night. I just kept driving the ball past his left side, and he couldn't stop me. I still can't believe I scored thirty points against the best point guard in the nation."

Coach Green took a seat behind his desk. "Believe it, Shawn. But don't get too cocky or overconfident. We can't let this media hype overexpose you. Believe me, I know all about the media. They love a star. They love to build up a star, just so they can tear him down. It's not really you they love; it's their stories. And whether their story depicts you in a good light or bad light, they could care less. They just want to sell newspapers or magazines. They don't give a damn about you."

Shawn nodded.

"That's why I'm only letting you do these two interviews. Once we win the Big Central Championship and head into the NCAA Tournament, I'll let you do a couple more. But right now we have to stay focused on winning basketball games. We can't get distracted."

"I know, Coach. The season is still early, and we have a long way to go."

"I'm glad you realize that, Shawn. And remember it takes a whole team to build success, not just one player. Never forget that."

"So, Coach, what's the surprise you called me here to see?"

Coach Green walked over to the door and put on his gray overcoat. "Grab your gear and follow me. We have a meeting at Deluxe Auto Sales."

"Deluxe Auto Sales?" Shawn grabbed his gym bag and followed the coach out of the office.

****

The smile on Latisha's face really wasn't a smile at all. It was a mask to hide the pain. It hurt like hell finally accepting the truth. *The relationship's over*, she kept telling herself. *Shawn never loved you, he just used you, and like a damn fool, you let him.* "But no more," Latisha whispered, as she loosened Miss Gloria's blond braids. "No more."

"You talkin' to me, Latisha?"

Miss Gloria had a knack for showing up at the worst possible times. Latisha had contemplated calling in sick and not reporting to work. She really didn't feel like facing Miss Gloria and all her questions, but she needed the money, and Miss Gloria was her best paying customer. She decided to keep her mouth shut and just let Miss Gloria do all the talking. She didn't want Miss Gloria finding out about Shawn or the stunt she pulled punching Tammera in the face in front of three thousand screaming fans. Fortunately, Miss Gloria was preoccupied with her own enemy, Miss Shirley Martha Lee, to notice Latisha's sullen mood.

"Latisha, you should have seen Miss Shirley last night, sittin' there at the Elks Club, old evil thang. Tellin' everybody she was originally from Chicago and had Mississippi written all over her."

Latisha pretended to listen to Miss Gloria's story. She looked across the shop floor and noticed Nickea watching her. *What's Nickea up to?* she wondered.

"Latisha, I'm telling you," Miss Gloria went on. "All night long, Miss Shirley was perched up on that bar stool, turnin' and twistin' her smelly self around like somebody really wanted her. If she had said one word to Tethonie, I swear I would have rammed her upside her oblong head …"

"Let me see that picture again of the hairstyle you want Miss Gloria." Latisha hoped Miss Gloria would shut her damn mouth long enough for her to collect her thoughts about her own situation.

Miss Gloria pulled a picture of a glamorous-looking actress out of her purse. "Here it is, child."

Latisha looked at the picture and sighed. There was no way in hell Miss Gloria was going to leave the Boutique looking like Halle Berry. "I'll do the best I can, Miss Gloria, but you ain't got the same grade of hair as Halle."

"I know, honey. Just make the braids thin and pull them back off my face like she has here in this picture. What was that movie she was in when she wore this hairdo?" Miss Gloria put her index finger against the side of her cheek. "You know I can't remember, and it wasn't even that long ago. I think it was one of those made-for-TV movies, and she played a sex goddess. Tethonie just loved her in that movie. Anyway, where was I with the story about Miss Shirley?"

"If she would have said something to Tethonie, you were going to knock her upside her oblong head."

"Oh yeah," Miss Gloria resumed, waving her hand in the air. "And you should have seen what she had on. It is November—right, Latisha? Well, let me tell you. Miss Shirley had on white shorts and a peekaboo blouse. I've never seen such a thang in the dead of winter. Then I overheard her tellin' these two mens that she likes getting it from both ends. Looord, I looked over and whispered to the bartender, Smitty, that they need to shut down both Miss Shirley's ends because she stank. And, Latisha, do you believe she heard what I said? As hard of hearing as that old battle-ax is, she overheard my comment to Smitty. Well, the next thang you know, she all up in my face sayin' I'm uppity. It's a good thang Tethonie came and dragged me away before I pulled that hateful old wig off her head."

As Miss Gloria continued on with her story, Latisha's mind drifted back to Shawn. She got a good look at his face before she ran out of the gymnasium. He was madder than hell, and it was just a matter of time before he confronted her. But at least she finally got his attention.

"Look, someone sent flowers. Oh, I wonder who they're for." Nickea ran over to greet the deliveryman at the door.

All the women in the shop stopped talking, including Miss Gloria as they waited to hear the name of the girl to whom the card was addressed.

"And the lucky girl is Latisha Wright." Nickea walked a bouquet of red roses over to Latisha.

"For me?" Latisha knew they couldn't be from Shawn. Not unless he planted a bomb in the blossoms.

"They sure are beautiful. I bet they from that Collins boy," Miss Gloria stated, trying to read the envelope Latisha opened. "That boy sure is fine. If I was only ten years younger, you'd have some serious competition on your hands, Latisha."

Latisha cut her eyes down at Miss Gloria as she read the card.

Dear Latisha,

I hope you are feeling better. I just wanted to let you know, I enjoyed meeting you, and I hope we can go out together again soon.

Darius

Latisha didn't feel like smiling but the ends of her mouth curled up. She looked over at Nickea. "Did you know about this?"

Nickea shook her head no, but the mischievous gleam in her eyes said otherwise.

"Who they from, Latisha?" Miss Gloria asked. "They from that Collins boy, ain't they. I knew it. You see, when it comes to matters of the heart, I know."

"Miss Gloria, why you all in someone else's business? Shut the hell up and let Latisha tell us who the flowers are from!" Nickea exclaimed.

Without saying a word, Latisha turned the card around so Nickea could read it.

Nickea smiled. "Remember—you have to name your first child after me."

"Are you pregnant, Latisha?" Miss Gloria asked.

"No, Miss Gloria, and don't go spreading false rumors around."

"Now you know I'm not like that," Miss Gloria replied.

Latisha shook her head. It was almost six thirty, and Jamal would be at the shop any minute. She picked up her pace to finish Miss Gloria's hair. She didn't want Miss Gloria's nosy ass in the shop when Jamal arrived.

****

Shawn checked out his new car. "A BMW, a red convertible BMW, and its mine. I can't believe this."

"Believe it, Shawn. It's leased to you for four years. The only string attached is you have to remain a Tiger. As long as you remain on the team, the car is yours." Coach Green opened the door for Shawn to get inside. "And look, it has a leather interior, a CD player, and a navigation system."

"Damn, Coach."

"That means you like the car?"

"Hell yeah! Who wouldn't?" Shawn plopped into the bucket seat and grabbed the leather-wrapped steering wheel.

"Okay, Shawn, before you get too attached to the car, we have a little paperwork to take care of first. C'mon, let's go inside and see Tony. He's the person who put this deal together for us. You remember Tony, don't you? You met him in the locker room after the game last night."

"Oh yeah, the guy with the plaid jacket."

"That's right," Coach Green answered.

Shawn stepped out of the car and took one more look at his new set of wheels. "Wait till Tammera sees me in this," he said, followed by a long, slow whistle as the coach led him into the showroom.

"Tony, I think he likes the car."

"Have a seat, gentlemen." Tony motioned in the direction of two cushioned chairs opposite his desk.

Shawn sat in the chair next to the coach but turned his head to look at his new car. He visualized himself driving through the streets of Pittsburgh with the top down and Tammera by his side.

"Shawn, I'm glad you like the car, but there are a couple of things we need to get straight before you drive it back to campus."

Shawn turned and listened to what Tony had to say.

"First and most important, you're paying for the car. Do you understand what I am saying, Shawn? If anyone—and I mean anyone—asks you about the car. You tell them your family is paying for it. That's all you have to say. Do you understand that?"

Shawn nodded.

"I don't think I need to remind you, it's a major recruiting violation for a college athlete to receive gifts. If word ever got out about this little transaction, you'd be kicked off the team. and Coach Green could lose his job."

"I already know all of that," Shawn responded.

"Good," Tony continued. "Now, Coach Green and I will really be making the payments. We've set up a bank account in your name. The monthly lease payments along with the insurance payments and the cell phone payments will be automatically deducted from that account. All you have to worry about is playing basketball. Second, no drunk driving or letting your friends drive the car. We don't want an accident to happen for the police to start snooping around. And make sure your license and registration are kept current. Finally, the car is yours as long as you remain on the Tiger team. If you flunk out, transfer to another school, or leave the school early to enter the pros, we take the car back on the spot. Do you understand the conditions of this deal, Shawn?"

"Yeah, I understand."

"And one more thing," Coach Green chimed in. "I think it's best if you don't drive the car around your mother. I think it's best if she doesn't know anything about this little transaction. And if she does see you driving the car, tell her it belongs to one of your assistant coaches."

"I got you, Coach. Don't worry. I know how to handle my mother."

"Well, all right, gentlemen. I think we all understand one another. Shawn, I need your signature here on this document and on the bank authorization."

Shawn eagerly grabbed the pen. "Just show me where to sign." He signed the documents without reading what they said.

Tony shook Shawn's hand. "Okay, Shawn, I think we have a deal. Here are the keys to your new car. Bring it in every ten thousand miles for an oil change and maintenance check."

"Got it. Every ten thousand miles," Shawn repeated as he dashed out of the door.

Coach Green and Tony Costello shook hands as Shawn drove the car off the lot.

****

Shawn couldn't believe his good fortune. Everything was turning out just the way he had hoped. His love life with Tammera was in high gear, he had a brand-new BMW, and he didn't have to worry about his schoolwork anymore. Although Jamal hadn't accepted the offer yet, he knew Jamal wouldn't let him down. He picked up the cell phone to call Jamal at the dorm.

"Hello?"

"Hey, Jamal, guess what I'm driving?"

"No, this is Robert."

"Oh, Robert, I thought you were Jamal. Is he there?

"No. Is this you, Shawn?"

"Yeah, Robert, it's me. Do you know where Jamal is?"

"He went down to East Liberty to get his locks tightened at Latisha's shop."

"Latisha's shop!" Shawn almost dropped the phone. "All right, thanks for the info, Robert. Peace."

The sound of Latisha's name made Shawn's excitement over his new car fade. It was time he paid Latisha a little visit. While stopped at a traffic light, he reached across to the passenger seat and unzipped his gym bag. The condom box was lying at the bottom of the bag. Latisha tried to trick him into getting her pregnant. Plus, she gave Tammera a black eye in front of a nationwide audience. Latisha was out of control, and it was time she was cut loose. Shawn lifted the condom box from the bag and placed it inside his jacket pocket. The more he thought about Latisha, the angrier he became. "No one is going to diss me like that and get away with it."

Shawn pressed down on the accelerator and headed up Fifth Avenue towards East Liberty.

****

Jamal arrived at the shop just as Latisha finished Miss Gloria's new do. Miss Gloria had decided to get her nails done and was seated with the manicurist next to Latisha's station. Latisha could tell Miss Gloria was listening to every word of her conversation with Jamal. She tried not to talk about Shawn, but unfortunately Jamal raised the subject.

"Latisha, you really shouldn't have punched Tammera in the face last night. I'm surprised you got away before the security guards got a hold of you. And you're lucky Shawn talked Tammera out of filing assault charges."

"Jamal, can we talk about something else?"

"Latisha, I think you have a lot going for yourself. You're beautiful, you're smart, and I bet you do the best braiding at this shop, don't you?"

"Well, she certainly gets my vote," Miss Gloria butted in.

"See, Latisha? Your customers seem to agree with me," Jamal answered with a smile. "Latisha, I hope you don't think I'm stepping out of line or getting into your business, but I think it's time you stop wasting so much energy on Shawn and concentrate on yourself."

"Jamal, you don't understand. It's not easy to shut down feelings. Believe me, I've tried. The problem is I love Shawn. And you can't just stop lovin' somebody. Even if that person mistreats you."

"I feel you, Latisha, but lovin' somebody doesn't mean giving up your self-respect."

"I heard that on a talk show the other day," Miss Gloria interrupted. "The poor child up on the stage just let her man walk all over her. Don't tell me that's what's going on with you. Has that Collins boy been hittin' you, honey?"

"No, Miss Gloria."

"Latisha, exactly what do you have planned for your future?" Jamal asked. "And please don't tell me you expect Shawn to take care of you."

Jamal looked up at Latisha. "And why don't I see any licenses up on your wall? Do you really just wanna braid hair for the rest of your life?"

"Jamal, I'm poor, and I can't afford to go to college. Yes, I had dreams of Shawn taking me away to a better life. Is that so bad to have dreams?"

"Only when you're living someone else's dream. Latisha, you don't need Shawn to take you to a better life. You can do that all by yourself. But first you need to stop trying to fulfill Shawn's needs and start working on your own."

"That's easy for you to say, Jamal." Latisha swiveled Jamal's chair around to face her. "Look at you. You're getting a college education. When you graduate, you're gonna be able to get a good job and make something out of your life."

"That's right, Latisha. Look at me. I'm poor too. I'm from the poorest neighborhood in Newark, New Jersey. But I didn't let that stop me. And the reason I can afford to go to college is because I'm on a scholarship. I knew my parents couldn't afford to send me to college, so I worked my ass off to get a scholarship. I admit it wasn't easy. It wasn't fun. I made a lot of sacrifices along the way."

"I've made sacrifices too, Jamal."

"Latisha, I'm gonna tell you this because I think it's something you need to hear. You've sacrificed your future for Shawn. What's gonna happen if Shawn decides he wants another woman? Are you prepared for a future without Shawn in your life?"

Latisha remained silent. She turned Jamal toward the mirror and slowly worked conditioner into his scalp.

"Latisha, do you have any goals?"

"My goal is to survive. You don't know what it's like growin' up in a house where your father's in jail. You don't know what it's like havin' to take care of your momma's kids and your sister's kids because they too damn busy running the streets. You don't know what it's like ..." Latisha knew Miss Gloria was listening and decided not to say anything else about her family.

"That just goes to show you, Latisha." Jamal turned around and looked up at her. "You're a strong person. Look at the adversity you've already overcome. You graduated from high school, I can tell you don't do drugs, and you already have a job. Now you need to concentrate on advancing your skills. Since you can't afford college, why don't you get your cosmetology license?"

"Yeah, I've thought about getting my license."

"Then why don't you? And after you achieve that goal, set another one. Maybe one day you can open your own shop."

"My own shop?" Latisha laughed. "Now that's really a dream."

"Yes, but it would be your dream, Latisha."

"My own shop." Latisha envisioned a shop with her name written in bold white letters across the front window, Latisha's House of Beauty.

"Look at that fine car that just pulled up," Miss Gloria stated, as a red BMW parked in front of the shop.

"Who is that?" Nickea asked, walking over to peek out the window. "Oh shit!" Nickea turned around to look at Latisha. "It's Shawn."

"Shawn?" Latisha repeated.

Jamal stood from his seat and walked over to the window. "Where did he get that car?"

"I don't know about the rest of y'all, but I think we're in for a little action up in here," Miss Gloria stated, blowing air onto her wet nails.

Shawn stormed into the shop and slammed the door. "Where's Latisha!"

The receptionist dropped her magazine and pointed into the styling room.

Nickea put a roadblock between Shawn and the entrance to the styling room. "Shawn Collins, don't you come in here buggin'."

"Move your fat ass out of my way. This is between me and Latisha!"

"No you won't push me out the way." Nickea bobbed her head from left to right.

Jamal ran up and put his arm around Shawn. "C'mon, Shawn, let's go. Take care of your private business in private. Not here at the shop."

"Not until I do what I came here to do. Now where is she? Where's Latisha?"

Latisha boldly walked up to confront Shawn. "You got something you wanna say to me, Shawn? Here, you wanna hit me? You wanna hit a woman? Go ahead. Take your best shot. You bastard."

All the hoods on the hair dryers went up, and heads still dripping wet with shampoo rose from the sinks as all the other women in the shop tuned in to the developing showdown.

"Where the hell do you get off, Latisha?" Shawn pushed Latisha back into the styling area. "Just who the hell do you think you are? I'm sorry I ever got hooked up with your crazy ass. What was on your mind punching Tammera in the face like that last night, huh? Answer me. Did you think I was just gonna sit back and let you get away with it, huh? Answer me!"

Latisha was frightened by the anger in Shawn's eyes. She reached for the stability of her workstation but accidentally knocked over the vase with the twelve red roses. The vase crashed against the floor next to where Miss Gloria was sitting.

"I'm gonna tell your momma you comin' in here causing all this ruckus." Miss Gloria backed out of Shawn's way. "And you lucky you didn't get any water on my new shoes."

"Shut up, you nosy-ass, baldheaded bitch. Try mindin' your own fuckin' business for a change."

"Shawn, have some respect. These are women," Jamal pleaded. "Come on, man, let's step." Jamal grabbed Shawn's arm. "Let's get out of here before you do something you're gonna regret."

"Let go of me!" Shawn pulled his arm back. "I'll go, but first I have something I need to return to Latisha." He reached into his jacket and removed the box of condoms. "Remember these! The next time you try to get your little, slutty ass pregnant, remember to take your goddamn evidence with you!" Shawn struck Latisha in the face with the condom box. "Nobody plays me like that, Latisha! You got that? Nobody!"

"It's your fault! You cheated on me, Shawn!" Latisha grabbed Shawn's arm, causing him to tumble on top of her.

"Latisha, what are you doing?" Nickea tried to pull Latisha up.

Shawn pushed Nickea away. "No, Nickea. I'm gonna give Latisha what she wants."

Shawn started grinding Latisha against the floor. "This is what you want, Latisha, isn't it? A piece of dick, right? You little whore. A goddamn piece of dick. Well, here it is. You happy now? Enjoy it, because it's the last you'll ever get from me."

"Shawn, have you lost your mind? Get off her!" Jamal shouted. "Get up, Shawn!"

Nickea reached for the phone. "I'm callin' the police!"

"Don't bother, Nickea. I'm leavin'. But you better keep her crazy, demented ass away from me."

"Shawn, don't you understand! I did it because I loved you. I didn't wanna lose you. Can't you understand … I didn't wanna lose you!"

"Latisha, you don't need that fool," Nickea shouted, trying to hold Latisha back from Shawn.

"Why wouldn't you listen to me, Shawn?" Latisha continued, breaking away from Nickea's hold. "Why wouldn't you return any of my phone calls? Why did you treat me like dirt? I loved you. I loved you, and you played me."

"I played you? I played you? You're the one who cut the hole in the condom. Remember? You're nothin' but a deceitful little ho." Shawn turned and headed toward the door.

Latisha ran after him. "I wasn't thinking straight. I'm sorry, baby. Please forgive me. Please don't leave me like this. Can't we go somewhere and talk this out?"

All the women in the shop looked on in silent disbelief as Latisha begged for forgiveness.

Shawn looked around at his audience. "Sorry is right. You make me sick. C'mon, Jamal, let's get the hell out of here before I kill this bitch."

"Don't you call me a bitch. I don't deserve that!"

Shawn put his hand in Latisha's face and shoved her away. "Get away from me!"

Latisha fell against her workstation, cutting her lip on the broken glass of the vase. She touched the back of her hand against her lip and drew blood. "I didn't do it to hurt you, Shawn."

"You're pathetic."

Miss Gloria jumped out of her chair. "If you hit her again, you gonna have to come through me!"

Nickea reached for her scissors and waved them in the air. "Get him out of here now, Jamal! Get him outta here now, or he ain't gonna have all the pieces he come in here with."

Jamal put his arm up to keep Nickea and Miss Gloria away. "Shawn, you've done enough! Now, let's just step." He slowly backed Shawn toward the door.

"I didn't mean to hurt her," Shawn said softly as Jamal backed him out of the shop and onto the street. "I didn't mean to hurt her. It was an accident."

Latisha retrieved a wet towel from her workstation and placed it against her bleeding mouth. She crept over to the window and witnessed Jamal taking the keys from Shawn. She cried as the car pulled away from the curb.

CHAPTER 18

After the incident at the beauty salon, Jamal was glad to get away. The turmoil Shawn and Coach Green inflicted on his life had taken a toll. His trip home couldn't have come at a better time.

He gazed out the window and watched the individual elements of the city of Newark become larger. The Performing Arts Center that the city was banking on to spur economic development had become a reality. The gleaming glass and stone structure added to the growing Newark skyline, allowing the city to legitimately claim its title as the Renaissance City. Across from the Art Center, a new riverfront park had also sprung up, replacing the giant, rusty oil tanks with shiny, green grass that followed the Passaic River along its winding path to the Newark Bay. Jamal's eyes sparkled as he proudly viewed his city. Although he wasn't alive when riots decimated the city over forty years ago, he was glad to see the city rising from the ashes and finally claiming a new image.

As the wheels of the plane touched the ground, Jamal decided to go directly to the hospital rather than visiting the family. He could hardly contain his excitement to see his father. He would tell his father about his classes, his roommates, his professors, and his plans for the rest of the semester.

Jamal navigated his way out of the plane and through the busy terminal. He caught the transit bus loading up at its designated stop. He squeezed in between two women discussing their Thanksgiving plans. He ignored their talk of cranberry sauce and mushroom stuffing and concentrated on what he would say to his father.

When he arrived at Newark Penn Station, he boarded the local transit bus for the short trip up Market Street. He frowned at his reflection in the bus window. He knew exactly what his father would say about the coach's offer. *Son, your self-respect is worth more than any amount of money that man could offer. Money is a fleeting thing, but self-respect, that endures.*

Jamal shook his head. He wasn't living up to his father's standards. But he couldn't sit idle and watch his father's health deteriorate under the financial strain. He couldn't let the family struggle to pay the overwhelming hospital bills. He had to do something.

The sign for Mount Hope Hospital erased Jamal's reflection from the window. He signaled for the driver to stop. He hustled his bag off the bus and braced himself for reality. He knew his father wouldn't look the same. His father had undergone lung surgery and, according to his mother, was currently having radiation treatments. His father would look frail and weak, but as long as he was still alive, that was all that mattered.

Jamal walked up to the front desk. "Can you give me the room number for Lloyd Lewis?"

"Room 508," the attendant answered, handing Jamal a small plastic room pass and a sign-in sheet.

Jamal signed his name. "Is anyone else in the room?"

"No, visiting hours just started, and you're his first visitor."

Jamal took the elevator to the fifth floor. He hated hospitals. The cold antiseptic smells and sterile stainless-steel environment made him uncomfortable. Before entering his father's room, he took a deep breath. He was thankful his father wasn't in intensive care.

He pushed open the door and stepped inside. The room was quiet except for the sound of the equipment hooked up to his father's bedside. There were tubes and wires running everywhere, connecting the equipment to his father's nose, chest, and arm. He stepped further into the room and sensed something was wrong. At first glance, it appeared his father was asleep, but upon further examination, he realized the truth. His father wasn't sleep; he was hooked up to a respirator.

"Dad." Jamal reached for his father's hand. "Dad, can you hear me?" His father's hand was cold and clammy and indicated no response to his touch. Jamal shook his head in disbelief. He looked closely at all the devices hooked up to his father. In addition to the respirator tube placed inside his mouth, there was an intravenous bottle dripping liquid into a tube attached to his arm, and a monitor set up above his bed to track his heartbeat. The faint beep of the monitor acted in unison with the bright green dot that zigzagged repetitively across the screen. He patted his father's hand. "Dad."

Jamal was disturbed by his father's appearance. His father had wasted away to skin and bones. He stepped back to read the nameplate attached to the foot of the bed. It identified the patient as Lloyd Lewis, but Jamal couldn't believe it was his father. His father was a strong, proud man. The person in the bed was a mere wisp of a man, barely clinging to life.

"Dad!" Jamal raised his voice, hoping his father would wake up. "It's me, Jamal. Dad, I don't know if you can hear me, but I'm here. I wanted to surprise you. I needed to see how you were doing."

The door to the room opened, and a nurse entered.

"Nurse, why isn't my father responding?"

The nurse walked up to the foot of the bed and picked up a chart.

"Is he heavily sedated?"

"This is your father?"

Jamal nodded.

The nurse made some notations on the chart before answering. "Honey, I'm sorry. I guess no one told you."

"Told me what?"

"Your father fell into a coma yesterday." The nurse returned the chart to the foot of the bed. "I'll get your father's doctor. He's right down the hall. He can answer your questions better than I can."

Jamal's eyes filled with tears. "Why didn't anyone tell me? I had the right to know."

The nurse touched Jamal's shoulder. "I'll be right back."

Tears rolled down both sides of Jamal's face and met underneath his chin. "Why God? Why my father? It's not fair." He picked up his father's listless hand. "I'm so sorry, Dad. I'm sorry I wasn't here for you. But I promise, I'll take care of the family while you're sick. You don't have to worry about that. I'm gonna take care of the family. Just like you did when you were able. Please don't leave us. We need you."

Jamal sat on the chair next to his father's bedside. The constant hum of the equipment continued to take deep breaths of air for his father. He couldn't imagine life without his father. His father was the glue that held the family together. Suddenly, the monitor indicated a spike in his father's heartbeat. He looked down at his father's face. A slight grimace flashed across his father's face. Jamal searched for some positive sign of hope. "Are you trying to speak? Are you trying to tell me something?" He moved closer toward the bed and lowered his ear down to his father's mouth. "I'm listening." Jamal waited for his father to speak. "You can tell me now, Dad. I'm listening." The alarm on the monitor sounded.

"Dad, what's going on?" The bright green dot on the monitor went flat. "Please don't die. Dad! Dad! Noooooooo! Doctor! Doctor!" Jamal ran into the hallway. "Something's wrong with my father. Somebody help me! Doctooor!"

"Code red, room 508." The announcement blared across the intercom.

The nurse grabbed Jamal's arm and pushed him toward the doorway. "Son, you're gonna have to leave the room."

Jamal stepped into the hallway as the doctor and his assistants rushed into the room. The piercing sound of the monitor continued. *This can't be happening.* He closed his eyes. "Please, God, let me wake up and all this go away." Jamal opened his eyes, but the nightmare remained. The sights and sounds of the hospital surrounded him like a glove. He sat down on the floor and covered his ears from the high-pitched alarm. He tried to stifle the sound with a prayer. "The Lord is my shepherd: I shall not want. He maketh me lie down in green pastures. He leadeth me besides the still waters. He restoreth my soul. He leadeth me in the paths of righteousness for his name's sake. Yea, though I walk through the valley of the shadow of death, I will fear no evil."

Jamal paused and raised his head. Attendants rushed in and out of his father's room.

"For thou art with me; thy rod and thy staff, they comfort me. Thou preparest a table for me in the presence of mine enemies."

The sound of the alarm stopped.

"Thou anointest my head with oil; my cup runneth over. Surely goodness and mercy shall follow me all the days of my life, and I will dwell in the house of the Lord forever."

After completing his prayer, Jamal sat quietly on the floor and waited for God to hear his words. "God, please don't take my father away."

After what seemed like an eternity, Jamal rose from the floor and crept over to his father's door. He peered through the window. The doctor and nurses were unhooking the equipment from his father's bedside. He rushed inside the room. "What are you doing? He needs those. He needs those. Don't take them away!"

"Son, I'm sorry, but your father's dead." The doctor pushed Jamal away from the bed.

The doctor's words didn't penetrate Jamal's spirit. He tried to stop the doctor from writing the time of death on his father's chart.

"I'm sorry, there was nothing more we could do."

"Yes you can. You're not trying!" Jamal reached for his father's hand. "He can't be dead. Please, Lord, don't let him be dead. Don't let my father be dead. Dad!" Jamal frantically patted his father's hand. "Dad, answer me! Tell me you can hear me. Please tell me you can hear me!"

The nurse gently pried Jamal away from his father. "Come on, son. He's in God's hands now. There's nothing more anybody can do." She pulled Jamal away from the bed and led him out of the room. "You gonna have to be strong now. You have to be the one to tell your family."

"I can't!" Jamal screamed.

The nurse squeezed Jamal's hand. "Yes you can."

"How can I?" Jamal sobbed onto the nurse's shoulder. "How can I possibly do that?"

"Listen to me, son." The nurse raised Jamal's head with her index finger. "It's better they hear it from you than from a stranger." She led Jamal to a chair in the visitor's lounge. "Have a seat and gather yourself."

Jamal slumped onto one of the narrow chairs. The watchful eyes of the other people in the lounge area looked at him with compassion, but he didn't want their pity; he wanted his father back.

"Concentrate on pulling yourself together. Let me know when you're ready to make the call. I'll help you through it," the nurse said.

Jamal nodded.

"I'm gonna get you a cup of coffee. It'll help clear your head."

Jamal watched through tear filled eyes as the nurse walked away. He knew she was right. He had to make the call home. But what on earth was he going to say? How could he tell his mother the man she loved for thirty years was gone? That she would never see him again—never hear him laugh or tell a funny joke—never watch him read the evening paper or sing in the church choir—never see him give away his daughter or hold his first grandchild. How could he possibly tell her that?

Jamal drank the coffee the nurse brought. The hot liquid warmed his throat but not his soul. He was empty and cold inside. Like a part of him was lost. A hole that would never feel complete. He decided not to break the news over the phone. It was something he needed to do in person.

When the orderly wheeled the covered body of his father out of the room, Jamal stopped him before he reached the elevator. He bent down and kissed his father through the thin white sheet that covered his face. "I love you, Dad, and if love could have saved you … you never would have died."

The orderly wheeled his father into the elevator. The stainless steel doors closed and the illuminated numbers transported his father away to another life.

****

Jamal 's oldest brother, Ali, answered the intercom when he buzzed up to the apartment. The crisp November air had cleared Jamal's head, and he was strong enough to deliver the awful news. Having Ali by his side would be a great comfort.

Ali greeted him at the door with a big hug. "Jamal, why didn't you tell anyone you were coming home? Let me get a look at you, little brother—or should I say college man."

"I've missed you, Ali. I'm glad you're home."

"We tried calling you this morning, but your roommate said he didn't know where you were."

"I know. I told him not to say anything if my family called. I wanted to surprise you all."

"You certainly did that." The smile faded from Ali's face. "Sit down, little brother. I have some bad news to tell you."

Jamal sat his bag next to the door and took a seat on the living room sofa. He knew the news Ali was about to deliver would be a tremor compared to the earthquake he was suppressing.

Ali sat on the sofa next to Jamal. "We tried to call you this morning to tell you about Dad. Jamal, Dad's in bad shape. He fell into a coma yesterday. He's on a respirator."

Jamal tried to appear strong but his voice quivered. "How's Mom doing?"

"Not well. After seeing Dad last night, she refuses to go back to the hospital. She said she can't see him in that condition again. Jamal, I've tried, but I can't convince her to go back to the hospital with me."

The hole in Jamal's soul expanded to encompass his heart. "Where is she?"

"She went over to the church to pray. She's a strong woman, but I'm worried about her. Between Dad's illness and all the other things going on with this family, I'm afraid she's at the breaking point."

"What other things?"

Ali took a deep breath. "Aaliyah's pregnant. She moved in with Bobby Rodgers."

"Pregnant! She told me they were breaking up."

"Yeah I know," Ali answered with a heavy sigh.

"How could she be so stupid to get pregnant, especially by him?"

"She says he loves her. Mom warned her if she kept seeing him, she'd have to move out. Aaliyah chose Bobby."

"Where are they living?"

"Somewhere up on Fourteenth Street. She hasn't had much contact with the family since she moved out. The baby's due in about six months. When Dad found out she was pregnant, it broke his heart. But that's not the worst of it, Jamal."

Jamal didn't want to know what could be worse. He was still trying to digest everything he already heard.

"Malik joined the West Side Kings." Ali shook his head in disgust.

"The West Side Kings!"

"Malik believes he can make more money on the street than with a legitimate job. He comes home occasionally to get clothes, but that's the only time we see him. Jamal, I think he's selling crack for the Kings."

"Good Lord!" Jamal put his head into his hands in utter frustration. His worst fears had come true. Not only had the disease of violence knocked at their door; it ripped it off its hinges. "Why didn't anyone tell me all of this was going on?"

"Mom and Dad didn't want to worry you. They see you as the savior of this family. They desperately want you to escape all this violence and poverty. They believe if you make it, you can pull the rest of the family up with you."

"But that's not fair, Ali. They called you for help. Why not me?"

"Because I'm the oldest, and I agree with them. You have enough to worry about without taking on the burdens of this family. All your life, you've been the one that's taken responsibility."

"I never complained, Ali."

"I know you never complained. But it should have been my job. I'm the oldest. But when things got rough, I bolted without thinking about the family. I was too caught up in my own world to worry about the family.

"You had problems, Ali."

"I abandoned you all. I left without telling a soul where I was going. I thought running away would help me escape my problems."

"But you've turned your life around."

"Yes, I've turned my life around, Jamal. But I still feel guilty. I feel guilty for leaving you all the way I did, especially you. That's why I'm here now, and that's why I told Mom and Dad not to call you. It's my turn to take on some responsibilities." Ali paused. "Being in the military taught me to be a man and to step up to my responsibilities. I'm on a two-month leave, and I told our parents I would be the one to take care of the family this time."

Jamal gave his big brother a hug. "I understood why you left, and I understand why you're back. But don't shut me out. We need to work together to get through this crisis. We can't let the family fall apart, especially now, Ali, especially now." Jamal turned away to hide his tears.

"What do you mean, especially now?"

Jamal looked at Ali. A tear floated down his face. "Before I came here, I stopped at the hospital to visit Dad." Jamal's entire body quivered. "While I was there … while I was there …"

"Jamal, what happened?"

Jamal walked over to the window and looked down at the street. The view looked the same, but the world had changed. "While I was there ... Dad died. Ali, I saw him die."

Ali was silent.

Jamal turned to face him. "Dad's gone. Ali, what are we gonna do?"

"Jamal, we knew this was going to happen. The doctors told us it was inevitable. It was just a matter of time. They couldn't stop the cancer from spreading. After they removed the first lung, the cancer spread to the other lung. They told us to prepare ourselves, to pray. They said the only thing they could do was lessen his pain. Make him comfortable. But we thought Dad had more time. We thought he would make it through Christmas. We thought you would have a chance to see him." Ali joined Jamal at the window. "I know you're sad, Jamal. But Dad was in a great deal of pain. Now he's free from that pain. We have to take some comfort in that. Dad is finally free."

Jamal's throat was tight with grief. "How do we tell Mom? How are we going to tell Mom and the rest of the family?"

"We'll tell them all together." Ali put his arms around Jamal. "We'll tell them all together, little brother. But first, let's go get Cleo and Jerel. They're down the street at the Laundromat. By the time we get back, Mom should be here. We'll tell them all together, as a family." Ali walked over to the closet and retrieved his coat.

"How about Malik and Aaliyah? We have to tell them too?"

"I don't know how to get in touch with them. They haven't given us their phone numbers, but I'll put word out on the street. Hopefully they'll come home."

Jamal followed Ali to the door.

Before opening the door, Ali turned around to face Jamal. "Would you believe Malik never visited Dad when he was in the hospital? Dad would ask about Malik every day. As sick as he was, he was more concerned about Malik than about himself."

"What's happened to this family, Ali? We used to care about each other."

Ali opened the door. "I don't know what happened, Jamal. I really don't know."

CHAPTER 19

I t was Saturday afternoon, and Robert's mind swirled with nervous anticipation. As he searched his closet for something to wear, he accidently knocked over the cardboard box that had been sitting on the top shelf. The box contained a collection of memories from his private boarding school days. His heart skipped a beat when he saw his tenth-grade yearbook laying open at his feet. He picked up the book and thumbed through the pages. He stopped when he got to the picture of Stephon. Although the picture had been taken over three years ago, it still conjured up strong emotions. Robert knew the emotion was love, because lust surely could not have endured the cruel test of time.

A tidal wave of memories crashed against Robert's mind. He recalled sneaking over to Stephon's bed that eventful night. He recalled being a willing participant in their sexual adventure. But most of all, he recalled the beginning of the end of their friendship.

"Are you worried about winning the swim meet tomorrow, Stephon?"

"No way. With you in the stands watching me, I'll do the best dive ever."

"How do you know I'll be there?"

"Because we're kindred spirits, Rob. You'll be there to support me."

"You think you know me, don't you?"

"I know what you like. Remember?"

"Stop that, Stephon. Someone is gonna see us."

"C'mon, Rob, stop being so scared. You liked it the last time we did it, didn't you?"

"Yeah, but ... but it was sinful."

"If it was so sinful, why are you so excited?"

"I don't know, Stephon. All I know is Father Reese says it's a sin."

"You wanna know what I heard? I heard Father Reese likes to do it too."

"You're lying, Stephon."

"No I'm not. Ask anyone."

"Don't you wanna know what it feels like, Rob?"

"I … I … I don't know."

"You're not gonna run away again, are you, Rob?

"No."

"Then let me put some lotion on you."

"Um, I don't …"

"Feels good, doesn't it, Rob?"

"Here—put some on me. Make me feel good."

"Like this?"

"Yeah, Rob, that feels good, baby. Do it faster."

"Ssssstephon."

"Yeah, that's right, baby. Let it go … Are you all right, Rob? Wait, where are you going? Don't run away again."

Robert's hands trembled with emotion as he returned the yearbook to the box. The bittersweet moment with Stephon had changed his life forever. He wondered if he was about to make the same mistake with Jelin. He put on his coat and headed for Jelin's apartment on the other side of campus.

****

A heavy dusting of snow had transformed the dull, gray campus into a brilliant white wonderland. Robert trudged through the snow-covered sidewalks trying to keep negative thoughts from entering his mind. After a ten-minute walk, he stood in the lobby of Jelin's building. He looked through the directory and then dialed the four-digit code.

"Jelin, it's Robert. I'm downstairs."

"C'mon up, bro. I'm in suite 207."

Robert took the elevator up to the second floor. "If it looks like a setup, I'll leave," he told himself, before lightly knocking on the door.

Jelin opened the door with a wide grin. "Whaz up, Robert? I wasn't sure I'd see you today."

"I said I would help you pass your accounting test, right?"

"Yeah, right." Jelin ushered Robert inside and directed him toward a sturdy-looking sofa in the living room area. "You're a true man of your word. Have a seat. I'm gonna get my stuff."

Robert watched Jelin swagger down the hallway. Jelin was dressed in his team jersey, a pair of fleece sweatpants, and unlaced work boots. Everything about him exuded a raw masculine sexuality that made Robert nervous. He removed a Kleenex from his shirt pocket and wiped the perspiration from his forehead.

After regaining his composure, he inventoried the surroundings. Jelin's suite looked very similar to his, except the living room appeared bigger and contained a large-screen TV and an elaborate-looking entertainment center. He sat on the sofa opposite the TV and stared into the sixty-five-inch flat screen. It seemed strange that such an expensive entertainment center would be in a college dorm room.

Jelin reappeared carrying his accounting book and worksheet.

Robert pointed to the TV. "Where'd you get that?"

"Uh, let's just say it was a gift." Jelin situated himself close to Robert on the sofa.

Robert could smell Jelin's deodorant mixing with the clean scent of his soap.

"I've been working on this worksheet all afternoon, but I can't get the damn thing to balance."

"Here, let me take a look." Robert's fingers accidentally brushed across Jelin's outstretched hand. He laid the worksheet on the table and scrutinized the entries.

"What's the problem, bro? What am I doing wrong?"

"Umm, I think you logged a couple entries as debits that should have been logged as credits." He did a quick calculation in his head.

"Damn, why is this shit so confusing?"

"It's not confusing if you think about it logically," Robert erased the incorrect entries and reentered them on the other side of the ledger. "Just remember the basic principle of accounting. A debit is an item of debt, and a credit is an item of payment received. See this entry? It should have been booked as a credit because it was a payment for a shipment of goods."

"Is everything so black and white, Robert? I mean, couldn't something be both a debit and a credit?"

"No, I don't think so. Not in accounting anyway."

"How about in real life?"

Robert wasn't sure how to answer. He handed Jelin back his worksheet. "Once you understand the basic difference between a credit and a debit, this stuff will be a lot easier. See, look. Now your worksheet is balanced."

"Damn, Robert, you really know how to keep everything in its right box, don't you?"

"I've had a lot of experience."

"Experienced at being boxed in?"

Robert remained silent. The conversation had taken a dangerous turn.

"All this talk is making me thirsty. Can I get you somethin' to drink?" Jelin rose from the sofa and headed into the kitchen

Robert's eyes widened when he noticed Jelin wasn't wearing any underwear. "What ... what do you have?"

"Let's see ... orange juice, water, or pop?"

"I'll have a water."

"One water coming up." Jelin removed two small water bottles and tossed one to Robert.

Robert caught the bottle in midair.

"You have quick hands. Are you as good with your hands as you are with numbers?"

"I guess so," Robert answered nervously.

Jelin walked back into the living room.

Robert tried to act calm and unbothered but couldn't remove his eyes from the bulge in Jelin's fleece pants that jiggled back and forth to the rhythmic gait of his strut. Robert's manhood stiffened.

Jelin raised his container in the air. "To my new tutor. May this be the beginning of a beautiful relationship?" Jelin grinned.

Robert raised his container in the air and saluted Jelin's toast. "A beautiful relationship," he repeated.

Jelin tapped his container against the side of Robert's.

Robert nervously tried to open his container with one hand.

"Why you so nervous, bro?"

Robert struggled with the lid of the water bottle.

"Did you come over here to teach me accounting or is there something else on your mind?"

"Something else?"

"Yeah, something else."

Robert tried to take a sip of water, but the opening missed his mouth. His attempt to brush away the water only brought more attention to his unruly erection.

"C'mon, Robert, don't play games with me. You know what time it is. You didn't come over here to help me with my accounting. You want something else, don't you? Don't you?"

Robert wiped the water from his chin with the back of his hand.

Jelin smirked. "Admit it, Robert. You want some of this, don't you?" Jelin groped the crouch of his sweatpants.

Robert didn't respond. He closed his accounting book and shoved it inside his book bag.

"Shawn thinks you're a faggot. Is that true?"

Robert's worst fears had come true. The situation was a trap, and like a damn fool, he had fallen for Jelin's charade.

"Aren't you gonna answer me, Robert? I saw the way you looked at me in the shower. I know what you want."

Robert finally found his voice. "I made a mistake comin' here. We were supposed to study in the library, remember? You're the one who changed the meeting location, not me. I came over here to help you with your accounting, not to be teased and ridiculed. So if that's your plan, Jelin, save it!" Robert stood to leave. "I'm tired of playing your stupid games!"

"Stupid games?" Jelin laughed.

"That's what I said!" Robert stepped toward the door. "So run back to Shawn and tell him, his little ploy worked. You got me."

Jelin blocked Robert's path. "You think Shawn put me up to this? Hell, if Shawn even knew I invited you over here, he'd go ballistic on my ass."

"Then why did you invite me here, Jelin? To tease me some more like you did in the shower? Do you get some sick, demented enjoyment from parading your big dick in my face?"

"Is that what you think I'm doing?"

"I don't know what the hell you're doing. But I'm not gonna stay around here and be made a fool." Robert swung his book bag over his shoulder and tried to push past Jelin.

"Hold up, bro." Jelin reached for Robert's shoulder. "Slow down … I don't want you to go."

Robert stopped and turned around.

"Robert, you don't understand."

"No, Jelin, you don't understand."

"I know, Robert. Believe me, I know. But this isn't some setup. I invited you over here because … because I thought maybe we could … you know." Jelin removed the book bag from Robert's shoulder and for the first time that afternoon looked Robert square in the eye. "Get to know each other a little better."

"What the hell is going on, Jelin? First, you're calling me a faggot. Now you wanna get to know me better. I'm a faggot! Okay? You're right. What else do you need to know?"

Jelin sat on the sofa and ran his hand across the top of his head. "Robert, I'm sorry. I wasn't calling you a faggot. It's just … this is hard for me."

"What's hard for you?"

"Robert, this isn't some ploy I cooked up with Shawn. The thing is …" Jelin looked down at the floor and then back up at Robert. "You bring out something in me. Something I don't know how to handle."

"Handle?" Robert asked.

Jelin maintained eye contact with Robert. "To be totally honest with you, I felt it the first day I met you at the Big O. You looked so scared, so helpless. I wanted to reach out to you. I wanted to protect you. To tell you everything was going to be alright. But I couldn't. Shawn already told me he thought you were gay. I couldn't risk my image."

"Your image?"

Jelin shook his head. "Robert, my life is a fuckin' lie. I'm always pretending. Pretending to be that image I've created for myself. Pretending I'm not attracted to guys, pretending I'm something I'm not. I know sooner or later someone's going to pull my punk card."

Robert couldn't believe the words coming from Jelin's mouth.

"Shawn's already broadcasted all over campus that he thinks you're a faggot. If I got caught associating with you … well, I think you get the picture."

"Yeah, I think so, Jelin. You're ashamed to be seen with me in public, right? That's why we couldn't meet at the library, isn't it?"

Jelin looked at the floor

"Jelin, what are you saying … you're gay?"

Jelin pulled Robert down onto the sofa. and looked at him with a twisted, angry expression. "I really hate that word. Whenever I hear the word *gay*, I envision a bunch of feminine men sitting around sipping tea. That's not me, Robert. I don't want that word to define who I am. I'm a man. I look like a man, I act like a man, and I have feelings like a man. Yes, I might find myself attracted to other men, but don't pin that gay shit on me. I don't accept that label."

"So what label do you accept, Jelin?"

"None! It's nobody's damn business what I choose to do behind closed doors, and it's nobody's damn business who I choose to do it with!"

"But it's okay for me to carry the banner, right? Is that what you're saying?" Robert rose from the coach and marched around the room. "Look at Robert, the campus faggot! Just don't get caught associating with him."

"No, Robert." Jelin motioned Robert back to the sofa. "I'm not asking you to carry the banner for me. It's just … it's different for me than it is for you." Jelin looked Robert in the eye. "I can't let the rest of the world find out the truth about me. I don't think you understand; the truth could ruin my career. You have to promise you'll never tell anyone what I just said. I'm an athlete, and athletes aren't supposed to have these kinds of feelings. In two years, I plan on playing in the pros, having endorsements. You know what something like this could do to me?"

"Yeah, Jelin, I know." Robert drew an imaginary cross across Jelin's heart. "I promise; I'll keep your secret. I already know what it feels like to have your sex life exposed and your future ruined."

"I'm sorry it has to be this way, Robert, but I'm glad you understand. Maybe one day I'll feel comfortable enough to tell the rest of the world. But now is not the time. Not for me."

"Yeah, maybe one day." Robert wondered if Jelin would ever be ready.

Jelin raised Robert's chin with his index finger. "Don't look so sad, yo. It's not the end of the world. We just have to be discreet. You know what I'm sayin'?"

Robert gave Jelin a weak smile.

Jelin returned Robert's weak smile with a broad grin. "This will be our little secret. Nobody needs to know except you and me. Nobody needs to know you turn me on."

"You turn me on too, but I guess you already knew that, didn't you?"

"Well, bro, when you had that full-fledged boner in the shower, it was pretty obvious."

"I tried to hide it, but being beside you in the shower was a fantasy come true. You have no idea how many times I fantasized over you. But I never in my wildest dreams believed it could come true."

Jelin ran the back of his hand against the side of Robert's face. "Truth be told; I've fantasized about you too. I've wondered what it would feel like to touch your face, to hold you in my arms ... to be with you."

Robert's body quivered.

"What's the matter? Do I make you nervous?"

Robert nodded. "I don't know what I'm supposed to do."

"Just relax and don't be afraid. I promise I won't bite. At least not where it hurts."

Robert slid his hand up Jelin's arm and squeezed his bulging biceps. "It's not that I'm afraid. It's just ... I was alone with someone before, and it didn't work out."

Jelin smiled at Robert's naiveté. "Robert, trust me. I'm not gonna hurt you."

"I got hurt before, Jelin, and I don't want to go through that again."

"Robert, I don't know what happened to you in the past, but I'm not that person that hurt you. I just want the opportunity to get to know you better. A lot better." Jelin grabbed Robert's hand and entwined their fingers.

Robert looked at the door.

"What's the matter? I thought this was what you wanted."

"It is, I think, but ... but what if ..."

"What if what?"

"What if Shawn's comes through that door?"

"Robert, do me a favor and don't mention Shawn's name again tonight? I want tonight to be about you and me. You understand what I'm sayin'?" Jelin untied his sweatpants and let them drop to the floor. "Just you and me. I locked the door after you came in, and my roommates are away for the weekend. We won't be disturbed. So just kick back and relax. I want us to enjoy each other."

"Are you sure no one can get in?"

"I'm sure." Jelin removed his jersey. "It's just you and me tonight. Do you think you can handle it?"

"I don't know."

"Maybe I can make you know." Jelin removed his boots. "C'mon, Robert. I don't like being the only naked person in the room."

Robert wanted to live out his greatest fantasy, but his fantasy seemed wrought with danger.

Without saying a word, Jelin slowly unbuttoned Robert's shirt.

Robert wanted to object, but he didn't. He wanted to run, but he couldn't. He wanted his body to stop responding, but it wouldn't.

Jelin put his index finger against Robert's lips. "Sssshh, don't say anything. Just relax and stop fightin' it. Everything's gonna be all right." Jelin bent down and removed Robert's boots and socks.

Robert remembered how Stephon persuaded him to have sex. He remembered how sex ruined their friendship.

Jelin looked in Robert's eyes. "Do you want me to stop? No ... that's not what you want, is it, Robert?"

Robert couldn't command his vocal cords. He allowed Jelin to unhook his belt buckle and pull the belt through the loops of his jeans.

"Now, that wasn't so bad, was it?" Jelin threw the belt across the room and reached for the tab of Robert's jeans.

Without putting up any resistance, Robert allowed Jelin to remove his pants.

Dressed in only a pair of powder blue boxer shorts, Robert looked into Jelin's eyes. He knew the situation was at the point of no return. He and Jelin were about to cross the line.

Jelin pointed to Robert's boxer shorts. "Are you going to take those off, or you gonna make me do all the work?"

Without taking his eyes off Jelin, Robert slid out of his shorts.

Jelin smiled. He placed his hands around Robert's waist and gently pushed him back across the sofa.

Nothing appeared normal to Robert anymore. The sofa, which once seemed so strong and sturdy, now was warm and subtle as it welcomed him into its comforting fold. Jelin's hands, which once seemed so big and rough, now were soft and gentle as they encircled him in a tender embrace.

Jelin stretched out on top of Robert. "I knew you wanted it. You just needed someone to show you, didn't you?"

Robert closed his eyes and tried to make sense out of it all. His whole world seemed flipped upside down. Everything that once seemed so fearful was now comforting.

Jelin sucked on Robert's earlobe. "I knew we would be good together."

Robert moaned as his fantasies of Jelin soared into reality. Jelin's tongue visited parts of his body he never knew existed. He was completely under Jelin's spell.

"You like it, Robert. Don't you?"

"I dreamed of this moment, but I never thought it would come true."

"Tell me about your dreams, Robert. Tell me how I can make your dreams come true."

"You already have."

Jelin's tongue danced around the perimeter of Robert's nipple. "Did I do this in your dream? Is this what you dreamed about?"

"In my dream, you put your arms around me and held me tight. Like I was the only person in the world."

"Did it feel like this?" Jelin put his massive arms around Robert and encircled him in a tight embrace.

Robert's body trembled from the forceful embrace. He enjoyed the curve of Jelin's arm, the ripple of his abs, the force of his thighs.

Jelin placed his ear against Robert's chest. "I can hear your heart, Robert. It's telling me you want more."

Robert marveled at the sight of Jelin's strong back. The slants of light from the late afternoon sun made the beads of sweat that trickled down the center of Jelin's back, glitter like shining stars. Robert ran his hands across the shimmering drops and watched the liquid fade into Jelin's smooth, dark skin. "Make love to me, Jelin."

Jelin rose from the sofa and motioned for Robert to follow.

Robert followed him to the bedroom.

Jelin closed the door and then pushed Robert down on the bed.

The rhythm of their hearts beat as one.

Jelin reached up to turn off the lights, but Robert stopped him.

"No, Jelin. I want to live my dream in color. Black and brown."

Jelin smiled. "This isn't a dream, Robert. I'm here, and I'm real. Better than any dream."

"Better?"

"In the morning, I want you tell me what was better, your dream or the real deal."

"In the morning?"

"You have a problem with staying the night?"

"No, not at all." Robert closed his eyes and the existence of time slipped away.

As the subdued shadows of evening faded into the darkness of night, their interlocking bodies melted into one. They held on to each other as though someone was trying to rip them apart.

****

The glow from the morning sunrise crept through the partially open blinds. Robert opened his eyes and looked around for Jelin. Jelin had left the bedroom but the sound of pots and pans rattled from the kitchen. Robert grabbed the pillow and inhaled Jelin's lingering scent. He drifted back to sleep, remembering their passion-filled evening.

Jelin walked into the bedroom carrying a breakfast tray loaded with scrambled eggs, ham, toast, and orange juice. "Wake up, sleepyhead. I have practice in an hour."

Jelin placed the tray on his lap.

Robert was glad Jelin had dropped his macho image and had allowed his gentle nature to take over.

"Since we skipped dinner last night, I thought maybe you'd be hungry."

Robert tasted the scrambled eggs. "I didn't know you could cook."

"There's a lot of things you didn't know."

"I'm starting to find out." Robert smiled.

"Robert, remember what we talked about last night." Jelin sat on the bed. "You promised this would be our secret." Jelin gently stroked Robert's face. "You have to keep your promise."

"Trust me, Jelin." Robert grasped Jelin's hand. "I know what it feels like to have your sex life exposed. To be hated—to hear constant whispering behind your back—to lose your best friend. I know because I've lived it."

Jelin stood from the bed. "How do you handle it, Robert? How do you learn to live with something that arouses so much hatred?"

Robert looked down at his plate and picked at his eggs. "That's the problem, Jelin. I haven't handled it, not really. I thought when I moved here to Pittsburgh, I could escape my past. I thought I could push it away, pretend it wasn't there. I thought I could make myself into someone the rest of the world would accept. I thought I could become a different person. But it hasn't worked. I haven't fooled anyone, not even myself."

Jelin walked over to the window and raised the blinds. "Robert, why does anyone have to know? My sex life is my own damn business."

Robert nodded his agreement. "I thought the same thing, Jelin. But the truth has a way of getting out … no matter how careful you are. Maybe it's time we stop running and accept who we are."

Jelin turned to face Robert. "Even if I do accept it, Robert, I'm not ready to tell the rest of the world. Why should I?"

Robert didn't answer. He picked up his glass and drank his orange juice.

"Let's not talk about this anymore. The important thing is we understand each other. Fuck the rest of the world." Jelin bent down and kissed Robert on the forehead. "I'm gonna jump in the shower."

"Do you need any help?"

"That's all right. I've already seen your shower routine, remember?" Jelin flashed a devious smile before walking out of the room.

Robert finished his breakfast and decided to wash the dishes while Jelin was in the shower. As he stood naked at the kitchen sink, he could hear Jelin in the bathroom. He hoped Jelin was as happy about the past twenty-four hours as he was. He put away the last of the breakfast dishes and then walked into the living room to retrieve his clothes.

His clothes were still piled up in the corner where Jelin had thrown them. He walked past the sofa and remembered how apprehensive he was when he first entered the apartment. But everything was different now. Robert smiled. He was standing naked in the middle of Jelin's living room, and he was no longer alone. He was finally rescued from the cold, isolated feeling of loneliness.

CHAPTER 20

What Jamal recalled most about his father's funeral was his mother never cried. She put on a valiant show of strength and character, welcoming friends and relatives, cooking food, and acknowledging cards and gifts. But her strong appearance was only a mask to hide her pain. Sooner or later she had to let her emotions out. Unfortunately, he wouldn't be around to help her. He had already missed two weeks of school and needed to get back to take his final exams.

The flight to Pittsburgh seemed even faster than the flight to Newark, Jamal thought as the city rose from below the clouds. The events of the past two weeks had crystallized his decision. The cost of the funeral amounted to $3,000, and the hospital bill totaled over $12,000. The only way to help his family was to accept the coach's offer.

Without his mother's knowledge, he had devised a plan to secretly pay the hospital bill. He arranged for the final medical bills to get sent to him in Pittsburgh. He also drafted a fake letter to his mother informing her that the hospital's charity fund would be paying her husband's medical bills. Jamal knew it was deceitful but it was the only way to resolve the issue without his mother finding out the truth.

As the wheels of the plane touched the ground, Jamal's self-pride crumbled. He was about to make a deal with the devil. But he was determined to retain one shred of dignity. He would accept the coach's offer but on his terms. He would agree to do Shawn's remaining class assignments and take three of his final exams. But the coach had to agree to the continuation of Shawn's tutoring sessions. Jamal was determined to drill the information into Shawn's brain no matter how much he protested.

****

"Listen up, men." Coach Green blew his whistle and called the squad to stop their practice drill. "I want you to work on your picks. I want Collins to have a clear lane when he drives the middle. Brian Short, I'm talking to you. Clear those men out of the lane. Do you understand what I'm tellin' you? I don't want Collins touched. Okay, let's try that play again."

Shawn drove the lane untouched but missed an easy layup.

Coach Green blew his whistle. "Take a break, guys. Collins, come over here."

"Yeah, Coach I know what you're gonna say. I missed that easy layup." Shawn bent over and grabbed the bottom of his shorts. "My timing is a little off. Give me a minute to catch my breath, and let me run the play again."

"What's going on with you, Collins? You've been dragging lately."

"Nothin'. Just give me the ball again."

"I think you've been spending too much time with that girlfriend of yours. She's draining all your energy. We've only been practicing for thirty minutes, and you're already out of breath. I'm warning you, Collins—if you don't shape up, I'm going to let Brian Short be the go-to guy instead of you."

Shawn fired a harsh stare at Coach Green.

"I mean it. The Christmas tournament starts in a couple of weeks. The team needs you at full strength." Coach Green looked at Shawn curiously. "Have a seat on the bench and catch your breath. I'm going to run the team through some defensive drills."

"A'ight, Coach." Shawn answered, grateful to get a breather.

Coach Green signaled for the rest of the team to take the floor.

Jelin ran over to check on Shawn. "Is everything all right, Shawn?"

Shawn took a deep breath to stop his heart from racing. "Yeah, I just needed a break."

"Okay, but if you're not feeling well, let the coach know. Don't make yourself sicker."

"I said I'm all right! Just leave me alone!" Shawn motioned for Jelin to go back on the court.

Jelin looked at Shawn for a couple of seconds before trotting back onto the court.

Shawn grabbed the Gatorade bottle and squirted the liquid into his mouth. The incidents of his heart racing when he wasn't really winded were occurring more and more frequently.

"Collins, do you think you can rejoin the team now?"

Shawn ran back onto the court. "Yeah, Coach."

****

Jamal took a cab directly from the airport to the Omni Center. He didn't want to think about his decision. He wanted to get it over with. He paid the driver the seven-dollar fare and then headed for the coach's office.

"Is the coach in?" he asked the pretty young secretary seated behind the desk in the outer office.

"No, he's at practice. Is there anything I can help you with?"

"I don't think so," Jamal answered. "I'll catch up with him later."

Jamal left the office and proceeded directly to the gym. As he walked down the long, empty corridor, he ignored the sound of his heels clanking against the linoleum floor. *Don't do it, don't do it, don't do it.*

He reached the double doors and peered through the windows. Coach Green was leading the team through some rigorous drills. He entered the gym and stood against the back wall.

"Church and Short, I want you guys to dominate the paint. Be aggressive. Don't give the opposition a chance for a rebound."

Coach Green spotted Jamal standing against the back wall. "Coach Fleming, take over for a minute." He handed his assistant the clipboard. "I have some personal business I need to attend to."

Jamal leaned against the wall for support as the coach approached.

"Jamal, I didn't know you were returning today. Shawn told me about your father. I'm very sorry."

Jamal nodded.

"I don't mean to press you, but we're running out of time. Did you have a chance to think about the business opportunity we discussed?"

"That's why I'm here. I need to see you and Shawn together."

"Together? No, Jamal. This opportunity is between you and me. Shawn has nothing to do with it."

"Shawn has everything to do with it."

Coach Green shook his head. "All right, Jamal, we'll do it your way. Give me a minute to dismiss the squad. Shawn and I will meet you back at my office."

"Okay." Jamal turned and walked out of the gym. As he headed down the corridor, he looked toward heaven. "Father, please forgive me for what I'm about to do."

He took a seat in the outer office and informed Marjorie that the coach was on the way to meet him. He folded his hands together and placed them against his lips. He looked past Marjorie to the window in the corner of the small office. The sun that had been shining brightly was suddenly covered by a dark cloud. Jamal interpreted the cloud as a sign of disapproval from his father. "I'm sorry, Dad."

"Excuse me?" Marjorie looked up at Jamal. "Did you say something?"

"I was just thinking out loud." Jamal turned from the window and looked at the floor.

"Are you a new recruit?" Marjorie asked.

Jamal looked up at Marjorie, but before he had a chance to answer, Coach Green and Shawn entered the office.

"Jamal, let's go back to my office. Marjorie, you can leave for the day." Coach Green opened the door to his inner office and motioned for Jamal and Shawn to go inside.

Marjorie reached for her purse and coat. "Thanks, Coach," she answered.

Shawn took a seat next to Jamal. "Jamal, I know what it feels like to lose a father. My father died when I was ten years old. I think about him every day."

"Have you ever betrayed him, Shawn?"

"All right, Jamal." Coach Green entered the office and closed the door. "I don't know why you're insisting on this cloak-and-dagger routine, but you certainly have my undivided attention. Am I to understand you've made a decision?"

Jamal nodded. "I've decided to accept your offer but on my terms."

"Your terms?" Shawn interjected.

"Continue, Jamal," Coach Green said, motioning for Shawn to quiet down. "I'm listening."

"I'll accept your offer. But only on the condition Shawn attends all his classes and allows me to tutor him on his assignments. I'll test Shawn on the material at the end of the semester. If he fails, he continues to take my test until he passes."

Coach Green cleared his throat. "That's a tall order, Jamal."

"Wait a minute, you two." Shawn stood. "Don't I get a say in this arrangement? Jamal, you know that wasn't the deal we agreed to."

"No, it wasn't the deal, Shawn. But it's the only deal I can live with. Take it or leave it."

"I'll leave it!"

"Wait a minute, Shawn," Coach Green interrupted. "Jamal, are you still agreeing to do Shawn's assignments and take three of his final exams?"

"Yes." Jamal choked on the word.

"Shawn, I think we need to give Jamal's condition some serious thought."

"Hell no!" Shawn picked up his gym bag and threw it against the coach's blank wall. "We had a deal, Jamal! What kind of shit is this?"

"What's the matter, Shawn? Afraid of a little education?"

Shawn looked at Jamal with bewilderment.

"Think about your future for a minute, Shawn. What would happen if for some reason you couldn't play ball anymore, huh? What other type of job do you think you could get without a college education? I'm making this condition for your sake, not mine." Jamal looked over at Coach Green. "The coach could care less if you get an education. His only interest is exploiting your abilities so he can hang some damn trophy on that stupid wall. My interest is protecting your future."

"Hold on, Jamal. You know that's not true. I care about my players."

"If you cared, you wouldn't have hired me to take Shawn's tests."

"Jamal Lewis, I don't need this shit from you. If you don't want to accept my offer, fine! I'll find someone that does."

"How many of your ex-athletes have ended up on street corners, Coach Green? Huh? Answer me that! How many?"

"Not that it's any of your goddamn business, but since I've been head coach here, I've sent two players to the pros. Now, go ask them how they're doing!"

"How about the other couple hundred players, Coach Green? Where are they? What are they doing? From my calculations, about 1 percent of your players make it to the pros. I'm asking about that other 99 percent. What have you done for them?"

Coach Green lurched forward and pointed toward the door. "Get your ass out of my office! I don't need this shit from you. I don't know who the hell you think you are coming into my office and talking to me like this."

"I'm someone who's not going to sit back and watch you destroy another future."

Coach Green sat down and tried to regain control of the situation. "I've had as much of you as I'm going to take. You're not the only person on this campus capable of taking Shawn's tests." He pointed to the door. "Get out of my office!"

"I may not be the only person capable of taking Shawn's tests," Jamal said, standing to leave, "but I am the only person who knows what you're up to."

"Why, you ungrateful son of a bitch! Are you threatening me?"

"Wait a minute, you two," Shawn said, standing between the Coach and Jamal. "It's getting too late in the semester to go looking for another tutor. This is my career." Shawn reached over and stopped Jamal from leaving. "I'll be the one that makes the decision. Jamal's right; a little education won't hurt me. I'm gonna accept Jamal's condition."

"Are you sure, Shawn?" Coach Green lowered his voice.

Shawn nodded. "I'm sure."

Jamal was stunned by Shawn's sudden turnaround.

Coach Green leaned across his desk and stared into Jamal's agitated eyes. "Well then, Mr. Lewis, it looks like our deal is back on. But let me give you a word of advice. If you ever threaten me again, consider this arrangement over. I won't stand for it. You got that?"

"And you remember what I said," Jamal answered. "My priority is Shawn's education, not your goddamn wall!"

Coach Green and Jamal eyed each other in a moment of silent hate.

Shawn intervened. "When do you want to get started, Jamal?"

"Let's discuss it back at the dorm. In private. I need a chance to look over your material."

Coach Green pointed his finger at Jamal. "If you think you have the upper hand in this situation, you're dead wrong. If word gets out about our little arrangement, I'll make sure I destroy you. You can kiss your education good-bye."

"You know something, Coach? The only person you're gonna end up destroying is yourself." Jamal headed for the door.

"Hold up, Jamal. I'll walk back to the dorm with you."

CHAPTER 21

Latisha squeezed the apricot-scented facial scrub onto her fingertips and stared into the mirror. What on earth had she been thinking, concocting that outrageous scheme to get pregnant? Shawn didn't lover; and slicing a hole in that condom was a pathetic attempt to get something she could never have. Shawn's heart. Thankfully, the week off from the shop had given her time to think about her life. For seven whole days, she sat up in her room feeling sorry for herself, listening to Aretha Franklin sing "Ain't No Way." Oddly, the song gave her a sense of peace and convinced her to move on with her life. A life without Shawn.

After rinsing the scrub from her face, she removed a variety of makeup bottles and lipstick tubes from her cosmetic bag. The first step to recovery was returning to work and facing the women at the shop. She didn't want to walk into the shop looking like the battered woman from hell.

First, she applied liquid foundation evenly across her face. Next she applied a light covering of pressed powder, concentrating on the bruise beneath her lip and the dark circles under her eyes. To conceal her sadness, she drew an outline around the edges of her eyes, subtly sweeping the shape of her eyes upward. She followed the eyeliner with a couple strokes of mascara and a touch of eye shadow. To complete her look, she applied a generous coat of auburn lipstick and then brightened up her cheeks with a hint of blush.

She smiled into the mirror. But the smile quickly faded. She could cover the bruise to her face but not the bruise to her heart. She wondered if she would ever experience a relationship based on true love. A relationship where love was both given and received. She remembered the advice Jamal gave her at the shop. *"It's time you stop wasting so much energy on Shawn and start concentrating on yourself."*

She picked up her comb and drew her hair into a modified French twist. She thought the style would give her an understated yet sophisticated look for her first day back at the shop. Her hair had finally grown out from that in-between stage and was back to a length she could do something with.

"Latisha, when you comin' outa there!" Her brother Hennie banged on the bathroom door. "I have to take a piss. You been in there all damn morning."

"Give me one minute, Hennie." Latisha gathered her belongings. Every damn morning, it was the same thing, someone yelling for her to come out of the bathroom. She hated living in her mother's house, and lately things had gotten worse. Ruby was pregnant with her fourth child, Hennie had gotten kicked out of school, and her mother's drinking had increased. Consequently, she changed her move-out date. She couldn't wait for June as originally planned. She had saved over $2,500, and since her plan to have Shawn's baby backfired, she was convinced the money would be enough to move into her own place.

"Your minute's up, Latisha!"

"All right." Latisha opened the door and stepped into the hallway.

"It's about damn time." Hennie rushed into the bathroom and slammed the door.

Latisha walked back to her bedroom to prepare for the first day of her new life. She changed into a pair of blue jeans, a soft pink sweater, and a pair of low-heeled pumps. After approving of her understated appearance, she sat down on her bed and pulled out her checkbook.

"Latisha, there's somebody here to see you," Pearl called from downstairs.

"Who is it, Ma?"

"Come down and find out."

It must be Nickea, Latisha thought. But why was she so early? It was still a full hour before the shop opened. Latisha shoved her checkbook inside her purse and headed downstairs.

"Nickea, is that you?"

"No, it's not Nickea," a deep voice answered.

Latisha was shocked to see Darius standing in the middle of her living room. "Darius. What are you doing here? Who told you where I lived?"

Darius looked at Latisha with a coy smile. "I pried the information out of Nickea. She told me you were coming back to the shop today, so I convinced her to let me pick you up."

Latisha placed her hands on her hips. She was going to have a long talk with Nickea about poking her nose into somebody else's business.

"I really wanted to see you again, Latisha, and since you weren't returning any of my phone calls ... well, let's just say I resorted to desperate measures."

"I wished you would have sent a text instead of poppin' up at my door like this."

"If it's a problem, I'll go." The dimples faded from Darius's smile.

The last thing Latisha needed was another man in her life, but she didn't have the heart to turn him away. Before she had a chance to respond, her sister Ruby walked into the room.

"Latisha, I didn't know you had company." Ruby flashed a jagged, discolored smile at Darius. "How you doin'. I'm Ruby. Latisha's sister."

"I'm Darius."

Ruby looked Darius up and down. "Latisha, I know this ain't the brother you been puttin' off."

"I'm the one," Darius answered.

"I think I might find a minute or two for someone as fine as you. What you say your name is?"

Darius observed Ruby's obvious state of pregnancy. "Darius. And it looks like you're already spoken for."

"But I ain't married though. Until you see a ring on this finger, I'm a free woman."

"Free is not exactly the word I would use," Latisha growled. "Don't you have three kids you need to go check on, Ruby?"

"Don't worry 'bout my kids. They fine."

"Latisha," Darius interrupted, "since you don't want me to drive you to work, I guess that means I can't show you the surprise I have for you."

"You're just full of surprises today, aren't you?"

Darius nodded.

"Listen, Darius, like I told you on the phone. I'm just getting out of a bad breakup. I need some time before I get back in the dating game."

"Who said anything about a date? This is merely a ride to work. No strings attached. I promise."

"Then what's the surprise?" Ruby asked.

"Latisha's gonna have to come with me to find out."

"Well, all right. Girl, you better go on. Don't keep this man waitin'."

"Ruby, isn't that Shequann I hear cryin' in the kitchen? Why don't you act like a mother for a change and go see what's wrong with him?"

"Like I said," Ruby answered, pointing her six-inch nails, "don't you worry 'bout my kids; they my kids, not yours."

"Ahh ... well, Latisha." Darius touched Latisha on the shoulder. "What do you say? Are we gonna go for a ride?"

"Anything to get the hell out of here." Latisha retrieved her coat from the closet next to the front door.

Darius helped Latisha into her coat. "It's been nice meeting you, Ruby."

"You remember what I said, Darius. If Latisha don't treat you right, you come back and see me."

"I'll remember that." Darius pushed Latisha toward the door.

"I'm sorry about my sister, Darius," Latisha apologized as they walked toward his car.

"She thinks the only thing she has to offer a man is what's between her legs. She doesn't have respect for herself—or anybody else for that matter."

"Don't worry about it. I know a lot of women just like Ruby."

"So what's this surprise?"

Darius opened the car door. "Get in, and you'll find out in about fifteen minutes."

"Fifteen minutes?"

Darius took his seat behind the wheel and started up the engine. "Are you all set?"

"Yeah, I guess so. I wish I knew where we we're going."

"Relax, Latisha." Darius slipped a jazz CD into the CD player. "I promise; I'll have you to work on time."

Latisha looked at Darius with a puzzled expression and then relaxed her head against the soft leather headrest. As the car pulled away from the curb, she closed her eyes and allowed the soothing rhythm of the music to dance around her soul. After being cooped up in the house all week, the soft music and the smooth ride was a refreshing treat. She looked at Darius and wondered how long he would keep up his gentlemanly ways.

"A penny for your thoughts?" Darius asked.

"Oh nothing." Latisha looked out the window.

Darius drove the car out of Garfield, through East Liberty and down the hill toward Oakland. When they passed Pittsburgh City University and Shawn's dormitory, her heart sank.

"Hold on, we're almost there." Darius turned off Broad Avenue and headed down one of the narrow side streets that ran parallel to the avenue. He parked the car in front of a large white building with a sign that read the Morrison School of Beauty.

"What are we doing here, Darius?"

Darius shut off the engine and unlocked the doors. "Come inside and find out."

Latisha grabbed her purse and followed Darius into the building.

"Darius, what's all this about?"

"Just follow me and you'll see."

Latisha followed him through a large, bright room filled with workstations and sinks. All the women in the room seemed to know Darius and greeted him warmly as they walked by. After exiting the large room, they walked down a short hallway and stopped in front of an office door. The name on the door read Neubie Williams. Without knocking, Darius opened the door and poked his head inside.

"Aunt Neubie?"

"Well, if it isn't my favorite nephew. Come on in, baby."

"Aunt Neubie, this is the young woman I was telling you about." Darius pulled a reluctant Latisha inside the room.

"You two have a seat," Aunt Neubie instructed, pointing to two chairs opposite her desk. "Just give me one second to finish up this paperwork."

Latisha sat down on one of the cushioned chairs. She looked around the small, cluttered office and was impressed with all the certifications and awards addressed to Neubie Williams.

"Now, young lady." Aunt Neubie removed her glasses and looked up at Latisha. "My nephew tells me you're interested in enrolling in our school."

Latisha was speechless. She had never discussed enrolling in beauty school with Darius.

The gall of him springing this on me without warning. "Well, I have been thinking about it, ma'am ..." She cut her eyes at Darius. "But I haven't completely made up my mind yet."

"What's there to think about? Either you want to be a professional stylist, or you don't. This school is considered one of the best training academies on the East Coast. Our graduates have gone on to work for some of the best salons in the country."

"Oh really," Latisha replied.

"Darius tells me you braid hair over at the Braid Boutique. He also tells me you're the best stylist in the shop. Is that true?"

"Well, my customers seem to think so." Latisha looked over at Darius.

"By the looks of your own hair, I can tell you have talent. Now, exactly why haven't you made up your mind? Do you just want to braid hair for the rest of your life?"

"No, ma'am. I just don't think I can afford school right now."

"Oh I see," Aunt Neubie answered. "Latisha, are you aware you can get financial aid to attend this school? Our students are eligible for loans, grants, and even scholarships. If you qualify, you won't have to pay back the grants and scholarships."

"I won't?"

"Well, of course not, honey. Here, let me get you some forms." Aunt Neubie removed a packet of forms from her file cabinet. "Why don't you take these back with you and read them over. They explain everything about the school and the financial obligations." Aunt Neubie handed the forms to Latisha. "If you decide the school is something you want to do, just fill out the forms and bring them back to me. I have some connections over at the bank, and I'll make sure your paperwork gets processed in time for you to start our winter semester next month."

Latisha looked at the smiling faces depicted on the brochures.

"I'll also check around and see if any scholarship money is still available." Aunt Neubie leaned across the desk. "Let me give you a word of advice, Latisha. You are far too talented to waste your skills. The hairstyling industry can be a very lucrative field if you have ambition, talent, and people skills.

"She has all three." Darius looked over at Latisha. "She just hasn't realized her potential yet."

"Latisha, please don't feel pressured. This is your decision, and whatever you decide to do, it has to be something you want. That's the key to being successful in this world."

Latisha was dumbfounded. No one had ever talked to her about being successful. "I ... I don't know how to thank you, Mrs. Williams."

"Call me Neubie,"

"Thank you very much, Miss Neubie." Latisha put the information packet under her arm so she could shake Miss Neubie's hand. "I'm gonna give what you said a lot of thought."

"That's all the thanks I need, honey."

Darius gave his aunt a knowing wink.

On the drive back to East Liberty, Latisha didn't know if she should hit Darius for not warning her about the surprise or kiss him for helping her move on with her life. As Darius parked the car in front of the Braid Boutique, she decided on the kiss.

"Darius, I've never met anyone quite like you before. I'm not sure what to say."

Darius smiled.

"I'm still mad you cooked up this scheme without telling me, but I do want to say thank you. Thank you from the bottom of my heart." Latisha kissed Darius on the cheek.

Darius took his index finger and pointed to his lips. "I think you can do a little better than that, girl."

"You do, huh? Well, how's this?" Latisha planted a big wet kiss on Darius's lips.

"Now that's what I'm talkin' about." Darius grinned.

"Good-bye, Darius. Thanks again for everything." Latisha opened the car door and stepped onto the curb.

Before she had a chance to close the door, Darius grabbed the handle. "Can I call you later?"

"I get off at seven."

Latisha sashayed into the shop.

Nickea could hardly contain her excitement. "Girl, I saw what happened out there. It won't be long before you-know-who is just a distant memory."

Latisha removed her coat and handed the packet of information to Nickea to hold. "Did you know about this?"

"Yeah, I knew. But I also knew if I told you, you wouldn't let Darius take you down to that school. Do you forgive me?"

Latisha smiled and gave Nickea a hug. "I forgive you—this time."

"Now don't hold back on me, girl. I saw the way you looked at Darius when he dropped you off. You're starting to like him a little bit, aren't you?"

"I really don't know him yet, Nickea. And the last thing I need is another man messin' up my life. But I will tell you this. I've never met anyone like him before. He actually did something nice for me. I'm not used to men treating me that way. He's the complete opposite of Shawn. At least he appears to be."

"Didn't I tell you there are some good men out there? Now give the brother a chance." Nickea placed her hand on Latisha's shoulder. "I know he's not rich, and he doesn't have a future in the pros, but, Latisha, he won't treat you like dirt."

"How can you be so sure, Nickea? How can you be so sure after he gets what he wants he won't move on? I don't think I could survive another broken heart."

"Trust me on this one. I get good vibes from Darius. And like I said before, the best way to forget about a man is to replace his ass."

"I don't want to end up cryin' my eyes out over another man, Nickea."

Nickea smoothed back the loose hairs from Latisha's French twist. "I know, honey. But you can't go through life being afraid of love. You have to be willing to let your guard down every now and then. If you don't, you might pass up your only true chance at happiness."

"Humph, happiness. I don't think I know the meaning of the word."

"It means having the pleasure of joy in your life. And I think Darius might give you that, if you give him half a chance."

Latisha looked at Nickea and wondered if she could possibly be right. "Well, I can't promise you anything will happen between me and Darius," Latisha answered, "but I'll think about giving him a chance."

Nickea smiled. "Now that's my girl."

Latisha retrieved the packet of information from Nickea and walked over to her workstation. Ignoring the silent stares from the whispering women in the shop, she laid the information packet on her workstation and looked at her watch. She still had fifteen minutes before her first customer was due to arrive. She started reading through the information about the school. The glossy pictures and heartfelt testimonies caught her eye. The more she read, the more she thought about the question Miss Neubie had asked. "Do you just want to braid hair for the rest of your life?"

By the time Latisha finished reading all the material, she was convinced enrolling in beauty school was something she truly needed to do. She picked up her pen and started filling out the enrollment application. After completing the enrollment application, she filled out the loan and grant forms. Proud of her decision to better her life, she looked up at herself in the mirror.

But this time, instead of seeing a girl with a battered face, she saw a girl ready to take control. Instead of seeing a girl with low self-esteem, she saw a girl ready to grow. Instead of seeing a girl trapped in the past, she saw a girl poised for the future. For the first time in her life, Latisha saw a woman. A woman with a dream based on her own achievements.

CHAPTER 22

J amal looked around the crowded library. It was early Saturday afternoon, and the library was packed with students cramming for the start of finals. All the private study booths were occupied, so he and Robert settled for one of the small tables in the center of the study area on the second floor.

"I know why they call finals hell week," Robert said, looking across the table at Jamal. "Because it's hell trying to cram four months of information into your brain over one weekend."

"Don't worry," Jamal answered. "You'll do fine. You already know the material. Do what I do. Read over your notes, but only concentrate on the areas you were weak in during the semester."

"That's easy for you to say, Jamal. You weren't weak in any areas."

"Robert, you're an intelligent brother. You did well on your midterms, and I'm sure you'll do well on your finals."

"I wish I had your confidence."

Jamal winked. "Trust me."

Robert turned to a blank page in his notebook and started doodling.

"Well, at least we don't have to worry about studying for our Urban Management final," Jamal said.

"What, Jelin—I mean Jamal?"

"I was reminding you that Dr. Altenburger isn't giving us a final in Urban Management; all we have to do is write a paper on one of the guest speakers who lectured during the semester."

"I finished my paper already. Haven't you?" Robert asked.

"No, I wanted to wait and listen to the last speaker."

"Who's the last speaker?"

"The chief of police from Penn Highlands."

"What's so special about him, Jelin—I mean Jamal? You're gonna have less than a week to write your paper."

Jamal looked at Robert inquisitively. "I have a lot of issues with the police, Robert. Actually, I've already started the paper. It deals with racial profiling and the Black Lives Matter movement. I need to get the point of view from the police chief."

"Oh, I see." Robert returned his attention to his doodling.

Jamal looked at Robert's notepad and noticed he was doodling Jelin's name. He wondered if there could be something going on between Robert and the star basketball player.

Robert's whole demeanor had changed lately. Plus, Robert was spending a lot of unexplained time away from the apartment. *No, that's ridiculous*, Jamal thought. There was no way Robert and Jelin could be involved in a relationship. Jelin and Shawn were best friends, for God's sake, and if Shawn ever found out his best friend was gay, all hell would break loose. Jamal shook his head. There was no way something could be going on between them.

It's a foolish thought, Jamal convinced himself. He reached into his book bag and pulled out his journal. Besides, he had his own problems to worry about. He was documenting his dealings with Coach Green and needed to log in the most recent events. Coach Green already gave him the payoff money—$12,000 in cash. Now he was obligated to take three of Shawn's final exams.

Jamal documented his final thoughts with the notation, "I've let myself become a victim." With a heavy sigh, he closed his journal and opened Shawn's Introduction to Psychology book.

****

Robert tried to focus on his studying, but his thoughts kept going back to Jelin. He dreamed of the day he and Jelin could go to the movies or eat lunch together in the cafeteria. He longed for the day he and Jelin could study together or take long walks in the park. But most of all, he prayed for of the day he and Jelin could openly display their feelings without fear of recrimination. Unfortunately, he knew that day would never come, at least not any time soon. Jelin was too afraid of the consequences.

Robert closed his notebook in frustration and looked across the table at Jamal. He was surprised to see Jamal reading a psychology book.

Jamal looked up. "Why are you staring at me?"

"I was just wondering."

"Wondering what?"

Robert pointed to the psychology book. "You don't have that class until next semester."

"Oh … it's for a new student I'm tutoring."

"Another new student?"

Jamal nodded.

"You better slow down, Jamal. You're already overloaded."

Jamal sighed and lowered his head. He nervously tapped his pen against the side of the table. "Robert … have you ever done something you really didn't want to do but felt compelled to do it?"

Robert narrowed his eyes, hoping he hadn't heard the question correctly. "What?"

"Have you ever been forced into doing something?"

The question caused Robert to think about Stephon.

"Have you, Robert?"

Robert stared down at the table. In the back of his mind, he heard Stephon's cries. *Rob, why'd you do it? Why didn't you tell the truth?*

"Robert, aren't you gonna answer me?"

"Jamal, can we change the subject?"

"No, Robert, I need to know."

Robert wasn't sure how to answer the question.

"I'm your friend, Robert. You can be honest with me."

"Yes, Jamal, I was forced into something I didn't wanna do. And I regret it. I regret it every day."

"Forced into what?" Jamal asked.

The door to Robert's past swung wide open, and the painful memories marched in. "I was forced to tell a lie." Robert hands trembled. "If I could change one thing I did wrong in my life, I would change something I did three years ago."

Jamal leaned across the table. "What did you do?"

Robert paused. He looked at Jamal with an empty, hollow stare. "I told a lie on my best friend."

"We all tell lies, Robert."

"No, it was a vicious, hateful lie. I thought I was doing the right thing. I thought I had no other choice. But I did have a choice. I could have told the truth. But I was afraid of the truth."

"And you've been carrying around the guilt for three years?"

Robert nodded. "So if you're being forced into something you don't want to do ... don't do it. Don't do it, Jamal ... unless you're ready to deal with the guilt."

"You don't understand, Robert. It's not that simple. My decision could affect the lives of a lot of people. People I've promised to protect."

"I thought the same thing, Jamal. I thought I was protecting my family. But I ended up hurting them as well as myself." Robert reached across the table and grabbed Jamal's arm.

"The truth always finds the light."

"Robert, what the hell happened to you?"

"I thought by lying I could hide the truth. I thought my lie would make the truth disappear. But it didn't disappear, and no matter how hard I tried, I could never escape it. I could never escape it, because it was here." Robert pointed to his head. "Inside my head ... tearing at me ... never letting me forget."

"Escape what? Robert did ... did your lie have something to do with your sexual orientation?"

Robert slowly nodded. He wasn't surprised Jamal finally asked the dreaded question.

"Except at the time, I didn't understand my sexuality."

"Do you understand it now?"

"I'm beginning to."

"Robert? If we go back to the dorm, will you tell me what happened? Will you tell me what you were forced to do?"

Robert nodded. "I've been waiting for the right time to talk to you, Jamal. I guess this is it, huh?"

"C'mon, buddy." Jamal closed his book. "We need to talk."

*****

Jelin rushed into the locker room.

"You're late, Church," Shawn warned.

"I know I'm late. I was studying and lost track of time."

"You studying." Shawn laughed.

"Yeah, do you understand what that word means, Collins? You know, actually opening up a book and reading the words."

"Chill, yo. I'm not the reason you're late." Shawn sat on the bench next to Jelin. "So what's her name? Wait—don't tell me. I bet it was Erica Taylor, wasn't it? You had Erica up in your room, didn't you?"

Jelin looked at Shawn but didn't answer.

"Okay, if it wasn't Erica, I bet it was Maxine do-me-one-more-time Walker, wasn't it?" Shawn jumped from the bench and performed a gyrating imitation of Maxine. "Now tell me I'm right. Tell me I'm right." Shawn laughed.

"Man, stop actin' stupid."

"Why do you let your women get to you? You need to learn from me. Do you see me having any problems?"

Jelin unzipped his gym bag and removed his practice gear.

"Come on, you guys," Brian Short shouted from the open doorway. "Stop clowning around. Coach Green is ready to get started."

"Tell him his number one and two stars are on their way." Brian left the locker room. "That Brian Short is an asshole, and I've seen the way he's been looking at Tammera lately. If we weren't on the same team, I'd ..." Shawn punched the locker.

"Man, you need to settle your ass down," Jelin said.

"I'm just hyped over the game against the Bobcats Tuesday night." Shawn grabbed his basketball and practiced his fifteen-foot jumper. "I'm going to be on fire. I can feel it pumpin' through my veins."

Jelin remained silent.

Shawn returned the basketball to his locker. "Take your time getting dressed, yo. I'll tell the coach you're getting a new knee brace from the trainer; that should buy you some time."

Jelin slapped Shawn a high five. "Thanks, bro."

"Anytime for my main homey."

As Shawn exited the locker room, Jelin pulled out the letter he had written Robert.

"So how's that new knee brace working out, Church?"

Jelin slid the letter back inside the envelope. "Coach Green, I didn't hear you come in. The new brace is good."

"Hurry up, Church. There's a new strategy I want to go over for Tuesday night's game, and you're pivotal to its success."

"Give me a minute, Coach."

"That's all I'm going to give you." Coach Green stared at Jelin before walking away.

Jelin changed into his workout gear and then trotted onto the court.

****

"Church, glad you could finally make it." Coach Green blew his whistle and motioned for his team to gather around him.

"Now, men, as you know, we have an important game against the Bobcats Tuesday night. The Bobcats play an aggressive man-on-man defense. Their strategy will be a full-court press every time we have the ball. That's why I called this special practice session. I want to go over a strategy to handle that press."

"I've got the strategy," Shawn yelled out. "Just throw me the ball."

"C'mon, Collins, listen up." Coach Green raised his hand to stop any further outburst.

"Teams that press don't like to get pressed. So do you know what we're going to do?"

"We're going to press them!" Brian Short yelled.

"That's exactly right, Short. I know we usually start our games out in a zone. But against the Bobcats, I want you guys to start out with an aggressive man-to-man defense. Right from the start, I want you guys to attack the man with the ball. We'll have the advantage because the Bobcats haven't seen us do much of that. I anticipate we'll throw them off their rhythm early."

"How about our offensive strategy?" Jelin asked.

"I'm glad you asked that. Our offensive strategy will be a breakdown of their press. On the inbound pass, I want Short to get the ball over to Church. Since you have the best arm on the team, Church, I want you to throw the ball up court for the fast-break opportunity. That's where you come in, Collins." Coach Green pointed to Shawn. "You're the fastest man on the team. When you see Church with the ball, do a quick pick and then make your cut for the fast-break opportunity up court. Remember, Collins—keep your eye on the ball and be ready for the pass from Church. That's how we'll break the press. Do you all understand that?"

"Yes, Coach," the team answered in unison.

"I can't hear you!

"Yes, Coach!"

"All right, men. Take the court and show me how our strategy is going to work. I want the first string to play offense and the second team to play defense."

The players took the floor and ran through the coach's drill, over and over again.

"Collins, I need you to get up court faster." Coach Green blew his whistle and instructed the team to replay the drill. "Start running up court as soon as you see Church grab the ball."

Shawn followed the coach's instructions and sprinted up the court. He couldn't recall the coach practicing the team so hard on one drill before. But Tuesday's game was the final game before the Christmas Tournament, and Coach Green wanted to go into the tournament undefeated.

After twenty minutes of constant running, the pain retuned. It started out as a slow, dull thud but gradually intensified into a sharp, piercing pain. "Not again." Shawn bent over and grabbed the bottom of his shorts.

"C'mon, Collins, you're dragging again!" Coach Green shouted.

Shawn tried to ignore the pain. When Jelin grabbed a rebound, he hustled up court and positioned himself under the basket. He jumped to catch the pass, but his timing was off. The ball sailed through his hands and bounced off the back wall.

Then it happened, a pain in his chest so intense it knocked him off his feet. His vision blurred, his muscles locked, and he fell against the hardwood floor. His teammates called out his name, but he couldn't respond. Coach Green shook his body, but he couldn't move. As the gymnasium faded into blackness, he wondered who turned off the lights.

*****

Jamal and Robert walked back to the dormitory in a peaceful silence. Broad Street looked like a picturesque postcard with the multicolored Christmas lights of the decorated storefronts reflecting off the newly fallen snow. They reached the revolving doors of the dormitory and headed up to their suite. As they entered their apartment, Robert volunteered to make a pot of coffee, and Jamal agreed to wash out two coffee cups. Once the coffee was ready, Robert sat the pot in the middle of the dining room table and took a seat opposite Jamal.

Jamal filled the two cups with the steaming hot coffee and handed one to Robert.

Robert sipped his coffee and braced himself for the inevitable. He hoped Jamal would accept what he was about to tell him. He prayed their friendship would remain intact.

"Jamal, I know you've heard the rumors about me around campus. And I'm sure you and Shawn have discussed it."

Jamal nodded and took a sip of coffee.

"You asked me over at the library if my sexuality had anything to do with the lie I told three years ago. Well, to answer your question, my sexuality had everything to do with it."

Before Jamal had a chance to respond, Robert put up his hand. "Just know this. After I finish telling you my story, I hope we can still be friends."

Jamal nodded and waited for Robert to continue.

Robert took a deep breath. "The truth is I'm gay. It's taken me a long time to accept that fact. Actually, I've never said those three words out loud before. I know it's hard for you to understand, but it's something I've been struggling with for a long time. The lie I told three years ago was based on my denial of those words. But for you to understand my struggle, I have to start my story from the beginning."

Jamal leaned forward.

"It's hard to pinpoint a specific date when I realized I was gay. But for me, I think it started earlier than most. You see, I was thrust into adulthood almost without warning. I remember having strange sexual feelings as early as the sixth grade. Certain things would make my body respond, and I didn't know why. But as I grew older, I began to recognize the stimulus my body was responding to. What the hell was happening to me? I would ask myself.

"My parents noticed it too. As they watched me withdrawal further and further into my shell, they knew they had to take drastic action. Their action was sending me away to a Catholic, all-boy boarding school. I didn't want to attend a religious boarding school, but my parents insisted. They said the structured environment and religious discipline would help mature me into a man. I silently prayed they were right. I knew there was something wrong with me, something I couldn't control. I convinced myself being away from home would help resolve the conflict waging war inside my head.

"Our Lady of Fatima was the name of the school my parents sent me to. It was located in the mountains about fifty miles southeast of where my parents lived. It was a beautiful place, surrounded by lush trees and calm lakes. Unfortunately, no one realized that this beautiful, peaceful place contained the one stimulus that would plunge my life into utter chaos.

"I met Stephon Matthews on my very first day. Although we were the same age, Stephon had matured early and was big for his age of fifteen. For reasons I didn't understand, I was drawn to Stephon. He sensed my need for friendship and took me under his wing. It wasn't long before we became best friends. Unfortunately, that's when the trouble started. I found myself having special feelings for Stephon, feelings I knew weren't normal.

"Stephon and I bunked together in the same large bedroom designated for sophomores. Stephon's bed was located directly across from mine. Every night after Father Reese sounded the night bell and turned off the lights, I would lie in my bed and watch Stephon. I could see his body silhouetted by the subdued moonlight that filtered through the large open windows.

"Stephon knew I watched him. One night he convinced me to come over to his bed. He said he wanted to talk. Other boys did the same thing, so I didn't think I was doing anything wrong.

"Stephon showed me pictures of naked women from a magazine he stole from his brother. Eventually, the pictures of the naked women turned to pictures of naked men. Stephon could tell the pictures of the naked men excited me more. It wasn't long before the pictures led to touching.

"The first time I let Stephon touch me, it frightened me. I ran back to my bed. I vowed never to let it happen again. But the sensation of Stephon's gentle touch was too powerful to erase from my mind.

"So I continued to sneak over to his bed night after night. It was always the same routine. I would sit on the edge of Stephon's bed, and Stephon would fondle me under the blanket. Then one night, Stephon asked me to touch him. I was nervous and scared, but I wanted to know what it felt like.

"To my surprise it didn't feel wrong or weird; it felt right, normal. The following night, we jacked each other off. I experienced my first orgasm that night. It was the most exhilarating moment of my life.

"But after I ejaculated, I knew I had done something wrong, something sinful. I jumped off Stephon's bed and ran to the showers. I tried to wash away my sin. I tried to make myself pure again. I rubbed myself raw trying to make the guilt of my actions disappear. But no matter how hard I scrubbed, I couldn't make it go away.

"After my shower, I ran to the chapel and prayed for the Lord's forgiveness. I prayed nobody would find out what I had done. I prayed for my soul. When I walked back past Stephon's bed, I told him I didn't want to do that anymore. He looked at me and smiled. He knew I liked it.

"The next morning, everything appeared normal, but late that afternoon, we were summoned to Father Bullock's office. Father Bullock was the head administrator of the school. He had received reports from some of the other boys that Stephon and I had been seen touching each other. We both denied the accusation, but Father Bullock didn't believe us. He warned us if he received any more reports about homosexual activity, we'd be kicked out of school. He said he didn't like having fags at his school. I didn't want to be a fag. I stopped going over to Stephon's bed. Nothing else happened for about three weeks, but then came that horrible October night."

"What happened that night?" Jamal asked.

"I've never told anyone other than my mother what happened that night." Robert trembled as the memory of that night flooded his mind. He looked over at Jamal and took a deep breath before continuing.

"About three weeks later, the spiritual director, Father Murphy, summoned me into his office on the first floor. He said he needed to talk to me. He asked me how I was doing and if I had made many new friends since coming to the school. I said yes. He asked if Stephon Matthews was one of my new friends. I said yes, Stephon was my best friend.

"He wanted to know if the rumors about Stephon were true. He asked if Stephon liked touching other boys. He asked if Stephon ever touched my private parts. I sensed danger and decided to keep my mouth shut. My silence irritated Father Murphy, and he stepped up his interrogation.

"'Is there something sexual going on between you and Stephon?' he shouted. 'Touching another boy is an immoral act. If you allowed Stephon to touch you, you're going to burn in the eternal flames of hell!'

"I was petrified by Father Murphy's dire warnings. He kept asking me the same question over and over. 'Is there something sexual going on between you and Stephon?' I finally answered, 'No!' But Father Murphy wouldn't take no for an answer. He pounded his fist against the desk, demanding I tell him the truth. When he realized I wasn't going to give him the answer he wanted, he reached into his desk and pulled out a Bible. He said lying was a sin. He said some of the other boys had seen Stephon and me. He shoved the Bible under my hand.

"'Tell the truth before God!' he shouted. I was afraid of the truth. I pushed the Bible away. I laid my head on his desk and started crying. But Father Murphy was relentless. He showed no mercy or compassion. He pulled me up by my hair and once again shoved the Bible under my hand.

"'Tell me the truth, before God!' he demanded. I was terrified by the anger in Father Murphy's voice. I was terrified by his threats of eternal damnation. I jumped from my chair and paced back and forth across the floor. Finally, I broke down. 'Yes, it's true, it's true, it's all true!' I shouted, but I painted it all as Stephon's fault."

"Why didn't you tell the truth?" Jamal asked.

"I couldn't tell the truth." Robert sobbed. "Don't you see, Jamal? I was afraid of the truth. The truth meant I was gay. The truth meant I would burn in the eternal flames of hell. I never told Father Murphy that I let Stephon touch me. I never told him that I liked it. I never told him how attracted I was to Stephon. I blamed it all on Stephon. I said it was all his fault. I said he made me do it!"

Robert laid his head down on the table and continued crying.

Jamal embraced his friend. "It's all right, Robert, I can see how painful this is for you. You don't have to continue. I understand."

"No." Robert lifted his head. "I've been running away from my lies for far too long. I need to talk about it." After gaining his composure, he continued. "After Father Murphy got the answer he wanted, he sent me back to my classes. I had a late study hall that evening. I dreaded going to that class, because I knew Stephon would be there, sitting at his desk in the rear of the classroom. I couldn't look at Stephon when I walked past. Stephon touched my arm and tried to talk to me, but I didn't answer. I ignored him and went directly to my chair. I sat in the row of desks closest to the windows. Just outside my window, I saw the headlights flash against the building. I knew it was Stephon's parents coming to get him. I knew Stephon was getting kicked out of school because of my lies.

"Father Murphy come into the classroom and stopped at Stephon's desk. I heard the torturous sounds of Stephon's sobs and the rustle of his books and papers as he was ushered out. He cried out to me. 'Rob, what did you say? Why didn't you tell the truth?' I knew what was happening in the back of the classroom, but I wouldn't let myself turn around. I couldn't let myself turn around. I couldn't bear to see the look on Stephon's face.

"Stephon was forced to go to the dormitory and pack up his belongings while his parents filled out his release papers in the head administrator's office. Unfortunately, they left Stephon alone in the dorm room. He couldn't deal with the embarrassment of being kicked out of school because he was gay. He couldn't understand how his best friend had betrayed him."

Robert stopped his story and put his hand across his mouth.

"What happened next?" Jamal asked.

With his hand partially covering his mouth and his voice barely above a whisper, Robert continued. "I kept a framed picture of Stephon and me hidden in the bottom of my foot locker. It was a picture of Stephon with his arm around me. Stephon knew how much I cherished that picture. He broke into my locker and ripped the picture into a hundred small pieces. Then he took the glass from the frame and smashed it against the bed. With the jagged edge, he slit both his wrists."

"Good Lord, Robert. I had no idea you were harboring such pain. I'm sorry. I'm sorry I made you tell me this story. You we're only a kid, Robert. You can't blame yourself."

"I do blame myself, Jamal. I could have told the truth, but I didn't. I lied. It was all my fault. It was all my fault what happened to Stephon!"

"No, Robert, it wasn't all your fault. You have to believe that. It wasn't your fault."

Robert looked up at Jamal and finished his story. "Stephon used his blood to spell out the word *why* across the floor. By the time they found him, he had already lost a lot of blood. They rushed him to the hospital that night, and all I could do was watch. The last memory I have of Stephon is his blood-soaked body being carried out on a stretcher because of my lies. I never got the chance to tell him I was sorry. I never got the chance to say good-bye."

"Listen to me, Robert," Jamal said, "you can't blame yourself forever."

"The only thing I had left of Stephon was that torn picture. The pieces were stuck against the floor with his blood." Robert looked up at Jamal. "But the saddest thing of all … I never found out if Stephon lived or died. I left school two weeks later. And to this very day, I don't know what became of Stephon Matthews. I tried calling him once, but the operator said his parents' number was disconnected. You see, Jamal, I've been carrying around the guilt of my lies for three years."

Jamal was speechless.

Robert shook his head. "Jamal, don't go where I've been. Don't let anyone force you into doing something you'll regret. It's not worth it. It's not worth the pain."

"I understand where you're coming from, Robert, but my situation is different."

"It's not different." Robert pounded his fist against the table.

Jamal remained silent.

Robert realized Jamal wasn't going to divulge his problem. He picked up the empty coffee cups and carried them over to the sink. "Jamal, are we still friends, or does my sexuality change things?" Robert was afraid to turn around to face Jamal's answer.

"My father taught me a long time ago not to judge anybody until you've walked in their shoes. Now I feel like I've walked in your shoes. I'm still your friend. I'll always be your friend."

"But I'm not a good person, Jamal. I'm a murderer. I killed my best friend."

"If he's dead, he was killed by hate and intolerance, not by you."

Robert turned on the water in the sink. He wished he could believe Jamal.

"You're a good person, Robert. I wish I could make you understand that. You've dealt with a lot of shit from a lot of assholes around here. But through it all, you've remained a kind, sensitive, caring person. Even with that horrible pain you've been carrying around inside of you. That's the type of person you are. You should be proud of those qualities."

Robert was able to muster a weak smile, realizing he and Jamal were still friends.

He turned around to face Jamal. "Thank you, Jamal. Thank you for accepting me."

Jamal joined Robert at the sink. "Robert, I consider you the best kind of friend. A true friend. And your sexuality doesn't change that. If you know in your heart that you're gay, and you accept that, I say live your life the way that makes you happy. Don't live it to please anyone else." Jamal placed his hand on Robert's shoulder. "You know something else my father used to say?"

"What?" Robert asked.

"You become strongest in your broken places."

Robert wasn't sure he understood what Jamal meant.

"If you break a bone, the body heals that bone stronger in the place it was broken. Don't you see, Robert? What you've been through has strengthened you. You may not realize it. But adversity has made stronger."

Robert hugged Jamal. "Your father was a wise man. I wish I'd known him."

"He would have liked you, Robert."

"I wish you could tell me what's going on in your life. Maybe I can help."

"You already have, Robert. And as soon as I figure out what I'm going to do, I'll tell you everything."

****

Dr. Perez closed the door to his examination room and joined Coach Green in the adjoining office. "I think Shawn's needs to be checked out by his personal physician. I was only able to run some preliminary tests, but from my quick diagnosis, I believe Shawn may have a heart condition."

"A heart condition," Coach Green repeated. "How serious?"

"At this point, I can't be sure, but it could be very serious. It appears Shawn's heart isn't pumping enough blood. The heart is supposed to pump 60 percent of the blood out with every stroke. I believe Shawn's heart is pumping 40 percent or less. I've seen this condition before in other athletes."

"Good God." Coach Green sat down and ran his hand across his receding hairline.

"Are you all right, Coach?" Doctor Perez asked.

"Yeah, I was just wondering what to say when Shawn comes out."

"I think we better be honest. I don't want to alarm him, but he needs to know the seriousness of his condition."

"But you said you weren't sure?"

"Yes, Coach Green, but—"

"What would happen if Shawn continued to play?"

"I would strongly advise against it. Shawn should stay off the basketball court until his condition has been thoroughly checked out. What happened today was a warning sign, a very serious warning sign. Shawn was only unconscious for a few seconds, but it could have been a lot worse."

"What's the verdict, Doc?" Shawn asked, joining the coach and the doctor in the office.

"Have a seat, Shawn."

Shawn sat next to Coach Green.

"I don't want to alarm you, Shawn. But I believe you may have a heart condition known as cardiomyopathy."

"Cardio what?"

"Cardiomyopathy. It's a weakening of the heart muscle. To put it simply, your heart isn't pumping enough blood."

"What do you mean, Doc? I'm as healthy as an ox. That little thing that happened to me out there on the court today was nothin'. I just didn't have enough to eat before I came to practice today. It happens all the time. Right, Coach?"

"Shawn, without further tests, Dr. Perez can't be sure of his diagnosis."

"Shawn, as the team physician, I strongly urge you not to play any more ball until you've received a clean bill of health from your family physician."

"But we have that game against the Bobcats Tuesday night," Shawn protested.

"Shawn, today was a warning. Next time it could be a lot worse," Doctor Perez advised.

Shawn looked over at the coach. "Does this mean I'm off the team? Does this mean I can't play ball anymore?"

"No, of course not, Shawn. That's not what the doctor's saying."

"Shawn, the decision will be between you, your parents, and your family doctor, not me or the coach. It's against school policy for us to make such decisions. Who is your family doctor? Let me give him a call and see if we can't get those tests started right away."

"No, that's okay, Doctor," Coach Green interjected. "Let me speak with Shawn's mother first. Then we'll contact the family doctor."

"All right. Just let me know who I should send my preliminary evaluation to."

Doctor Perez handed Shawn his card.

"We'll do that, Doctor. And thanks for seeing Shawn so promptly."

"It's my job. I am the team doctor, remember. And, Shawn, I want you to slow down and take it easy for a while. No more basketball or any other vigorous activity until you get a complete examination."

"A'ight, Doc. I hear you."

"Thanks, Doctor." Coach Green shook the doctor's hand.

Coach Green put his arm around Shawn's shoulder and guided him out of the office and down the corridor toward the gymnasium. "Shawn, I think Dr. Perez may have been overly cautious with his diagnosis. What do you say if we wait and get you tested after the Christmas Tournament? That way, you'll be able to get national exposure from the tournament. You won't have to practice, and I'll only use you sparingly during the tournament games. If you feel yourself getting winded, just signal me, and I'll take you out of the game."

"I like the sound of that, Coach. I think Doc's diagnosis was off. I feel fine now."

"Okay, Shawn, but let's keep this between you and me. Don't tell your mother, and let me handle Doctor Perez."

"You're the man in charge." Shawn smiled.

When they reached the locker room, Coach Green stopped Shawn. "I think the team's waiting inside. Don't tell anyone what the doctor said or what we decided. We don't want to alarm anyone needlessly now, do we?"

"Don't worry, Coach. You know I can keep your secrets."

Coach Green opened the door and walked Shawn to his locker.

"All right, guys," Coach Green shouted, "Shawn's going to be okay. You can all leave now. Shawn's fine. The doctor said he just overexerted himself. He needs to take it easy for a few days." Coach Green motioned for the rest of the players to leave. "Jelin, can I see you before you go?"

As the rest of the players patted Shawn on the back and expressed their relief over his diagnosis, Jelin ran over to Coach Green.

"Yeah, Coach."

"I want you to walk Shawn back to his dormitory and make sure he gets plenty of rest over the weekend. We need to make sure he's well rested for Tuesday night's game."

"I think I can handle that, Coach. Is that all?"

"Yeah, that's all. Now go get Shawn out of here."

"Right, Coach." Jelin ran back over to where Shawn was standing.

"It's a damn shame," Coach Green mumbled as he watched Jelin and Shawn joking around.

"Man, you better not scare me like that again." Jelin put his arm around Shawn. "You almost gave me a heart attack. I thought they were going to have to carry me out of there too."

"Yeah, well next time don't throw the ball so hard." Shawn laughed, pushing Jelin back against the lockers. Jelin's bag slide off his shoulder, and the flap flew open.

"You're lucky the coach gave me strict orders to make sure you get plenty of rest, because otherwise we would have to go a few rounds over that push, man." Jelin picked up his bag and demonstrated his best Mohammed Ali imitation.

As Shawn and Jelin walked toward the exit, neither noticed the letter that had fallen out of Jelin's bag.

****

After watching Shawn and Jelin leave, Coach Green begun shutting down the lights to the locker room. Before turning off the last of the lights, he noticed a letter lying on the floor. He walked over to where Jelin and Shawn had been standing and picked up the letter.

"Well, well, well, what do you know? I never would have guessed."

Before leaving for the day, he locked the letter in his desk drawer.

CHAPTER 23

"Shawn, I just had to call you. I received the latest report on your grades, and I can't believe how quickly you pulled your grades up."

"I told you I would do it, Moms."

"Getting you that tutor was a great idea. Tell Jamal whatever he's doing, to keep it up."

"How about me? I think I had a little something to do with too."

"I know you did. I'm proud of you, Shawn."

"Moms, where's Damar? I wanna say hello."

"He went to the movies with his friend Jonathan. Hold on, Shawn. Someone's at the door."

Martha walked into the living room and looked through the peephole. "What is she doing here?" she uttered into the phone.

"Who is it, Moms?"

"It's Miss Gloria."

"Moms, you know all she likes to do is spread gossip."

"I know. Hold on a minute, Shawn." She opened the door.

"Good afternoon, Martha."

"Miss Gloria, what a surprise."

"Put the water on, Martha."

"Shawn, I'll call you back."

"Moms, don't believe anything she says. Especially if she says anything about me."

"I know, Shawn. I'll call you back later."

"Wait. Remember, Mom—don't believe anything."

"Okay, Shawn, I'll call you back. Bye."

"I tried callin', but I couldn't find your number. Why ain't you listed in the book? How's somebody supposed to get a hold of you? I thought I would see you at church last Sunday, but you weren't there ..."

"I know. Damar was sick, so we stayed home." Martha closed the front door.

"Sick? Is he all right?"

"It was just a slight cold; he's fine now. Excuse me for a second." Martha turned off the phone. "I was on the phone with Shawn."

"Like I said, put the water on, Martha. We need to talk. And I need some hot tea to warm up these old bones."

"Come into the kitchen, Miss Gloria."

"I'm glad Damar is feeling better, 'cause I heard that Hong Kong flu was going around again. But I didn't come over here to talk about Damar. I came to talk about Shawn."

"Shawn? What about him?"

Miss Gloria removed her fake fur. "It sure is cold out there, but I guess I shouldn't complain since we ain't had nearly as much snow as we did last year. Your kitchen sure is pretty."

Martha laid Miss Gloria's coat across the back of one of the kitchen chairs.

"How much this kitchen set you back?"

"I really don't think that's any of your business."

Miss Gloria removed a pack of cigarettes from her purse. "Do you mind?"

Martha retrieved an ashtray from the china cabinet.

"Thank you, precious." Miss Gloria lit her cigarette and exhaled a puff of white smoke.

"Now, what is it you feel you need to tell me about Shawn?"

"I hate to be the one to tell you this." Miss Gloria exhaled another puff of smoke and watched it float through the air. "But I think you need to know what your son's been up to."

"What's he been up to?" Martha lit the fire underneath the water kettle.

"Do you have any cake?"

"No," Martha answered.

"How about cheese?"

Martha removed a package of mixed cheeses from the refrigerator. She sliced a few strips of cheese and laid them on a plate.

"Now you know I ain't the type to gossip." Miss Gloria shoved a piece of cheese into her mouth. "But you and me been friends since you first come up here from Virginia."

"Uh-huh." Martha turned off the whistling kettle.

"And you know Albert was my second cousin on my father's side once removed. So I feels we kin. And it wouldn't be right if I didn't come over here to tell you what I saw your son do."

"For God's sake, Miss Gloria. What did Shawn do?"

Miss Gloria waited until Martha poured hot water over her tea bag. "Well, as you know, I gets my hair done over at the Braid Boutique." She flicked the braids off her shoulders. "By the way, how do you like my new color? It's called Summer Time Sunshine."

"It's very … bright," Martha answered.

"Tethonie thinks it brings out the light brown in my eyes."

"Well, it certainly does make you … stand out." Martha took a seat across the table from Miss Gloria. "Now as you were saying …"

"Oh yeah. I was getting my hair done a couple weeks ago over at the Braid Boutique. And you know my stylist is Latisha Wright, don't you? That child sure is talented. See how thin and tight she makes the braids?"

"I know she works there."

"Well, apparently her and Shawn had a fallin' out over some condoms. Now, Martha, I don't know if the story is true or not, but Shawn accused Latisha of puttin' a whole in one of the condoms so she could get herself pregnant. Like I said, I don't know if that part of the story is true or not, but what I do know …" Miss Gloria took another drag from her cigarette. "Shawn come bustin' in the shop, yellin' and screamin' and just carrying on like a fool. Pushin' and shovin' folks out the way. And I won't even repeat what he called me." Miss Gloria clutched her fake pearls.

"I'm not one bit surprised Latisha would pull such a stunt. The first day that little tramp set foot in this house, I knew she was trouble. I'm just surprised it took Shawn so long to find out."

"Even if it's true, Shawn ought not have done what he did." Miss Gloria rolled her eyes and took another sip of tea.

"Done what?"

"Martha, after he pushed his way in the shop, he knocked that poor girl down on the floor and jumped on top of her. Looord, I thought they was gonna have relations right there on the shop floor. I screamed at the top of my lungs for him to get up off of her, but he wouldn't listen to me. It's a good thang his roommate was there. Seems he was the only one capable of talkin' some sense into Shawn. Now don't get me wrong, Latisha made a fool out of herself too. Shawn did try to walk away, but she wrapped herself around him like a dog in heat."

Martha sipped her tea, waiting for Miss Gloria to finish.

"Well, Nickea and Shawn's roommate, I can't remember that boy's name." Miss Gloria snapped her fingers. "I think it was one of them Muslim names … Abdul … Kareem … Mohammed …"

"Jamal," Martha answered. "Shawn's roommate is named Jamal."

"Yeah, that's it, Jamal. Well, Jamal and Nickea tried to pry Latisha away from Shawn, but she wouldn't let him go. The next thang I know, he done knocked that girl down on the ground. Martha, you should have seen the blood."

"Blood!"

"Straight from Latisha's mouth." Miss Gloria slapped her hand against the table. "I'm not sure, but I think he knocked out a couple of her teeth. Well, by this time, I couldn't sit back any longer. So I jumps out of my chair, and me and Nickea—we pushes Shawn out the door before he had a chance to do any more damage. Then I sees him get into this fancy red sports car and drive away, all high and mighty. Now it ain't none of my business." Miss Gloria extinguished the butt of her cigarette in the ashtray. "But I don't think you need to be buying that boy such an expensive car at his age. I know you got a lot of money from Albert's accident, but I think you done spoiled that boy rotten."

"You're right, Miss Gloria, it ain't any of your business. Now you listen to me." Martha snatched Miss Gloria's plate and cup away. "I don't need you coming over to my house trying to tell me how to raise my son! I'm a grown woman, twice grown. And I'll raise my sons the way I see fit. I don't give a damn what you or any of those other gossipmongers down at the beauty shop think. I know my son. You hear me, Miss Gloria! I know Shawn, and he would never hurt a woman. Not unless he was pushed too far!"

"Now don't get your tail feathers all riled up. I just wanted to let you know what your son's been up to. The whole town's been talkin' 'bout it, not just me. I didn't want all the gossip goin' on behind your back. That's why I come over here, to tell you to your face."

Martha walked over to the counter and gently placed Miss Gloria's plate and cup into the sink. "Well, you've said what you came over here to say. Now I would appreciate it if you would leave." Martha turned around to face Miss Gloria. "I'll find out what really happened from my son."

Miss Gloria got up from the table and snatched her coat. "I suppose I'll be seeing you in church on Sunday. Lord knows you could use the prayer."

Martha gripped the edges of the counter. After gathering her composure, she walked Miss Gloria into the living room and opened the front door.

"Looks like you got some more company." Miss Gloria stated as a gray Mercedes sedan pulled into the driveway. "That looks like Judge Patterson's car. I didn't know the two of you were still friends."

"And that's all we are Miss Gloria—friends."

"Now I wasn't implying anything, but you know he is a married man."

"Good-bye, Miss Gloria." Martha assisted Miss Gloria into her car and closed the door.

Miss Gloria started up her engine but didn't immediately pull away.

"Martha, it's freezing out here. Where's your coat?" Lincoln asked, joining Martha on the walkway. "I'm sorry, is this a bad time? I can come back later."

"You're timing couldn't have been more perfect," Martha said as Miss Gloria drove away. "I can really use a friend right now."

"Was that Miss Gloria?"

"Yes. I don't know why some people think they have the right to tell you how to raise your kids."

Judge Patterson put his arm around Martha's shoulder. "Don't let that old battleax get to you. Shawn's a fine young man. I think you did a damn good job raising him. Now let's get out of this cold."

Martha laughed. "Yeah, before Miss Gloria drives back around and sees you with your arm around me."

Judge Patterson joined in the laughter as he led Martha inside the house.

"I'm surprised to see you, Judge. What brings you by?"

"I remember back in the day you used to call me Lincoln."

"Yes, but that was before you became a judge." Martha motioned for him to remove his coat and have a seat on the sofa.

"Well, for your information, my name is still Lincoln."

"Okay, Lincoln." Martha smiled, taking his coat and hanging it in the living room closet. "But I'm still surprised to see you."

"I tried to call first, but your number wasn't listed."

Martha took a seat next to Lincoln on the sofa. "I know. I got so tired of all of Shawn's girlfriends constantly calling. I got a private number. But I must say, I was quite pleased to find out Shawn's dating your daughter Tammera. She certainly is a lovely child."

"Well, I've had my share of problems too. It's not easy raising a child these days."

Martha nodded. "I heard that."

"That's partially why I'm here. I got the message from Tammera about joining your family for the holidays. I think that's an excellent idea, Martha. I don't know why we let our friendship fade away over the years. It's funny though, isn't it? It took our kids to make us realize how far apart we've drifted."

"I guess we got too caught up in trying to raise our children and scratch out a decent living for ourselves."

"I think you're right. But I must admit, Martha. The years certainly have been kind to you. You still look like that beautiful young woman that you used to sing like an angel over at the Pyramid Club."

Martha's eyes flickered. "You still remember that?"

"Vividly."

"That certainly was a long time ago. Where are my manners? Can I fix you a cup of tea or coffee? The water's already hot."

"A cup of tea would be nice."

Martha fixed the tea and then walked a tray with cream and sugar into the living room.

"So what was Miss Gloria doing here?" Lincoln asked.

"Spreading gossip about Shawn and his ex-girlfriend. Seems they got into an argument down at the Braid Boutique where Miss Gloria gets her hair done."

"Oh I see. So she had to come running over here to tell you about it."

"Lincoln? Do you know anything about Shawn driving a fancy red sports car?"

Lincoln looked surprised. "It's a red convertible BMW. He brought Tammera home a couple of times in it. He told me the car was a gift. I assumed it was a gift from you."

"No, I would never buy Shawn such an expensive car at his age."

"Maybe it belongs to one of his coaches or another player. You know how kids exaggerate."

Martha folded her arms across her chest. "Well, I know one thing. I'm going to have a long talk with that boy after the game tomorrow night. I know I didn't raise no fool."

"Now don't go thinking the worst. I'm sure there's a rational explanation for the car."

"There better be." Martha picked up her teacup. "There better be."

"That reminds me. The other reason I stopped by was to ask you to join me at the game tomorrow night. It's ridiculous for us not to sit together and cheer our children on."

"That would be nice. It's usually just me and my son Damar. It certainly would be a pleasure having some adult company for a change. Will your wife, Linda, be joining us?"

"You mean Miss Gloria didn't tell you?

"Tell me what?"

"Linda and I separated over three months ago."

"Separated? No, I had no idea."

"After twenty-one years of marriage, she decided she needed to find herself. She moved out of the house and rented a condo over on the North Side."

"I'm so sorry, Lincoln."

"Don't be. Linda and I haven't been happy for a long time. I think she was just waiting for Tammera to turn eighteen before she made her move."

"Do you still love her?"

"Yes, I suppose I do. After being together with someone for twenty-one years, it's not easy letting go. If she loves me, she'll come back. But if she doesn't, I'll move on with my life." Lincoln smiled and took Martha's hand into his. "I hope you'll help me do that."

Martha removed her hand from Lincoln's grasp. "So why don't you pick me and Damar up around seven o'clock?"

"Where is Damar? I'd like to meet him."

"He went to the movies with some friends." Martha looked at her watch. "As a matter of fact, it's about time for me to go pick him up."

"Well, I guess that's my cue to leave."

Martha retrieved Lincoln's coat from the closet. "So I'll see you tomorrow night around seven?"

"Wouldn't miss it." Lincoln walked with Martha to the door.

"Thanks for coming by. I'm glad we're reestablishing our friendship."

"Me too." Lincoln winked.

Martha escorted Lincoln onto the porch. "Good-bye, Lincoln."

"Good-bye, Martha." Lincoln smiled and then walked away.

CHAPTER 24

J amal slid from under the covers and crept over to the window. The dreary, winter sky looked ready to dump another load of snow on the already ice-covered walkways. He glanced at the clock; it was already eight o'clock. He wished he could stay in the bed and hide beneath the warm covers, but he had a full day ahead of him. First, he had to attend his Urban Management class and then take two of Shawn's final exams.

The thought of cheating for Shawn made Jamal's head ache. He removed a bottle of aspirin from his desk drawer and headed for the bathroom. He hoped the aspirin combined with the warm shower would relieve his stress. He stepped inside the shower stall and let the pulsating water cascade over his throbbing temples. His life was out of control. His father was dead, his brother was a member of a violent street gang, and his sister was pregnant by a drug dealer. But his greatest pain was selling himself out for $12,000.

Jamal looked at the water below his feet. "Damn you, Coach Green. Why am I letting you turn me into a victim?"

As Jamal left the bathroom, Shawn was standing in the hall with a towel in his hand.

"It's about damn time you came outta there. What were you doing all that time?"

"Watching my future go down the drain," Jamal answered.

"You haven't changed your mind about our appointment, have you? I'm counting on you, Jamal. We have a deal, remember."

"I'll be there."

"You better be!" Shawn slammed the door in Jamal's face.

Robert, who had been sitting at the dining room table eating a bowl of cereal, asked, "What was that all about?"

"I'll tell you later. And, Robert, I won't be walking to class with you today. So go ahead and leave without me."

"But we have that guest speaker from the police department today. I thought you needed the information to finish writing your report."

"I do. I'll be there. I'm just gonna be a little late."

"Are you all right, Jamal? You're not acting like yourself."

"Yeah, I'm fine. I'll meet you in class later." Jamal walked back to his bedroom and closed the door.

Once inside his room, Jamal prepared for the day. He dried his hair and then pulled his locks into a ponytail. He changed into a warm wool sweater, corduroy pants, and insulated work boots. Before leaving, he wrote down the room numbers where Shawn's finals would be held and stuck the paper inside his book bag. He was glad Robert wasn't in the dining room when he walked out of the suite. He exited the revolving doors and ran across campus to Fitzgerald Hall.

****

By the time he met Robert, Jamal was sweaty and out of breath.

"What's going on, Jamal? Why are you out of breath?"

"I ran all the way from Fitzgerald Hall." Jamal removed his coat and took his seat next to Robert.

"Fitzgerald Hall?"

"I was taking care of some personal business. Did I miss anything?"

"Personal business?"

"Shh, I'll tell you later." Jamal took out his notebook.

Robert turned away from Jamal as Dr. Altenburger introduced the guest speaker.

"Class, I would like to introduce the police chief of Penn Highlands, Chief Roger Gateman. He's the final speaker this semester in our series on running city government. Remember your final reports on 'How to Make City Government Better' are due to me by Friday. No excuses. You've had all semester to work on this assignment. Please hold all your questions for Chief Gateman until after he finishes his presentation. Chief Gateman, I give you the floor."

"Thank you, Dr. Altenburger. It certainly is a pleasure to be invited here to address your class today ..."

After Chief Gateman finished his half-hour presentation, Jamal raised his hand to address one of the chief's comments. "So let me get this straight. You say your officers routinely stop motorists driving through Penn Highlands for probable cause."

"That's right."

"How do you define probable cause?"

"Probable cause is a reasonable assumption of suspicion. For instance, an officer might stop someone for driving erratic, driving too slow, or driving with an obscured license plate. There are many reasons for probable cause."

"Is race a reason for probable cause?"

"Excuse me?"

"What percentage of Penn Highlands is African American, Chief Gateman?"

"About 10 percent I believe."

"Okay then, let me give you this scenario," Jamal continued. "Let's say I wanted to visit my professor, Dr. Altenburger, who lives in Penn Highlands. Let's say Dr. Altenburger lives on Chester Lane, and I was driving down her street late at night looking for her house number. Would I be stopped?"

"It's possible."

"Why is it possible? What law have I broken?"

"You haven't broken any laws, but you might appear suspicious."

"Why would I appear suspicious? Don't I have a right to be in that neighborhood?"

"Of course you have the right to be in that neighborhood. What I'm saying is it's your actions that may provoke suspicion."

"Is looking for a house number a suspicious act?"

"Not in itself, but your speed combined with the fact you weren't recognized as a member of the community might raise suspicion. Especially if there had been recent robberies in the neighborhood. It could be assumed you were casing houses."

"Do you assume all unrecognized motorists driving slowly through Penn Highlands are burglars, or just the unrecognized minority drivers?"

"We stop anyone who looks suspicious."

"Don't you mean anyone who looks like a minority? Based on what you've been telling this class; you condone skin color as grounds for probable cause. It sounds to me like you encourage your officers to treat minority drivers as potential suspects until we prove ourselves innocent. Is that your policy, Chief Gateman?"

"Jamal, I think you're putting words in Chief Gateman's mouth," Dr. Altenburger intervened.

Chief Gateman uncrossed his legs and sat upright in his chair. "Like I said before, if you look out of place and are acting suspicious, it could be grounds for reasonable cause. Does anyone else have any questions?"

"Chief Gateman," Jamal continued, why does the color of my skin equate with probable cause? Don't you know stops based primarily on race are against the law? It's called racial profiling."

"Jamal don't be disrespectful; Chief Gateman is our guest," Dr. Altenburger interrupted.

"Listen, young man, we don't discriminate in Penn Highlands. We stop anyone who looks suspicious."

"Statistically speaking," Jamal continued, "what's the percentage of minority motorists stopped in your town versus white motorists?"

"We don't keep those records."

"Of course you don't. And you know why you don't? Because they would show race is the factor most often used in determining who gets stopped."

"That's categorically untrue, and I don't like the accusations you're making against my police department."

"I'm only repeating your words."

"You're twisting my words."

"You're twisting the law."

"Jamal, this is your last warning." Dr. Altenburger stood from her desk.

Chief Gateman leaned against his chair and tucked his thumbs inside his gun belt. "Well then, let me give you this statistic. Most of the arrests we end up making during routine traffic stops that involve drugs and other contraband are against minority motorists. So I would say we have justification for our suspicion."

"Of course, it's basic arithmetic. If most of the drivers you stop are minorities, most of the arrests are going to involve minorities. It doesn't take a brain surgeon to come to that conclusion. But how many of those minority drivers are stopped and let go? How many of those minority drivers are harassed and victimized for no reason at all?" Jamal stood from his seat. "Let me see a show of hands of all the students in this classroom who have been stopped for no reason at all and then let go."

Of the five minority students in the classroom, all five, including Robert, raised their hands. None of the white students raised their hands.

"How many times? How many times in the last two years have you been stopped?"

"Three times."

"Five."

"Twice just this year."

"Twice."

"Four times."

"You see, Chief Gateman, your policy is just another example of the daily indignities that people of color suffer in this society. Do you ever wonder why the minority community distrusts the police? It's because of policies like yours. Policies that treat us like criminals based solely on the color of our skin. Why don't you just issue us passes and stop us at the border? I'm sure South Africa has some leftover passes from their Apartheid days."

"Jamal, I think that's enough," Dr. Altenburger interjected. "Take your seat and calm down."

"Calm down? Calm down?" Jamal shouted. "It's okay for him to sit up there and brag about his policy of racial profiling, and you expect me to calm down! You expect me to take my seat and not have anything to say about it. I'm sick of it, Dr. Altenburger. I'm sick of being treated like a criminal, and I'm sick of being denigrated based on the color of my skin!" Jamal reached for his notebook. "I refuse to sit here and accept a racist policy that empowers him to exercise harassment without provocation and systematically victimize me as a target."

As Jamal prepared to leave, the rest of his class started to protest against the chief's policy.

"That's right. Whatever happened to the Constitution!"

"You tell him, man!"

"How many more of us have to be killed by trigger-happy cops before your racist policy gets changed?"

Jamal was encouraged by the outburst from his classmates but wasn't interested in hearing any more of Chief Gateman's empty proclamations. It was always the same old answer. *Racial profiling has never been condoned by the police department.* He put on his coat, grabbed his book bag, and headed for the door.

Robert grabbed his coat and followed him. "Wait a minute, Jamal. I'm coming with you."

Dr. Altenburger tried to regain control of her class. "Chief, I think the class has certainly given you something to think about."

"Jamal, wait up! Wait up!" Robert called.

Jamal slowed his pace, and Robert caught up with him in the corridor. "That was some speech you gave in there. I can't wait to read your paper." He put his hand on Jamal's shoulder. "Jamal, will you please tell me what's going on? You haven't been acting like yourself lately. I know what Chief Gateman said in there was offensive, but let's face it, it's no secret."

"I know, Robert. I know it's no secret, at least not among the African American community, but why do we have to accept it? Why do we have to accept the role of being victims? Why?" Jamal kicked his boot against the side of the wall. "Why have I been so stupid?"

"What do you mean stupid? You're the smartest person I know."

"Look at us, Robert. You, me, and Shawn. Look at us."

"What about us?"

"We've let other people control, manipulate, and use us to the point where we have nothing left. No pride, no self-esteem, no dignity."

Robert cocked his head to the side.

"It wasn't until I heard those words come out Chief Gateman's mouth that I realized just how pathetic we are. We've let other people turn us into victims. We've sat back and let it happen. I've made up my mind, Robert. I'm not going to let it happen anymore."

Robert ran his hand across the top of his head. "Let what happen?"

"Don't you see, Robert? We're all victims." Jamal paused and then looked Robert in the eye. "You were the victim of unsympathetic priests. Instead of helping you deal with your sexual confusion, they coerced you into giving up your only true friend in order to save yourself from eternal damnation. They didn't try to help you, Robert. At fifteen, they stripped you of your pride and self-esteem. But instead of blaming those uncaring priests for the tragic events that happened to Stephon, you blamed yourself. You accepted the role of a victim. You shut yourself off from the rest of the world. You accepted the meager existence of living among the shadows of your past rather than expressing your beautiful inner soul. Robert, you have a lot to offer this world, but they've made you too damn scared to come out into the light!

"And look at Shawn," Jamal continued. "He's even worse. He doesn't even realize he's being victimized. His coaches have manipulated and controlled his every move since puberty. They've forfeited his educational opportunities for the sake of their win-lose records. Shawn's been fooled into believing his only success in this world will come with a basketball in his hand. They don't give a damn about Shawn. They never have. The only thing they care about is winning and keeping their damn jobs. After they finish using Shawn, draining him of his athletic abilities, they'll toss him aside like yesterday's garbage and move on to their next victim. Look around at the street corners, Robert! They're full of ex-athletes just like Shawn. I see them every day … standing there … hopelessly clinging to their past glory. Shawn's no different."

Jamal looked down at the floor. "Then there's me."

"Are you a victim too, Jamal?"

Jamal shook his head. "It's ironic, Robert. I thought I was stronger than you and Shawn. But in reality, I'm weaker. You and Shawn were blindsided by your victimization. I had a choice."

"What do you mean?"

Jamal looked past Robert toward the windows at the far end of the empty corridor. "For the past two months, Coach Green has been bribing me to take three of Shawn's final exams. At first I said no. Taking the money went against everything I stood for. But then my father died, and everything changed."

"I think I understand," Robert answered. "You had to protect your family."

"I promised my father on his death bed I would take care of the family. Coach Green's money was the only answer." Jamal shook his head. "Coach Green agreed to pay my father's entire hospital bill. I took Coach Green's $12,000. That's why I have to meet Shawn at eleven o'clock—so I can take his final exams."

Robert looked at his watch. "You don't have much time, Jamal. It's almost eleven o'clock."

"Time is the one thing I do have, Robert. I have my whole future ahead of me. And I'll be damned if I'm gonna let Coach Green take that away from me. Chief Gateman may have the power to victimize me on the road, but I'm not going to be victimized in the classroom."

"But you've already accepted the money."

"I'm sick of being used, Robert. I'm not going to take Shawn's exams. I'm only going to pretend to take them."

"You're what? How … I mean, what if Coach Green finds out?"

"So what if he finds out. What's he going to do? Go to the police? Report me to the university? No, he'll be the one with dirt on his hands. He'll be the one who tried to violate school policy, not me."

"You're going to keep the money?"

"I could keep the money, but I'd still be a victim. Don't you see, Robert? I'd still be under Coach Green's thumb."

Robert nodded. "Just like me. Forced into something you didn't want to do."

"I don't want to live like that. I see what it's done to your life and what it's beginning to do to mine."

Robert nodded.

"I'm going to turn the tables on Coach Green. I'm going to make him the victim. He won't have anything to hold over my head. I'll have all the power. And with that power, I'll force him to stop exploiting his players. If he doesn't, I'll threaten to go public with everything I know."

"I don't know how you're going to pull this whole thing off, but it's a hell of a plan. Good luck."

"Thanks, Robert. I'll see you later." Jamal gave Robert the power sign to stay strong and then dashed down the hall and out the side exit.

CHAPTER 25

J amal was relieved he fooled Shawn into thinking he took the exams for him. In reality, he switched both tests, and Shawn had signed his name without realizing he was signing his own work.

With the exams behind him, Jamal headed back to the dormitory. He wanted to write down his thoughts while they were still fresh in his mind. After describing the events of the afternoon, he opened his desk drawer and looked at the insidious cash from Coach Green. The sight of the money made him sick. He slammed the drawer and noted in his journal it was time to stop being a victim.

As Jamal contemplated his options, the muffled sounds of a Christmas party coming from the suite next door filtered into the room. He smiled, remembering the happy times Christmas used to bring to his life. Suddenly an idea popped into his head. He rushed to the closet and removed the bag of Christmas gifts he had purchased for his family. He pulled a decorative box out of the shopping bag. "This is perfect," he whispered to himself. He could wrap the money up like a Christmas gift and drop the package off at Coach Green's house during the Bobcat game.

The box was just the right size; he didn't even need to wrap it. He placed the money inside the box and envisioned the look on Coach Green's face when he opened the box on Christmas morning and saw $12,000 staring up at him.

Jamal considered placing a note inside the box but quickly changed his mind. Coach Green would know who the money was from. Besides, he wanted the opportunity to tell the coach face to face.

But there was one problem; he didn't know where the coach lived. He remembered it was somewhere on the outskirts of the city but couldn't recall the exact location. "Maybe Shawn has the address somewhere in his room." Jamal rushed down the hall and into Shawn's room.

He searched for ten minutes, with no luck. "Maybe I can get the address from Marjorie over at the Omni Center." He rushed into the kitchen and picked up the phone. Before dialing the number for customer assistance, he noticed a leather address book lying on the counter with the name S. Collins engraved on the cover. He flipped through the pages and found the coach's name and exclusive Fox Hills address. In addition, Shawn had left his car keys on the counter. "I'm sure Shawn won't mind." Jamal put the keys in his pocket along with the address book. He retrieved the gift box, put on his thick winter coat, and headed for Shawn's car parked in the rear of the dormitory.

****

Shawn rummaged through his gym bag for his address book. "Where is it?" The book contained the good-luck picture of his father. He retraced his steps and remembered he left the book on the kitchen counter next to the phone. "Damn it." He would have to play without his good luck charm.

"Collins!" Coach Green hollered. "I need to see you in my office, now!"

Shawn didn't like the tone of the coach's voice. He finished getting dressed and then walked into the coach's office.

"What is it, Coach?"

"Come in and have a seat."

Shawn entered the office. Quadre Jones and Brian Short were already seated.

Coach Green motioned Shawn to the last open chair. "I wanted you to hear this from me."

"Hear what?"

"I'm changing tonight's lineup. I'm moving Short over to the starting guard position and starting Quadre at forward."

"You're what!" Shawn jumped from his chair. "Wait a minute, Coach. You promised I was going to start as usual tonight."

"I know what I said, Shawn. But I've changed my mind. You're still not at 100 percent. I've decided to use you as a reserve."

"A reserve! I've never played reserve in my life, and I'm not gonna start now!"

"I'm the coach here, not you. You'll do as I say. You got that!"

Shawn looked down at Quadre. "And how long is this weak lineup supposed to last?"

"Who you callin' weak?" Quadre jumped up.

"I'm calling you weak, Jones! You flathead, no-talent punk."

"You got somethin' to prove!" Quadre shoved Shawn. "C'mon wit' it, man."

Coach Green jumped between his players. "Cut it out and sit down, you two! I won't have this on my team. You understand me! Any more actions like that, Jones, and I'll have your ass on a train back to New York quicker than you can say probation."

Quadre cut his eyes at Coach Green then at Shawn but returned to his seat without further confrontation.

Coach Green glared across the desk. "This is an interim strategy. Once Shawn's back to full strength, we'll go back to the original starting lineup."

"Unless you have a reason not to—right, Coach?" Brian smirked.

"Well, that remains to be seen," Coach Green answered.

A tightness consumed Shawn's chest. He clinched his eyes and hoped the pain wouldn't start.

"All right, men, I want you to go back to the locker room and get dressed. I'll be there in a couple of minutes to start the pregame meeting. And remember—you guys are teammates. Act like it."

Shawn jumped from his chair and stormed out of the office.

****

Robert headed toward the Omni Center. His mind was filled with jittery excitement. Jelin wanted to meet before the game. As usual, they agreed to meet in their secret location underneath the bleachers in the practice gym. Robert wondered what could be so important it couldn't wait until after the game. Jelin's voice sounded happy, and Robert took that as a positive sign.

The long line of fans waiting to buy tickets reminded Robert how important the game against the Bobcats was for the Tigers. He walked up to the students' window, hoping to see Jamal. He had searched for Jamal before leaving the dormitory, but Jamal had mysteriously disappeared.

After showing the guard his ticket, he bypassed the entrance to the large gymnasium and headed down the corridor to the small practice gym. Just as Jelin had advised, the lights were dimmed and the door was unlocked. He quietly slipped inside. The cool ventilated air washed across his face and smell of bounced rubber filled his nostrils.

"Pssss, Robert. Over here."

The sight of Jelin dressed in his team uniform, cloaked by the surroundings of their secret hiding place, heightened Robert's anticipation.

"Hi, baby," Jelin said as Robert approached.

Robert smiled. He liked it when Jelin called him baby. "Hi back." He took a seat next to Jelin on the bleachers. "What was so important you had to see me before the game?"

"I wanted to give you a letter I wrote. But after I talked with you on the phone, I realized I lost it. I think it fell out of my bag back at the dorm."

"A letter?" Robert asked.

"I wanted to let you know how I feel."

Robert swallowed. "How you feel?"

"Robert, I know it's not fair the way I treat you in public. Ignoring you all the time, pretending we're not friends. I wanted to let you know it won't be this way forever. I wanted to ask you to go away with me over spring break."

"Spring break?" Robert mentally calculated the number of days remaining before spring break.

"I know these past couple of months haven't been easy. But don't give up on me, bro."

Robert was speechless.

"Don't get bored with our relationship."

"Bored? How could I get bored? I don't see you enough to get bored."

"Seriously, Robert." Jelin reached for Robert's hand. "I need you to understand why I act the way I do."

Robert enjoyed the touch of Jelin's hand. "I know how important basketball is to you, Jelin."

"It's everything to me. It's my life. It's my future. Since I was a little boy, I've dreamed of playing in the pros." Jelin looked around the empty gymnasium. "I hate meeting here in the dark. But I have to be careful."

"I like meeting you in dark places." Robert smiled.

"Robert, I'm telling you all this …" Jelin paused and then looked Robert in the eye. "I'm telling you all this … because I want you to know something."

"Know what?"

"How much you mean to me. I want you to be a part of my future. I just haven't figured out how I can have both my loves, you and basketball together in my life."

The word love circled Robert's head. He wondered in what context Jelin meant the word. Was it just a figure of speech, or was Jelin expressing a true emotion?

"Do you understand what I'm sayin', Robert?"

Robert nodded. "I would never do anything to jeopardize your dream. I promised you that. Remember?" Robert placed his hand against Jelin's heart. "Listen to me, Jelin. I would do anything to make your dream come true … even if it meant … letting you go."

"I don't wanna to lose you." Jelin embraced Robert.

"I don't want to lose you either."

"Robert, I love you," Jelin whispered.

Robert heard the word again. But this time it sounded forceful and direct. This time Jelin said it with emotion. A door somewhere deep inside of Robert swung open. A door he thought was locked forever. "I love you, too, Jelin."

"I gotta go, Robert." Jelin kissed Robert's forehead.

"Good luck. I'll be cheering for you."

Jelin jumped from the bleachers and headed toward the exit. Before reaching the doors, he turned around. "Robert?"

Robert looked up, his head still spinning with emotion. "What?"

"Never mind." Jelin headed out the door.

Robert sat quietly in the dark and replayed Jelin's words over and over in his head.

CHAPTER 26

J amal drove north on Route 51 toward Fox Hills. Pittsburgh's lone black radio station played selection after selection of Christmas music. He reached for the radio and pushed the scan button hoping to hear something more in tune with his emotions. As he listened to each pathetic offering, he realized how much he missed Newark. He missed his friends, he missed his family, and he missed having a variety of radio stations. He opened the glove compartment and searched for a CD. He grabbed the top CD and slid it into the CD player. The harmonious jazz sounds of Joshua Redman surrounded him on the quadraphonic speaker system.

The music temporarily took Jamal's mind off of his troubles. He focused back on the winding road. Although the snow had stopped, the unsalted road was slick with patches of black ice. He skillfully maneuvered the car around the dangerous ice patches and up the winding curves. In the distance, he could see the twinkling Christmas lights reflecting off the exteriors of the extravagant homes built into the sloping hillside. It was obvious Coach Green lived in a very wealthy neighborhood. Each home looked large enough to contain six to eight bedrooms. He wondered if any black people lived in the homes but then remembered an article he had read about Pittsburgh demographics. Of the 318 metropolitan areas studied, the Pittsburgh metropolitan area ranked among the top fifty most racially segregated places to live. He wasn't surprised Coach Green had selected such a place.

Jamal glanced in his review mirror and noticed a police car was following him. Although he was traveling well below the speed limit, he tapped the brakes. He didn't want to give the police any reason to pull him over. As he continued up the winding road, he kept an eye peeled in the rearview mirror. He hoped the police car would pass, but to his dismay, the police car turned on its flashing lights and motioned him over. Jamal pulled off to the side of the road. The police car pulled up behind him.

The officer got out of his vehicle and approached the BMW. His arrogant, self-confident swagger made Jamal nervous. The officer first inspected the exterior of the car and then approached the driver side window. Jamal hadn't done anything wrong but braced himself for the inevitable harassment.

The officer tapped on the glass.

Jamal rolled down the window. "What's the problem, Officer?"

The officer shined a harsh light into Jamal's face. "You were driving erratically. Can I see your license and registration?"

"The road is slick. I was trying to avoid the ice patches."

"I didn't ask for an analysis of your driving. I asked to see your license and registration."

Jamal unfastened his seat belt and reached into his back pocket for his wallet. "Here's my license." He handed the document out the window. "I'm a student at Pittsburgh City University. The car belongs to my roommate, Shawn Collins. His registration and insurance papers are in the glove compartment."

The officer nodded and motioned for Jamal to open the glove compartment.

Jamal withdrew Shawn's registration and insurance papers. "My roommate plays for the PCU Tigers. They're playing a game against the Bobcats tonight over at the Omni Center."

The officer scrutinized the documents. "What are you doing way out here?"

"Shawn asked me to deliver a package to his coach's house."

"Where does the coach live?"

The oncoming red and blue flashing lights caught Jamal's attention. "On Valley Road."

The second car blocked the BMW between the two police vehicles.

Officer Number One stepped away from Jamal and went over to talk with Officer Number Two. Jamal heard them talking but couldn't make out their conversation.

After a short discussion, Officer Number One returned to his police vehicle and picked up the radio.

Officer Number Two approached the BMW and pointed a weapon at Jamal's head.

"Put your hands on the steering wheel where I can see them."

Jamal placed his hands against the steering wheel but kept his eyes focused straight ahead. As the flashing lights turned his black hands red then blue, he thought about his father and what his father said to do if he got stopped by the police. "Keep your cool, son, and do what they say." He could hear portions of the conversation Officer Number One was conducting over the radio.

"Roger, I've just pulled over a lump of coal ... I need backup ... license number L0691-66800 ... red convertible BMW, registration number ... I think you need to send over Officer Franski. Looks like a possible Johnnie."

Jamal closed his eyes and shook his head. The term Johnnie referred to a drug dealer. He prayed the situation would end without incident. But he was a black man, in a white neighborhood, driving an expensive sports car. He fit the racist police profile. Out of the corner of his eye, he saw the barrel of the gun pointed at his head. In the distance, the siren of yet another police car approached. He assumed it was the officer that had been requested over the radio. He wondered why Officer Franski had been specifically requested. Unfortunately, it didn't take him long to find out.

Officer Franski brought his car to a screeching halt and jumped out. He ran up to Officer Number Two, talked briefly, and then approached the BMW.

"Step out of the vehicle."

"I already gave my license and registration to the other officer. The vehicle hasn't been reported stolen. Why do I have to get out?"

"Because I said so, nigger!"

The word struck Jamal like an ice pick ripping apart his pride. "No! I haven't done anything wrong. I wasn't driving erratically, and I'm not getting out of this car. I have rights."

"Oh I see. You're one of those smart-ass niggers, aren't you? Get your black ass out of that car now, or I'm gonna pull you out!"

"No!"

"What did you say to me, boy?"

"I said hell no!" After hearing the words pour from his mouth, Jamal regretted saying them.

"He's from out of state," Officer Number Two intervened. "Newark."

"Oh, I see. Well, maybe we ought to give him a lesson on how things are done around here. Have you checked inside the vehicle yet?"

"No, not yet. I was waiting for Arnie to finish running the plates."

"What's that in the backseat?"

"Possible drugs or weapons. That's why we called you."

Fear shot through Jamal's eyes. They were going to check inside the package. How could he explain $12,000 in cash? He turned his head to see where he had left his cell phone and the address book. He needed help.

"Keep your eyes straight ahead, boy," Officer Number Two advised, still pointing the weapon at Jamal's head.

Jamal tried to prevent the situation from getting any further out of hand. "This is ridiculous. Let me make one phone call, and this whole situation can be cleared up." He removed his hands from the steering wheel, reached across the seat, and picked up the cell phone and address book.

"He's going for a weapon!"

"Freeze!"

A shot was fired. Jamal realized he had violated his father's advice.

"Don't move. Keep your hands visible at all times."

Jamal slowly raised his hands in the air.

Officer Franski snatched open the car door and yanked Jamal out. "I don't think you understand who's in charge here. Just because you drive around in a fancy car, you think you're a big man, don't you! Don't you!"

Jamal looked up at Office Franski but didn't answer.

"Answer me!" Officer Franski slapped Jamal across the face with his eight-battery flashlight.

The address book and cell phone fell from Jamal's hands.

"Now, you gonna answer me!"

A large welt developed above Jamal's left eye, but he remained silent. He knew the officer was trying to strip him of his dignity. He was determined not to give him the satisfaction.

Officer Number Two pulled Officer Franski aside. "Calm down, Keith."

Officer Franski ignored the warning and stepped back into Jamal's face. "He needs to understand who's in charge around here. When I say jump, you ask how high. When I say talk, you start flapping those big lips. You understand me, porch monkey?"

Jamal refused to respond.

"What's in the package?" Officer Number Two intervened.

Jamal didn't want to respond, but knew he had to give an answer. "Like I said before, it's a gift for my roommate's coach."

"A gift, huh?" Officer Franski replied. "Well, let's just take a little look."

"Wait a minute!" Jamal shouted. "You have no right to search my vehicle. If you want to arrest me, go ahead. But I want to call my lawyer. I know my rights."

"He wants to call his lawyer. Did you hear that, Jimmy? The nigger wants to call his lawyer." Officer Franski placed the butt of his flashlight under Jamal's chin. "The only right you have is the right to remain silent."

The cold steel dug into Jamal's skin.

"Stand back." Officer Franski pushed Jamal aside then reached into the backseat for the box.

Jamal looked down at the ground. He felt like a criminal although he hadn't violated any laws.

"Well, well, well, what do we have here?" Officer Franski looked up with a smirk.

Jamal knew he was better off keeping his mouth shut. If they arrested him and took him down to the station, at least he could call for help.

"Hey, Arnie," come over here and look at what I found."

Officer Franski held open the box so the other two officers could look inside.

"What you doin' with all this money, boy? Answer me when I speak to you. You been sellin' drugs. You bringing drug money into my community?"

Jamal maintained his silence.

"You son of a bitch, I said answer me!" Officer Franski turned Jamal around and pushed his face against the hood of the car. "You think you can drive around here in your fancy BMW, transporting drugs, and flashing all this money around?"

Jamal closed his eyes and silently prayed. All his life, he had fought against violence. All his life, he had rejected drugs. All his life, he had tried to do the right thing. But none of that mattered now. The officers were so blinded by their racism the only thing they could see was a nigger with $12,000.

"You gonna answer me! I got ways of makin' you talk!" Officer Franski struck Jamal in the back of the head with the flashlight.

A fire ignited deep within Jamal's soul. He turned around and wrestled the flashlight from Officer Franski's hand. "Now, tell me who the big man is!" he yelled, throwing the flashlight against the ground.

Officer Number One and Two immediately intervened, wrestling Jamal to the ground.

Jamal struggled for his life. The cell phone and address book lay within reach. He scrambled toward them, but Officer Franski kicked them away.

Officer Number One pinned Jamal against the front fender of the BMW. Jamal noticed the picture of Shawn's father, dressed in his policeman's uniform, lay face up on the road watching the confrontation.

"You ought not have done that, boy!" Officer Franski grabbed Jamal by the braids and pounded his face into the dirt. "Who the hell do you think you are? You ain't in nigger town anymore, boy. You're in my neck of the woods now."

Adrenaline flooded Jamal's body. His muscles tensed, his blood pressure rose, and his heartbeat quickened. He turned over and pushed Officer Franski away.

"You son of a bitch!" Officer Franski shouted.

"Grab his arms," Officer Number One instructed. "Hold him down so I can cuff his black ass!"

Jamal refused to be cuffed. He lay prone on his back with his hands underneath his body.

A fourth police car pulled up. Officer Number Four immediately jumped out of his car.

"He's resisting arrest!" Officer Number Two shouted.

Officer Number Four pulled out his collapsible baton. Without asking any questions, he ran up to the confrontation and started beating Jamal.

The baton struck Jamal in the neck, the right side of his face, the left side of his face, his throat, and finally his head. The officer struck him so many times the baton flew out of his hands.

The strength drained from Jamal's body. The blood from his wounds obscured his vision, but he refused to submit. He couldn't let them cuff him.

"Assume the position!" Office Number Two shouted, trying to grab Jamal's arms from underneath his body.

The sting of a billy club tore through Jamal's right shoulder. He raised his hands to protect his face.

The officers pinned Jamal's arms against his chest and turned him onto his stomach.

Jamal tasted the dirt from the road. An Officer gripped his head in an illegal choke-hold, shoving a thumb into his mouth.

"Aiiiiiggh that black bastard bit me! Cuff his mother-fuckin' ass. Cuff him now!" Officer Franski screamed.

A fifth police car pulled up, and a police captain emerged.

"He's refusing to assume the position!" Officer Number One yelled.

"The nigger bit me!" Officer Franski held his hand up in the air. "He probably gave me AIDS!"

Office Number One returned to his vehicle to call EMS.

"Grab his legs," the police captain instructed. "Get out the restraints. Stop him from kicking. Subdue him! Subdue him!"

A blackjack rose above Jamal's face. The intensity splintered his jawbone. Handcuffs jingled above his head. The cold steel surrounded his wrists. A pair of restraints were laid by his side. The leather straps bound his legs.

Somewhere in the distance, a train whistled across the landscape. Jamal wondered if the passengers could see him lying on the road. He wondered if they could see his future being beat out of him. The sound of the whistle faded into the reality of the voices above him.

"If the son of a bitch gets up, put him down with this."

"I don't think he's gonna move, Keith. I think we taught him a lesson."

Jamal tried to yell, but the scream was trapped inside his head. He saw his future rise from his body and float in the air between the blurred faces of the police officers. He saw it swept through the valley and sucked into the clouds to fall as tiny drops of moisture that weighed heavy on the shoulders of his tormentors.

"This is our third Johnnie for the week. Congratulations, men. We're ahead of schedule."

As Jamal drifted into blackness, he uttered, "I'm only eighteen, Keith. I'm only eighteen."

****

"That wasn't no foul. I didn't touch him!" Quadre ran up to the referee to protest the call.

"That's your second warning. You're out of the game!" The referee pointed to the locker room.

"What! You're not listening to me!" Quadre stood in the middle of the court and pleaded his case. "I didn't touch him! I didn't touch him!"

The spectacle caused the Bobcat fans to rise to their feet and sing in delight.

"Na-na-na-na. Na-na-na-na. Hey, hey, hey. Good-bye."

Coach Green rose from the bench and motioned Quadre to leave the court.

"We want Collins! We want Collins! We want Collins!" the Tiger fans roared, stomping their feet against the bleachers.

Coach Green motioned Shawn off the bench. Shawn stood from the bench and threw off his warm-ups. The Tiger fans erupted into applause.

Quadre was led off the court to the locker room, still arguing with the referee.

Shawn checked into the game. He knelt in front of the timekeeper's table and looked up at the scoreboard. His team was behind sixty-six to sixty with four minutes remaining on the clock.

The buzzer sounded, and Shawn entered the game. All the Tiger fans were on their feet except for Dr. Perez, who sat behind the Tiger bench, stunned Coach Green had defied his warning.

Shawn took his spot around the perimeter of the foul line and watched as the Bobcats made all three of their shots. Since a technical foul had been called on Quadre, the Bobcats retained possession of the ball. The Tigers now trailed by nine points. On the inbound pass, Brian Short stole the ball from the Bobcats. He immediately passed the ball to Jelin, who looked for Shawn up court. Like clockwork, Shawn had already escaped from his man and was headed up court. He caught the pass from Jelin, jumped high above the rim, and slammed the ball through the hoop with one hand.

The fans screamed with delight and chanted, "Collins! Collins! Collins!"

Shawn bathed in the admiration as he returned to play defense.

"Why did the coach wait so long to put Shawn in the game?" Martha screamed over to Lincoln.

Lincoln shrugged. "I don't know. We could have been winning this game."

The Bobcats inbounded the ball and passed it around the perimeter. After running down the shot clock to ten seconds, they passed the ball inside to their big man. The big man attempted a hook shot but was blocked by Jelin. Shawn picked up the rebound. He dribbled the ball up court and sank a three-pointer. The Bobcat lead was cut to four points. The Bobcat coach called a time-out to stop the Tiger momentum.

"Remember what we practiced," Coach Green implored. "If we keep pressure on the ball, we'll keep the Bobcats rattled. Now, we're only down four points. We have plenty of time, so don't do anything stupid. Collins has the hot hand, so work the ball inside to him to take the shot. Okay, men, get out there and show me why we're ranked number one."

The team clapped in unison then hustled back onto the court.

Shawn took his position then looked around for Tammera. She was standing on the sidelines with her pompoms raised in the air. He tried to get her attention but noticed Brian Short smiling at her. After the game, he was going to get something straight with Brian. Either he kept his eyes off of Tammera, or he ended up with one eye permanently shut. The whistle forced Shawn's attention back to the game. His heart palpitated with excitement.

The Bobcats once again inbounded the ball. They spread out into a four-corner offense. Shawn knew their strategy was to run down the clock. He watched the Bobcats pass the ball around the perimeter. With the shot clock down to ten seconds, the Bobcats worked the ball inside and then scored on a short jumper.

The clock was down to two minutes and thirty seconds. The Bobcats were ahead by six points.

Shawn looked over at the bench for the play. Coach Green signaled the high-low play. Brian Short inbounded the pass to Shawn. Shawn dribbled the ball up court and passed it underneath to Jelin. Jelin immediately passed the ball back out to Shawn on the perimeter. Shawn connected on a three-pointer. The Bobcat lead was cut to three points with less than two minutes to play.

The Bobcats quickly inbounded the pass, but again the fast hands of Brian Short stole the ball away. Shawn had already broken free from his man and was headed up court. Short fired the ball to Shawn. Shawn jumped, caught the ball in midair, and slammed a two-handed dunk over his opponent. The noise level was electric. The Bobcat lead was cut to one point. Coach Green called a time-out and motioned his team to the bench.

As Shawn ran toward the bench, his heart was beating wildly against his chest. He looked up at the cheering fans, but their cheers were drowned out by his beating heart. Then it hit, a pain so piercing it knocked him to the ground. He tried to stumble to his feet, but the pain overwhelmed him. He tried to crawl to the bench, but his arms wouldn't carry him. He fell facedown against the hardwood court.

The fright on Coach Green's face suspended time. He ran onto the floor and tried to hoist Shawn onto his feet.

Shawn looked into Coach Green's blurred face. "I'm sorry, Coach."

****

A hush fell over the gymnasium, amplifying the sound of Martha's scream. "Shaaawn!"

Dr. Perez jumped from behind the Tiger bench and rushed onto the court. "Someone call the paramedics! We need to get him to the hospital. Get everyone back! Get everyone back! He needs air!"

Coach Green gently laid Shawn down and then directed his players over to the bench. "Shawn's going to be all right. Just relax. Shawn's going to be okay. Give him some air."

A disturbing silence hung over the gymnasium.

"That's my son!" Martha screamed, piercing the silence. "Lord have mercy, that's my baby. Get out of my way! Let me through!" Martha pushed her way through the crowd and onto the court.

Doctor Perez stood to address Martha before she reached Shawn. "Mrs. Collins?"

"Are you a doctor? What's wrong with my son?"

"Do you really need to ask? I warned you all not to let Shawn play. I warned this could happen!"

"What the hell are you talking about?" Martha reached for Shawn's hand. "What's wrong with my baby?"

"Didn't Coach Green or Shawn tell you?"

"Tell me what?"

"Dear God." Dr. Perez put his face into his hands and shook his head. Before he had a chance to respond, the onsite paramedics rushed a stretcher onto the court and checked Shawn's vital signs.

"We have a weak pulse. Are you the team doctor?"

"Yes," Dr. Perez answered.

"Do you have any idea what we're dealing with here?"

"Possible cardiomyopathy." Doctor Perez cut his eyes at Martha.

"What!" Martha screamed. "How do you know that? How do you know that's what's wrong with him!"

Doctor Perez looked over at Coach Green. "Because I diagnosed Shawn over a week ago with the condition after he collapsed at practice."

"Collapsed at practice! Why wasn't I told?" Martha grabbed the doctor's coat collar. "Why wasn't I told of his condition? I'm his mother!"

"I think you better ask Coach Green that question."

Martha looked over at Coach Green.

Coach Green avoided Martha's stare and focused on the paramedics strapping Shawn onto the stretcher.

"I'll get my car and meet you at the hospital," Dr. Perez said, watching the paramedics prepare Shawn for transport.

Martha cupped her hand around Shawn's face. "You're going to be all right. Hang in there, baby."

Martha ran along side the stretcher toward the exit. When she passed by Coach Green, she lost control.

"You did this! You've destroyed my son! You promised me you were going to take care of him, and look what you've done!"

"Martha, no!" Lincoln grabbed Martha's fist from the air. "Now is not the time."

Martha buried her face against Lincoln's chest. "He knew Shawn was ill, and he didn't tell me. He made him keep playing!"

"We can't worry about that now, Martha." Lincoln looked for Damar, whom he had left standing by the exit. "C'mon, you need to get into the ambulance. I'll get Damar, and we'll meet you at the hospital."

Lincoln grabbed a frightened Damar and then escorted Martha into the waiting ambulance.

"What hospital are you taking him to?" Lincoln shouted to the paramedics.

"Allegheny Memorial!"

****

By the time Robert made his way down to courtside, the ambulance had already sped away with his roommate. He needed to find out where they were taking him. He pushed his way toward the Tiger bench. The scene inside the gymnasium was still chaotic. Fans were running around everywhere trying to get some word on Shawn's condition. As Robert neared the Tiger bench, he looked into the shallow faces of the players. They all seemed to be in a silent state of shock, except for Coach Green, who paced back and forth in front of the bench.

"Jelin," Robert called. "What hospital are they taking Shawn to?"

Jelin motioned the security personnel to let Robert through.

"Jelin, do you know what happened? Is Shawn going to be all right?"

"I pray so. They took him over to Allegheny Memorial. Wait for me outside of the locker room, and we'll go over to the hospital together. Where's Jamal?"

"I'm not sure, but I'm gonna to try calling him at the dorm."

Coach Green stopped his pacing long enough to watch the interaction between Jelin and Robert.

"Get your team ready. We're going to finish the game." The referee blew his whistle and indicated to the timekeeper to set the thirty-second time-out clock.

Coach Green gathered his team around him. "Let's win this game for Collins," he instructed before sending his players back onto the court.

Robert went to the lobby to call Jamal on his cell phone. The call went straight to voice mail. "Where is he?" Robert left a message and then went to wait for Jelin outside the locker room.

CHAPTER 27

When the paramedics arrived at the scene, five police officers were huddled over the suspect.

"Who's the wounded officer?" the lead paramedic asked.

"Officer Keith Franski," Police Captain O'Reilly stated.

"What's the injury?"

"Hand laceration. He was attacked by the suspect."

The paramedics rushed their medical gear over to the crowd of officers. Two of the officers stood with their guns drawn while the other two crouched above the suspect.

"Which one of you is Officer Franski?"

"That's me." Officer Franski looked up at the paramedics.

"Let us take a look at that hand."

Officer Franski held his finger in the air.

"Can you still move it?"

"Yeah, I think so."

"Were you cut?"

"The bastard bit me! What if he has AIDS?"

The lead paramedic swabbed the wound with antibacterial ointment. "It doesn't look that bad, but you may have ligament damage. We're going to put a splint on it to keep it from moving. You won't need stitches, but I suggest you see a hand specialist within the next couple of days."

"Damn that black bastard."

"What exactly happened here?"

"We stopped the suspect for a routine traffic violation. He became combative, and we had to subdue him."

The lead paramedic looked down at the suspect. "We better take a look at him. I think I see blood."

The assistant paramedic bent down to get a closer look. "Hey. I don't think this guy is breathing."

"What?" The lead paramedic shoved his way past Officer Franski. "Tell your men to get back. Let us take a look!"

"Don't tell us how to handle our suspects!" Officer Franski yelled. "He's a dangerous criminal. We can't take the chance of him getting up and hurting another officer."

"He's handcuffed. What the hell is he gonna do? Tell your men to step back, now!"

Officer Franski motioned for the other officers to stand back. "But if the son of a bitch moves, put him down."

The assistant paramedic turned Jamal onto his back.

"Holy shit! This man has blunt-force trauma to the head. You called us here for a fuckin' finger laceration when you have an injured suspect? What the hell were you thinking?"

"Those injuries occurred after we put in the call," Officer Number One advised. "He resisted arrest."

"Tommy, get the defibrillator!"

As the assistant ran back to the ambulance, the lead paramedic started CPR.

"He's already lost a lot a blood. I don't know if we're going to be able to revive him."

"You wanna know what we were thinking?" Officer Franski answered. "We were thinking we just got another one. We just got another scumbag drug dealer off the streets. If you think we should feel sorry for his ass, well, you thought wrong."

"This man is critical." The lead paramedic grabbed the defibrillator from his assistant.

"He's still not responding. We're losing him!"

The lead paramedic placed the electrodes against Jamal's chest.

Jamal's body convulsed.

"He's still not responding. Get him on the stretcher. We'll continue this in the ambulance. We gotta get him to the hospital—now!"

The lead paramedic turned to the five officers. "Would somebody take off those damn handcuffs! How the hell are we supposed to work on him?"

Officer Number One walked over and unlocked the cuffs.

The paramedics rushed Jamal into the ambulance.

"In case you care, we're taking him to Allegheny Memorial."

The door to the ambulance slammed shut, and the ambulance roared up Route 51.

"I'll go to the hospital," Officer Number One advised. "They're gonna want a report on what happened."

"Remember, Arnie—the suspect sustained those injuries resisting arrest," Officer Franski warned.

"I know the drill." Officer Number One returned to his vehicle and followed the trail of the ambulance up Route 51.

"I hope the bastard dies," Officer Franski said. "Who the hell does he think he is? Driving around like he belongs here. Waving that goddamn cell phone in our faces, actin' like he's the fuckin' president."

Officer Franski turned and looked at the BMW. The caution lights were still blinking, and music still played over the CD player. "Would someone turn off that jungle music and call a tow truck so we can get this piece of shit outta here?"

****

"Momma, is Shawn going to be all right?" a frightened Damar asked.

"I think so, baby," Martha answered, pulling Damar closer.

"Momma, can we go see Shawn?"

"We have to wait until the doctors say it's okay."

"When will that be?"

"I'm sure it will be soon, son," Judge Patterson intervened.

Martha ran her hand across Damar's smooth, brown face.

"Lincoln, why didn't Shawn tell me about his heart condition?" Martha shook her head. "I could have sent him to our family doctor. I could have yanked him off that damn basketball team. I'm his mother. I'm supposed to be the one making the decisions. Where did I go wrong, Lincoln? Where did I go wrong?"

"It's not your fault," Lincoln answered. "Coach Green kept important information from you. He deliberately concealed Shawn's condition."

Martha's eyes narrowed. "He's gonna pay for what he's done to my son. I'm gonna see to that, Lincoln."

"Shawn's going to be fine. I'm sure of it. He's gonna be fine." Lincoln embraced Martha with a strong, firm hug.

"I wish I could be as sure as you." Martha looked up at the clock; it was 10:34 p.m.

"Mrs. Collins! Mrs. Collins!" Jelin and Robert rushed into the waiting room. "How's Shawn? Is he going to be all right?"

"We don't know yet. They won't let us into the emergency room, and they haven't told us anything."

"Is Dr. Perez in there?"

"I think so," Martha answered.

"Shawn's going to be all right," Lincoln repeated, trying to calm everyone's nerves.

"How can you be so sure?" Martha asked. "What if he isn't all right? What happens if he doesn't regain consciousness? What happens if I lose my baby? Lincoln, I don't think I could survive that."

"Martha, listen to me. Shawn's gonna make it. He's young, he's strong, and he's a fighter. Just like his mother. Now you have to be strong for both your sons. They both need you right now."

Martha looked down at Damar and nodded.

"Let us pray." Lincoln motioned for everyone to hold hands. "We're going to pray, and God's going to hear our voices."

With Damar cradled against her arm, Martha took hold of Jelin and Robert's hands and then bowed her head.

Lincoln completed the prayer circle. "Dear Lord, please hear the sorrow of our hearts. Please take away the pain I see in this mother's eyes. Please give this young child the chance to grow up with his brother. Dear Lord, we pray you lift up our souls and allow us to share another day with our brother Shawn. We pray you allow us to sing ol' happy day and rejoice in the light of your compassion and understanding. Dear Lord, we pray you spare the life of this young man and open his eyes so he can see the love in our hearts. In God's holy name, we pray. Amen."

Martha couldn't hold back the tears. "Thank you, Lincoln."

"Mrs. Collins." Dr. Perez approached Martha with a smile on his face. "Shawn is alert, and he's asking for you."

"What?" Martha couldn't believe her ears.

"Shawn's conscious. He's asking for you."

"Thank you, Jesus!" Martha shouted. "And thank you, Doctor." She gave the doctor a heartfelt hug.

"Can we see him?"

Doctor Perez nodded.

"C'mon, Damar, let's go see Shawn."

As Martha left the waiting room, Lincoln turned to the doctor. "What's Shawn's prognosis? Is he going to be all right?"

"Are you Shawn's father?"

"No, Shawn's father is dead. I'm a close friend of the family."

"The prognosis looks good, but I'm afraid his basketball-playing days are over. The important thing is Shawn is going to be all right," Dr. Perez advised before returning to the emergency room.

"That's right," Lincoln answered, turning to face Robert and Jelin. "Shawn's going to need our support to get through this. We have to make him understand his life is a lot more important than a basketball career."

Jelin nodded.

"Jelin, did you know anything about Shawn's heart condition? Had Shawn or Coach Green said anything about it?"

"No, Judge, but Shawn did pass out at practice."

"When?"

"About a week ago. But Coach Green said Shawn just overexerted himself. He said it was nothing for us to be concerned about."

"I see." Lincoln nodded.

"Code red! Code red!" The announcement blared across the intercom like acid rain, sending the emergency room staff into a frenzy.

The sliding glass doors opened, and paramedics rolled a stretcher into the entrance.

"Room one!" the head emergency room nurse shouted.

"Blunt-force trauma to the head, multiple contusions, excessive internal bleeding …"

****

The list of injuries buzzed past Robert's head, quicker than he could comprehend what they meant. He saw the victim's face and for a brief second thought the victim looked familiar. His mind flashed back to the last time he saw Stephon. He remembered rushing over to the stretcher and seeing Stephon's blood-soaked wrists wrapped in gauze. *"I'm sorry, Stephon. I'm so sorry."* Robert closed his eyes and then opened them. But to his horror, illusion changed into reality. It wasn't Stephon; it was Jamal.

"Jamaaaallllll! "That's Jamal! Oh my God!" Robert rushed over to the stretcher. "Jamaaalll! Jamaaaall! What happened?"

"Careful, son." The nurse pushed Robert away as the victim was rushed through the waiting area and into the emergency room.

Ignoring the nurse's warning, Robert followed the stretcher into the emergency room and watched as Jamal was lifted off the stretcher and onto the operating table. Jamal's face was covered with blood.

"The patient is convulsing!"

Jamal's body shook violently against the table.

"Diazepam, 2 mgs stat!"

The nurse shot liquid from a needle into the intravenous bottle above Jamal's bed.

"Someone get him out of here!"

Robert was pushed back into the waiting area. All the sights and sounds from the hospital blurred with his tears.

Jelin cradled Robert against his shoulder.

Judge Patterson demanded answers from the police officer. Unsatisfied with the response, he turned to the paramedic.

"What the hell happened?"

"I don't know, Judge. When we arrived at the scene, that poor boy was already beat half to death."

"We had evidence of drug dealing," the police officer intervened. "When we asked the suspect to get out of the car, he became combative. He wounded one of the other officers at the scene and had to be restrained. He refused to be handcuffed and resisted arrest. He sustained those injuries resisting arrest."

"That's a lie!" Robert finally organized his sights and sounds into a concrete reality. "Jamal doesn't do drugs. Jamal's a straight-A student. How can you say he's a drug dealer! Jamal's never done drugs. He hates drugs! He told me so!"

"Did you find any drugs?" Judge Patterson asked.

"We found $12,000 in cash. That's what provoked the suspicion. When we questioned the suspect about the money, he lunged at one of the officers."

"That's a damn lie!" Robert shouted.

"I asked if you found any drugs!"

"No, we didn't find any drugs."

"Then why the hell are you saying he was a drug dealer!"

"Listen, Judge Patterson, that's all I'm going to say. If you want to find out the specifics of the arrest, you're going to have to get a copy of the police report when it gets filed."

"You bet your ass I will. This case smells to high heaven like a profile stop. Believe me, it will be thoroughly investigated. God help you if this boy dies and this case turns out to be another instance of racial profiling. I'm sick and tired of seeing the civil rights of our children violated, just so you can pad your damn arrest statistics!"

The word *victim* struck Robert like a missile. "I know why Jamal had $12,000," he whispered into Judge Patterson's ear. "It wasn't drug money."

The doors to the emergency room opened, and the doctor that had been working on Jamal emerged.

"Is there a next of kin here?"

Jelin tightened his grip around Robert's shoulder.

Judge Patterson walked over to the doctor. "No, he's a student at Pittsburgh City University. I believe his family lives out of town. His roommate is here." Judge Patterson pointed to Robert.

"Son, do you know how to get in touch with the patient's family?" The doctor knelt down in front of Robert's chair.

Robert couldn't stop his hands from shaking. "Why?"

The doctor clasped Robert's hands into his. "I'm afraid we have some bad news about your roommate."

"His name is Jamal." Robert's tears froze against his face.

"I'm sorry to have to tell you this, but Jamal died on the operating table. He sustained massive head and chest injuries. He regained consciousness but suffered a massive aneurysm on the operating table."

"Nooooo! I don't understand! I just saw Jamal a couple of hours ago. How could this happen?"

"Robert," Judge Patterson said. "C'mon, son, get a hold of yourself. I know this is a difficult time, but we need you to stay calm. We need to contact Jamal's family. They have to know what happened right away."

"I need to know what happened!" Robert cried. "Jamal was my best friend. What did he do to die like this? Oh, God help me!" Robert fell back against his chair and buried his face into his hands.

"I'm going to prescribe him some sedatives." The doctor wrote Robert a prescription and handed the piece of paper to Jelin. "This will help calm him down."

Jelin took the prescription and put it in his coat pocket. "I'm gonna take Robert down to the pharmacy and get his prescription filled, then go back to the dorm."

"I'll contact the appropriate authorities at the university," the doctor said. "They need to be advised of the situation so they can contact the family." The doctor looked down at Robert then walked away.

"Jelin, while you're at the dorm, can you look through Jamal's things and see if you can find his home number? I need to talk with his family." Lincoln reached for his wallet. "Here's my cell phone number. Give me a call when you find it."

"Yes, sir." Jelin took the card and placed it in his pocket. "C'mon, Robert, lets go."

Robert rose to his feet. He had to grab hold of Jelin's arm to keep from falling.

Jelin ushered Robert toward the elevator.

Robert stopped and looked around the waiting room at all the silent faces watching him. His anger turned to rage. "Don't look at me! Look at him! He's the murderer!" Robert pointed to the police officer standing at the nurse's station. "I hate you! I hate you for what you've done! I hate you for the way you see us! I hate you for the way you treat us!"

Jelin tightened his grip around Robert's arm. "C'mon, Robert, this won't do any good."

"Jamal wasn't a criminal! Why'd you have to kill him?"

Jelin pulled Robert into the elevator.

"Whyyyy! Whyyyy! Whyyyy!" The elevator doors closed, leaving Robert's words hanging like icicles from the waiting room walls.

Lincoln turned and looked at the police officer. His intense stare caused the officer to turn around.

Lincoln pointed his finger. "You just murdered the wrong person."

The officer gave Lincoln a blank stare.

"And if it takes me the rest of my life trying, I'm going to prove it was murder."

CHAPTER 28

C oach Green purchased a copy of the morning paper and then hurried to his office. He ignored the front page and thumbed through the pages until he reached the sports section.

The phone disrupted the coach's reading pleasure.

"Hello."

"Melvin, I think we have a problem."

"Tony?"

"Yeah, it's me. Have you read the morning paper yet?"

"I was just reading it when you called. Isn't it great? They're predicting the Tigers to win the Christmas Tournament, even without Collins."

"That's not the story I'm talking about. Did you read the front page?"

"The front page?"

"Turn to the front page, Melvin."

Coach Green turned to the front page. The bold-face headline glared at him: "Student Dead after Traffic Stop."

Under the headline was a picture of a red convertible BMW. The dead student was identified as Jamal Lewis, roommate of the freshman basketball sensation Shawn Collins.

"Oh my God," Coach Green gasped.

"Isn't that the car we leased Collins?" Tony shouted into the receiver. "I thought we made it clear no one else was to drive that car! You know what's going to happen now? The police are going to start snooping around. Our butts are going to be on the line, Melvin!"

"Calm down, Tony. Let me finish reading the article. I'll call you back." Coach Green hung up the phone.

After finishing the article, he slammed the newspaper against the desk.

He picked up the phone and called Tony. "I read the article, Tony. Don't worry. I'll take care of it."

"What do you mean, you'll take care of it? How are you going to stop the police from snooping around?"

"Look, Tony, there are only four people who know about the car. You, me, Shawn and possibly Jelin Church. I know I can keep Shawn and Jelin's mouths shut. And like you said, there's no way the paperwork can be traced back to you or me. It will identify Shawn Collins as the lessee. So just sit tight, Tony. If the police or the media start asking you questions about the car, just play innocent and show them the lease agreement. Tell them Shawn came in with his mother and leased the car. End of case. Besides, I think the police have something to hide. They're going to want this case to disappear just as much as we do."

"Yeah, how can you be so sure?"

"It's just a hunch I have. I know for a fact Jamal wasn't a drug dealer. The police fabricated that story to make the victim look like a criminal. Believe me, it happens more often than you think."

"Well, what about Shawn's mother? She knows that car doesn't belong to Shawn."

"Let me take care of Mrs. Collins. I know her. She's gonna want to protect Shawn. Remember her son isn't completely innocent either. He accepted illegal recruiting gifts. She's gonna wanna keep that private."

"It sounds like you have it all figured out, Melvin."

"I do. So relax, Tony. You're gonna keep your job, and I'm gonna keep my team."

"Do you think you can still make the NCAA Tournament without Collins?"

"Yeah, I do. Quadre showed me a lot of talent. And I think I have a way of harnessing that temper of his."

"You never cease to amaze me, Melvin. I'll let you go so you can take care of business. Call me and let me know how everything is working out."

"Sure, take it easy, Tony. And remember—if anyone asks about the car, it belongs to Shawn Collins."

"I understand. Bye, Melvin."

Coach Green hung up the phone and stared at his empty wall of achievement. He opened his desk drawer and removed the letter Jelin had dropped on the locker room floor.

He picked up the phone and dialed Jelin's dorm room.

****

Shawn sat up in bed and looked around his hospital room. He was still groggy from his medication, but the events from the last twenty-four hours were beginning to surface. He remembered collapsing during the Bobcat game. He remembered being rushed to the hospital. He closed his eyes and tried to erase the last twenty-four hours from his mind. But the memories continued to surface. He remembered being transported to a semiprivate room with a view of the river. He remembered having a roommate that talked too much.

He looked out the window at the river. A fragile layer of ice had formed across the water, stopping the mighty river in its tracks. He grimaced at the sight, realizing his basketball career had also been stopped. Stopped by the fragile beat of his heart. He looked at the monitor set up to track his heartbeat. It was obvious his heart was in bad shape. The doctors hadn't said anything yet, but he could feel the tension in the air. It was just a matter of time before they broke the bad news.

He turned from the monitor and looked at the patient in the bed next to him. The patient had introduced himself as John Martin Turner. A junior high school principal at Harriet Tubman Middle School. During the night, Mr. Turner had rambled on about his recovery from a massive heart attack and how he was due to be released in the morning. Now Mr. Turner was dressed and sitting on the side of his bed, reading the morning paper. He wanted to ask Mr. Turner if he could borrow the sports page but didn't want to start his roommate talking again.

Mr. Turner peered past the paper at Shawn. "It sure is a shame, isn't it?"

Shawn gave Mr. Turner a puzzled look.

"About that young man the police killed. That makes the third one in less than two years. And just like the other two times, I bet the police get off scot-free."

Shawn didn't have a clue what Mr. Turner was talking about.

"This article says he was stopped for a routine traffic violation. Yeah, *routine*—we all know what that means. He was driving in the wrong neighborhood, at the wrong time, in the wrong car. Now you tell me—how could the situation have gotten so out of hand they had to use deadly force? It says right here he didn't have a weapon. I bet it was because of that fancy sports car he was driving."

Mr. Turner turned the paper around so Shawn could see the picture of the car.

"I bet they said, 'Yeah, you driving around here in your fancy BMW like you belong here. Yeah, we're gonna teach you a lesson.'"

Shawn looked at the picture. It looked like his car.

"Okay, Mr. Turner, your ride is here." A nurse rolled a wheelchair into the room and stopped in front of Mr. Turner's bed.

"Why do I have to ride in that thing?"

"It's hospital procedure, Mr. Turner."

"I'm perfectly capable of walking out of here on my own. I don't need that thing."

"Mr. Turner, you've been the perfect patient the entire time you've been here. Now you're gonna give me a hard time on your last day? C'mon, put that newspaper down and climb aboard."

"Oh, all right, Nurse." Mr. Turner climbed into the chair. "Here, son, you can have the paper."

Shawn took the paper and nodded thank you.

"You don't talk much, do you, son?"

"Are you ready to go, Mr. Turner?"

"Put this baby in gear and get me the hell outta here."

Shawn was relieved to see Mr. Turner rolled out the door. He opened the paper to the front page and looked at the picture of the car. After reading the first two paragraphs, he dropped the newspaper onto the floor. His brain turned to a blank page, his emotions crawled into a tight ball, and his tongue withdrew to the back of his mouth. He lay against his pillow and stared aimlessly at the ceiling.

****

"Have a seat, Jelin." Coach Green motioned Jelin into his office.

"Is this about Shawn? Do you know more about his condition?"

"It appears Shawn's going to be fine ... except ..."

"Except what?"

"Except Shawn's can't play basketball anymore. His heart's too weak."

Jelin shook his head. "Does Shawn know yet?"

"I think the doctors are waiting for him to get a little stronger before they break the bad news. But he probably has some idea what's going on."

Jelin stood and walked over to the window. "I can't believe this. Since we were kids, we planned on playing in the pros. Me and Shawn, Frick and Frack. We've played basketball together since we were in grade school. Now this has to happen." Jelin punched the windowsill. "It isn't fair. Why Shawn? Why did this have to happen to him?"

"I know, Jelin. It's a shame. But you still have a chance to make it. You can make it for the both of you. That is … as long as we understand each other."

Jelin looked over at Coach Green.

"You heard me right, Jelin. You're a good basketball player. Damn good. But there are a lot of good basketball players out there. And just like you, they all have dreams of making it to the top. Most of them would do anything to get a shot at the pros. How about you? What would you be willing to do to make it into the big leagues?"

"I don't know, Coach. I never really thought about it that way. I always believed my talent and hard work would get me there."

"Don't be so naïve, Jelin. Talent and hard work will only get you so far. To make it into the pros you need that extra little push. You need someone behind you, pulling strings, making phone calls, arranging meetings."

"You mean like an agent?"

"No, I'm talking about that person who controls your college career. The person who designs the plays to showcase your talents. The person who makes the well-timed phone calls to the right pro scouts."

"You're that person, Coach."

"Now you're getting the picture. I always knew you were a smart kid."

"Is all this leading somewhere, Coach?"

"Sit down, Jelin. We need to talk."

Jelin returned to his chair.

"It was a tragedy what happened to Shawn's roommate, wasn't it?" Coach Green handed Jelin a copy of the morning paper.

Jelin looked at the headlines. "I still can't believe it."

"Did you know Jamal Lewis?"

Jelin nodded. "I'm gonna miss him."

"Did you know they found $12,000 on him?"

"Yeah, I know. So what."

"What do you suppose he was doing with all that money?"

Jelin remained silent.

"Shawn told you, didn't he?"

"Told me what?"

"Don't play games with me, Jelin. I'm the one who controls your destiny. Remember?"

"What do you want from me, Coach?"

"I want the truth!"

Jelin was silent for a moment. "All right, Coach. Shawn told me about the money. I wasn't surprised. Hell, you bought me that entertainment center and my mother that Buick. I know the deal. I'm not stupid. I'm not gonna tell anyone about the money or the car. So if this meeting is about me keeping my mouth shut, you don't have to worry."

"The police are saying Jamal was a drug dealer."

"That doesn't surprise me. The police always come up with some type of excuse when they unjustifiably kill a black kid. Everyone in my world knows that."

"So you're telling me, you'll allow Jamal's good name to get dragged through the mud, and you aren't going to say anything?"

Jelin hung his head. "I guess that's what I'm sayin'. It hurts—it hurts like hell what happened to Jamal. He was good a kid. He didn't deserve to die that way. But he's dead, and there's nothin' I can do to bring him back."

"Well, just to make sure there's no misunderstanding, I have one more thing I need you to know." Coach Green opened his desk drawer and removed a letter. "You dropped something in the locker room the other day." He held the letter up. "Does this belong to you? Did you write this?"

Jelin jumped up and tried to grab the letter from Coach Green's hands. "That's my personal property! You have no right to my private life."

"Don't even think about it, Jelin." Coach Green snatched the letter from Jelin's reach. "This is my insurance policy. What do you think Shawn would say if he found out his best friend was sucking sausages with his roommate? What do you think would happen if the sports wires got a hold of this information?" Coach Green stood and looked Jelin in the eye. "Let me tell you what would happen. You wouldn't have a career. Nobody would want you on their team. You'd been finished!"

Jelin sat back down. "I've already told you, I'm not going to say anything. What the hell do you want from me?"

Coach Green reared back against his chair. "I want you to make sure Shawn keeps his mouth shut. You and Shawn are the only two people who know the truth about the car and the $12,000. I want to make sure it stays that way. Do you understand what I'm saying?"

Jelin slid his hand across the crown of his head and down the back of his neck.

"I don't understand you, Jelin. A big, strapping boy like you. I never figured you the type." He smirked. "You don't fit the mode."

"The fuckin' *mode*." Jelin shook his head.

"I guess you're the don't-ask, don't-tell type, huh, Jelin? Trying to keep your sick perversion under wraps? Well, the cat's out of the bag. And I'm the one holding the cat's tail."

Jelin uttered a sick laugh. "How's my type supposed to act?" Jelin asked, standing up and enacting effeminate mannerisms. "Should I start taking showers in the girls' locker room? Or maybe I should wear a pink armband around my wrist. What if I pranced around the court in a pair of high-heel sneakers? Would that make me fit the mode? Is that how I'm supposed to act?" Jelin paused and then looked Coach Green up and down. "All my life. All my fuckin' life, I've been afraid of what people like you would say if the truth got out. But you wanna know something? Now that the truth is out, I don't give a damn!"

Coach Green crossed his arms. "You sure about that, Jelin?"

"You sit there behind that big desk actin' like you da' man. Like you got all the power and all the answers. The judge and the jury, ready to hang my ass if I don't do your dirty work. Well, let me tell you something." Jelin leaned across the desk. "I don't give a damn, because I know I'm more a man than you'll ever be. You see, Coach, I don't have to go around threatening people to get what I want."

"No, you just unzip your pants and pull out your dick for some faggot to suck. What kind of man is that!

"It's a man who accepts who he is!" Jelin slammed his fist against the desk. "Not some lying, fake, bastard wannabe who has to exploit teenagers to get what he wants! That's not a man; that's a fuckin' coward."

"If I were you, Mr. Church, I wouldn't be standing there acting so high and mighty. Maybe you accept yourself. Maybe you can live with yourself knowing you're a sinner, a queer, a homo. But I don't think the rest of the sports world is gonna be so open-minded. If I were you, Mr. Church, I'd sit my ass back down and think about my future. It only takes one phone call for me to ruin your career." Coach Green picked up the phone. "Don't make me do it!"

Jelin reached for the arm of the chair and guided himself back down.

"I thought you would see it my way." Coach Green put the phone down. "And one more thing. Make sure your little boyfriend keeps his mouth shut too."

Jelin nodded.

Coach Green locked eyes with Jelin. "All right, Jelin. I think we understand each other. Remember I know your dirty little secret. I have the power to make your dreams come true or be your worst nightmare. It's your decision."

Jelin rose from his chair and silently exited the office.

CHAPTER 29

"P ost-traumatic shock."

The words crackled through Martha's head like kindling wood.

"Your son can't deal with the sudden trauma that's impacted his life. His mind is blocking it out. It's a mental disorder, not physical."

Martha removed a tissue from her purse. "He suffered a similar condition eight years ago after his father died." Martha wiped her eyes. "But the symptoms were different then. He didn't completely shut down. He suffered awful nightmares and would wake up screaming in the middle of the night. The episodes lasted over a year."

"Post-traumatic shock can manifest itself in many ways. I'm no psychiatrist, Mrs. Collins, but I believe your son's condition is much worse this time around. He's refusing to accept reality."

"I wish he hadn't seen that damn newspaper. I wanted to keep that awful news away from him until he was stronger. I was afraid something like this could happen."

"Mrs. Collins, I'm going to refer your son to a psychiatrist experienced with working with post-traumatic shock patients. His name is Doctor Coronado. He's located right up the street at University Hospital. If you'd like, I'll give him a call right now and set something up. We need to start working on this problem now before Shawn falls any deeper into withdrawal."

"By all means, Doctor James. It's been three days, and Shawn hasn't uttered a word."

"There is some good news. Your son's cardiomyopathy isn't as severe as we first believed. As long as Shawn takes his medication and stays away from any vigorous activity, he should be able to live a long, healthy life."

"That is good news, but I won't be able to rest until my son's completely out of the woods, physically and mentally."

"I have two children of my own, Mrs. Collins. I know how difficult this must be for you. Keep talking to Shawn. Try keeping his spirits up. Sometimes the smallest ray of hope can trigger a positive reaction."

Martha rose from her chair and reached for her coat and purse. "I wish I knew what that ray of hope could be. Shawn's dealing with a lot of bad news. And to make matters worse, he has to watch the basketball game from his hospital bed." Martha shook her head. "I know that's not going to be easy on him."

"We'll get Shawn through this, Mrs. Collins. It's going to take some time, but we will get him through this. Now go visit your son. I'll call and arrange for Dr. Coronado to see Shawn this afternoon."

Martha exited the doctor's office and walked toward the elevators. "I won't let you break my son, Coach Green," she uttered.

Martha reached Shawn's hospital room and peered through the small window. Shawn was lying in his bed, his face void of emotion. "I glued that coffee mug together, and I'm going to do the same with you," Martha whispered before reaching for the door handle.

"Mrs. Collins?" Martha heard a familiar voice. She turned around to see Latisha.

"Latisha, what are you doing here?"

"I came to see Shawn."

"I thought you and Shawn broke up."

"We did, but I wanted to make sure Shawn was all right. But if it's a problem, I'll go. I don't want to upset you or him. Not at a time like this."

"Are you aware Shawn's dating someone else?"

Latisha looked at the floor. "I know he's dating Tammera Patterson. I didn't come here to worm myself back into his life."

"You didn't."

"No." Latisha looked up at Martha. "I'm just concerned. I still care for Shawn. I probably always will. I just need to make sure he's all right. That's all, Mrs. Collins."

"Did you know Shawn can no longer play basketball? Did you know he'll never make it into the pros?"

"I read all about it in the papers." Latisha's eyes filled with tears. "I loved Shawn for all the wrong reasons. I know that now. I was caught up in the glamour of being the potential wife of a pro basketball star. I know that was wrong, Mrs. Collins. But I did love your son, and no matter what you think about me or what you say about me, that's one thing you can't change."

Martha nodded. "We all make mistakes, Latisha. Lord knows I have. And as long as you don't judge me on mine, I won't judge you on yours."

"I 've moved on with my life, Mrs. Collins. I have no intentions of rekindling a relationship with Shawn. I'm concentrating on getting my own life together. I enrolled in cosmetology school. I start in January."

"That's wonderful, Latisha. It makes me proud to see a young person doing something positive with their life. Most of the news we hear about our children these days is the negative type. Good luck to you."

Latisha smiled. "How's Shawn doing?"

"Physically he's going to be fine, but mentally he's in bad shape. The news about his basketball career combined with Jamal's death was just too much for Shawn to handle. He's refusing to accept reality. The doctors call it post-traumatic shock. Don't be surprised if he doesn't respond to you."

"Are you sure my visit won't make matters worse? Shawn and I didn't exactly part as friends."

"No, I don't think so. Just tell him what you've told me, about moving on with your life. Somehow we've got to convince Shawn to move on with his life as well."

"That's not gonna be easy. I know how much Shawn loves to play basketball."

"No, it's not. And, Latisha, do me a favor. Don't mention anything about Jamal while you're in there. He's not strong enough to deal with that issue right now."

Pain flashed across Latisha's face. "I owe so much to Jamal. He's the one who convinced me to move on with my life. To love myself before tryin' to love somebody else."

Martha reached into her purse for a tissue. "I guess it's true what they say about the good dying young."

"I wish it wasn't true." Latisha wiped her eyes. "Why did they have to kill him? Why don't they go after the real drug dealers and leave the innocent people alone?"

"Shawn's father, Albert, was a cop. He was a good cop. His precinct was located in one of the most dangerous sections of the city. But he believed if you treat people with decency and respect, they'd return that respect. He was on the force for ten years and never once fired his weapon. Unfortunately, some officers have no respect for people of color. They see us all as criminals and treat us that way. Until that thinking is changed, innocent young men like Jamal will continue to die, and the racial scars of this country will continue to fester."

Latisha leaned against the wall for support. "Why does it have to be that way? Why can't they see us as individuals?"

Martha shook her head. "I don't know, Latisha. Albert used to say racism was built into the system. He used to constantly complain about racial profiling and the police union. Unfortunately, it's an unwritten policy that goes on and on. I don't know if it will ever change." Martha handed Latisha another tissue. "But right now I'm more concerned about Shawn. It's going to take all our attention to bring him back into reality. So dry that pretty face of yours and go in there and talk to him. Be positive and maybe something you say will get through to him. I'm going to wait out here for his psychiatrist."

Latisha nodded. After drying her tears, she turned the handle and entered Shawn's room.

****

The harsh winter wind blowing against Robert's face didn't chill him. The cold, wet snowflakes accumulating on his lashes didn't make him blink. He was numb. The cruel reality of death covered him like a blanket. It was two days before Christmas, but the only thing he felt was emptiness.

As he watched the cars creep past him on the slush-covered road, he couldn't help but think about Jamal. Just three days ago, he and Jamal were happy, looking forward to their Christmas vacations. Now he was making plans to attend Jamal's funeral. Jamal's brother, Ali, was coming to transport his body and personal belongings back to Newark. Robert decided to wait outside, rather than inside where every stick of furniture and fiber of carpet shouted Jamal's name.

It was hard, but somehow Robert found the strength to get out of bed and face the grim sadness of the day. Jelin had spent the last two nights comforting and consoling him, convincing him he couldn't spend the rest of his life in mourning. Although Jelin's words spoke of healing and survival, his voice indicated trouble and separation.

A car pulled up and parked next to the curb, and then a man emerged. The man looked up at the dormitory and then approached the revolving front doors. He was taller and a little heavier, but he had the same forceful stride and proud strut as Jamal.

Robert brushed the snow from his face and waved his hand.

The man waved back. "Robert?"

Robert reached out his hand. "Ali?"

"Nice to meet you, Robert."

Ali's voice sounded more like Jamal in person than it did over the phone. "Nice to meet you, too." Robert pushed back tears. He promised himself he wasn't going to cry. He was going to make it through the whole day without crying. "Follow me. I'll take you to Jamal's room."

Robert led Ali into the elevator and up to the twentieth floor. "Jamal's room is down here." Robert wasn't sure if he should refer to Jamal in the present or in the past. "I was going to start packing his things ... but ..."

"I know," Ali answered. "It's still too hard to face the truth. It seems I'm becoming an expert at this. Just a month ago, I packed up my father's things."

Robert opened Jamal's bedroom door. It was the first time he had ventured inside the room since Jamal's death. It seemed strange, almost as if Jamal was still alive. His books were still open on his desk. His sweater was still draped across the back of his chair, and his bed was still unmade. The room was alive with Jamal's spirit.

Ali walked up to Jamal's desk and started removing a few personal belongings. "Robert, can you see that Jamal's clothes and books are given to a local charity? I'm only going to take a few things back with me."

Robert nodded and then sat on Jamal's bed. He remembered all the late-night discussions he and Jamal had sitting on the bed. Jamal had a knack for always knowing the right words to say. Robert wished he knew the right words to say to Ali. "How's your family doing, Ali?" Robert knew it was a stupid question.

"My mother's devastated. I really don't know how she's going to survive losing a husband and a son. We had to hospitalize her." Ali stared into the distance. "Jamal was the light of her eye. He was the great hope of the family. It's funny, Robert. We always believed Jamal was going to be the one to make it."

Agony was engraved on Ali's face.

"In a blink of an eye, Jamal was ripped away from us. Crucified by something we can't understand." Ali pounded his fist against the desk. "We just don't understand what happened here. What happened, Robert?"

Robert shook his head. "I don't know. I keep hoping I'll wake up and all of this will just be a bad dream."

"Now they're saying Jamal was a drug dealer. Do you know how much that hurts our family? Anyone who knew Jamal knows that can't be true."

Robert nodded.

"My family's been contacted by a Judge Patterson. Do you know him?"

"Yes, he's the father of my roommate's girlfriend."

"I'm meeting with him after I leave here. He's agreed to hire a lawyer and take care of all the legal fees. Our family gave him permission to have a private examiner do another autopsy on Jamal's body. I can't tell you how grateful we are. I know we can't bring Jamal back, but at least we can clear his name

"I heard Judge Patterson used to be a top-notch lawyer. If anyone can get to the bottom of this mystery, I'm sure he can."

"It's no mystery, Robert. It was murder. Those damn cops murdered my little brother."

"I know they did, Ali."

"The thought of what those cops did to my brother makes me want to throw up." Ali walked over and raised the window. The cold winter air turned Ali's breath into angry puffs of white smoke.

Ali looked down at the view. "My brother was so happy coming to this city. His dream was finally coming together. Did you know Jamal planned on going to graduate school at Wharton?"

"Yeah, I know," Robert answered sadly.

Ali turned around to face Robert. "After he got his master's degree, he planned to return to Newark. He wanted to open up a community outreach center for small minority businesses. That was my brother, always trying to help someone. Always fighting for the underdog. He was determined to transform Newark into the promised land. But all his hopes and dreams are gone now. Beat out of him by a bunch of racist cops." Ali paused and then shook his head in disbelief. "They didn't think his life was worth spit! No, they couldn't see the person my brother really was. I keep having these visions. Visions of my brother lying against that cold cement road, begging for his life. Pleading for those cops to listen to him. But they wouldn't listen. They didn't give a damn. For God's sakes, Robert. He was only eighteen! His life was just beginning."

"Listen to me, Ali!" Robert pulled Ali away from the window. "We have to keep Jamal's dreams alive. We can't let them take his dreams away too." Robert embraced Ali, and they cried together.

After gathering himself, Ali took one final look around the room. "Well, I think I have everything I need. I better go. I have to meet with Judge Patterson before my flight back to Newark."

"How about his journal?" Robert picked up Jamal's journal from the floor.

Ali took the journal and flipped through the gold leaf pages. "Why don't you keep this?" He handed the journal to Robert. "I think you and Shawn might get more out of it than my family."

"Thanks. It will be nice having something to remember Jamal by."

Ali placed the remainder of Jamal's personal belongings inside a duffel bag. "I can see why my brother spoke so highly of you, Robert. I hope you and Shawn can make it to the funeral next week."

"I'll be there, but I don't know about Shawn. He's still in the hospital."

"Yeah, Judge Patterson told us. We're all praying for him."

Robert walked Ali to the door.

"You don't need to take me to the lobby. I remember how to get there."

"All right." Robert gave Ali a final hug. "I'll see you next week."

"Bye, Robert."

"Bye, Ali."

After Ali disappeared into the elevator, Robert closed the door and looked at Jamal's journal. A strange sensation forced him to read Jamal's words. He opened the journal and stared at the inscription written inside the cover.

> To my son,
>
> Whenever you pick up this journal,
> know I am with you.
>
> Love,
> Your father, Lloyd

Robert began reading and was surprised by the detailed information Jamal included in the journal. He read about Jamal's family. Jamal's struggle with his father's death. Jamal's attempt to pay the hospital bills. He read about Jamal's desire to bring his two roommates together as friends, and Jamal's knowledge of his relationship with Jelin. Finally, he read about Jamal's decision to accept Coach Green's money and his fateful decision to return it.

The date of the last entry was written the night of Jamal's death. Robert finally understood where Jamal was headed that night. He was returning the money to Coach Green.

Robert closed the book and walked over to the window. The snow had stopped, and a ray of light was streaming through a small opening between the dark clouds. "I know what you want me to do, Jamal." Robert directed his voice to the ray of light. "I know what I have to do."

CHAPTER 30

Coach Green walked down the hallway of Allegheny Memorial Hospital until he came to the gold nameplate that read Dr. Dan James, Cardiologist. He lightly knocked on the door.

"Come in."

"Dr. James?"

"Yes."

"I'm Melvin Green. Shawn Collins's basketball coach."

"I got the message you called, Mr. Green. Come in and have a seat."

Coach Green shook the doctor's hand. "Call me, Melvin."

"What can I do for you, Melvin?"

"I was hoping you could update me on Shawn's condition. I understand he's going to be all right, but I needed to hear the news firsthand from his doctor."

Dr. James removed his glasses and laid them against the top of his desk. "We've updated Shawn's condition to stable. His cardiomyopathy isn't as severe as we once believed. We're very optimistic about his physical prognosis. But of course, you know his basketball-playing days are over."

Coach Green nodded. "You say his physical prognosis looks good?"

"It's his mental condition that has us concerned."

"His mental condition?"

"Shawn's suffering from a condition known as post-traumatic shock. He knows he can't play basketball anymore and then that awful news about his roommate's tragic death." Doctor James shook his head. "It was too much for Shawn to handle. He totally shut himself down. Refuses to accept reality."

"What are you telling me, Doctor? Has Shawn gone crazy?"

Dr. James narrowed his eyes and looked at Coach Green curiously. "What I'm saying is Shawn's blocking out the tragic events. It's not an uncommon reaction under the circumstances. When someone experiences events in their lives that are too horrible to think about, the mind has a way of blocking those events out. It's a defense mechanism in which the existence of unpleasant realities is kept out of conscious awareness."

"Shawn's repressing what happened to him?"

"No, not exactly. Repression stems from an internal source such as a fantasy or an impulse. Shawn's pain stems from external sources. The end of his basketball career and the death of his roommate being the sources. Usually the patient is able to snap back into reality pretty quickly. But in some cases, such as Shawn's, it takes a little longer."

"How much longer?"

"I can't answer that. But I can tell you Shawn's under the care of a renowned psychiatrist."

"Has Shawn said anything about what happened?"

"Other than asking for his mother when he was first brought into to the emergency room, Shawn hasn't said more than two words."

Relief flashed across Coach Green's face. "Is it all right if I visit him?"

"Of course. Shawn's in room 504. But, Melvin, make sure you only discuss positive things. Things Shawn might like to hear. Whatever you do, don't mention anything about Shawn's replacement on the team. I'm afraid if Shawn hears any more negative news, it might push him even further into withdrawal."

Coach Green nodded. "I understand, Doc. Don't worry. I know just what to say to Shawn."

"Good. Shawn needs all the positive encouragement he can get."

Coach Green shook the doctor's hand. "Thanks for seeing me."

"My pleasure. And good luck in the Christmas Tournament tomorrow night, Melvin."

"Thanks, Doc. Without Shawn in the lineup, we're definitely going to need it. Good-bye."

"Good-bye, Melvin."

Coach Green exited the office and headed for room 504. After reaching the room, he pushed open the door and stepped inside. He walked up to the side of Shawn's bed.

"Shawn are you awake?"

Shawn didn't flinch; not even a blink crossed his face.

Coach Green scrutinized his stolid face. Shawn was awake but focused on the frozen river outside his window.

Coach Green stepped in front of the window, blocking Shawn's view. "Shawn, it's me."

Shawn blinked but made no acknowledgment of the coach's presence.

"Shawn, I know you can hear me. I'm going to say what I came here to say, then leave so you can get some rest. Okay, big guy?"

Shawn continued his blank stare.

"I hate like hell what happened to you. I hope you can believe that. But life must go on. It must go on for you, it must go on for me, and it must go on for the team. It's my responsibility to move the team forward. Even without you, I'm still expected to win the Christmas Tournament and the Big Central division title. Do you know how difficult that's gonna be without my ace guard?"

Shawn showed no response to the coach's patronizing tone.

"I'm sure you know we play the Huskies tomorrow night in the finals. The guys dedicated the tournament to you. They even sewed a patch with your number eleven onto their jerseys." Coach Green touched Shawn's shoulder. "We need your support, Shawn. Your support would go a long way in helping the team win the tournament. Do you think you're strong enough to give the team a little pep talk? I brought a tape recorder with me."

Shawn blinked but made no acknowledgment of the coach's request.

"I know it was your dream to win the Christmas Tournament and to capture the NCAA crown. It was our dream together. Remember? We can still have that dream, Shawn. If you don't want to talk to the team, I understand. But I do need you to do one thing for me."

Shawn closed his eyes.

Coach Green bent down and whispered into Shawn's ear. "I need you to keep your mouth shut. Keep your mouth shut about all the things I did for you. You remember, don't you? The fake SAT score, the car, the money, the payoff to Jamal. Nobody needs to know about those things. I want your agreement to keep it that way. Do you understand me? Do you hear what I'm saying, Shawn?"

Shawn turned away.

Coach Green grabbed Shawn by the shoulder. "Listen to me, Shawn. If word gets out about our little arrangement, the Tigers will be sanctioned. Do you know what that means? No post-season play. No Big Central Championship. And it will be all your fault." Coach Green lowered his voice and spoke through gritted teeth. "Is that what you want, Shawn? Huh? Answer me, goddamn it! Do you want all that guilt hanging over your head?" He let go of Shawn's shoulder.

Shawn buried his face in his pillow.

Coach Green walked away from the bed and looked out the window at the frozen river below. He turned around to face the situation at hand. "Do you want Jelin to lose his shot at making the pros?" He inched closer to the bed and lowered his voice. "Did you hear what I said, Shawn? Do you want Jelin to have a shot at making the pros?" He paused to let the words sink in. "You see; I can deny him that chance. I found out some very interesting news about your best friend." He bent down closer so he could whisper directly into Shawn's ear. "Did you know Jelin was a faggot? Did you know he was sleeping around with your roommate, Robert? Well, I have proof. Right here in my pocket."

Coach Green removed a copy of the letter and waved it in the air.

"It's all right here in Jelin's own handwriting. There's no way he can deny it. That's why I had a little talk with Jelin. And guess what? He's agreed to keep his mouth shut. And as long as you agree to do the same, we won't have any problems. Do you get my drift?"

Shawn looked up at Coach Green.

"Remember, Shawn—you're as guilty as I am. I didn't twist your arm to accept that car or the money. So if I go down, I'm taking you, Jelin, and your mother with me." He stared into Shawn's empty face. "Your mother's not stupid; she knew what was going on."

Shawn's face remained void of expression.

"By the way, this is your copy of Jelin's letter. I thought you might enjoy some reading material while you're stuck here in the hospital." Coach Green threw the letter on Shawn's bed. "I'm warning you. Don't push me, Shawn. I'm not playing any games this time."

Coach Green walked toward the door and then turned around. "Oh yeah, I almost forgot. Make sure you watch the game tomorrow night.

Your replacement, Quadre Jones, has filled your position like a pro. We don't need you after all." Coach Green grinned and then walked out of the room.

****

Robert glanced at his bus ticket. He found it hard to believe he was looking forward to returning to a place he once despised. His bus was scheduled to leave the following day, Christmas Eve. He planned to spend Christmas Day with his family then fly to Newark for Jamal's funeral. But before he left, there was something he needed to do.

"Robert, you have a lot to offer this world, but they've made you too damn scared to come out into the light."

Robert had decided to come into the light. He had decided to make the information in Jamal's journal public. He knew it meant exposing Shawn's activities with Coach Green and announcing Jelin's sexuality to the world, but it was something he had to do for Jamal.

He looked at his watch; it was a quarter after three. He had made arrangements to meet Jelin in their private rendezvous location at three thirty. Although his plan could derail Jelin's dreams and end their relationship, it was time they stopped being victims and started fighting back. He put on his coat and headed for the Omni Center.

****

Robert approached the double doors to the small practice gym. The dull thud of a basketball bounced against the hardwood floor. He looked through the windows. It seemed odd Jelin was in the open shooting baskets. Usually he'd be hiding underneath the shadows of the bleachers. Robert pushed open the double doors and stepped inside. He smiled as Jelin dashed across the floor to retrieve a rebound.

He took a seat on the bleachers and watched as Jelin continued to shoot baskets. Jelin was doing what he loved most in the world, playing basketball. Unfortunately, he was about to ask Jelin to sacrifice that love.

"Hey Robert how about a game? You and me, one on one?"

Robert pointed to himself. "Me? I'm awful."

"No you're not. You just haven't practiced enough." Jelin dribbled the ball between his legs. "I've been practicing this game since I was ten years old. I finally have my jump shot perfected." He connected on a fifteen-foot jump shot. "See, it's all in the flick of the wrist and the arc of the ball."

The ball swished through the net and rolled toward Robert's feet. He picked up the ball and heaved it at the basket. His shot missed the basket and the entire backboard.

"Robert, you throw like a girl. That's all wrong." Jelin retrieved the rebound. "First, you have to center the ball in your hands. See these veins in the skin of the ball, that's what they're for. Use the veins to find a comfortable position in your hand. Aim at the target, then release." Jelin threw the ball over to Robert. "Try again."

Robert followed Jelin's instructions. He positioned the ball in his hand, concentrated on his target, and attempted a short ten-footer. He was surprised to see the ball go through the hoop.

"I knew you could do it if you tried."

Robert smiled. "I wish everything could be that simple."

"Yeah, I know. It's easy when you don't have any opposition." Jelin slammed a dunk shot.

Robert nodded.

Jelin demonstrated a fancy behind-the-back dribble and then looked over at Robert. "Coach Green knows about us, Robert."

"What?" Robert's word echoed off the walls.

"He called me into his office yesterday and gave me an ultimatum."

"An ultimatum. Wait a minute, how did he … find out?"

Jelin faked out his imaginary opponent, drove the lane, and then gently laid the ball into the hoop. He dribbled the ball back to the foul line. "You remember that letter I lost? The letter where I confessed my feelings for you?"

"I remember."

"I didn't lose it in my dorm room. It fell out of my gym bag in the locker room. Coach Green found it." Jelin dribbled the ball and looked up at the backboard.

Robert was speechless. He wished Jelin would look at him.

"He called me a faggot, Robert. Do you know how that made me feel?" Jelin finally looked over at Robert.

"I'm sorry, Jelin." Robert couldn't maintain eye contact. Being called a faggot was Jelin's worst fear. He wished he could think of something comforting to say, but his mind was too cluttered with emotion.

"Coach Green read my words to you, Robert." Jelin attempted a three-point shot, but his aim was off. "He knows about our relationship."

Robert swallowed. "What did you say?"

Jelin retrieved his rebound. "What do you think I said? He threatened to end my career. He threatened to use the letter against me if I didn't keep my mouth shut."

"He threatened you?"

Jelin bounced the ball twice and looked up at Robert. "Did you know Coach Green was paying Jamal to take Shawn's tests?"

"Yeah, I knew."

"He's blackmailing me. He said if I told anyone about the money or the car, he'd release the letter to the press." Jelin turned and took another jump shot.

The ball bounced off the rim. "So you agreed?"

"Robert, you know how important basketball is to me."

"Yeah, I know."

Jelin retrieved the ball and then walked over and sat next to Robert on the bleachers. "Well, I still feel that way. I told Coach Green I'd keep my mouth shut. As long as he kept my secret."

Robert shook his head no.

"But I've had some time to think about my decision." Jelin placed the basketball on the seat between them. "I've decided I can't play for a man like Coach Green. I can't play for a man I don't respect. A man that would risk the health of one of his players in order to win a damn basketball game." Jelin paused. "So last night I made a couple phone calls."

Robert avoided Jelin's eyes. He didn't want to know. He didn't want to know who Jelin called.

"The coach at UCLA is still interested in me."

The words penetrated Robert's body like bullets.

"I've decided to transfer to UCLA. I'm going to sit out the rest of this year and join the Bruins next season as a red-shirted junior."

One of the bullets penetrated Robert's heart. "What about Coach Green?"

"Fuck Coach Green. I'm going to make it clear—if he outs me, I'll out him. He's a coward, Robert. I'm not afraid of his weak ass."

"What about us?" Robert held back tears.

"Robert, you once said if you had to let me go, you would."

Robert closed his eyes and felt his tears.

"Maybe one day we can be together. But now is not the right time."

"Will there ever be a right time, Jelin?" A tear rolled down his cheek.

"I'm not saying it's over." Jelin wiped the tear from Robert's face. "I'm just saying you have to give me two years. You have to give me time to have my shot at the pros. To have my shot at my dream. We'll stay in touch. We can see each other during spring break and over summer vacations. You can come out to California."

"Then what, Jelin?" Robert wiped away his tears. "Will I have to hide in your room? Or maybe you can tell everyone I'm your cousin. Jelin, I can't deny myself any longer. I won't." Robert turned away.

"Robert, don't take this attitude." Jelin turned Robert around to face him. "I'm just asking for some time."

"And what happens after you make it into the pros?" Robert shoved Jelin in frustration.

Jelin didn't answer.

"What's that going to change? You'll just come up with another excuse why we can't be together. What would your fans say? What would your sponsors say?" Robert paused. "Jelin, why can't you just accept the fact that you're gay!"

Jelin froze. He looked Robert in the eye. "I do accept it. But that doesn't mean I have to give up my life because of it!"

Robert stood up. "What about Jamal? He gave up his life. He gave up his life because he stood for something! He stood for what's right and decent in this world. Now they're trying to drag his name through the mud. And you're not only letting them; you're helping them ... because you want to protect your damn image!"

Jelin stood and grabbed Robert's shoulder. "What am I supposed to do? I can't bring Jamal back. Nobody can!"

"Maybe we can't bring him back, but we can save his name and let him rest in peace."

"Rest in peace? C'mon, Robert." Jelin pushed Robert away.

Robert grabbed Jelin's warm-up jacket. "Jamal left a journal. He described everything that happened. His agreement with Coach Green, the money, the car, where he was headed the night of his death. Did you know he was returning the money to Coach Green? It's evidence, Jelin. Evidence in Jamal's own handwriting. We have the power to clear Jamal's name and bring his killers to justice."

"And what about my name?" Jelin snatched his jacket from Robert's grasp. "Did Jamal mention anything about our relationship in that journal?"

Robert looked up at Jelin but didn't answer.

"He did, didn't he? Jelin looked away then turned back. "That information could destroy me!" Jelin glared at Robert. "Is that what you want? You want to destroy me!"

"No, I don't want to destroy you. I want to save Jamal."

"Jamal's dead!" Jelin shouted.

"Jamal will never be dead. Not for me! Jamal lives in my heart." Robert beat his fist against his chest. "He was the only person who accepted me. He made me see the good inside of me. He taught me how to fight."

"So who are you fighting, Robert? You're fighting me. I thought you loved me!"

"I do love you, Jelin." Robert picked up the basketball from the bleachers and threw it across the gym. "But I'm finally starting to love myself too."

"So you're gonna make our relationship public and drag my name through the mud?"

Robert watched the ball roll into the shadows. "Jelin, I'm tired of living in the shadows where I don't belong. Afraid of what people might say or think about me. I'm tired of feeling trapped, always looking for a way to escape. I've done that all my life. Now it's time I stand up and fight."

Jelin looked at Robert with bewilderment. "Robert, I understand where you're coming from, but I'm just not ready yet."

"Don't you see, Jelin? You'll never be ready."

"Robert, what do you want from me?"

"I want your support. I want you to come with me to see Shawn. To convince Shawn to tell the truth. It's time we expose Coach Green for what he is. A low-down, cold-blooded leach. He's the one who almost killed Shawn. He's the one responsible for Jamal's death. He's the one driving us apart." Robert reached out to Jelin. "It's time we stopped being Coach Green's victims."

"I can't Robert." Jelin stepped back. "I won't stop you from doing what you think you have to do, but I can't support you. I'm sorry. This is all too much for me. I never asked for all this. I want to live my life in private, not splattered across some fuckin' headline."

"Jelin, listen—"

"No, Robert, you listen. My mind's made up. I'm leaving. I'm getting the hell out of this place. As far away as I can get. You go carry your banner for honor and righteousness. Do what you think you have to do. But do me one favor. Wait until I'm gone. Hopefully I'll be far enough away, I won't get damaged by all this … mess." Jelin turned and walked away.

Robert wanted to beg Jelin to stay. He wanted to tell Jelin he understood his fears. But he knew their lives had come to a crossroads. Jelin wanted to live his life behind a wall, cloaked between reality and fantasy. Robert wanted to live his life in the light, free from the hiding places that provided a false security.

Robert watched the man he loved head for the exit. He knew once Jelin walked out the door, he'd be walking out of his life.

"Jelin!"

Jelin stopped and turned around.

"Do you remember the last time we were together, here in this gymnasium?"

Jelin nodded. "I remember."

"You said you loved me. Before you walk out of that door and out my life, I need to know. Did you mean it?"

Jelin retrieved the basketball from the corner. He bounced the ball twice against the floor and then looked up at Robert. "Yeah, I meant it."

"If you love me, then why are you leaving me?"

Jelin looked down at the ball. "Robert, when I told you I loved you, I started to say something else, remember?"

Robert slowly nodded.

"I was going to tell you, you made me happier than anyone else in the world. But I didn't finish the sentence. Do you know why?"

Robert shook his head no.

"Because I knew I had another love." Jelin twirled the basketball on his index finger. "Another love by the name of basketball. I've been in love with her since I was ten years old. And she loves me back. See how gracefully she dances on my finger? She does whatever I tell her to do. She's always there for me, and no one condemns me for loving her. She's an easy lover." Jelin looked up at Robert.

Robert looked away.

"Your love is hard, Robert. It tears at my pride. It challenges my manhood. It makes me doubt who I am." Jelin walked up to Robert and touched his face. "I love you, Robert. Lord knows I do. But if I choose your love, the doors will close on my career. I can't let that happen."

The air deflated from Robert's body. Jelin was going to leave him just as he found him—empty and alone.

"I know deep down inside you agree with me, Robert. You know it's best if I leave. I can't give you what you need, what you deserve to have. We'd only end up resenting each other."

"Can't we at least try?" Robert grabbed Jelin's hand.

Jelin shook his hand loose. "No, bro. It won't work. You see, it's all about image. To be the next Michael Jordan or Kobe Bryant, I have to have an image. I can be that all-American wholesome boy next door. Or I can be that bad boy with an attitude. But I can't be that boy in love with another boy. That image won't fly. That's why I've created this illusion. I won't be a person. I'll be a number. I'll give the fans what they wanna see. What they expect to see. I'll keep hiding behind my illusion, pretending to be something I'm not. On the outside, I'll be number thirty-four … but on the inside … I'll still be loving you."

Robert looked up into Jelin's eyes. "And I'll still be loving you."

Jelin dribbled the ball against the floor, positioned the ball in his hand, and aimed at his target.

Robert watched the ball fall through the net. He turned his head in time to see Jelin exit through the doors.

CHAPTER 31

R obert opened the door to Shawn's hospital room. "Mrs. Collins? Is it all right if I come in?"

"Of course, Robert. C'mon in."

"How's Shawn doing?" Has there been any change?"

Martha looked at Shawn's peaceful face. "No, not really. The doctors say we just have to wait. Give him time."

"Time for what?" Robert asked.

"Time for him to accept what happened … and …"

"And what happened to Jamal?"

Martha nodded. "There is some good news. Shawn's cardiomyopathy isn't as severe as the doctors once believed. They expect him to make a full recovery as long as he takes his medication and avoids strenuous activity."

"Mrs. Collins, is it true Coach Green knew about Shawn's illness?"

Martha closed her eyes and nodded. "I still can't believe what that man did to my son."

Robert bit down on his lip. He wanted to tell Martha the truth. The list of people Coach Green hurt included more than just Shawn.

"He's sleeping right now, but when he's awake, all he does is look out the window at that frozen river down there. I keep hoping he'll open up and talk to me."

"Has he talked at all?" Robert asked.

"No, not a word."

Robert wanted to tell Martha about the information in Jamal's journal, but he needed to talk with Shawn first.

"The doctors say the smallest ray of hope may trigger a positive reaction. I keep racking my brain, trying to figure out what that ray of hope might be."

Robert wondered if Jamal's words could be that ray of hope. He hoped to get a minute alone with Shawn so he could discuss the journal before he left. "I'm leaving for home tomorrow evening, Mrs. Collins. I just stopped by to tell Shawn good-bye. I'm not sure I'll be returning next semester."

Martha looked into Robert's eyes. "I'm sorry to hear that, Robert. But I know this has been a very difficult semester for you. It's been difficult for all of us." She stood from her chair. "Have a seat. I'll give you some privacy to say your good-byes. I'm gonna get a cup of coffee and make a few phone calls." She placed her hand on Robert's shoulder. "If I don't see you before you leave, have a happy holiday. For what it's worth, I hope you decide to come back next semester. I'm sure Shawn would like that too." Martha gave Robert a hug before leaving the room.

Robert watched Mrs. Collins walk out of the room. He took a deep breath and then looked down at Shawn. "I'm sure you'd be happier if you never saw me again."

Shawn opened his eyes.

"So you are awake."

Shawn blinked, but his stare remained vacant.

"Shawn, you really need to talk to your mother. She's worried sick about you. We all are."

Shawn showed no reaction.

"Listen, Shawn. I know you don't like me. I'm not gonna stand here and pretend you do. The reason I'm here is to talk about doing something for Jamal." Robert hoped the mention of Jamal's name would spark a reaction, but Shawn remained listless.

"I know it's hard to accept Jamal's death. But, Shawn, you have to go on with your life. We all do. That's what Jamal would have wanted." Robert paused. Jamal's spirit had entered his body and was directing his words.

"Jamal's memory lives on. It lives on in you, and it lives on in me. That's something you and I share. A common memory of someone we both cared for. Someone we'll both miss." Robert shook his head. "Shawn, can't we put our differences aside, just this once, and focus on that common bond that ties us together?"

Shawn continued to look past Robert out the window.

Robert turned and looked out the window. He wanted to know what had captured Shawn's attention. The water had broken through cracks in the ice, causing the river to flow once again. But now the angry river carried big chunks of ice downstream.

"It's beautiful—isn't it, Shawn?"

Shawn didn't respond.

Robert wanted to give up, but the spirit of Jamal urged him on.

"It's beautiful seeing something you thought was trapped break free." Robert removed his coat and sat on the chair next to Shawn's bedside. "That's how I felt for a long time. Trapped." Robert looked down at his feet. "I know you hate me because of my sexuality. Hell, I hated myself. I hated myself so much I withdrew from the world. I hid inside a box in the corner of my mind. I allowed my pride and my self-esteem to be stripped away from me." Robert's voice quivered with emotion. "I didn't think I deserved them."

The spirit of Jamal carefully chose his every word.

"But Jamal made me realize that I do deserve those things. He made me realize my sexuality doesn't make me a bad person, and I don't have to hide anymore. Jamal taught me to never let anything get taken away from me again. Not without a fight." Robert balled his hands into fists and placed them against the side of Shawn's bed. "But now they've taken Jamal away, and it hurts, Shawn! I hurt just as much as you do. But don't you see? The pain we share over Jamal's death is the bond that ties us together. It's a bond stronger than hate. It's Jamal's legacy he left us. Now, the question is, what are we going to do with that legacy? Are we going to continue to let our differences divide us? Or are we going to stand together and fight for something that was taken from us?"

Tears formed in the corners of Shawn's eyes, and his lips quivered, but he remained silent.

"Shawn, the night of Jamal's death, he was returning the $12,000 to Coach Green. He didn't want to be another one of Coach Green's victims. He didn't want to be like us. All our lives we've let other people control us … tell us what to do and when to do it. It's ironic, but Jamal was killed because he didn't want to be like us."

Robert pulled his chair closer to Shawn's bedside and removed the journal from his pocket.

"Shawn, together we can be a strong force. Jamal left a journal. He described the deal he made with Coach Green to keep you eligible to play on the team. I have the journal. I have it right here. Together we can expose Coach Green. We can tell the world how Coach Green destroyed so many lives. But the best thing is we can clear Jamal's name. The police are saying Jamal was a drug dealer. With your testimony and the words Jamal wrote in this journal, we can prove why he had $12,000 on him the night of his death. We can prove Jamal wasn't a drug dealer. We can bring the officers who murdered him to justice."

Robert placed the journal on Shawn's bed. "Unfortunately, the journal also exposes your wrongdoing. You'll have to admit all the things you allowed Coach Green to do for you. You'll have to admit it all." Robert took a deep breath. "There's something I'll have to admit, also."

Robert looked down at his feet. "Shawn, I know you figured out that I'm gay. I've tried to hide that fact from myself for a long time. But not anymore. I'm not afraid to tell the world that I'm gay, but I am afraid to tell them that ... that I ... that I've been having a relationship with Jelin."

When he didn't hear a reaction from Shawn, he looked up. Shawn's face remained void of emotion, but Robert noticed a glimmer of reaction ignite in Shawn's eyes. He didn't know if he had kindled a firestorm of hope or stroked the embers of hate. But it was evident Shawn was listening.

Jamal's spirit pushed him to the finish line.

"Shawn, we all have broken places. You, me, and Jelin. But they say when you heal, you heal strongest in your broken places. It's time we heal, Shawn." Robert looked into Shawn's eyes. "It time we become strong."

Shawn looked at Robert but remained silent.

"Jelin knows about the journal. He knows it describes our relationship, and he knows I want to make the information public. I discussed it with Jelin before coming here. I tried to convince him to come with me." Robert paused. "Jelin couldn't face you with the truth. He treasures your friendship and couldn't bear the thought of losing it."

Robert took a deep breath to gain control of his emotions. "But Jelin is being strong. He's moving to California after the holidays. He's gonna play for UCLA. He said he can't play for a man like Coach Green. A man that almost killed his best friend. He knows the information in the journal may ruin his career, but he said he wouldn't stop me from making it public. He's gonna take his chances in California."

Robert stood from the chair and placed the journal in Shawn's hand. "Jelin made his decision. He's not going to remain a puppet on Coach Green's strings. Now it's your turn, Shawn. It's your decision whether we remain victims or stand united and fight."

After getting no response from Shawn, Robert reached for his coat. "I'm going home for the holidays. My bus leaves tomorrow evening at eight thirty. If you need to reach me, I wrote my home number on a piece of paper inside the journal. You have a lot to think about, Shawn. I'm gonna leave you alone." Robert put on his coat and walked toward the door.

"Good-bye, Shawn. I really wish we could have been friends."

****

Shawn watched Robert leave. He regretted the way he treated Robert. From the first day they met, Robert tried to be his friend, but he pushed Robert away. He couldn't be seen hanging out with someone the entire campus knew was gay. Shawn laugh to himself. In the back of his mind, he always knew Jelin was gay. He remembered that night many years ago. That night he and Jelin camped out in the backyard. They pitched a tent under the old maple tree and stayed up half the night talking. He remembered Jelin explaining how babies were made.

"If you do it hard, it makes a boy. If you do it soft, it makes a girl."

He remembered Jelin crawling on top of him and doing it hard. It only happened that one time, and they never discussed it again. But he knew Jelin never grew out of those feelings. He knew Jelin looked at boys differently than he did. But Jelin kept his sexuality a secret, and as long as he kept it a secret, it hadn't mattered.

Shawn remembered the William Lynch story Jamal told him. How William Lynch kept his slaves divided by exploiting their differences. Shawn shook his head. He wasn't going to let William Lynch win. Jelin and Robert were his true friends. They were the only ones who supported him when he was down. But he was driving his true friends away. He looked down at the gold leaf book in his hand. He wasn't going to let their differences keep them divided. All the emotions bottled up inside of him exploded in his head and escaped through his tear ducts. For the first time in eight years, he cried.

His emotion changed to anger. Coach Green destroyed his life, and now he was threatening to destroy the lives of everyone around him. Shawn opened the journal and read the inscription.

> Whenever you pick up this journal,
> know I am with you.

He turned to the page dated September 7.

September 7

I met my roommates for the first time today. I don't think they're going to get along. I think Robert's gay and Shawn's homophobic. It's going to be hard, but I'm determined to make them friends before the end of the semester. I've got to make them understand that the bond of friendship is stronger than the bond of hate.

September 21

I met Shawn's mother and little brother today. It's Shawn's dream to be a superstar. But all he needs to do is look into his little brother's eyes, and he would see he's already a superstar. I wonder why Shawn can't see that.

October 14

I received a letter from home today. My father has lung cancer. I have to find a way to help pay the medical bills.

October 27

Shawn's girlfriend, Latisha, has a kind heart and a generous soul. She's agreed to tighten my dreads in exchange for a ticket to Shawn's game. I wish Latisha could see the good inside of her. I believe she truly loves Shawn, but she needs to understand she doesn't need Shawn to fulfill her dreams.

November 11

Today Shawn almost found out the meaning of responsibility. He was fortunate Latisha's plan didn't work. If it had, Shawn would be a father in nine months. I believe Shawn's luck is running out. Eventually, someone is going to hold him responsible for his actions. Shawn's not prepared to handle responsibility. The day he's forced to handle it will be a sad day.

November 20

I just left a meeting with Shawn's coach. He made me an offer. If I agree to take three of Shawn's final exams, he'll pay Dad's entire hospital bill. Now I know what it feels like to come face to face with the devil. I really don't want to accept the coach's offer, but I don't have a choice. I'm flying home over the weekend to visit the family. I'll make my decision after I get back.

November 24

Dad died today. I've never felt so much pain. My family needs me now more than ever.

December 3

I decided to accept Coach Green's offer but on my terms. I've devised a plan that will allow Shawn to get his education. It will be hard living with the knowledge that I helped him cheat, but I couldn't live with myself knowing I took away his educational opportunity.

December 5

I tried to make Shawn understand the importance of his education. God forbid if something happened to him and he could no longer play basketball. Shawn believes everything should be handed to him on a silver platter. He doesn't realize that platter has strings attached. Coach Green is pulling those strings tighter and tighter. Eventually, Shawn's going to be his puppet. I'm afraid Shawn's going to end up being another one of those pathetic souls I see standing on the street corners hopelessly clinging to their lost splendor.

December 12

I think Robert and Jelin are involved in a relationship. I'm happy for Robert. He's such a sad person. I wish I could make him understand his sexuality doesn't make him a bad person. I hope Shawn doesn't find out about the relationship. I don't know what he'll do.

December 17

Robert opened up to me today and told me the reason for his sadness. Because of his sexuality, he allowed his pride and self-respect to be ripped away from him. He was in love with his best friend at boarding school. A priest found out and forced Robert to expose the relationship. Robert was petrified of his sexuality. He believed if he admitted he was gay, he would burn in hell. So he blamed the entire affair on his friend. Later that night, his friend committed suicide. Robert feels responsible for the death of his friend. He's been carrying around guilt and self-hatred for three years. Robert's living among the shadows of his past, afraid to stand up for himself. I've tried to convince him to stop being a victim. Not to let anyone take something away from him again without a fight. I think eventually, Robert will gain back those things he lost. I think Robert will come back into the light.

December 19

Today was the day I took two of Shawn's exams. Shawn doesn't know I switched the exams. I handed in his copies, not mine. I looked at Shawn's answers. I'm positive he did well. I can't wait to tell him he passed both exams on his own. Maybe now I can finally convince Shawn that basketball doesn't have to be his only road to success. Maybe I can prove to him he has a brain.

December 19 (Revision)

This nightmare must end. I'm returning the $12,000 to Coach Green's house tonight. I wrapped the money up like a Christmas present, and I'm going to use the BMW he bought Shawn to drive to his house in Fox Hills. I'll drop the present off while he's coaching the Bobcat game tonight. I refuse to be another one of Coach Green's victims.

After reading the last entry, Shawn closed the journal. He remembered the last time he saw Jamal. The day Jamal had taken his Management and Psychology exams. Jamal had looked up at him with a wink and a smile.

Shawn shook his head. Jamal had been proud of him. For the first time in his life, someone was proud of him for something other than his athletic abilities. He couldn't let Jamal be buried under the label of a drug dealer. Jamal was a true hero.

"We'll see who gets destroyed, Coach Green."

Shawn opened the drawer to his nightstand and pulled out a telephone book. After finding Judge Patterson's number at the courthouse, he reached for the phone.

Martha entered Shawn's room and dropped her Styrofoam coffee cup against the floor.

Shawn handed his mother the phone.

"Call Judge Patterson. I have a lot to say, and I want you both to hear it together."

CHAPTER 32

Shawn noticed Jelin pacing back and forth outside his hospital room and motioned him in.

"Come in, Jelin. I'm watching the game."

Jelin eased into the room and sat down on the chair next to Shawn's bed. "What's the score?"

"Seventy-four to eighty-two, Tigers," Shawn answered, avoiding direct eye contact with Jelin.

Jelin looked up at the screen. "It looks like Coach Green's gonna get his wish. He's finally gonna win the Christmas Tournament."

"Yeah, with a weak starting lineup of Quadre Jones and Brian Short, two assholes."

Jelin tried to laugh. "Shawn … I really don't want to talk about the game. We need to discuss—"

Shawn interrupted him. "Look at Coach Green's face. He's such an asshole."

"The Tigers are up by ten points, and there's only a minute left in the game. He's a winner, Shawn. He's the winner, and we're the losers."

"Is that what you think, Jelin? You think we're losers?"

Jelin ran his hand across his freshly shaved head. "Listen, Shawn. I didn't come here to talk about Coach Green. I stopped by to say good-bye. I'm leaving for Los Angeles after the holidays. I've decided to play for the Bruins."

"Yeah, I heard."

"I can't play for Coach Green anymore. That man valued a damn basketball game over your life. The life of my best friend. How could I play for someone like that?"

"Jelin, I allowed Coach Green to treat me like that. I danced on his string like a damn puppet. I danced until I got choked."

"I got choked too. Now I've got to get away." Jelin folded his hands together and leaned toward Shawn's bed. "Coach Green threatened to destroy my reputation if I didn't do what he asked." Jelin looked up at the screen. "I'd rather have no career than do what that bastard wants me to do."

Shawn appeared absorbed in the final seconds of the game.

"Shawn, did you hear me?"

The final buzzer sounded, and Shawn broke out in a huge smile. "Look at that fool frontin'. Jumpin' up and down, actin' like he's king of the fuckin' world. I hope that bastard enjoys his moment in the spotlight because it's all about to end."

"Shawn, you're not making any sense." Jelin pointed to the TV. "That man used us. Now he's basking in the spotlight, and we're the ones paying the price."

The smile faded from Shawn's lips. "Jamal told me one day I'd wake up and realize the price I paid. I never imagined it would be my health."

"Shawn, I just came to say good-bye. I'll call you from LA next week."

Shawn finally looked at Jelin. "Wait, Jelin. Don't go. Not until you hear what I have to say. I know about Coach Green's threats, and I know about your relationship with Robert."

'What?"

"I know, Jelin."

Jelin regurgitated a rehearsed line. "Shawn, I know it's hard to understand how I could have feelings for another man. I don't understand them myself. But I didn't come here to explain my sexual preference. I just came to say good-bye. I want us to part as friends." Jelin stood to leave. "I don't wanna screw up your image like I have mine."

"My image ... that's a fuckin joke. What kind of image do I have? Look at me, Jelin. I'm lying here in this damn hospital bed, flat on my back, watching my team play before a nationwide audience. A team I helped get there based on my blind stupidity! You know what type of image I have? The image of a fool."

"You're nobody's fool, Shawn."

Shawn looked up at the screen. "I was Coach Green's fool. I did everything he asked. I believed he had my back. I believed he was lookin' out for me. I let him control everything. He decided my major, he picked out my classes, and he bought my books. Hell, he even selected the type of car I would drive. But now I know the truth." Shawn shook his head. "The only thing he was lookin' out for was his damn self. He exploited me, and like a damn fool, I let him." Shawn looked over at Jelin. "I may have been Coach Green's fool, but I'll be damned if I'm gonna be William Lynch's fool."

"William Lynch?"

"Jelin, I'm not gonna let our differences divide us. You're my friend, goddamn it. You've been my friend since kindergarten. I'm not letting you move to LA."

"Shawn, didn't Robert tell you? I'm gay!"

"He told me. So the fuck what."

Jelin sat back down. "What are you saying, Shawn? ... That it doesn't matter?"

"I'm not the one running away. You are."

"I don't understand you. I know how you feel about Robert. You hate Robert. You hate gay people. You've made that painfully clear. I'm no different than Robert. So if you hate Robert, why don't you hate me?"

"I don't hate Robert. I never have." Shawn locked eyes with Jelin. "I was jealous of Robert. I didn't want the two of you to get together. I wanted your friendship all to myself. I was afraid Robert would come between us. I didn't want to lose my best friend."

"Why didn't you tell me?"

"I didn't want you to be gay, Jelin. I didn't want your sexuality to come between our friendship."

"It doesn't have to. Not if we don't let it."

"I know that now, Jelin. Jamal wrote in his journal that we're all brothers. I finally understand what that means. That's why you can't leave. We have to stick together and fight. You, Robert, and me. It's time we stand together and bring Coach Green's conniving ass down."

"How? How can we bring him down without hurting ourselves?"

"We can do it, man. If we stick together."

"That's a nice speech, Shawn. Unfortunately, it doesn't work for me." Jelin reached over and picked up the love letter from Shawn's nightstand and waved it in the air. "Coach Green holds my punk card. He said if I didn't convince you to keep your mouth shut, he'd expose me to the media. That's why I have to leave. To protect my future."

Shawn nodded. "You can protect your future right here."

"Shawn, don't you understand? I still want to play basketball. You of all people should know that."

"Jelin, I know how much you love basketball." Shawn looked up at Jelin. "I also know how much you love Robert.

"How ... how long have you known?"

"For a couple months. I saw it in your eyes, man."

"But you didn't you say anything."

"What the hell was I gonna say? Stop being a faggot?" Shawn laughed at how absurd that sounded to him now. "Jelin, I didn't wanna lose you as a friend. I thought as long as you kept it a secret and no one else knew about it, it wouldn't matter."

"Does it matter now? Now that other people know?"

"No, Jelin. It doesn't."

Shawn picked up the remote control and turned up the volume on the television. Coach Green was giving an interview. "I wanna hear what this fool has to say."

"Coach Green, how does it feel to win the Christmas Tournament?"

"It feels great. The guys really played their hearts out tonight."

"How were you able to win the Christmas Tournament without the talents of Shawn Collins and Jelin Church?"

"We have a strong bench. The guys really stepped up big tonight. Especially Brian Short."

"Do you think the Tigers can carry the momentum of this win into the final stretch of the season?"

"Yes I do. I believe we'll win the Big Central division title. I've been predicting that all season."

"Why wasn't Jelin Church on the court tonight?"

"Jelin has some personal problems he's trying to work out."

"Do you expect him back?"

"That's up to Jelin."

Jelin grabbed the remote and turned down the volume. "Do you believe that asshole up there perpetratin'? Personal problems. He's my fuckin' problem."

"He has a problem too, Jelin. He just doesn't know it yet."

"What?"

"Coach Green has someone waiting for him at his office."

"Who?"

"My mother."

"Your mother?"

"I told my mother and Judge Patterson everything."

Jelin dropped the remote.

"They know about the car, the money, the cheating, everything. In addition, I gave them Jamal's journal."

"They have the journal?"

"My mother and Judge Patterson had a meeting with the university chancellor. They threatened to bring a lawsuit against the university if something isn't done about Coach Green." Shawn smiled and looked up at the screen. "Bro, you just watched Coach Green's last game."

Jelin balanced himself against the back of his chair.

"That's why we need you to stay here, Jelin. It's time we bring that chump down. Judge Patterson says we're going to need your deposition to help prove our case against Coach Green and against the police. And maybe your testimony in court."

"In court?" Jelin stood and paced the room. "Shawn, I don't know if I can do that. I don't want my sex life splattered across the headlines. You might accept me … but I don't think the rest of the sports world will be as forgiving."

"Judge Patterson believes Coach Green will step down voluntarily. He thinks this whole ugly matter will get settled without draggin' your relationship with Robert through the media. But we're gonna need your help."

Jelin stopped his pacing. "You're sure the Tigers will get a new coach?"

Shawn nodded. "Coach Green's history. So what do you say? Are you gonna stay here and fight or run away?"

Jelin gave Shawn a strange look. "When did you become so wise, Shawn?"

"I grew up, Jelin. Lying here in this hospital bed gave me a lot of time to think about my life. I didn't like what I saw. I've been so blinded by hundred-dollar sneakers and promises of fame I didn't realize I was being exploited. I didn't realize the important things in life. The things that were staring me right in the face. My family, my education ... my true friends."

"You know I can't let you beat me at anything. Not even growing up."

"Does that mean you're gonna stay?"

Jelin smiled and nodded.

Shawn motioned Jelin over to his bedside. "Remember our secret handshake? The one we used to do in grade school?"

"I remember."

Shawn tapped his fist against the top and bottom of Jelin's fist and then wrapped their index fingers together. "Frick and Frack, through thick and thin. Friends are friends to the very end."

Jelin couldn't help laughing. "Man, why'd you have to go there."

"Because it's still true. Friends?"

"Friends," Jelin repeated.

"Yo, Jelin, if you hurry, I think you can catch Robert before he leaves. His bus isn't scheduled to leave until eight thirty."

Jelin looked at his watch.

"Tell Robert I'm sorry. Tell him I want him to stay."

Jelin smiled.

"Now get outa here, punk." Shawn laughed.

Jelin grabbed his bag and rushed out of the room.

****

Coach Green didn't see the person sitting on the couch in his dimly lit outer office. He passed through the outer office and went directly to his desk. He picked up the phone, ignoring the red message light flashing on his answering machine.

"Pierre, this is Melvin Green. Can you deliver my wife's fur coat to my office at the Omni Center by eight thirty? ... Great, I'll be waiting."

Coach Green hung up the phone and smiled at his wife's picture.

"If I were you, I wouldn't look so pleased with myself."

Coach Green looked up to see Martha Collins standing in the doorway. "Mrs. Collins, what are you doing here?"

"I have some news, and I wanted to deliver it personally."

"If it's about Shawn's recovery, I already heard. I can't tell you how happy I am about it."

"Oh, I'm sure you can't."

"Don't mention this to Shawn yet, but I'm working on a deal to make him an assistant coach."

Martha took a seat opposite the coach's desk. "That won't be necessary. Shawn's gonna be too busy to be your assistant."

"Too busy?"

"Shawn's going to be in court."

"In court?"

"Testifying." Martha smiled.

Coach Green's face turned red. "Testifying about what?"

"About you, Coach Green."

Coach Green leaned across his desk. "Is this some type of a joke, Mrs. Collins?"

"I like referring to it as payback. And payback is a bitch, isn't it?"

The perpetual grin disappeared from Coach Green's face. "What exactly are you trying to say, Mrs. Collins?"

"Remember the day you sat at my kitchen table? The day you promised to take good care of my son? You said his education was the most important thing on your list of priorities. Well, you lied, Coach Green. The only thing you cared about was your damn self. You used me and you used my son. I'm gonna make sure you pay for that."

"Now hold on, Mrs. Collins. Don't you sit there and play little miss innocent with me. You knew what was going on. If it wasn't for me, your son never would have made it into college. You knew he didn't pass that SAT on his own."

"I admit I made mistakes. I admit I let you slither into my son's life." Martha shook her head. "I'll never forgive myself for that. I can't change the past, Coach Green, but I sure as hell can change the future."

"Mrs. Collins, if you're threatening me, I suggest you think again. I'll tell the world you were in on this from the start. I'll say you put Shawn on the auction block to the highest bidder. It just so happens I put in the highest bid." Coach Green grinned.

"You disgust me. From the first day I met you, I never trusted you. I couldn't put my finger on exactly why. But now I know." Martha stood up and looked directly into Coach Green's eyes. "But it was always there, that look in your eyes. That cold, hollow emptiness. That lack of compassion and emotion. Now I can see it. Now I can look into your eyes and see straight down to hell."

"Save the dramatics for someone that cares."

"Oh, I found someone that cares." Martha placed her fists on Coach Green's desk. "You see, I have the goods on you, Coach Green. My son told me everything. I know about the money, the car, the payoff to Jamal. Yeah, I know how you forced Jamal into your web of deception. Hell, I even know how you're blackmailing Jelin, you conniving bastard."

"You'll never prove any of it!" Coach Green sneered across the desk.

"The hell I won't!" Martha slammed her fist against the desk. "You see, Coach Green, you didn't cover all your tracks. In addition to my son's testimony and Jelin's testimony, we have testimony from Jamal."

"That's impossible. Jamal's dead."

"Thanks to you."

"That's ridiculous. Now you're accusing me of Jamal's death. You're a sick, deranged woman. I'm calling security." Coach Green reached for the phone.

"Go ahead, call them!" Martha grabbed the phone and threw the receiver at Coach Green. "You think you can control people's lives, don't you? You think you can wave your hand and make us do whatever you want, don't you? Don't you?" Martha reached into her coat pocket and pulled out a copy of Jamal's journal. "Well, you thought wrong. But Jamal says it best. He left a journal, Coach Green. He documented all his dealings with you." Martha threw the copy of the journal onto his desk. "I made this copy especially for you. Read it and you'll find out what we all know. The night Jamal was killed, he was returning your payoff money. The $12,000 you gave him to take Shawn's test. It's all right there in black and white. Read it and weep."

Coach Green looked down at the journal in horror.

"It didn't take much convincing after I showed it to the university chancellor."

"You told your pack of lies to the chancellor!"

"I told my pack of truths to the chancellor and to the local media. And guess what? They were all very interested in what I had to say. As a matter of fact, you're gonna be featured on the eleven o'clock news tonight. Be sure to watch."

Coach Green stared at Martha with the look of a crazed man.

"By the way, I also had a little chat with the team doctor. He had a lot to say about the little stunt you pulled with my son's life. Judge Lincoln Patterson thinks I have enough to charge you with attempted murder." Martha stepped away from the desk. "You knew my son was ill, you bastard!" Martha pointed her finger toward Coach Green's stunned face. "You almost took away my son's life. Maybe I can't take away your life, Coach Green, but I'm sure as hell gonna take away your freedom to live it."

Coach Green sat in stunned silence.

Martha walked toward the door and then turned around. "I hope your wife enjoys her new coat. It's gonna be the last thing you're able to buy her. And by the way, that blinking light on your answering machine? That's a message from the university chancellor. He's calling to ask for your resignation. Have a good day, Coach Green." Martha slammed the door on her way out.

Coach Green sank into the cushion of his chair as Martha's words caved in around him.

He reluctantly pushed the red blinking light on his answering machine.

"Melvin, this is Chancellor O'Leary. Call me immediately. I just heard some disturbing news. We need to talk!"

Coach Green picked up the journal and read the information Jamal left behind.

The telephone rang, and the answering machine picked up.

"Melvin, it's Tony. There's a problem. Judge Lincoln Patterson subpoenaed my records on Shawn's car. There's a team of investigators going through them right now. I'm not gonna take the fall for you, Melvin. This was your idea. If they find out anything, it's gonna be your ass, not mine."

The knock on the door startled him.

"Mr. Green? I have a delivery for you."

Coach Green stared at the door. "Come in." He voiced strained and weak.

"Are you Melvin Green?

Coach Green nodded.

"Pierre said you wanted this coat delivered right away."

Coach Green pointed to the chair in front of his desk.

"I just need your signature here, sir." The deliveryman handed Coach Green the invoice.

Coach Green's hand shook as he scribbled his initials.

"Thank you, sir."

Coach Green opened the box and pulled out the coat. He rubbed the coat across his face and let the soft, silky fur tickle his nose. He visualized his wife wearing the coat to the NCAA championship game. He pictured her standing next to him on the podium as he accepted the tournament trophy.

He looked across the room at his wall of achievement. The wall was no longer empty. The championship trophy was proudly displayed atop a lighted glass shelf. The bronze and gold colors of the trophy reflected shimmers of light into his eyes. His named was etched in gold letters across the front of the trophy. Melvin Green—Coach of the Year.

He walked across the room to touch the trophy, but the instant his fingers touched the wall, the trophy and shelf disappeared.

He fell back against the wall and slid down onto the floor. He pulled the coat against his face and cried. The voices of failure began to echo in his head. The voices started out low but grew louder and louder, consuming the room in a choir of song that bestowed his failures.

"You'll never amount to anything more than a two-bit, glad-handling, ghetto hustler."

"You're a lying, fake, bastard wannabe who exploits teenagers to get what you want. That's not a man; it's a fuckin' coward."

"This is Chancellor O'Leary. I just heard some disturbing news. We need to talk!"

"Melvin, this is Tony. We have a problem. If they find out anything, it's gonna be your ass, not mine."

"I hope your wife enjoys her new coat. It's gonna be the last thing you ever buy her."

"Maybe I can't take away your life, but I'm sure as hell gonna take away your freedom to live it."

"Stop it! Shut up! Shut upppppp! It not my fault. I can't go to jail. I'm just a man! A man who wanted to support his family! A man who wanted to be accepted!" He placed his hands against his ears to stop the voices, but the voices were coming from inside. He had to shut them up. He had to make them stop.

"I'll show you. I'll show you all!"

He reached into his pant's pocket and removed a set of keys. He unlocked his bottom desk drawer and pulled out a lock box. He used the small key to unlock the tiny cylinder. The voices still screamed in his head.

"Do it."

"You coward."

"You loser."

"Do it."

"You'll never amount to anything anyway."

"You'll never be accepted."

Coach Green removed a .45-caliber pistol from the box. He walked over to his wall of achievement. He placed his head against the wall and pulled the trigger.

****

Robert reached into his mailbox and removed the mail that had gathered over the week. He placed it in his book bag, deciding to look it over once he got on the bus. He glanced at his watch. It was already eight o'clock. He needed to hurry or he would miss his bus. He returned to the suite and surveyed the surroundings one final time. He had decided to pack only one bag; his father would drive down and pick up the remainder of his belongings after the holidays.

He backed his way out of the suite and locked the door. He ran his fingers across the number 2020 and thought about all the events that had transpired over the last four months. He wished he had the power to rewind time. He wished he could bring Jamal back and start the semester all over again, but he couldn't change the past. It was time he moved on.

Robert turned his back to the room and headed down the circular hallway. He pushed the button for the elevator and watched the lighted numbers climb toward him. When the doors opened, he was almost knocked over by Jelin rushing out.

"Robert, I'm glad I caught you."

"Jelin, what … what are you doing here?"

"C'mon, I'll ride down with you."

The two stepped inside the elevator. When the doors closed, Jelin grabbed Robert and kissed him forcefully on the mouth. "Robert, I love you, and I want you to stay."

Robert was lightheaded. He didn't know if he was responding to the downward surge of the elevator or Jelin's whirlwind kiss.

"You were right, Robert. I need to stay and fight. Shawn told me the same thing."

The lobby light illuminated, and the doors opened. They stepped into the lobby.

"Shawn said what?"

"He told me to tell you he's sorry. He wants you to stay."

Robert searched Jelin's face for an explanation. "Shawn wants me to stay?"

"He doesn't care about our relationship. He said together we can bring Coach Green down."

Robert's heart pounded against his chest. He wanted to believe Jelin, but everything seemed too good to be true. "Jelin, I have to catch my bus. I only have thirty minutes to make it downtown."

Jelin took Robert's bag and followed him out the revolving doors. "Robert, you said it yourself. Together we can save Jamal's name and bring his killers to justice. All we have to do is tell the truth."

Robert stopped in the middle of the plaza and turned to face Jelin. "I don't think you know what the truth is."

"The truth is I don't wanna lose you."

Robert didn't know what to say. He didn't want to fall back into Jelin's confused world. He continued down the hill.

"Did you hear what I said?" Jelin grabbed Robert's shoulder and turned him around. "Look at me."

Robert looked up at Jelin. "What about your career? Your image? Are you saying you're ready to throw all that away for me?"

"Shawn said the information about our relationship could be kept confidential. It has no bearing on the case. Robert, I think I can have you and basketball together in my life."

"And which one comes first?" Robert continued down the hill, already knowing the answer to his question.

"You."

Robert turned around. "I don't want you to give up basketball for me. It won't work. I can't compete with her, and I don't want to. You have an image to uphold, remember? I want off your damn emotional roller-coaster. I need to get on with my life."

"Who's the one walking away now, Robert?" Jelin stopped walking. "If you really love me, you'll stay."

Robert stopped and turned around. "That's not fair, Jelin. You're holding all the cards."

"But you're holding my heart."

Robert was stunned. He didn't know what to say. He knew their relationship would have too many hurdles, and he didn't want to hide anymore. He wanted out of the shadows. He wanted to live his life in the light. But he still loved Jelin and wanted to follow his heart.

"Jelin, I need some time to think it over. If the only way I can have you is to deny myself … that's a difficult decision."

Jelin nodded. "That's fair. Just give me the chance to prove myself. To prove my love for you. Promise me you'll come back next semester."

"There's the downtown bus."

Jelin handed Robert his bag. "Promise me that much, Robert."

Robert looked deep into Jelin's eyes. "Okay, I promise." He gave Jelin a quick hug before boarding the bus.

****

The lights of the city faded into the distance. Robert closed his eyes and drifted into a heavy sleep. He hadn't gotten much sleep since Jamal's death, and he was physically and emotionally exhausted. When he awoke, he was only ten miles from Cambridge Falls. He remembered the mail in his book bag and decided to sort through it before arriving home. There were two letters addressed to him, and everything else was junk mail. He opened the first letter. It was from Jamal's brother, Ali. It identified the time of Jamal's funeral and the directions to the funeral home. Robert folded the letter and put it in his jacket pocket. He looked down at the second letter. It was postmarked Akron, Ohio. But there was no return address. Robert's pulse quickened. The only person he knew from Akron was … *That's impossible. Not after all these years.*

Robert's mind flashed back to the time he tried calling Stephon in Akron three years ago. The operator's words were etched into his memory. *"That number has been disconnected. No further information is available."*

Robert had convinced himself that Stephon was dead and his parents had moved away. He looked back down at the letter. The sweat from his fingers rubbed off the first two letters of his name. Whoever wrote the letter used a marker instead of a pen and called him Rob instead of Robert. Robert wiped his hands against his jeans and then slowly opened the letter.

Dear Rob,

I know you're surprised to hear from me after all this time. I tried writing you over the years but could never find the right words to express my feelings. For many months, I blamed you for what happened. I couldn't understand why you betrayed our friendship the way you did. After my suicide attempt, I was hospitalized in a psychiatric ward of a local hospital here in Akron. I was forbidden to have any contact with you. I obeyed everyone's wishes. I wanted you to think I was dead. Because I was dead. I was dead to myself.

Everyone told me how horrible and sinful my ways were. They told me I had to change. But, Rob, no matter how hard I tried, I couldn't change. I couldn't change who or what I was. My parents put me into a program run by religious conservatives. They said they had the power to make a gay person straight.

I believed them. I followed their strict guidelines. But they had no power; they couldn't change me. However, my prayers were answered in another way. They were answered by God. God told me he created me and loves me. He opened my eyes to the truth. I no longer hate you or myself. I understand I was put on this earth for a reason. To preach against hate and intolerance. I understand why you did what you did. You were afraid. You were afraid of what it meant to be gay. That's why I'm studying to become a priest. It's my hope to counsel other gay adolescents so their lives aren't destroyed the way our lives were. Rob, I'm sorry for what I did to you. It wasn't your fault, and it wasn't mine. We needed guidance. We needed someone to reach out to us. Someone to help us cope with our feelings. But instead of receiving spiritual guidance, we received hate and intolerance. We were taught there was no place for us in this world. We were forced to either deny ourselves or end our lives. You chose denial, and I chose death.

I've been speaking out about the suicide rate among gay teenagers. It's an issue that's very near and dear to my heart. Who better than me to address that issue—right?

Last week I was fortunate to run into your mother. She was visiting a local church here in Akron where I was speaking. She told me about the brutal death of your roommate Jamal. She urged me to reach out to you and renew our friendship. She gave me your address and the courage to write. Something I've wanted to do for a long time.

I hope this letter reaches you before you leave for Christmas vacation. Your mother told me the date and time your bus is scheduled to arrive in Cambridge Falls. I convinced her to let me pick you up at the station. The best Christmas gift I can think of is seeing you again.

Rob, I want you to know I don't blame you for what happened, and I'm not dead. I'm very much alive.

Love,
Stephon

Just outside his window, Robert saw the sign welcoming him back to Cambridge Falls. Main Avenue looked the same, but everything appeared different now. The muted colors of autumn were replaced with the festive colors of winter. The giant oak trees that lined the avenue now flaunted white branches. And the farmers' market across the street from the bus depot now displayed a gold-and-red Merry Christmas sign. Robert put his hand against the glass and watched the sights filter through his fingers. The sights of Cambridge Falls no longer haunted him.

The bus pulled into the station. Stephon was standing inside the terminal door. He had grown into a man—a handsome man.

What do you say to someone you thought was dead?

Robert retrieved his bag from the overhead bin and stepped off the bus.

Stephon greeted him with a big smile. "I knew I would recognize you, Rob."

Stephon's voice sounded like a harmonic melody playing in Robert's ear. But he couldn't speak. He was still in shock. Still searching for words. Any words.

"Rob, didn't you get my letter?"

Robert nodded.

"Good. I didn't want you to faint when you stepped off the bus. Don't I even get a hello?"

Robert finally found his voice. "It's been a long time."

"Exactly three years, two months, four days, and"—Stephon looked at his watch—"two hours."

"You remember?"

"How could I forget?"

"Stephon, there's something I never got the chance to tell you." Robert looked at the ground and then back up at Stephon. "I'm sorry. I'm so sorry for what I did. For what happened to you."

"For what happened to us," Stephon replied.

Robert touched Stephon's face. "I still can't believe it's you."

Stephon drew Robert close. "I want my hug."

Robert was suspended in a cruel fantasy. If he opened his eyes, it would all disappear.

"It feels like old times, doesn't it?" Stephon asked.

Robert stepped back to take another look at Stephon. He needed to make sure Stephon was real. "Well, not exactly. You were a little shorter then. And what happened to that little Afro you used to be so proud of?"

"What, you don't like my fresh fade cut?"

"No, I like it. You just don't look the same. Not like I remember."

"And neither do you. Hell, you used to be a skinny runt. But look at you now, Rob. You must have kept up that weight-training program I put you on."

Robert smiled. "I did."

"You look great."

"So do you, Stephon."

"Okay, now that we got that over with, let's get out of this stupid terminal. Your family's expecting you."

Robert followed Stephon out of the terminal, he couldn't help but smile.

Stephon placed Robert's bag in the backseat.

"Is this your car, Stephon?"

"No, it's my parents' car."

"Do they know you came to see me?"

"I'm a man, Rob. My parents no longer control my life."

As they drove up Main Avenue, Robert wasn't sure what to say. He just kept looking at Stephon. He still couldn't believe it was true.

Stephon finally broke the silence. "I told you in the letter that I've accepted my sexuality. Have you?"

"Yeah, but only recently. After what happened to you, I tried to repress my sexuality. My sexuality and my guilt were intertwined. I couldn't separate them."

"Rob, can we leave our past behind us and move on?"

"I would like that, Stephon."

"So let's make a vow. From now on, let's agree not to mention my suicide attempt or your guilt. Life is too short to dwell in the past. Let's talk about the future."

Robert smiled. "I can't believe you're in seminary school."

"That's right. I want to be a priest. A priest who accepts everyone. It won't matter what your sexual preference is. Where you were born.

What type of music you like. What color shoes you wear, et cetera, et cetera, et cetera. How about you, Rob? What are you studying?"

"Urban management. I want to be a city manager."

"Oh yeah, I remember." Stephon smiled. "You wanted to come back and rule over Cambridge Falls. Get back at all those kids who treated you cruel in high school."

"I grew out of that selfish revenge vendetta. Now I want to move to Newark and finish something my roommate dreamed about."

"What was his dream?"

"To turn Newark into the promised land. So after I graduate, I plan to get a job working for the city of Newark."

"And work your magic?"

"That's right. So, Stephon, what else have you been doing with yourself?"

"What would you like to know?"

"Well, for starters, do you have a love life?"

"Just the church. Once I take my vows, my only personal relationship will be with God." Stephon looked over at Robert.

"Is it that simple, Stephon? I mean, we both know how hard it is to ignore our desires. They're a part of us. How can you deny that?"

"I'm not denying my desires. I'm just channeling them in a different direction. I won't lie to you, Robert. It's not easy. I pray every day to have the strength not to give in to temptation. I believe I have a higher calling. I've been called by God to deliver a message. So what happened to us doesn't have to happen to other confused kids."

Robert nodded. He wasn't going to argue with a message from God.

"So is there anyone special in your life, Rob?"

"I'm not sure."

"What does that mean?"

"There is someone, but … but I'm not sure he knows what he wants. I'm not sure I know what I want."

Stephon smiled. "Do you love him?"

"He's a basketball player."

"Wait—don't tell me. A confused jock." Stephon laughed. "Am I right?"

Robert nodded.

"My only advice to you is go with what you feel in your heart."

Robert was afraid of what he felt in his heart. His heart still had feelings for Stephon. He was glad when Stephon pulled into the driveway.

Robert retrieved his bag from the backseat. "Thanks for the ride. Are you coming in?"

"No, I'll let you have some time alone with your family."

"When will I see you again?"

"Your mother invited me over for Christmas dinner tomorrow. I'll be over around two o'clock."

"Okay, I'll see you then. Bye, Stephon."

"Bye, Rob."

Stephon backed out of the driveway and headed up the road. Robert watched the car disappear into the flow of traffic. He was numb over the turn of events that had rocked his world.

"Robert, you're home. C'mon on in here, boy." Robert's mother gave him a warm hug as she ushered him into the house. "How was your ride from the bus station?"

Robert smiled at his mother's veiled attempt to find out how things went with Stephon. "Mom, can we talk about it later? Right now I just wanna enjoy being home. Where is everyone?"

"They went over to your grandmother's house. They should be back soon. Why don't you go get unpacked before they get here."

Robert hauled his bag up the stairs but stopped midway and turned around. "Thanks, Mom."

"For what?"

"You know what. For always being there when I need you."

"That's my job. I'm your mother."

Robert smiled and then continued to his bedroom. He sat down on his bed and thought about the events of the day. Over the course of twenty-four hours, his life had gone from empty and alone to overcrowded. He wondered if it was possible to be in love with two men.

He lay against his pillow and closed his eyes. It really didn't matter since they were both in love with someone else.

CHAPTER 33

R obert put his confused feelings aside while he dealt with the rush of the holidays and the preparations for Jamal's funeral. He was the only one from Pittsburgh to make it to Newark for the funeral. He stolidly watched as Jamal was laid to rest in a somber celebration of his life. The minister tried to make everyone rejoice in the happiness Jamal inspired during his short time on earth, but it was hard to rejoice over a bright life cut down so brutally and senselessly. During the ceremony, Robert made the decision to return to Pittsburgh. It was his duty to bring the officers responsible for Jamal's death to justice. The winds of change had shifted, and Robert felt he was standing with the wind.

****

The candlelight vigil was Stephon's idea.

Robert looked at the sheet of paper in his hands and then out at the sea of faces. Every face glowed with the light of a candle.

"No justice, no peace! No justice, no peace!"

The chant of the audience grew louder with each speaker. After months of testimony, the grand jury was finally slated to hand down its verdict of whether the five officers accused of Jamal's death would be indicted for murder. Using his skills of persuasion, Stephon had organized the vigil. He put together a diverse group of religious leaders who called for a night of prayer and hope on the courthouse steps, the night before the verdict was to be read. The vigil attracted a much larger audience than expected. The crowd of over five thousand participants clogged the plaza in front of the courthouse and spilled out into the streets.

Stephon convinced Robert to deliver the keynote speech at the vigil. "You're Jamal's voice, and Jamal's voice must be heard." Robert couldn't argue with Stephon's logic. Delivering the speech was the best way to keep Jamal's memory alive. Robert looked down at the speech in his hands. It was the paper Jamal had written on racial profiling. Robert could still remember the class where Jamal spoke out so elegantly against racial profiling. He hoped reading Jamal's words would awaken a sleeping nation to an issue that had plagued the minority community for far too long.

The list of speakers Stephon had organized for the evening was impressive. Judge Patterson was first, followed by a state senator, a congressional representative, a former mayor, the head of the NAACP, representatives from the League of Minority Police Officers, Jamal's brother, Ali, and finally Robert.

Robert looked out into the audience. All his friends were there to give him support. He looked into each of their faces and realized how important Jamal's life had been. Learning, respecting, and overcoming had been Jamal's philosophy, and his philosophy had touched and enriched all their lives.

Ali finished his impassioned plea for justice, and the chant of the audience intensified.

"No justice, no peace! No justice, no peace!"

Robert looked out at the sea of candlelit faces. Jamal had touched not only the lives of him and his friends but also the lives of everyone at the march. They were all speaking out. They were all refusing to be victims.

"No justice, no peace! No justice, no peace!"

Robert stepped up to the microphone and into the light.

EPILOGUE

A year passed since Jamal was laid to rest. But his words still rang true—we do become strongest in our broken places. Latisha learned to reach for her own dreams and to love herself before loving someone else. She received a grant and enrolled in beauty school. Miss Neubie immediately took Latisha under her wing and armed her with the tools of success. In addition, Latisha finally moved out of her mother's house and into a two-bedroom apartment with Nickea. She and Shawn were still friends, but Latisha made it clear that her life had taken a different path. She now understood the meaning of true love, and her heart belonged to Darius.

Martha learned material possessions were no substitution for firm parental guidance. She acknowledged her vulnerability as a single mother and used her mistakes to help others. She sued the university and accepted an out-of-court settlement of 3 million dollars. She used the money to create a nationwide network of support groups for single mothers raising male athletes. But at the moment, she was busy preparing for her wedding. She and Lincoln were engaged.

Jelin learned accepting himself didn't mean giving up his dream. He managed to keep his personal life private and no longer feared the consequences. He finished his sophomore year with the Tigers and helped them capture the NCAA crown. He was awarded the most-valuable-player trophy, and in a touching interview after the game, dedicated the trophy to the real hero of the tournament, Shawn Collins. Pro scouts were already enticing Jelin to leave college early, and Jelin was seriously considering the idea.

Shawn learned to appreciate the things in life that really mattered—his family, his friends, and his education. He realized being a man meant accepting responsibility. His basketball-playing days were over, but he held on to his scholarship. He selected a major and was seriously pursuing a degree in criminal justice. He decided to follow in his father's footsteps and enter law enforcement. He believed it would be easier to fight racial profiling and police brutality on the inside rather than the outside. Finally, he realized he could keep the promise he had made to his dad and become a superstar without stepping foot on a basketball court.

But out of everyone, Robert's broken places grew back the strongest. He learned to focus on the brightness of his future rather than the darkness of his past. He learned to appreciate the good inside himself and to love himself for the person he had become. Fear and humiliation had driven him into darkness, but he came out fighting. He and Jelin were still working through their problems, but he decided to take their relationship one day at a time. The unexpected appearance of Stephon on the scene had certainly complicated things, but Robert decided to save that issue for another day. For the moment, he was just happy to be back in the light.